F   Morris, Gilbert
Mor   Dawn of A New Day

American Century #7

DATE DUE

Also by Gilbert Morris

THE AMERICAN CENTURY SERIES

1. A Bright Tomorrow
2. Hope Takes Flight
3. One Shining Moment
4. A Season of Dreams
5. Winds of Change
6. Pages of Promise

THE HOUSE OF WINSLOW SERIES

1. The Honorable Imposter
2. The Captive Bride
3. The Indentured Heart
4. The Gentle Rebel
5. The Saintly Buccaneer
6. The Holy Warrior
7. The Reluctant Bridegroom
8. The Last Confederate
9. The Dixie Widow
10. The Wounded Yankee
11. The Union Belle
12. The Final Adversary
13. The Crossed Sabres
14. The Valiant Gunman
15. The Gallant Outlaw
16. The Jeweled Spur
17. The Yukon Queen
18. The Rough Rider
19. The Iron Lady
20. The Silver Star
21. The Shadow Portrait
22. The White Hunter
23. The Flying Cavalier
24. The Glorious Prodigal
25. The Amazon Quest
26. The Golden Angel
27. The Heavenly Fugitive
28. The Fiery Ring
29. The Pilgrim Song
30. The Beloved Enemy
31. The Shining Badge
32. The Royal Handmaid
33. The Silent Harp
34. The Virtuous Woman
35. The Gypsy Moon

★ NUMBER SEVEN IN THE AMERICAN CENTURY SERIES ★

Dawn of a New Day

GILBERT MORRIS

Revell

a division of Baker Publishing Group
Grand Rapids, Michigan

Published by Revell
a division of Baker Publishing Group
P.O. Box 6287, Grand Rapids, MI 49516-6287
www.revellbooks.com

Printed in the United States of America

Library of Congress Cataloging-in-Publication Data
Morris, Gilbert.
    Dawn of a new day / Gilbert Morris.
        p.   cm. – (American century ; bk. 7)
    ISBN 978-0-8007-3265-3 (pbk.)
    1. Domestic fiction. I. Title.
PS3563.O8742D39 2008
813'.54—dc22   2008008806

Scripture is taken from the King James Version of the Bible.

This is a work of historical reconstruction; the appearances of certain historical figures are therefore inevitable. All characters, however, are products
of the author's imagination, and any resemblance to actual persons, living
or dead, is coincidental.

To Rick and Tracy Lineburger

My joy is to see young people like you two
fall in love with Jesus—then with each other!
You two have been a deep source of joy to me
ever since the old days at Ouachita!

CONTENTS

PART 1   SEEDTIME (1960-1964)

1. Man with a Lance   13
2. Concert in Fort Smith   30
3. A Rough Party   46
4. Growing Up—Hard!   59
5. The Big Time   71

PART 2   SOWING (1965-1966)

6. Sensation at the Prom   83
7. A Funny Way to Save the World   95
8. "Make Me a Chocolate Pie!"   107
9. Christmas in the Ozarks   121
10. Graduation Gifts   127
11. "I Don't Have a Life!"   139
12. Maxwell Gets a Shock   148

PART 3   THE FACE OF WAR (1967-1968)

13. The Star   157
14. Artists Need to Suffer   166
15. "You Grew Up and I Never Knew It"   179
16. A Surprising Evening   192
17. Success!   205
18. Men of Honor   220

PART 4   HARVESTTIME (1969)

19. "What Good Am I to Anybody?"   237
20. Prue Takes Over   256
21. Back Home   265
22. The Old Rugged Cross   277
23. Only a Minor Miracle   291
24. A Night to Remember   300

THE STUART FAMILY

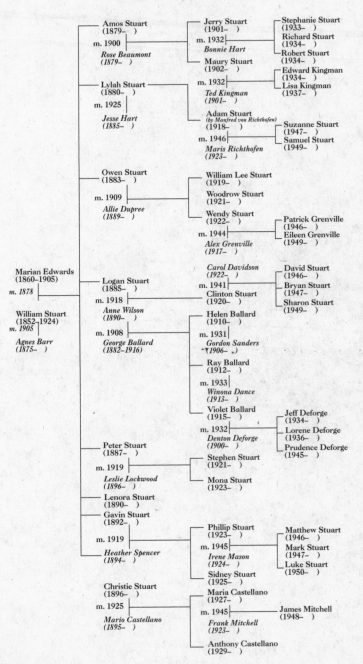

Part 1

Seedtime
(1960–1964)

1

MAN WITH A LANCE

I don't have any more figure than a *fence post*!"

Prudence Deforge had come to stand before the narrow, full-length mirror her father had fastened to her wall. She was fifteen years old, and now as she stood staring at her reflection, was filled with a combination of feelings: anger, disgust, humiliation. The dress she had on was only two months old, but already she could tell that she had grown—something she had come to dread like nothing else. The dress was a loose-fitting shift dress made of a soft, dark green fabric with yellow geometric designs running throughout. The neckline had a small, green collar, the sleeves came to the elbow and ended in a small cuff, and the hemline fell to about four inches above the knee; the dress was well made and stylish, and her mother had been excited when they had found it at JC Penney in Fort Smith, but now it seemed all wrong.

"I wish I looked like Momma instead of Daddy," Prue muttered as she tugged at the dress trying to get it to fall somewhat lower. She was exactly five feet ten inches tall and very slender—although she called herself "skinny." A sense of disloyalty suddenly swept over her, for she loved her father dearly—but of the three Deforge children she was the only one who seemed to have inherited Denton Deforge's genes. Her sister, Lorene, and her brother, Jeff, had inherited Violet Deforge's good looks, both having brown hair, brown eyes, and being small and well knit. Although Jeff was now twenty-six and had his own family, the last time he had come he had hugged her and said, "Why, you're taller than I am, Prue! When are you going to stop growing?" The memory of that had lingered, and the bitterness that only youth could know had caused Prue sleepless nights. Her sister, Lorene, at twenty-four was also married. She was only five feet five inches tall, and Prue found herself having to fight against the resentment, for she longed to be small and shapely like her sister and like *normal* girls.

"Prue! Come on down. Breakfast is ready."

Her mother's voice stirred the girl, and she quickly gathered her books, shoving them into a maroon canvas satchel. She started to leave the room but paused for one moment again before the mirror. Peering at herself, she took in the lean figure that had not yet developed like other girls her age, and she tried to take some comfort in her face and hair. Like her father, she had hair that was black as a crow's wing that glistened in the sun. Her eyes were dark blue, so blue that at times they seemed almost ebony. She did have eyebrows and eyelashes that would never need any "Maybelline" makeup as the other girls used, for they were black too. She studied the oval face, the mouth that seemed too wide, and the cheekbones that seemed too pronounced, all a gift from her father. Nothing pleased her, and her lips tightened into a pale line, and she muttered, "I'm nothing but a dope!"

Wheeling away from the mirror, she moved down the stairs holding onto the rail, and when she turned down the hall and entered the dining room, she found her father and mother already seated. Taking her seat, she muttered "Good morning" and bowed her head, waiting until her father had asked the blessing.

"That dress looks very nice," Violet said. She was a pretty woman of forty-five with hands toughened by farmwork, but a clear look, and a pleasing expression on her face.

Looking up from her oatmeal, Prue said rebelliously, "I'm already outgrowing it! It's too short! I'm nothing but an old giraffe!"

Denton Deforge laughed and pointed his knife covered with blackberry jam in his daughter's direction. "You've never even seen one of those things."

"I've seen pictures of them. All tall, and gawky, and clumsy just like me."

Denton did not answer for a moment. He had known for some time, both he and Violet, that this younger daughter of theirs was more of a problem than either Jeff or Lorene had been. She had come late in life, and Dent, at sixty, had found a very special love for her. He was grieved to know that she was unhappy. Now as he layered his fresh, crisp biscuit with blackberry jam he wondered, *It's not just her looks she's worried about. It's the bad grades she makes at school. Don't know what to do about this girl.*

Violet caught Dent's eyes and shook her head slightly. Ever since Prue had started school she had had trouble with her studies. She was a bright girl able to learn practically anything—except what was written in a book. Violet smiled and said, "I'll let the hem out of it when you get home today, Prudence. Now, eat your breakfast or you'll be late for the bus."

Prudence gobbled down her oatmeal along with two eggs, three biscuits, and two thick sausage patties. She scooted around, kissed her parents, and left at a dead run, slamming the door behind her. Violet got up and began to clear the table; she noticed that Dent was staring out the window, watching as Prue ran down their long, gravel driveway toward the paved road. She came over and stood beside him and ran her hand over his hair, which was still black with only a few silver threads. "You worry about Prudence, don't you?"

Dent Deforge shoved his chair back, reached out, and grabbed Violet, putting her onto his lap. He was strong and wiry as he had been all his life, and he seemed to elude age effortlessly. "You're still the best-looking woman I ever saw." He grinned and kissed her firmly. Then despite her protests, he held her pinioned on his lap, his eyes darting toward the window. Prue had reached the road now and was standing beside Mark Stevens. "She worries about being too tall," he said, "and she worries about her grades. I wish I could do something about it, but I don't know what."

Sitting on her husband's lap, Violet put her arm around him and whispered, "It'll be all right. She's a good girl, and she'll find her way. God has promised me that."

"He has?" Dent's voice was muffled, and he nuzzled her neck for a moment, making her squirm. "Well, that's all right then. I just wanted to be sure."

Prue hurried to the road where she had seen Mark emerge from the other side of the highway. The Stevens' place was just across from the Deforges', and she had never known a time when she had gone more than a few days without seeing Mark. She stood now looking up at him and taking pleasure in it, for so many of the boys were shorter than she. At sixteen years of age, Mark Stevens was six feet three and still growing. He had tawny hair that was long and needed cutting, deep-set gray-green eyes, a wide mouth, and high cheekbones. Prue had always thought he was the handsomest boy she had ever seen, although she had never breathed a word of this to anyone.

Mark had a small transistor radio with an earphone, and grinning at the young girl who had joined him, said, "Here. Have a listen."

Prue shoved the earphone into her right ear and listened as the song came through clearly from a Fort Smith station. It was "Itsy Bitsy, Teeny Weeny, Yellow Polka Dot Bikini." Prue's lips turned up into a smile, and she moved with the beat of it. "That's the silliest thing I ever heard, Mark," she said, removing the earphone and handing it back to him.

"Why, it was number one on the *Hit Parade* last week. Shows you what kind of music we're going to have in the sixties, doesn't it?" He turned the radio off to conserve the battery, shoved it into his shirt pocket, and then said, "Are you ready for that algebra test?"

"I guess so."

"You always do good on math and stuff like that," Mark said somewhat enviously, shaking his head. "I wish I could. That Mrs. Brown is one mean lady!"

"You do well in everything else, and I do awful!"

Mark glanced at the young girl, knowing that she was despondent over her grades. He had spent a great deal of time trying to help her, but somehow, except for math and things involving numbers, she simply could not grasp the other subjects. "Well, you'll do great on this," he said. "Come on. Give me a little help. Did you get number 7?"

He opened his book, and the two stood there, Prue explaining the problem until the yellow school bus lumbered up, and they climbed aboard. They sat down together near the back of the bus, and as Prue explained the problem, she was very conscious of Mark's arm pressing against hers, and she made the explanation as long as possible to keep him occupied.

★   ★   ★

"Hey, Prue!"

Prudence felt a hand shoving at her back insistently and dreaded what was to come. She sat directly in front of Leon Dicus, a big, brawny athlete who apparently never once considered studying outside of class. She tried to ignore him, wishing that Mrs. Brown would come in, but her hopes were unrealized.

"Hey, Prue!" A large hand seized her arm, and she found herself pulled around almost bodily. Dicus's grip was hard, and he was grinning at her with his big, fleshy lips drawn back to expose very large teeth. "You gonna do me right on this test, ain't ya, babe?"

Knowing very well that he expected her to help him cheat his way through, Prue said in a strained voice, "I can't do that, Leon! Mrs. Brown will be looking right at us!"

Dicus laughed, not caring who heard him. He liked an

audience, and he looked around to see most of the students taking in the little drama. "Aw, she wears bifocals. She can't see two things at once. Besides, she has to turn her back sooner or later. You write the answers down and just slip 'em over your shoulder. Okay?"

Mark Stevens was sitting directly across from Leon Dicus, and he saw the distress in the girl's face. He knew that Prue was too shy to do anything to draw attention to herself, and she hated it when someone like Dicus put her in this position. "Aw, let her alone, Leon," he said. "Do your own work."

Dicus turned quickly, his smile fading. "You keep your oar out of this, Mark! We're gettin' along fine without your help!" He turned back, squeezing Prue's arm again, saying, "You do me right, maybe I'll take you out for a party some night. You and me we'll—"

Dicus never finished his sentence, for Mrs. Brown opened the door and marched in, bearing the test in a brown manila folder. She was a small woman with brown hair and direct, brown eyes, and she began the class going through the little ritual: checking roll, making announcements, and then finally said, "Mark, would you pass these papers out, please?"

"Yes, ma'am." Mark got up, took the folder, and removed the test. Going to the front of each row, he counted the number of students and handed a sheaf to each student in the front seat. When he had distributed them, he went back and found one placed upside down on his desk. He winked at Debbie Peters, who winked back at him. Debbie was the best-looking girl in school, with large, blue eyes, fluffy, blond hair, and a pert figure. She was a little short for Mark, but it seemed that most of the cheerleaders were short and peppy.

"You may turn your papers over," Mrs. Brown said, "and begin work. If you finish before the bell, turn them over, and remain in your seats. There will be no talking during the test. If you have a question, bring your paper to me."

Soon the room was filled with the sound of pencils scratching across paper, of erasers being rubbed furiously to erase mistakes, heavy breathing, groans, and sighs. Mrs. Brown walked like a soldier on his post across the front of the room, her sharp eyes going over the students. She was a stringent teacher, always fair, and always ready to give help, but she was death on any form of cheating.

Prue finished her test in ten minutes, turned it over, and sat there looking down and saying nothing. She was praying that Leon Dicus would leave her alone, but she knew that if Mrs. Brown turned her head he would be after her for the answers. No more than five minutes after Prue had finished her test, a student entered the room and handed Mrs. Brown a note. Mrs. Brown scanned it, and giving one final look at the class, walked over to the door. She stepped into the hall to talk with the principal and closed the door behind her; Prue knew what was coming. She felt a sharp pinch in her back that almost made her cry out, and Dicus hissed, "Come on, Prue! Give me them answers!"

Without turning around, Prue bowed her head and shut her eyes. "I can't do it, Leon!" she whispered.

"Sure you can! Come on now!" Dicus caught a fold of flesh on Prue's side and squeezed. The pain was intolerable, and Prue could not keep back the cry of pain that rose to her lips. She could not get away, and the pressure increased; she began to tremble and said, "Please! Don't do that, Leon!"

"Give me them answers!"

Mark had been watching the two, and now he said, "Let her alone, Dicus!"

"Mind your own business!"

Mark saw that the hulking young man had increased his pressure and that tears were running down Prue's cheeks. He was an easygoing young man, Mark Stevens, but under his calm demeanor lurked a temper that could be ignited instantly. This is what happened now, for almost without thinking, filled with anger, Mark raised his right arm, and leaning over, belted Dicus in the ribs, bringing a grunt of pain from the larger boy.

Dicus had a temper too, and releasing Prue, he came out of his seat, and with a roar of anger threw a punch that caught Mark on the neck and shoved him over against Debbie, who cried out, "Look out, Mark. . . ."

Dicus was on his feet, reaching over for Mark, but Mark also rose and hit Dicus full in the mouth. This cut Dicus's lip so blood appeared, and with a cry of rage, he flung himself at Mark, throwing his arms around him. The two fell to the floor, Debbie began screaming, and Prue swiveled around, her eyes wide. The whole class began crying out as the two boys thrashed and pitted each other, awkwardly rolling and falling into desks.

The fight did not last long, for Mr. Brawner, the principal, came in, followed by Mrs. Brown. Brawner was a large man, well over six feet and very muscular. He reached down, grabbed Dicus by the collar, and jerked him upright. Mark scrambled to his feet as the principal said, "What's wrong with you two? Fighting in a classroom! Both of you come with me!"

Dicus whined, "It was his fault! He started it! He just up and hit me!"

"Shut your mouth, Leon! I've had enough of you! Now, come on! Mark, I'm a little surprised at you."

Prue wanted to cry out, "It wasn't his fault," but she could only stand there and watch as the two boys were hauled off by the husky principal.

"All of you get back in your seats and finish the test," Mrs. Brown said icily. She waited until they started and then stood looking at them. She had put in years of teaching, and a fight was nothing new to her, although in the classroom it was a little different. Finally the bell rang, and as she was taking the papers, she heard Debbie Peters say to Prudence Deforge, "It was all your fault! All you had to do was give him the answers!" Mrs. Brown caught this whisper and was able to figure out the rest. As Prudence started to leave, she stopped her and said, "I'm very happy with your work this year, Prudence."

She saw the girl's lips tremble and knew she was terribly disturbed by the fight. "Try not to let it bother you, dear," she said. "There'll always be bullies like Leon." She smiled and put her hand on the girl's thin shoulder. "But sometimes there are good boys around—like Mark Stevens."

★   ★   ★

Prue managed to avoid the students who wanted to talk about the fight all day, but after school when she got on the bus and sat down looking out the window, she heard many of the kids say, "I bet Mark and Leon really got it from Mr. Brawner. He knows how to use a stick."

Suddenly the seat settled, and she heard Mark saying, "Hey, that was some test, wasn't it?"

Prue turned to see that Mark had plopped down beside her and was smiling cheerfully. He was unwinding the chord of the earphone that was attached to his radio and plugged it into his ear. Turning it on, he listened for a moment and then removed it and said, "Listen to this." He held the earphone to her ear, and she heard Elvis singing "Are You Lonesome Tonight?" Mark grinned and said, "Do you like that bird, Elvis Presley?"

"I guess so."

"Seems kind of weird to me the way he twists and jumps around, but all the girls seem to be crazy about him." He listened to the song for a moment, then pulled out a packet of Juicy Fruit. "Here. Have a chew."

Prue took a stick and unfolded the wrapper, but before she popped the gum in her mouth she said, "I'm sorry you got into all that trouble because of me, Mark."

"Because of you? It wasn't because of you. It was that Neanderthal, Leon."

"Did Mr. Brawner paddle you?"

"Ah, he gave us a few licks. Nothing to worry about. I had

to go back and take the test over again. Didn't do too good,
I don't think."

Eileen Ferrell, sitting across from Mark, leaned over and
said, "Leon says he's going to stomp you, Mark."

"Let him fly right at it," Mark said cheerfully.

Prue bit her lower lip and shook her head. "I hope you
don't fight with him again."

"So do I. It's hard on the hide rolling around punching at
somebody. He'll probably forget it. He's too dumb to remember anything very long."

The bus rumbled on, and Prue was relieved to see that
Mark did not seem at all upset. She had been nervous all day
and unable to give more than scant attention to the teachers.
It didn't seem to matter though, for no matter how hard she
tried, she never could make good grades.

When they got off the bus and it went roaring off with a
cloud of diesel fumes, Prue felt she had to say something to
Mark. "I thank you so much for sticking up for me," she said
timidly.

Mark turned and looked down at Prue. The sun struck
her black hair, and her eyes looked almost black. He grinned
and tapped her on the shoulder with his fist. "Hey! We're
pals, aren't we? I can't have anyone trying to run over my
buddy."

"Thanks anyway." She turned to go away but heard him
call her name.

"Did you hear about the rally over in Fort Smith?"

"No, what is it about?"

"It's a political rally. John Kennedy thinks he's going to be
president. He's doin' pretty good too." Mark kept up with
politics closely, and now he ran his hand through his hair and
shook his head. "It looks to me like he's got a good shot at
being president. May not get another chance to hear him.
Don't know what he's coming to Fort Smith, Arkansas, for,
but he is. You want to go? Dad said I could borrow the car,
and I'm gonna go."

It was the first time Mark had ever asked her to go anyplace in a car, and a thrill ran through Prue Deforge. "I—I'd like to, but I'll have to ask Momma and Daddy."

"Ah, they won't care. They know old Mark Stevens is a trustworthy fellow. We'll leave right after school's out tomorrow. We'll have time to stop and get a burger somewhere after the rally. We'll be in late though. Tell your folks that."

Prue whispered, "All right, Mark." She turned and flew to the house and found her mother peeling potatoes in the kitchen. "Momma," she said, "Mark wants me to go to a political rally over in Fort Smith tomorrow."

"He does? Who all's going?"

"I don't know, but can I go?"

Violet Deforge turned and looked at this daughter of hers, and her heart seemed to swell. Other girls had had real dates at fifteen, although she knew she would not permit Prudence to do such a thing, but she knew Mark Stevens like he was her own. He had been in and out of the Deforge house since he could walk, and seeing the pleading look in Prudence's eyes, she said, "Well, you ask your daddy. He's out fixing the gate."

"All right, Momma." Prudence dashed out of the house and found her father wiring a gate together, and before he could say a word, she said, "Mark's going to a rally over in Fort Smith tomorrow. He's got his daddy's car, and he wants me to go with him. Can I go?"

"Whoa! Whoa up there!" Dent grinned. He got the story out of her and then pulled his straw hat off and stuck one thumb under the bib of his overalls. "I wouldn't even consider it if it was anybody except Mark," he meditated, "but I guess it's okay." He was driven backward as Prue threw her arms around him and kissed him on the cheek. "We'll be in late, Daddy," she cried. "Don't worry about us!"

★   ★   ★

Prue had spent two hours getting ready, scrubbing herself until her skin shone. She had only one dress that would be suitable for what she considered her first date with Mark Stevens, and after her shower she slipped into the polyester minidress in a bright, multicolored pattern with a scooped neck, short sleeves, and a dropped waistline where the bottom of the skirt was pleated. She worked on her hair, which she considered her best asset. It was thick and black, with a slight curl in it, and she had let it grow longer than the current fashion. There was nothing else to do, and she paced the room nervously; finally she went over to her chest of drawers and opened the drawer next to the bottom, which was filled with mementos and souvenirs. She withdrew a green, leatherbound volume, her diary, and carried it over to the desk and opened it. She took a gold Cross pen, also a gift from her parents, and began to write:

> *My first date, and with Mark Stevens! I'm so excited I can hardly hold this pen! We're going to a political rally over in Fort Smith. I'm wearing my new dress that Momma and Daddy bought me, and it looks all right, except I'm too skinny. I wonder if I'll ever have a bosom! Anyway, we're going to the rally, and we'll be late coming home, so we'll probably eat at a fancy restaurant.*

For a moment Prue paused and then added one sentence:

> *I don't know what I'll do if he wants to kiss me. I just don't know—but I think I'll let him.*

Prue's face flushed at the words, and she shut the diary quickly as if apprehended in a shameful deed. Quickly she went back and concealed it and for the next hour grew more and more nervous. She had taken a half day off from school, the first time she had ever done so, and by four o'clock she had driven her mother crazy.

"Well, there he is," Violet said. "You have a good time." She hugged her daughter and watched her as she ran out to the Chevrolet station wagon that had pulled up. She walked out on the porch, saying, "Now, you be careful. Drive slow. You hear me, Mark?"

"Yes, ma'am, I always do. Don't worry now. We'll be back pretty late. It might be one or two o'clock."

Prue settled down in the front seat, and Mark said, "Hey, you look nice. A new dress?"

"Yes," Prue said shyly. "I'm so excited to be going."

Mark was wearing a pair of charcoal gray slacks, a tan shirt, and a pair of brown saddle oxfords. As he drove quickly out of the driveway, he said, "We'll have to pick the others up, then we're on our way."

Prue sat silently for a moment and felt something close around her heart. "The others?"

"Oh, didn't I tell you? Yea, John Tyler's going with us. He's sold on Kennedy—and Debbie is going too, of course."

Mark continued to speak happily of the trip, but if Prue had had her way, she would have gotten out of the car and gone back home. She sat silently as Mark stopped to pick up John, Mark's best friend, who greeted them both cheerfully and got in the backseat, saying, "Better get back here with me now, Prue. You know who's gonna want to sit in the front with Mark."

Prue silently got into the backseat beside John, and he began at once talking about the primaries for the presidential election. She knew nothing of this and could only nod and make an agreeable noise from time to time.

Debbie's parents lived in a large house just outside Cedarville. Her father was in real estate, and the Peters were one of the wealthiest families in the county. Debbie came out wearing a light blue polyester minidress that clung to her figure provocatively, had a V-neckline, short sleeves, and was trimmed with a band of darker blue ribbon. Mark, who had gone in to get her, opened the door for her, then went around to take his seat behind the wheel. "You look like a beauty queen, Debbie," he said, grinning.

"Why, thank you, Mark." Debbie smiled and sat close to him as he started the car up. She turned toward the back-seat and said rather coolly, "Hello, Prue. Hello, John." She took their greetings, then turned around and scooted closer to Mark. "This is going to be such fun! You're going to tell me all about politics."

★   ★   ★

The rally was held in the Convention Center, a rather grandiose name for the largest building suitable for such a rally in Fort Smith, Arkansas. It was just off the square, very close to where Isaac Parker, the hanging judge during the days of the Indian territory, had stood and watched the men he sentenced hang. The gallows were still there, at least a replica of them, with the ropes dangling down, and Prue, who had visited the place once, felt a chill as she thought of the executions.

Now, however, they were inside the Convention Center, which was packed, and John Tyler constantly nudged her with his elbow or poked her with his fingers, a nervous habit of his. "You're gonna love this guy Kennedy," he said. "He's from the rich Kennedy family, you know."

As he spoke, the moderator finished introducing John Kennedy, and the politician came to stand before the podium.

"Why, he's so handsome!" Debbie exclaimed. "He looks like a movie star!"

Kennedy was, indeed, a handsome man—a florid face, a broad, white smile, tousled hair that gave him a boyish look. He looked trim and fit, and for forty-five minutes he spoke in his Boston accent, strange to the ears of these Arkansas folk, but whatever it is that gets a man attention, John Fitzgerald Kennedy had it. Prue understood little of what he said. She was still sick at heart for the disappointment that had come at discovering that this was not to be a date at all, at least not for her. She looked bitterly sometimes at Debbie and with almost something like pain at Mark who put his arm around the blond girl from time to time, but who mostly listened to Kennedy.

Finally the speech was over, and Kennedy smiled and said, "I would like to take a few questions. Our time is short, so I can only take three or four. If you will." He broke off, saying, "Well, young man, I see you're the first volunteer. What's your name?"

"My name's Mark Stevens, Senator Kennedy."

"What's your question, Mr. Stevens?"

Mark had a good, strong voice, and he said, "Mr. Kennedy, on our currency there are the words, 'In God We Trust.' Do you believe this?"

A shocked look swept across Kennedy's face. He was a Catholic, of course, and had already gone through intense grilling. He had not expected it from what appeared to be a high school student in the backwoods of Arkansas. Now he said, "I don't think my religion is the issue here."

"Why, Mr. Kennedy, the founders of our nation believed in God, and as I've said, our currency says we trust in him. I'd like to hear your comment on how that will affect you if you're elected president."

Kennedy's lips drew tight, and he lost his smile for a moment. "You're not a reporter in disguise, are you, young man?" Laughter followed his remark, and Kennedy regained his good humor. "When I'm elected president," he said, "you'll probably be a star reporter for the *New York Times*. I want you to come to my first news conference, and I'll guarantee you I will answer any questions." He sensed the mood of the audience, however, and said, "Of course I believe in God, and I believe in the values that the fathers of the nation have set before us. . . ."

After the meeting was over and the four students were

on their way home, Debbie said, "I was so thrilled that he answered your question."

"He didn't answer my question." Mark shrugged. "He just gave me a politician's noise."

From the backseat John said, "Why, he claimed to believe in God."

"Almost everybody in America claims that," Mark said as he swerved to miss a pothole in the road. "I caught him off guard a little bit, but he's a good man."

The car sped on through the darkness. As Mark settled down to the long drive back to Cedarville, Prue noticed that Debbie had moved as close as possible and Mark's arm had fallen around her shoulder. He steered the station wagon expertly with his left hand, and once she saw Debbie turn her face up and whisper something. Mark's head came around, and he gave her a quick kiss, then turned his eyes back toward the road.

Prue got out of the car when Mark stopped. He had let the others out already, and she had seen him take Debbie up to the front door, where they had remained longer than was necessary. When Mark had come back he was whistling and happy. Now Prue got out and said, "Thanks for taking me to the rally."

"It was fun, wasn't it?"

"Yes, it was. Good night, Mark."

She moved on into the house and found her parents still up.

"You didn't have to wait up," she said.

"Wait until you have a little girl going out on her first date and coming in at two o'clock in the morning," Dent said, but he was smiling. "Did you have a good time?"

"Yes. It was nice." She walked over to her parents, kissed them both, and went upstairs to her room.

"She don't seem very happy," Dent said. "I thought it was going to be fine for her."

"She'll tell me about it tomorrow, Dent."

The next day Prue did tell her mother the full story, and when she said, "I thought it was going to be a date, but it was Debbie that he was interested in. Not me," Violet remembered her own hard times. Now she came over and put her arms around this tall daughter of hers and said quickly, "Your turn will come."

"No. It never will."

2

CONCERT IN FORT SMITH

Prue entered her bedroom, singing under her breath Johnny Preston's version of "Running Bear," but as soon as she stepped inside she stopped dead still and looked wildly about. She had left her room in good order, but now it appeared as though a bomb had gone off. The drawers of her chest were opened, and clothes were pulled out; the snacks she kept on top of her desk were all opened, and over on her dressing table, beside her bed, sat the culprit, a yearling coon who had a jar of cologne in the clever fingers of his right paw and the top in the other. He stared at her, eyes beady, then dropped the bottle and cap, leaped off the dressing table, and scurried across the floor. When he reached the girl's feet, he reared up and pawed at her knee, his mouth open as if he were trying to speak.

"Bandit! What in the world have you done?" She stared down half filled with anger but amused at the same time. Her father had brought the coon home from a hunt, and she had raised it on a tiny doll's bottle filled with condensed milk. He had grown rapidly, and though she usually kept him outside in a pen, she had brought him up to her room earlier to play with him. A call from her mother had drawn her away, and now twenty minutes later she came back to the wreckage that had been her room.

"Bandit! You're a bad coon!" she scolded. The coon opened his mouth, and seeming to grin, pawed at her knees, making a plaintive noise in his throat. Stooping over, Prue picked him up and cuddled him as if he were a baby, holding his head beside her face. He nibbled at her ear gently, as he always did, and his tiny feet clutched her blouse. Despite herself, Prue laughed and shook her head. "You're a charmer," she said. "Now, look at this mess I've got to clean up." She put the coon down and wagged her finger at him. "Now you behave yourself while I clean up the mess you've made."

Quickly the girl started putting the room in order, stopping long enough to turn on the radio of her new stereo set. Ray Charles began to belt out "Hit the Road, Jack!" and when he had finished, Ricky Nelson's voice filled the room, and Prue sang along as he crooned "Travelin' Man."

Soon she paid little attention to the music and did not actually care for most of what she heard. Keeping one eye on Bandit, who seemed content with the stick of peppermint that she gave him as an offering, Prue completed her job, then hesitated for a moment and glanced at the clock. Quickly she turned, opened the door, and stepped into a room no more than eight by ten. It had been used as a storage room, perhaps as a bedroom, by her grandparents, but Prue had made it into her own special treasure room. She had transferred her diary there and for the past year concealed it in an old horsehide trunk with a curving top. The shelves were filled with items she had kept from her childhood on, including baby rattles and the toys that she had grown up with.

At one side of the room was an enormous chifforobe made out of cherry. It reached almost to the ceiling and was fully four feet wide. Taking a key from a gold chain around her neck, Prue unlocked the armoire and swung both doors open, thinking, *It's nice to have a private place like this.* She pulled out a twelve by fourteen pad covered with canvas used by artists, and snatched up a piece of charcoal. She glanced at the variety of paints that she had collected, mostly odds and ends, then turned and went out into the bedroom. Sitting down on the bed with her legs underneath her, she held the pad steady with her left hand and with her right began sketching the raccoon as he sat sucking on the peppermint. Her hand flew fast, and in a very short time she had captured the animal just as he polished off the candy. He dropped to all fours, came scurrying over, and clamored up on the bed, reaching for the pad.

"No you don't!" Prue scolded. "You can see it, though. That's you, Bandit." She studied the sketch she had done; it had caught the animal just as she wanted it. "Now," she said, "I'll begin painting it tonight if I have time, and you'll have your own picture." She reached over and picked him up, and he lifted his paws up to touch her face. She touched her nose to his and laughed. "I'll bet you'll be the only raccoon with a portrait by a famous artist." She laughed, put Bandit away, then went back and replaced the canvas and charcoal. Closing the door, she locked it and dropped the key back down the front of her shirt. She heard someone calling and stepped outside, then opened the door to her bedroom. Her mother was calling, "Come for supper!" and she called back, "All right, Momma. I'll be right there!"

She went down the stairs, taking them two at a time, and set the table for her mother. Soon her father came in and washed his hands at the sink in the kitchen despite his wife's protests. "We've got a bathroom for that!"

"If this sink is good enough," Dent grinned, "for my grandpa to wash his hands in, it's good enough for me." He dried his hands, came over, kissed her soundly, and she pushed him away. "That's the trouble with marrying a younger woman," he said. "They're hard to train up. I should have married an older woman." He had married Violet when she was extremely young, and he was a bachelor in his early thirties, but he had aged well, and people often took them to be about the same age.

They all sat down around the old oak table, and Dent asked the blessing, ending by saying, "And let the Wildcats win that football game tonight. Amen."

"Dent, you ought to be ashamed of yourself!" Violet said

with exasperation. "God doesn't care who wins that ball game."

"Lots of folks do, though," Dent said. "Don't see any harm in prayin' for a little edge. Louisville's got a bigger, faster team than Cedarville. Mark and John will have their work cut out for them with all those big linemen crashin' in." Mark Stevens was the quarterback and John Tyler played tight end for the Cedarville Wildcats; they had already been visited by college scouts.

Prue smiled at her father, who winked at her, and filled her plate full of green beans, fried okra, new potatoes, and two pork chops. She ate all that was on her plate, listening to her parents talk mostly, and then she polished off an enormous slice of fresh peach pie.

She got up to clean the table as her mother said, "Don't forget. I've got to go to the Missionary meeting tonight."

"Well, I did forget," Dent said. He reached over and grabbed Prue's arm as she started by and said, "Let's me and you go to that football game tonight."

Prue said, "It's too cold to go."

"You can wear your momma's fur coat."

"She cannot wear my fur coat, but she's got a perfectly good wool jacket. Do you want to go, Prue?"

"I guess so," Prue said. She helped her mother wash the dishes, then went back upstairs to dress for the ball game. She got ready early and entered the storage room and removed her diary. Coming back, she wrote firmly on the first clean page:

> *November the 5th, 1962. Daddy wants me to go to the football game with him tonight. Momma's going to a Missionary meeting, so I guess he doesn't want to be alone.*

She sat there for a moment staring at the page, then put down:

*I'd like to see Mark and John win their game. Everyone
says they're going to get scholarships at the University of
Arkansas. If they do, I'll never see them again, I suppose.
It's been a long time, it seems, since Mark took me to that
rally where John Kennedy spoke. A lot has happened since
then—for one thing I'm two inches taller! Will I ever stop
growing? I'm going to be a giant! I'm already taller than
nearly every boy in the senior class, but I will say that it's
nice to have filled out a little bit. I was as skinny as a rail
at that time, but now my figure's growing, and I've got hopes
that even if I am a giant, I'll be a well-shaped giant.*

The sound of the radio filled the room. It was Johnny Hor-
ton singing "Sink the Bismarck." She hummed along with
it for a while and thumbed through the pages of her current
journal. Kennedy had been elected president, of course, but
in April he had nearly lost his popularity when an invasion
of Cuba called the Bay of Pigs had failed. She turned a few
pages, noted that Gary Cooper, her favorite actor, had died
and that Alan Shepard had gone into space. A few pages later
she had made a note that Roger Maris had broken Babe Ruth's
home run record.

As she studied the pages, somehow she sensed that things
were not quite right. John Glenn had orbited the earth, but
the war in Vietnam had gotten worse. Just the previous month,
in October, President Kennedy was in trouble again when the
Russians were putting missiles into Cuba. She had sat up
with her family during what was called the Cuban Missile
Crisis, wondering, all of them, afraid that it might mean war.
She turned away from that page quickly, not wanting to think
about wars, and then read her entry stating that Marilyn Monroe had died. She remembered, for some reason, that the star's
death had made her cry. She was not a fan of Marilyn Monroe,
but the actress had seemed so beautiful on the screen, and
so full of life, and the thought of her lying cold and dead—a
suicide—had struck some chord deep in Prudence Deforge's

heart. She shut the book abruptly, put it back in its hiding place, then went downstairs.

Her mother had left, and her father was shrugging into his red and green mackinaw and pulling a wool stocking cap over his ears. "Well, we better get going." He stopped to look at this daughter of his critically. "You sure are gettin' pretty, Prue," he said, studying the oval face and generous lips of the young woman. "How old are you now? I forget."

Accustomed to his teasing, she said, "I'm seventeen, and I'm six feet tall. I wish I was six inches shorter. You think I can have the doctor shorten my legs? Cut a part of them out?"

Coming over to stand beside her, Dent, who was six foot three, said, "You're just right. A man likes a woman with some heft to her."

"Thank you, Daddy. Now come on, and let's go to the game."

The game was much like other high school football games. Partisans for each side seemed to grow crazy when their favorites scored or performed some good feat on defense. Even Prue, who did not understand all the intricacies of football, could appreciate Mark Stevens' play. He had a grace about him as he took the snap from the center, backed up, waited until the last minute, then fired a short pass right over the line, once in a while lifting one that carried fully fifty yards. Prue winced every time the bullish, opposing linemen knocked him down, but he always got up, and she could see a grin on his face.

It was a low scoring ball game, but the Wildcats won fourteen to ten. When it was over, Dent said, "You want to go down and congratulate Mark?"

"No. I'll tell him tomorrow on the way to school."

★　　★　　★

Leslie Stevens had just finished his pie at supper and was drinking his third cup of coffee, complements of his wife, Joy.

He had come to appreciate this wife of his more with every passing year. Joy kept her figure, and better than that, she had turned out to be an excellent mother for Mark. Les himself had grown frustrated at times with Mark when he was very small, but Joy had never wavered. His glance slid around the table, and he felt a satisfaction and a sense of well-being at his family. His business had prospered too. He had gone into electronics, and now everyone in the county knew that if anything electric went bad, Les Stevens was the man to see.

"Did you hear who's going to be in Fort Smith for a concert next Thursday?" Les asked.

"No. Who is it?"

"It's Bobby Stuart."

"Really? Prudence's cousin?" Joy said with surprise. "I can't believe he's coming to a little place like Fort Smith, Arkansas."

Bobby Stuart had become one of the rising rock-and-roll stars of America. He was the son of Jerry and Bonnie Stuart and the grandson of the late Amos Stuart. Bobby's brother, Richard, was now a minister in Los Angeles, and his sister, Stephanie, had married a newspaperman named Jake Taylor in Chicago. But it was Bobby who got the headlines.

Les shook his head. "I don't know whether the Stuarts should be proud of that boy or ashamed. Nice to see a young fella succeed, but this rock and roll—I just don't like it. Something is wrong. Kids seem to go crazy."

Mark had been eating his second piece of pie, and he swallowed a huge mouthful to say, "Well, like it or not it's here to stay. What with Elvis and people going crazy over him. I don't care much for it myself, but I have to admit it gives me a thrill to see one of Prue's kinfolk who's a star."

"Maybe you'd like to go over and see the boy," Les said. "I got two tickets." He fished into his shirt pocket and said, "I traded O. M. McCoy one of Henrietta's litter for 'em. I think he got the best of the deal. That's gonna be a fine coon dog!" He looked over and said, "Would you like these tickets, Mark?"

Mark nodded, his eyes brightening. "I sure would!"

"Wait a minute! You can't walk to Fort Smith," Les said.

"Well, maybe I could borrow your car, Dad."

"You can on one condition."

"Why, sure. What is it?"

"I think you ought to take Prudence with you. She hardly gets to go anywhere. Hearing her cousin would be a real treat for her."

Mark hesitated and frowned. "But I'm going steady with Debbie. You know that."

"I don't know anything about it. I know if you want to take the car, you'll take Prudence—and not *with* Debbie!"

The argument went on for some time, and Les leaned back, saucering his coffee and sipping it noisily, enjoying it. Finally Mark shrugged and said, "Well, all right, Dad, but Debbie's going to kill me."

★　★　★

Prue was painting the picture of the sketch she had made of Bandit when she heard her mother calling her. Quickly she moved into the storage room and locked the picture in the armoire. She did not know why she could not show her pictures, or sketches, or paintings to anyone. It had become a very private thing with her. She brought home report cards studded with mostly Cs and Ds, her good grades only in math, so when she had discovered at age eleven that she had a gift for drawing, it was something she kept secluded. She could not explain it to anyone. Perhaps she was afraid that she would fail at that as she did at everything else. At times she knew she was foolish and that she could get help from the art teachers in school, but somehow drawing had become a sanctuary for her. Many times she had gone into her room in tears over her failures in the classroom, but as she began to sketch, or to paint, somehow that all faded away and a sense of well-being and security would arise in her.

Now she went downstairs and found Mark standing in the kitchen talking to her mother. He grinned at her at once, saying, "Guess what you and me are going to do?"

Prue halted, and an alarm went off somewhere in her head. She had been nearly two years getting over what she thought would be her first date with Mark. It had left a tiny scar that was still sensitive, and now she said, "What do you mean? What are we going to do?"

Mark reached into his shirt pocket and pulled out two small pieces of cardboard. "Look at this. Two tickets to your cousin Bobby Stuart's concert."

Prue took the tickets, noted the date, then said, "This is in Fort Smith tomorrow."

"That's right. Dad says I can have the car, so I want us to go over and take it in. How about it?"

"What about Debbie? Is she going too?"

"Nope. This is just for you and me, Prue. I figure we could go give Bobby all the support we've got. Will you go?"

Prue turned and said, "Is it all right, Momma?"

"Why, of course. I think it would be fine, but I suppose you'll be home late."

"Probably will," Mark said cheerfully. "But you know me. Old reliable Mark. I'll take care of your little girl." He went over and put his arm around Violet and grinned down at her. "You trust me, don't you?"

Violet could not help but smile. "Yes I do, but you drive careful, you hear?"

After Mark had left, Violet said, "Isn't that nice?"

"At least it won't be like last time." There was a tone to Prue's voice that caught her mother's attention. She knew that the girl had never gotten over her disappointment, and now she said, "Well, this time it'll be just you and Mark, and you can have a good time."

★　　★　　★

As Prue got ready to go to Fort Smith, she remembered the last time she had gone to the same town—to hear Kennedy. This time she had not bought a new dress; the one she had was nice enough. Her mother and father had gone to Little Rock to visit one of her father's distant relatives. While they were there her mother had taken her to M. M. Cohen's, which had a tall woman's section, the first that Prue had ever seen. She had tried on dresses so often that simply did not fit, but here, for the first time in her life, she found that there were dresses made for tall women. The saleswoman had been very helpful, and finally her mother bought her three dresses; Prue had gasped at the price, saying, "Daddy will kill us!"

"You deserve them, Prudence. Now, just see how nice you look."

Prue stared into the mirror at the dress she had chosen. It was a purple and blue checkered print with a rounded neck, long, narrow sleeves, and a low, hip-hugging waistline, and it fell to midthigh. Her legs were covered with dark blue tights, and she had on a pair of black, low-heeled shoes. She could not help but admit that she looked better than she had two years earlier, for though she was tall, her figure had blossomed, and as she left the room and went downstairs, she was hopeful that Mark would notice.

Mark came up to the door, and when he opened it his eyes brightened. "Hey! We look good, don't we? Both of us."

Prue laughed shyly, saying, "Yes, you certainly do." He was wearing a dark blue sweater with long sleeves and a V-neck where a light blue knit shirt peeked out, a pair of khaki-colored slacks, and two-tone oxfords.

Mark opened the door for her when they were outside at the car, then got into the car beside her. "Here we come, Fort Smith! Hey," he said, "you remember the last time we went? It was to hear Kennedy."

"I remember."

Something about the brevity and terseness of her reply caught Mark, and he suddenly remembered that she had not been happy. But now he said, "Just you and me this time, Prue. I got enough money saved that we can go to that fancy Italian restaurant after the concert."

The drive to Fort Smith seemed to go by very quickly, and Mark, who could be highly entertaining, kept her laughing most of the way. When they arrived at the Municipal Auditorium it was packed, as they had expected. Shoving their way through the crowd, Mark muttered, "Not exactly what I expected. We look out of place here."

Prue had already discovered that. She looked vainly for others wearing nice, sensible clothing, but several of the teens looked like what had come to be called "Hippies." Most of them, boys and girls, wore T-shirts with various signs or symbols on them, some of them downright vulgar; blue jeans, either skin tight or sometimes exceptionally baggy; and penny loafers.

"Well, I guess this is the rock-and-roll crowd," Mark said, shaking his head. "They look pretty bad to me. Some of them need to take a bath."

Prue nodded, but before she could speak the program began. An emcee came out and introduced an act that proved to be loud: four men who could jump around the stage expertly while playing guitars. The lyrics were familiar, some of them, for most rock performers latched on to current hits. Prue settled down with Mark, aware that his arm was touching hers and of his pleasant cologne. It felt good that she didn't have to slump as she did with most boys to try to be shorter, and despite her distaste for some of the music, she enjoyed herself.

Finally Bobby Stuart came on. Prue knew him, of course, for he came to the Stuart family reunions, but he had not been there for the past two years, and he had changed. His auburn hair was longer, his blue-green eyes seemed almost electric, and his handsome face was rougher. It was not his looks alone, but something about his presence that came across. He sometimes stood at the piano and played standing up, his left hand pounding a steady beat while the fingers of his right hand flew over the keyboard. His hair fell in his face, and he moved his shoulders to the rhythm as the house went wild.

Mark watched, with shock, as the crowd seemed to lose all semblance of sanity, mostly young women who screamed and threw their arms around wildly. It interested him, but he raised his voice, and putting his head close to Prue's ear, said, "I hope you don't go into a fit like that."

Aware of his lips almost touching her face, Prue shook her head. "I don't think there's any danger. They all act like maniacs. Bobby can sing and play, but they act like he's a god of some kind."

That was the impression that both of them got. There was idolatry in the wave of adulation that swept through the auditorium, and when the act was over, several young girls broke through the guards and came pulling at Bobby, trying to tear his clothing off apparently.

"Come on," Mark said, standing up. "We're going back to see your kinfolk."

Staring at him, Prue shook her head. "They'd never let us in."

"That's what you think. Just stick with me, Prudence."

Mark's confidence was not unfounded, for after most of the fans had filtered away, he accosted a local policeman, saying, "Go tell Bobby his cousin is out here. Prudence Deforge."

It worked, somehow, and they were permitted to go back to Bobby's dressing room. He had taken off his coat and was removing his makeup when they came in. His eyes lit up when he saw Prudence, and he jumped up immediately. "Hey, this is great! Why didn't you come earlier? We could've gone out together."

"We didn't want to bother you, Bobby," Prue said. "This is Mark Stevens, and I guess you remember me."

Bobby shook Mark's hand, then turned to Prue. "No, I

don't remember you," he said. When Prudence looked disappointed, he grinned and said, "I remember a skinny, little girl with some kind of weird bangs, but this is another story." He put his arms around her and said, "You done growed up on me, Prudence." He kissed her on the cheek and laughed. "Well, let's go out and eat. I'm starved."

Bobby had become adroit at missing the crowds. He had called ahead, and they had a private room at the fanciest restaurant in Fort Smith. As they sat down to a table covered with a white tablecloth and candles gleaming, he said, "I can't go into McDonald's anymore. They tear my clothes off of me."

The waiter came, and Bobby said, "Order anything. I'll have spaghetti myself."

"That sounds good to me. What about you, Prue?" Mark asked.

"Oh yes. That'll be fine."

For the next hour and a half Mark and Prue sat there listening as Bobby talked and ate, dropping such names as Buddy Holly, Elvis, and other stars in the firmament of the rock world.

After the meal, Bobby said, "I've got a little partying to do. You two come along. It'll be fun."

Quickly Mark said, "We'd like to, Bobby, but I promised Prue's parents that I'd get her home as soon as possible. It's a long drive; we'll have to take a rain check."

Bobby twirled a wine glass in his fingers and leaned back in his chair. There was a strange light in his blue eyes, and he studied them clinically as if they were creatures from another planet. "I can remember," he said very quietly, "when Richard and I were growing up. He was always conscious of what our parents wanted. Always wanted to be home on time so they wouldn't worry, and I was always the one who stayed out until morning."

A pensive expression crossed his face, and he appeared to listen to the music that was playing softly in the background for a time. "Now Richard's preaching in the slums of Los

Angeles, and I'm making a million dollars a year." He said no more, but it was obvious to both of his hearers that it was a subject that preyed on his mind often. He spoke again, and it was as if he was talking to himself, not to the two who sat before him. "As long as the spotlight's on, and the kids are screaming my name, or as long as I'm partying, it doesn't seem to matter much. But every time I get quiet like this, I think about what it all means, and sometimes it just doesn't add up." Abruptly he shook his shoulders in a strange gesture of dissatisfaction, drank the rest of the wine, then stood up saying, "Well, the party's about to begin. Hey, Mark, do you like to hunt deer? How about if you and I go together while I'm here?"

"You mean it?" Mark demanded.

"Is the Pope Catholic?" Bobby grinned. "I'll be dropping by to see your folks, Prue—and you can take me hunting, Mark."

After they left the restaurant and began their journey homeward, Prue and Mark did not speak much for some time. It was a cold, starry night, and Mark turned the heater up full, and also the radio. He found a powerful station, and for a while the sound of music filled the car. Finally he said, "Did it seem to you that something was troubling Bobby tonight?"

"Yes, it did," Prue answered. "It's strange, isn't it? All that money, and everyone screaming his name, but I could see in his eyes that he's not happy."

They drove along quietly, and the twisting road took all of Mark's attention. Finally Prue grew sleepy and jerked several times, pulling herself out of sleep. But the music was soft, and the car was warm, and the meal had been heavy. She drifted off to sleep, and soon she began to slump over toward Mark. He glanced at her, and seeing that her head was dropping, carefully reached over and pulled her against him, holding her tight against the swaying of the car, steering skillfully with his left hand. A protective sense came over him as he held her, and a smile touched his wide lips. He had his long thoughts about this girl who was so strange to so many. The kids at school made fun of her, because she was overly tall in their opinion and because of her poor grades. But as he stole a glance at her face, which was in sweet repose, he thought, *She's a good kid. I've got to look out for her more than I have in the past. Maybe I can find her one of the guys to be her steady. I'll talk to Tim Netherwood. He's a nice guy and hasn't been much for girls. I'll talk to Tim*, he promised himself.

Prue came out of her deep sleep and for a moment could not remember where she was. Suddenly she became aware that her head was on a shoulder and she was clutching a sweater that covered a warm, living body; then it all came back and she sat up blushing, thankful for the darkness so Mark could not see her face. "I'm–I'm sorry. I must have dropped off to sleep."

Mark's arm was around her shoulder, and he squeezed her. Her hair smelled sweet, and there was something touching in her confused protest. "You sure did drop off. For about an hour and a half," he said. "We're almost home."

Prue was intensely aware of Mark's arm around her and did not know whether to pull away or let it remain. Finally he moved it and flexed it, saying, "My arm's asleep. You sure did get a good nap."

Soon they pulled up in front of the Deforge house. There was a light on in the living room, and Mark said, "I'd better go in and make my excuse. It's a little later than I thought."

"What time is it?"

"After two. Come along."

The two of them got out of the car, walked up the porch, and entered the house, but they were greeted with silence. "I guess they've gone to bed," Prue said. They were standing inside the hallway with a full view to the living room; she turned, and her eyes were bright, refreshed by her sleep. "It was such a good trip, Mark," she said quietly. "Thank you so much for taking me."

Mark started to say "Good night," but as she stood before

him, there was a vulnerability in her and a sweetness that touched him. "It was fun for me too," he said. He was standing very close to her, and he reached out and ran his hand over her hair. "I think it's one of the best nights I've ever had. You're fun to be with, Prue." Her perfume was very faint, but he caught the scent of it. He was accustomed to leaning over and peering down at Debbie from his great height, but Prue's face was not far below his own, and she was looking up at him, her dark eyes unreadable. Without meaning to, he reached forward, pulled her close, and kissed her on the lips, then released her. "Good night, Prue," he said huskily, then turned and left.

Prudence had been kissed before, but this kiss was somehow different. She touched her lips with her fingers and stood silently for a moment, listening as the car started up and pulled out of the driveway; then she turned and walked up the stairs. When she entered her room, she moved to retrieve her diary, brought it back, and sat down at the desk. Her lips still seemed to tingle from Mark's caress, and she wrote one item in a hand that was not quite steady:

Mark kissed me!

3

A ROUGH PARTY

Be still now, Elvis!"

The fledgling bird stirred frantically in Prue's hands as she tried to calm him down. She had found the baby mockingbird with an injured wing, apparently just out of the nest, and had nursed him back to health. Now as he fluttered wildly she saw that the wing was strong, and she waited until he calmed down. She had named him Elvis, hoping that she could keep him and that he would sing for her, but as with so many of the wild things she captured, she could not bear to keep the bird cooped up. She was standing now outside the barn and with a swift movement tossed the bird up in the air. She watched as his wings beat almost frantically; then as they caught the rhythm, he sailed off, flying directly for the green hedge where the mockingbirds always nested.

"Good-bye, Elvis! I'll be seeing you!"

Her head was full of schemes on how to feed the birds throughout the winter, and she had bird feeders all over the Deforge property, also birdhouses and everything that would entice any sort of bird to come. Now she made her rounds, replacing the peanut butter that the winter birds seemed to like, along with the suet and the wild bird seed. She was happy as she moved, for any kind of bird or animal attracted her, and she had had every sort of pet imaginable—to the despair of her parents.

The sound of her name being called caused her to lift her head, and she looked up to see Mark loping along in that easy gait of his that seemed to devour the distance. He was wearing a pair of black tennis shoes and a sky-blue running suit. His cheeks were flushed with the cool air, and he began speaking even when he was thirty yards away, his voice filled with excitement.

"Hey, Prue! Guess what?" He reached out and took her arm, grinning broadly. "We got a visitor coming."

"Who's that, Mark?"

"Bobby called this morning. Said he's coming for that visit he promised us. Won't that be a kick?"

"I'll be glad to see him."

Mark dropped his hand from her arm and cocked his head to one side. His tawny hair was mussed by the brisk November breeze, and perplexity showed itself in his gray eyes. "You'll be glad to see him?" he mocked her. "Every girl in Cedarville High School will be turning backflips just to get close to him, and you'll be glad to see him!"

Prue smiled then and brushed her dark hair back from her face. Her face was also flushed from her exercise in the cool wind. During the winter her complexion grew pale, but during the summers she tanned in one day, the envy of the girls who spent hours lying under a burning sun. She was wearing a pair of jeans that had been torn in both knees from her grubbing around in the garden during the summer and fall and a gray sweatshirt with a collar and sleeves of green exposed. "He's my cousin, and I'll be glad to see him," she said, "but not as glad as some of the other girls of course. They practically fall down and worship the ground rock stars walk on."

Mark nodded. "I'm glad you're not like that," he said fervently. "Well, I got to get going. I got to break the news."

The news spread all through the school, and no one was more excited than Debbie Peters. When Mark told her that Bobby Stuart was coming and might visit the school, her eyes flew open with a startled expression, and her lips formed a round "O." Then she began talking rapidly. "You've got to get him to go out with us. Oh, Mark, promise me!"

"Well," Mark said reluctantly, "he's coming mostly to visit Prue's parents and go hunting with me, but I'll see what I can do."

Debbie put herself against Mark in a way that she had used before when she wanted something. Her voice grew into a purr, and she reached up and stroked his cheek. "Now, honey, you can do this for me. After all, it's not too much to ask."

The pressure of her firm, young curves against him warmed Mark. "Sure," he said, "I'll do my best." He watched her as she ran off eagerly spreading the news to the other girls, and he realized that for her having Bobby Stuart come to her house would be a social triumph.

After school that day, the gang all went to McDonald's, where those with money crammed themselves with hamburgers and french fries buried under an ocean of ketchup.

"Hey, is that right, Mark?" Maxine Elders said. "Is it true that Bobby Stuart is coming to our school?"

"I think he will. It'll be a little bit different from the usual assembly program, won't it?" Bobby had tentatively agreed to speak to the student body and perhaps to perform just a few songs.

Mark's words were picked up, and he looked over to see that Debbie's face was flushed. Her eyes were flashing, and she was talking as fast as possible. He drew a sigh and thought soberly, *Well, Bobby, old son. I think if you knew all of this, you wouldn't have agreed to come for a visit!*

★   ★   ★

Bobby Stuart arrived in all of his glory on Thursday, driving a lavender Cadillac convertible. Mark first got a hint of it when Debbie came to him, grabbing his football sweater. "He's outside in his convertible! Come on, Mark!"

Mark did not have to ask who was outside, and when he cleared the front door of the red brick school, he saw Bobby sitting up on the back of the seat, the car already surrounded by milling students.

"Well, he's here," Mark said. "Come on. Let's go make him feel welcome." He made his way through the press of students, and when he got to the side of the car, having towed Debbie with him with his left hand, he reached up and shook hands with Bobby. "Didn't expect to see you here so early," he said.

"Can't wait to get that ten-pointer." Bobby grinned. He was wearing a black wool maxicoat; a bright red shirt that had a wide collar, long, full sleeves, and was unbuttoned quite far down the front; a pair of tight-fitting, black bell-bottom pants; and black boots with chunky heels. He winked at Debbie, who was still held by Mark's hand. "Is this your main squeeze?"

"Yes, this is Debbie Peters. Debbie, Bobby Stuart."

Bobby came down off the seat of the Cadillac in one easy leap. He was not quite six feet tall, much shorter than Mark, but since Debbie was short, he could look down at her. She was wearing somewhat more than the standard school uniform, having known that the rock star would be there. Her dress was a dusty rose color and was made out of a thin, knit orlon material. It had a round neck, was short in length, and was covered with a matching sweater that she kept unbuttoned. Bobby reached for her hand and winked at Mark, saying, "You better watch out. I'm liable to steal your girl."

Laughter and looks of envy went around, mostly from the other young girls.

"Come on. We've got to stop by Prue's house. Her folks are anxious to see you." A groan went up from the crowd, and Mark added, "I hate to put the arm on you, Bobby, but I sort of agreed that you'd come to assembly tomorrow. You know, just tell us a little bit about show business and maybe sing a song or two."

"Why, sure. Be glad to." Bobby grinned as the crowd burst into applause, and he looked at Debbie, saying, "I'll see you

again, little lady. Maybe you can find me a lady to go with you
and Mark, and we can all go out." He ran his eyes over the
crowd and saw a tall redhead who was looking at him with a
bold attitude. He seemed to freeze; then he smiled and lifted
his hand. "This lady right here, if she's not spoken for."

"Oh, sure," Mark said. "This is Margie Satterfield. Come
and meet Bobby."

Margie came forward. She was a senior, and her reputation
was none too good. There was a sensuous quality in the way
that she moved and looked, and she turned her head to one
side and smiled. "I'd be happy to go out with you, Bobby."

On the way to Prue's house Mark said, "How come you
picked Margie Satterfield?"

Bobby was driving the Cadillac carelessly at almost top
speed, so Mark had to hang on. He turned and grinned. "She's
a rebel."

"Well, I guess she is, sort of, but how did you know
that?"

Bobby shrugged. "Don't know, but I'm a rebel myself. It's
a funny thing," he said, swerving to dodge a mustard-colored
dog that yelped and tucked his tail between his legs as the
lavender Cadillac shot by, nearly touching him. "I can go into
a room with fifty kids there, and if there's one in that group
that's a rebel, it seems just like we're magnetized. Rebels
kind of draw each other, I guess."

"Well, you found the right one. Margie hasn't got too good
a name at school."

Again the rash grin creased Bobby Stuart's lips. "Just the
kind I'm lookin' for," he said as he reached over and punched
Mark in the arm. "Now, let's talk about that deer we're going
to get."

That night Bobby had dinner with Prue and her parents.
They enjoyed talking about the Stuart clan and reminiscing
about the reunions. After dinner Bobby walked over to Mark's
and decided to spend the night there.

★   ★   ★

The next day the two went to school early where, to the delight of the student body and even most of the faculty, Bobby made an appearance at the weekly assembly program. Usually it was a boring time with a local politician speaking earnestly about how the students of Cedarville High School could make America great. Always there was a great deal of dozing, punching, pinching, and all in all a real waste of time in the view of most students.

Bobby was introduced by the superintendent, Mr. Simms, and was greeted by thunderous applause and the stamping of feet as he came and began to speak. He was a polished speaker by this time, knowing exactly what to give each crowd. He spoke for some time about music of different kinds—bluegrass, blues, jazz, mainline—and then finally gave a brief history of rock and roll. He was witty and kept the faculty and the student body amused, amazed, and impressed as he spoke of the giants of the entertainment world as if they were his intimate friends—which some of them were.

Finally he walked over to the piano and gave a brief performance. It was not his usual performance, for he chose the rather placid standards such as "Roses Are Red," which was on the charts with Bobby Vinton's version. He played Ray Charles' "I Can't Stop Loving You," and the crowd went wild. He stayed away, however, from the more blatantly raw songs that were on the charts, and finally when it was over he said, "I know that some people have the idea that rock-and-roll stars are all terribly immoral and dangerous, and perhaps there's some truth to that. I want to encourage all of you," he said earnestly, "to stay in school, work hard, prepare yourself. I've seen a lot of young fellas and young girls put their hearts into being performers and then fail. Since they didn't do anything else to get ready for life, they went down the drain." He paused and then smiled at the faculty. "You people are doing a great job, and I honor you for it."

Afterward Mark left with Bobby, having obtained permission from the principal to take the day off. The two went to Mark's house, changed clothes, and left with two 30-30 rifles, one Mark's and one his father's.

The hunt proved very enjoyable. Bobby talked, not about show business but about his family mostly. This was surprising to Mark, but it suited him. Out of the spotlight, Bobby seemed to be quite different. He was quiet, and as the two sat on the stand with long silences, Mark would often look at Bobby thinking how strange it was that someone from Prue's family was a nationally known entertainer. He had no envy, however, and Bobby sensed this, for once he said, "You wouldn't care for my lifestyle, would you, Mark?"

"Not really."

"What do you want to do?"

"What I'd really like to do is become a writer, maybe a reporter like your grandpa Amos. I think he really did some good in the world with what he wrote."

Bobby turned his head slightly, letting his eyes fall upon the younger man. "Yes, he did," he said briefly. "Don't suppose I do much good singing the stuff I do."

Mark tried to think of a suitable reply but could only say, "Well, like Yogi Berra says, 'It ain't over till it's over,' Bobby."

The answer seemed to intrigue Bobby Stuart, and finally he muttered, "Well, I hope before it's over I do more good than just exciting a bunch of hysterical teenyboppers."

They got no deer that day, but the next morning they were out early, and Bobby got his trophy, a fine ten-point buck. It seemed to please him more than any of the awards he had gotten from the world of entertainment. They dressed the deer out and took the head to the local taxidermist. Bobby said as they left, "I reckon we ought to celebrate tonight. I'm looking forward to our party with your lady and Margie—what's her name?"

"Margie Satterfield."

"Yep! That girl's quite a swinger."

Clearing his throat, Mark said, "You better be a little bit careful. She's a local girl, and—"

"Oh, don't worry," Bobby said. "I'll treat her just exactly like she wants to be treated."

★　　★　　★

Bobby Stuart looked around the interior of the Blue Moon and grinned with satisfaction. "This looks like my kind of place," he said. He turned to wink at Margie, whose arm he was holding tightly. "What do you think about it, sweetie?"

"I been here before," Margie said, leaning against him. "The last time I came Pa found out about it and just about killed me."

"Well, let's hope Daddy don't find out about it," Bobby answered. "You ever been here before, Mark?"

"Nope. Never have. Kind of got a shady reputation." He shifted uneasily and glanced at Debbie. "I'm not sure I should have brought you, Debbie."

"Oh, don't be such an old stick-in-the-mud! It'll be all right." She was excited. Her eyes glowed as she looked around the room. "I've always wondered what it was like in here."

The Blue Moon was like dozens of other small places of entertainment scattered around the county. It was set back off Highway 23, a low, squat building with a flat roof and the windows blacked out. The parking lot usually sported more pickup trucks than anything else, for it was the home of the indigent redneck. The five-piece country western band was already at work, and the clientele were highly appreciative. A constant battle was fought between the local authorities, for although there was a liquor license in existence, the Blue Moon was the scene for underage drinking and activities such as drug dealing and fights between young, rawboned farmers wearing Tony Llama boots and Stetsons.

They found their way unassisted to a table, and a waitress wearing too much mascara came over and said, "What'll it be?"

Bobby said, "Bring us the best you got, and keep it comin', honey."

The waitress looked at him and chewed her gum intensely. "Ain't I seen you before somewhere?"

"Sure, I'm Elvis Presley's twin brother. Don't you see the resemblance?"

"Ah, get out of here," the waitress said scornfully, and twisted away, fighting off several eager hands as she made her way to the bar.

Actually there was little doing in the Blue Moon except for the purpose of consuming as much beer and hard liquor as possible. The band members took turns singing, and all of them had the same twangy voice that seemed prerequisite for a country western singer.

After an hour, the room was filled with the acrid smell of marijuana and cigarette smoke, and the noise had increased to an astonishing level so that the only way to be understood was to shout.

Mark leaned over and said, "Debbie, I feel as out of place here as a long-tailed cat in a roomful of rockers. There's gonna be trouble here sure as you're born."

"Oh, it's fun, Mark. Come on. Let's dance."

Mark did not consider himself much of a dancer, but at least he was sober, which could not be said for most of the other patrons. Debbie snuggled close in his arms, her eyes going all around the room. She danced twice with Bobby, and Mark danced with Margie. He asked her, "What do you think of Bobby?"

"He's really somethin'," Margie said. She was wearing a dress that revealed her charms, and she grinned wickedly. "He's got designs on me, I do believe."

Startled, Mark flushed and said, "Be careful, Margie. This is a different kind of world than Cedarville High School."

"You better believe it," Margie said, obviously pleased with the difference.

After two hours, Mark looked at his watch. It was only ten o'clock, but he said, "I've had about enough of this, Debbie. Come on."

Debbie protested, but Mark leaned over and said, "How about let's cut out of here, Bobby?"

Bobby had been drinking drink for drink with some of the rough-looking fellows that had come around to meet him. The word was out that he was Bobby Stuart, and they were all curious.

Bobby said, "No, I'm gonna give a little concert here. Stick around. You'll see somethin'."

The concert at the Blue Moon was not the same as the one Bobby had given at the high school assembly. He sang the raw blues of New Orleans, the lyrics being scandalous and blunt. He sang jazz, and then he moved into the senior side of rock and roll, which dealt almost altogether with sex and drugs.

As Mark sat there he kept his head down, for he felt embarrassed, and shocked, and ashamed by what was going on. When he did glance up he saw that Bobby had shed his coat and perspiration was on his forehead. He was on some sort of drugs, Mark figured, although he had not seen him take any. "I wish we could get out of here, Debbie," he said. "Maybe after he gets through singing."

But afterward Bobby clung to Margie, who seemed to melt against him. He leaned over and kissed her roughly, and she put her arms around his neck. Mark had been watching her and knew she had drunk hard liquor, and he did not know what else she had taken. Her eyes were getting glazed, and there was a looseness to her mouth and a suggestiveness in the way she leaned up against Bobby Stuart.

"Come on, Bobby. Let's get out of here," he said. But he had little hope of any response. He got none either, for Bobby simply shook his head, saying, "I'm having too much fun, Mark."

"Well, I've got to go and get Debbie home."

"See you tomorrow," was all that Bobby said; then he turned his attention back to Margie Satterfield.

Debbie protested but knew that it was hopeless. They drove home, and when Mark took Debbie to the door she leaned against him and he kissed her, but his mind was preoccupied. "I wish Margie and Bobby had come on with us. That's a pretty rough place."

Debbie was angry at having to leave the party, and angrier still that Mark paid no attention to her when she put her arms around his neck and pulled at him. "Well, go on then!" she said. "You're nothing but a blue-nosed Puritan!" She stepped inside, slammed the door, and Mark went back to the car feeling that the night had been a disaster.

★   ★   ★

"Mark, get up!"

He had been asleep, his head under the covers, but when he surfaced he saw his father standing there. "What is it, Dad?" he mumbled.

"Get your clothes on and come downstairs," Les said. There was a stiffness in his voice and a serious look in his eyes that brought Mark awake instantly. He did not question the orders, and after his father left, he jumped out of bed and pulled on a pair of jeans, socks and shoes, and a pullover. When he went downstairs, he found his father standing with Sheriff Zach Wilkins in the living room. Wilkins turned around, nodded, and said, "Hello, Mark."

"Why, hello, Sheriff," Mark said, and even as he stood there, a sense of disaster began to grow in him. "What's the matter?" he asked quickly.

Sheriff Wilkins was a tall, lanky man of thirty with a droopy mustache and a set of cool, blue eyes. He pulled his hat off now and asked directly, "You were at the Blue Moon last night, weren't you?"

"Yes, sir, I was. Debbie and I went with—"

"With Bobby Stuart and Margie Satterfield." Sheriff Wilkins nodded. "What time did you leave?"

"Oh, it wasn't late. About ten thirty, I guess."

"But Bobby and Margie didn't come with you?"

The sense of disaster grew within Mark. "Why, no. They were going to stay a little longer." He hesitated, then said, "What's wrong, Sheriff?"

The sheriff's eyes grew bleak, as cold as polar ice. "Margie Satterfield's parents have filed a complaint. They claim she was assaulted."

"Oh no!" Mark gasped. He looked at his father and understood the glance of disapproval. "She was all right when we left there," he said weakly.

"Well, she's not all right now. Did you see her take any dope?"

"Well, she had a few drinks—"

"How many?"

After Mark answered all of Sheriff Wilkins' questions, he finally asked, "What's going to happen?"

Closing his notebook with a vicious gesture, Sheriff Wilkins stuffed it in his pocket, then jammed his hat on his head. "Probably nothing to the one responsible!" He looked at Les and said, "I'm sorry that Mark had to get involved with this, Les, but it looks like he's clean, at least."

"What's going to happen to Bobby?" Mark burst out.

"Nothing probably." Disgust was rich in Wilkins' voice and he shook his head. "He's already made bond and skipped out. We'll never get him. Not with the money he's got to hire lawyers." He adjusted his hat and turned to face Les, saying again, "Sorry about this, Les."

"I'm sorry too. Margie's people are going to be pretty broken up."

"Yes, they are, and that—" Wilkins started to say more, but then pulled his lips together into a tight line and shook his head in disgust. He turned and left the house, and as soon as the door slammed Les said, "Sorry you got involved with this. It's going to be bad for Margie's family."

"Gee, Dad, I am too. I didn't want to go to that Blue Moon in the first place. I sure didn't think anything like this would ever happen."

Les Stevens' face suddenly reflected a sadness. "I'm sorry for Bobby's parents," he said. "They'll suffer the most over this."

"Do you suppose the newspapers will get it?"

"What do you think? You know journalism. It's what you want to do. Would you miss a story like this?"

Mark shifted nervously and clenched his fists. "I guess you're right. If I'd known about it, I'd never have let Bobby go to that place."

"You couldn't have stopped him. That young man's on a downhill run, and he's going to crash one of these days." A sense of doom and frustration seemed to hang over the two. They stood there, and finally Mark said, "I'm sorry, Dad. I should have been more careful."

"Not your fault. A man makes his own choices—and Bobby Stuart seems to be a genius at making the wrong ones!"

4

GROWING UP—HARD!

Prue stirred, bringing her head out from under the covers as her automatic alarm went off. She hated the harsh, ringing sound and had set the radio to play; Bob Dylan's voice filled the room, singing "Blowing in the Wind." She lay there drowsily until Dylan finished, and then she sang along with Andy Williams on "Can't Get Used to Losing You." At long last she threw the covers back, moved down the hall to the bathroom, and after washing her face, she came back and quickly dressed. As usual, she paid little attention to what she wore. She couldn't wear the three dresses bought from the tall shop at M. M. Cohen's in Little Rock all the time, so she pulled on a skirt that was too short and a blouse whose sleeves were two inches above her wrist bones, then shook her head with a sense of despair. She had refused to play girls' basketball primarily because she was ashamed to wear the brief uniforms, and she felt she was all bones. This had been several years ago, and despite pressure from almost everyone, except her parents and Mark, she had kept her resolve. Standing before the mirror, she pulled the brush and comb through her thick hair and analyzed herself. "Too tall, too gaunt, figure like a coat hanger!"

Abruptly she moved away, replaced the comb and brush, then grabbed her books and left her room.

At breakfast she was quieter than usual, and her father reached over and pinched her chin, grinning as she blinked. His face was fresh from a shave, and his eyes were fixed on her as he urged, "You need to get out more. What ever happened to that young fellow that was hanging around? What was his name?"

"George Featherstone."

"Yeah, that's it! Nice young fellow. What ever happened to him?"

"He got tired of reaching up to kiss me good night." Featherstone had been a respectable five ten, but the two inches between his own height and that of Prudence made a difference. She had seen it in his eyes and knew that he had taken considerable ribbing. Finally she had said, "George, go find a short girl. No point our carrying on like this." He had grinned and said, "Doesn't bother me if it doesn't bother you, Prue." However, he had taken her advice and dated one of the majorettes who was a diminutive five four.

"There must be some tall guy in that school who appreciates a good-looking girl."

"There is," Prue said, taking a bite of her toast and rising from the table. "His name is Leon Dicus."

"Oh yeah! Plays guard, doesn't he, on the football team?"

"That's him. You wouldn't like him." She paused at the door, turned around, and shook her head futilely. "I don't," she said, and then turned and left the house. She found Mark at the end of the driveway, as usual, and they exchanged greetings while waiting for the bus.

When they were aboard, she and Mark sat down next to each other. As soon as the bus lurched off, he said, "I been thinking, Prue. You know the tryouts for the school play are tonight. I think you ought to give it a whirl."

"I'm no actress."

Mark laughed and nudged her on the shoulder. "I'm no actor, either, but I'm going to try out. It's not going to be a very classy play, and it'll probably be bad. All high school plays are, I think. All I've seen anyway." He looked out the window for a time, examining the landscape as if he had never seen it before, then returned to his conversation. "Debbie will get the lead role, she always does, and I'm hoping to get the lead male role."

"You'll get it," Prue said firmly.

"Well, maybe so, but in any case, there are two or three more roles, and anyway, it's not the acting. Well, it's just the fun of it. The rehearsals, going out for hamburgers afterward, and it's always a lot of laughs. Mr. Spender will be directing it. He's a good egg. Full of energy and hoping to make this a great production that'll set the world on its ear." He laughed and turned to face her, his eyes bright with humor. "I told him waiting for the results of a high school play was like throwing a rose petal off the Grand Canyon and waiting for the effect."

Prue could not help but laugh. "You do have a way with words, Mark. I think you're right about that, though."

"Will you try out?" he asked eagerly. "Some of the rehearsals will be late, and I'll have the car, so gettin' back and forth won't be any trouble."

Prue had taken part in very few activities at school. A thought came to her mind, *This is Mark's last year. Next year he'll be off somewhere starting on a football team and surrounded by pretty girls. This is my last chance to get any time with him.* "All right," she said smiling. "It probably won't do any good. Do they have a part that calls for a female giraffe?"

Mark frowned, reached down, and took her hand and squeezed it until it hurt. "Don't say that!" he said. "I don't like it! You're always putting yourself down, Prue. All of us have things we can't do and things we can do."

Prue did not answer. She looked down at his strong, large hand that covered hers, then looked up and said, "What can I do?"

"You can take care of crippled birds, and you can bake the best coconut pies in the Western world. Maybe in the universe. Yes, in the universe." He began to tease her, and finally said, "All right. The tryouts are after school. We'll stick together. Right?"

All that day Prue looked forward to the tryouts with dread

and yet a faint ray of hope. She had no idea if she could be a competent actress, but she had a good memory and knew that she could memorize her lines quickly. The thought of stepping out on a stage before a crowd of people—well, she blotted that out of her mind. She had sung at church before— for she had a lovely contralto voice—but this was different.

That day at the tryouts Prue found herself almost ready to bolt. She might have run away, except one of her friends, Lylah Maddox, latched onto her, saying, "I'm so glad you came. Maybe we can both be in the play, and we could help each other with our lines."

Mr. Spender, the English teacher and director of the play, was a rather small man of thirty-three with thinning blond hair and pale blue eyes. He loved drama and inevitably directed all of the school plays. Now he stood up and said briskly, "This will just be a preliminary tryout.

"As some of you are aware, I will have each of you today read a small part, and then from these I will select some who will do a full-fledged scene. It's a difficult thing to cast a play, and I want us to have the best production possible. Now, let me pass these out. Who's trying out for the part of Helen Teague?" He smiled as only one hand went up. "All right, Debbie. No point in trying you out since you have no competition. Okay, what about the part of Harry Bowers?" He looked over three or four boys, Mark being one of them, handed out some sheets, then moved on down the line.

Prue took the sheet of paper and studied it. She had a phenomenal memory, and by the time she was called to stand up on the stage and read the part, she knew it perfectly. Her heart almost failed her, even though there were only a few students there, but she saw Mark wink at her and give her the high sign. Without glancing at the paper, she recited the part in a clear voice and stepped down off the stage, thinking, *Well, that's that!*

She was mistaken, however, in her feeling that she would not be chosen. Mr. Spender came to her and said, "I can tell you right now you're in the running, Prudence. You have a good, clear voice, and I think you might do well in the part of Sally. It's not a big part, but it's very important. The main character, Helen, will be defined by those around her, especially by the character called Sally." He handed her a few sheets of paper, and said, "We'll try you on a scene tomorrow with other actors and see how you do."

The next day after almost a sleepless night, Prue walked through the scene somewhat awkwardly, but not forgetting her lines. The scene involved Helen, played by Debbie Peters, and she knew her lines perfectly as well.

After the scene was done, Prue left the auditorium feeling that she had at least a chance. Debbie walked over to Mark, who had been watching, and said, "I know she hasn't had any experience. That might be a problem."

"Not a chance." Mark shook his head. "She doesn't do well in her subjects except for math, but she's got a memory like an elephant. She can remember everything that ever happened to her, I think."

His words somehow displeased Debbie, and she gave him an odd look. "We'll see," she said.

Later that day, after school, Mr. Spender was gathering his books together and preparing to leave when he had a visitor. He looked up as the door to his classroom opened and said, "Why, hello, Debbie."

"Oh, Mr. Spender, may I talk with you for a few moments?"

"Of course, Debbie."

Debbie came over and said with a worried look, "Mr. Spender, you're the director, and I know it's up to you, but one thing about the play concerns me."

Spender blinked with surprise. "What's that, Debbie?"

"Well, it's Prue. I don't think she's right for the part of Sally."

"Why, I thought she did very well. She hasn't had any experience, of course—"

"But it's such a terrible chance to take! She does all right when there's nobody there, but what about in front of an audience? Why, you know how Mary Ann Gateau froze up last year during the play. It ruined it!"

Spender rubbed his chin thoughtfully. "That's right," he said. "I hadn't thought about that." Then he added, "But I think she'll be all right."

"Oh, it isn't just that. She's so terribly tall, and I'm petite. Helen is supposed to be a strong person in the play, and here's this giantess towering over her. I don't think I can overcome that, Mr. Spender."

Spender walked over and sat down on his desk, his brow furrowed. He rubbed the wrinkles away, and for the next ten minutes the two talked earnestly. Finally he said, "Well, I'll think it over, Debbie. I wouldn't want anything to go wrong with the play."

"Of course, I'm sure she'll understand, and Dale Roberts would be perfect for the role." She added quickly, "And you could let Prue help with the costumes or something like that." She gathered her books up, held them to her breast, then said, "It'll be better. You'll see, Mr. Spender." She turned and walked out, a satisfied smile lurking on her lips.

★   ★   ★

Prue could not keep the good news to herself, and she excitedly told her parents that night at supper that she was going to be in the play. Her sparkling eyes and obvious good spirits made her father say, "Why, that's fine, Prue! I'll even come to it myself. Might be better than a Texas wrestling match."

Prue laughed at him and then went out the next morning with the same excitement. Mark met her with a smile and said, "I bet you didn't sleep a wink."

"Oh, I did too, but it is exciting. And I think, like you said, Mark, it's going to be fun."

The two talked about the play all the way to school, and

all that morning Prue thought about the days that were to come.

At lunch, in the cafeteria, she was almost through eating when Mr. Spender came by and paused beside her. "Prudence," he said very quietly, "after you finish eating, I need to have a word with you."

"Of course, Mr. Spender. I'll come to your classroom." Thinking that it was something concerning the part, Prue hurriedly finished, then made her way out of the cafeteria and down the halls. When she went into Mr. Spender's classroom, she saw that a troubled look was on his face. "Yes, sir?" she asked. "What is it?"

Ira Spender was not a man who could deal with difficult situations easily. He began talking in a rambling fashion about the integrity of a cast and how every member was a part, like a part of a machine. Prue listened to him, wondering where in the world he was going. Finally, almost in desperation, he said, "I know you'd like to do the part of Sally, but I just don't feel it's right for you." He saw the disappointment drive the smile from her face and hurriedly said, "You've got another year, and this would be a good time for you to get experience. Perhaps you could help with the costumes, or be a prompter."

All the joy left Prudence, and she said dolefully, "No thank you, Mr. Spender. Maybe I wasn't meant to be an actress anyway." She turned to leave, hearing him call out to her, "Now wait a minute, Prudence! Don't take it like that!" But she closed the door quietly, and for the rest of the day said not a word. The disappointment cut like a knife, and then she saw Mark and Debbie walking down the hall arm in arm late that afternoon headed for practice, obviously, and anger touched her. She was not a girl given to anger, as a rule, but somehow she just knew that Debbie Peters had something to do with her rejection. *She knows how to work men, and Mr. Spender wouldn't be anything for her*, she thought as she watched Mark and Debbie disappear into the auditorium.

"Hi, sweetie pie."

Prue turned to find Leon Dicus approaching, and, as usual, he managed to put his hand on her, this time on her shoulder, which he kneaded with his strong fingers. "Why don't you and I go out and hit a flick tonight? Maybe get something to eat afterward?"

"All right. I'd like that."

Leon Dicus's face assumed a comic air. "Why, I must've asked you a hundred times and you've turned me down a hundred times. You're gettin' smart, Prue." He squeezed her shoulder again, then winked. "I'll pick you up at six thirty."

"All right, Leon."

Prue watched him walk away in that peculiar walk that athletes have, those trying to be athletes, at least. It was a sort of a rolling swagger, and he acted as if his neck were so muscular that he could not twist it around, so he turned slowly to face people. "Why did I do that? I can't stand him." Prue knew with one part of her mind that she was getting revenge somehow on Mr. Spender, and Debbie, and even Mark. The bitterness that came to her did not allow for logical thinking. She lifted her head high and said, "I'll go out and have a good time." She left the school and went home, determined to show somebody that she could have a life without a role in a sorry little high school drama.

★   ★   ★

The movie was *Dr. No*, starring Sean Connery and Ursula Andress. It was the second of the series that Prue had seen, and she enjoyed the smooth antics of British Agent 707. She thought Connery was amusing, and as for the feminine star, her chief claim to acting fame came from her curvaceous body, which she displayed at every possible opportunity.

In one scene where Ursula Andress appeared to her best advantage, Leon put his arm around Prue and pulled her closer. He whispered hoarsely, "Her name ought to be Ursula

*Un*dress." His wit, such as it was, amused him, and he kept his arm around Prue, constantly caressing her. At one point, his caresses became so objectionable that Prue jerked herself away and said, "Keep your hands to yourself, Leon! This is a public place!" He grabbed her hand and grinned. "We'll go to a private place then after the show."

The private place proved to be something called the Blue Moon. When they pulled up in front, suddenly Prue remembered something. "Wait a minute!" she said as Dicus prepared to get out. "I'm not going in that place. That's where Bobby Stuart got into trouble and Maggie Satterfield was attacked."

"You don't have to worry about that, baby. I been here before. I can handle any trouble that comes."

Against her better judgment, and protesting all the way, Prue was dragged inside the nightclub. As soon as she stepped inside and looked around, her heart sank, and she knew she had made a terrible mistake.

★ ★ ★

Mark was up late studying; his parents had already gone to bed. He jumped when the phone went off right behind his head on the kitchen wall. Leaping up, he wondered who could be calling at eleven o'clock at night.

"Hello?"

"Mark—?"

"Prue, is that you?"

"Why—yes. Mark, I need you."

Mark clutched the phone harder and said, "What's the matter? Where are you? You're not at home?"

"No. I'm out on Highway 28 at a Texaco station, the one right across from the water tower."

"I know the place," Mark said. "What are you doing there?"

"Please, don't ask questions! Can you come and get me?"

"Sure. I'll be right there. Do your folks know you're out?"

"I don't want them to know anything. Please, just come and get me, Mark."

Fear shot through her voice, and she said, "Please," in a whisper.

"All right, Prue. Don't worry. You stay right there inside the station. I'll be there in twenty minutes. All right?"

"All right, Mark."

Mark hit the front door running, got into the Buick, the family's second car, and hoped that his parents wouldn't hear the engine start up. It caught at once, and he eased out onto the road, waiting until he got out to the blacktop before he opened it up. Floorboarding the accelerator, he shot through the night, a thousand things racing through his mind. He covered the distance in record speed, pulled up beside the Texaco station, which was still lit up, and by the time he got out of the car he saw Prue running toward him. Her eyes were wide, and her lips were trembling, and he said, "Prue, what is it?"

"Please, Mark, take me home."

"Sure. Get in the car." He walked over with her, opened the door, then shut it when she was inside. Quickly he moved back to his own position behind the wheel, put the Buick in gear, and drove away. Out of his rearview mirror, he saw the attendant standing outside scratching his head. Twisting his head, he saw that Prue was as far away from him as she could get, and she was staring out the window. He also thought he could see that her shoulders were trembling as though she were crying.

Reaching over, he touched her shoulder and said, "Look, Prue, you'd better tell me about it. What are you doing way out here in the middle of nowhere?"

Prue did not turn for a moment. She cleared her throat, searched through her purse for a Kleenex, and then blew her nose. Finally she turned and said, "I've been at the Blue Moon with Leon Dicus."

"What?" Mark swerved the car as he turned to face her. "Have you lost your mind, Prudence Deforge?"

"Please don't scold me. You can't say anything that I haven't said to myself."

Mark heard the plea in her voice and turned his attention back to driving. He said nothing, and she sat there quietly until he pulled in her driveway. "The lights are on," he said. "I guess your folks are up waiting on you."

"I know they are," Prue said. She had regained her composure now and added, "Mark, thanks for coming after me."

"Sure. That's okay."

"I–I guess I owe you an explanation. You heard about Mr. Spender deciding not to let me be in the play?"

Mark swirled in the seat. "What do you mean? I didn't hear anything about that!"

For an instant Prue thought of telling him that it was Debbie Peters' idea, but she had no evidence, so she said, "I felt so bad, like I'd been cut off at the knees, and then when Leon asked me to go out, I guess I just was so desperate I accepted. It was awful! Everybody was drinking, and there are rooms there that couples kept going off into. I begged Leon to take me home, but he was drunk. He started to drag me into one of those rooms, and I tore away from him and ran out the front door. He chased me, but he stumbled, and I disappeared into the woods, and then I came out down the highway and walked to the Texaco station, and that's when I called you."

She broke off suddenly, and Mark saw that she was crying again. He put his arms around her and held her close for a minute. "Look, we all make mistakes. You made one, so go in and tell your folks all about it. I hope your dad doesn't punch Leon out."

"You do? I thought you might like that."

"No, I'm planning to do it myself," he said.

"Oh, please, Mark! Don't do that!" Turning her face to him, Prue touched his chest, and then she whispered, "I don't know what I would have done if it hadn't been for you. I was so afraid."

She was soft against his chest, and her tearstained face was blurry in the moonlight. He did see her lips were trembling, and as he had done once before, he bent his head, meaning to give her a friendly kiss. It did not turn into that though. Her lips were soft under his, and vulnerable, and for a long moment he held her, and then she broke away. Her voice was thick as she whispered, "Mark, I've got to go in." She left and went up the walk, wiping her face on a Kleenex as she went. She turned back and waved at Mark, then took a deep breath, and stepped inside the house.

The next half hour was as bad as anything Prudence had known. She was very honest with her parents, as she always had been. She explained how hurt she had been by being cut from the play, and how she had made a foolish decision. She saw the anger in her father's eyes and the muscles of his shoulders bunched up, but she went to him and said, "Please, Daddy. I know you want to go beat him up, but that would just make things worse." She took a deep breath and shook her head. "You don't have to worry about him anymore. I hope I never see him again, or anybody like him!"

5

THE BIG TIME

Hey! You can't come in here!" Ossie Peabody, the drummer of Bobby's band, was well-built, but he had no chance against the burly man who simply pushed the door open and brushed him aside. Ossie made an angry noise, which caused Bobby Stuart to turn around and say, "That's all right, Ossie. Take it easy." He was exhausted after a tiring concert. It had gone on for more than four hours, and he had given it everything he had. Bobby was accustomed to backstage visitors, but usually they were fifteen- or sixteen-year-old teenyboppers.

The man who entered the room looked like a truck driver. He was short, muscular, and had hands like hams. His small-ish brown eyes were deep set and were regarding him care-fully. For a moment fear touched Bobby, for he was not yet clear on the charges he had incurred back in Arkansas. The girl's parents, whatever her name was, were pressing it, and Bobby had paid a mint to lawyers. This man looked like a policeman, or maybe a process server. "What can I do for you?" he asked.

"Nothing, but I can do a lot for you." The big man looked at Ossie and said, "Take a walk, fella."

Ossie straightened up, preparing to argue, but something about the man's demeanor impressed Bobby. "That's okay, Ossie. Go get the car ready. I'll be there as soon as I finish with this gentleman." He waved off Ossie's angry look, and when the door shut he said, "Now, what's up?"

71

"I'm R. D. Fitzgerald. Did you ever hear of me?"

Bobby swallowed hard and said, "Yes, sir! Of course I have!" He came forward at once, put his hand out nervously, and summoned a smile. "I'm glad to know you, Mr. Fitzgerald." Fitzgerald had a grip like a Stilson wrench, and Bobby pulled his hand back before it was mangled. "Why don't you sit down."

"Okay." Fitzgerald pulled a cigar from his inner pocket, bit the end off, and spit it on the floor. He pulled out a kitchen match, struck it with his fingernail, and held it to the tip of the huge cigar until it was burning with a cherry red light. He then leaned back and blew a perfect smoke ring up at the ceiling. "So . . . you've heard of me."

"Why, everybody's heard of you, Mr. Fitzgerald," Bobby said. This might not have been strictly true, but people in the entertainment world, at least on the inside, had heard of one of the biggest producers in Hollywood. Bobby kept close track on this, for he had a great desire to make a movie. He longed to see himself up on the big screen, and now he sat down thinking, *This is it! He wouldn't have come to see me unless he had moviemaking on his mind!* "Your last picture was great, Mr. Fitzgerald," he said. "I went to see it three times."

Fitzgerald had a tough face, but pleasure moved across his features. "Glad to hear that. Always like to hear a good word about the work I do." He blew another perfect ring at the ceiling, watched it until it dissipated, and appeared to have nothing to say.

Bobby thought, *He's pretty sharp. He knows I'm nervous, and he's letting it all build up. I can't let him con me like that.* He leaned back, stretched, and yawned, and said, "Were you out in the audience tonight?"

"Yeah, I caught your act." He waited for Bobby to ask how he liked it, but Bobby simply stretched again and kneaded his shoulder muscles.

"Pretty tough being out there that long. Sometimes I think I'd rather be pumping gas at Exxon."

This amused Fitzgerald. "No you don't, Bobby. You're doing exactly what you want to do."

Startled, Bobby laughed. "I guess you're right about that. I don't mind getting tired. After all, that's what puts the beans on the table."

Fitzgerald suddenly sat up straighter and said, "You're a pretty sharp kid. I've had my eye on you for a long time, and now I guess you know pretty well why I'm here."

"From what I hear, you don't have any hobbies. All you do is work, so if you're here I guess you want to talk to me about some sort of project you've got on your mind."

"Project. I like that. Yeah, a project. I got a project, all right. I want to put you in a movie, Bobby." He grinned, for despite his determination to be cool, Bobby blinked and for a moment could not speak. "What else would I be doing here?" he demanded.

"Well, I think it's kind of strange, if you don't mind my sayin' so. I mean, all you had to do was send for me and I would have come to your office, Mr. Fitzgerald."

"I wanted to see you in action. Hadn't caught your act, and now all those screamin' idiots out there convinced me. If they'll scream at a concert, they'll scream at a movie. Right?"

"Well, I hope so. You understand that I'm no actor."

"Ah, you don't have to be an actor. They won't come to see you act, they'll come to see you sing. Just give 'em that sexy look and swivel your hips, and they'll fill the theaters up."

"What sort of a movie do you have in mind?"

"None at all. That's up to my people. They'll find something that will fit you and will be brainless enough so that the kids who have to move their lips to read will catch on to the plot. Lots of singin', lots of hip swingin', moonlight, and kissing. That's it. Are you ready to talk contract?"

"Why, you'll have to talk to my agent, of course."

"That's all right. Dogs got fleas, and performers got agents—not much difference." Fitzgerald heaved himself out of his seat and moved toward the door. When he got there, he stopped and turned around. "You're gonna be big, kid. I'm gonna see to it. See you around."

As the door slammed, Bobby rose and was shocked to find that his hands were unsteady. He had to swallow twice before he could regain his composure, and then excitement flooded him. "It's all set," he whispered. "This is the big break, and I'm going to grab for the brass ring!"

★   ★   ★

Two weeks later Bobby arrived at Universal Studios. He had gone to see his parents, expecting them to be as excited as he was. Instead he found them somewhat less so. Quite a bit less so, to be truthful. His dad had given him a lecture on how dangerous Hollywood was and how many stars had killed themselves, or died miserable and unhappy, and nothing Bobby could say would change his mind. He stayed for two days, and although his father hadn't said anything else, nor his mother either for that matter, he felt uncomfortable and finally left early for the studio.

His agent, Happy Miller, was there and had already laid the groundwork. From the time Bobby first arrived he was given the red-carpet treatment. One of the vice presidents, a short, clever fellow named Lar Delmont, showed him around the studio. He met stars that he had seen, some of them years ago, and attended a whirl of parties. It was fun, but Bobby's mind was on making movies. Finally he was given a copy of the script and assigned a musician to go through the score with him so that he could begin to learn the words to the new music. They were relatively simple tunes, and Bobby picked them up almost instantly. "Not the greatest tunes in the world," he said to the piano player, whose name was Johnson.

"No, not what you're used to." Johnson shrugged. "You'll

have to make up the difference with a little jazz. You know the drill, Bobby."

"I know; I'll practice that."

The first meeting of the cast was something that Bobby looked forward to. He had been anxious to know who else would be in the movie, wondering if there would be an established star. He asked Mr. Fitzgerald, who grunted, "You don't want another star. They'll be looking at the star and not at you. This picture's to make you a star, Bobby. Don't you get that?"

"But won't there be anybody in it that's familiar? When I see a movie I like to know at least a couple of the people."

Fitzgerald grinned. "You'll have Lannie Marr. You ever see her?"

Bobby tried hard to think, and then suddenly it came to him. "Hey, yeah! I saw her! She was in that movie with Dana Andrews. She was some kind of a gangster's moll." He whistled slowly. "Boy, what a sexpot!"

"Can't act for sour apples, but she's got the body. She'll have to sweeten up a little bit. We're makin' this one for the kids."

"I don't think you'd shock 'em much," Bobby said with a smirk.

The cast met at one of the large stages at Universal, and Bobby was more nervous than he cared to admit. He was standing there uncertainly when a tall man with a mop of black hair came over and said, "I'm Abe Fontesque, your director. Glad to see you, Bobby."

"Nice to meet you, Mr. Fontesque."

"Come on in and let me introduce you to the people."

Fontesque made the rounds, and Bobby met several people, but the only one he remembered after the meeting was Lannie Marr. She was blonde and had large, dark blue eyes. Her face was sultry, and her lips, even in repose, had a sensual quality. As for her figure—well, it had put her in the movies. Bobby remembered reading that she had been in girlie magazines, and even X-rated movies, and resolved to look into that. When he was introduced, he nodded, saying, "How are you, Miss Marr? I've seen your movies. Great!"

"Have you?" Lannie gave him a closer inspection. "I haven't been to any of your concerts. You'll have to give me one so I know what to expect."

There was something in her voice, and in her eyes, that made her words seem to mean more than their dictionary meanings. Bobby was used to being successful with women, but this one was different. He said no more to her during the meeting but listened as Abe Fontesque outlined the work schedule. He listened only with half of his mind, for the other half was on the sleek woman who sat lounged back in her chair swinging one leg slowly. Her eyes came around to him and studied him as if he were an interesting specimen; then he saw approval come, and the lush lips turned up in a smile, and she nodded imperceptibly, almost. But he knew what Lannie Marr was thinking.

After the meeting, Bobby thanked Fontesque. "I'll do the best I can, Mr. Fontesque, but I may need a little help. All I've ever done is sing. That's different from acting."

"That's all right. We got you an acting coach, and Lannie here will give you all the tips you need. We start shooting day after tomorrow," he said. "Start on these first scenes, and we'll see how you do."

Bobby turned and found Lannie Marr standing with her eyes on him. "Is it too late to go out and get a bite to eat, or do you have other plans?"

"That would be nice; I don't have any plans."

The two of them went out to the restaurant of her choice, where she was apparently well known. After they ordered, Bobby looked across and said, "I don't mind telling you, Lannie, I'm scared green. I don't know beans about acting."

The actress picked up her cocktail, sipped it, and then leaned forward, giving him an excellent view of her figure in the low-cut dress. "I don't think you'll have any trouble. You never have trouble with women, do you, Bobby?" The directness of her words and the boldness of her eyes startled Bobby, and this amused Lannie. She leaned back then and said, "We'll talk about it, and like Abe said, I can give you a few lessons."

★ ★ ★

By the time the first scenes were due to be shot Bobby was nervous, almost terminally so. He made his way to the studio that morning, but everything he said onstage was stiff, and his movements seemed clumsy. Fontesque was patient enough, but at the end of the day's shooting he shook his head, saying, "Bobby, I don't want to make you more nervous than you are, but you're going to have to loosen up a little bit."

"I'll do my best, Mr. Fontesque." Bobby went to his dressing room feeling miserable. He had almost finished dressing when a knock came to his door. He got up, opened it, and found Lannie standing there. "Mind if I come in?"

"No. You might as well." He tried to grin. "Nobody else is beating a door to the famous actor's dressing room."

Lannie was wearing a dress made out of a thin, light blue clingy silk. It had short cap sleeves, a low, revealing sweetheart neckline, and a short, tight skirt with a slit up the right thigh. Her legs were covered with a pair of stockings with an opalescent shimmer, and her shoes were open-toed and had very high heels. She came over and stood so close that she almost touched him. "Feeling pretty low, aren't you?"

"Pretty low, Lannie. Pretty low."

"Well, I've got the medicine for that. Come on. We'll go out and have something to eat at a place I know."

Bobby shrugged. "I don't think food's going to help any, but thanks. It'll be nice to get away from this place."

Lannie took him in a fancy sports car, so expensive Bobby didn't even know the name of it, to a restaurant in the heart of the city. She was well known there, and after the maître d' had led them to the table and taken their order, she leaned back and studied him. There was a sultriness in her air, even when she did not intend it. "You don't want to worry too much about these things. You're worried because you did poorly for the scenes."

"Well, of course, I am!" Bobby exclaimed. The waiter brought the drinks, and he downed his instantly. "Who wouldn't be worried? If I don't learn how to act quick, I think they'll call the whole thing off."

"Yes, they might do that, but I don't want you to worry about it. Let's just eat, and drink, and dance, and then when you get loosened up we'll go to my place and talk about it."

This was the way the evening went. Lannie Marr might not have been the world's greatest actress, but she was certainly world class in making a man unwind, and by the time they got to her apartment, Bobby, after several drinks, was feeling much better.

"Will you come in?" Lannie said, gazing at him directly. Then without waiting for an answer, she turned and went inside.

The apartment was about what Bobby had expected. A large area with art deco, lots of black-and-white marble, with pictures on the wall that looked like the artist never had any lessons. The couch was huge and overstuffed, looking more like the Goodyear blimp than anything else. It was also an odd color, sort of a mixture of lime and apricot. But it was comfortable enough, and when Bobby sank into it Lannie stood over him. "You're feeling better," she said.

"Yeah, quite a bit—but I still have to go to the studio tomorrow and make a fool out of myself."

"Don't you know what's wrong, Bobby?"

"I can't act! That's what's wrong!"

"I can't act either. Most people in the movies can't. Now on the stage, that's different. They've got to stay up there for hours." She shook her head, saying, "I don't see how they remember all that. All I have to remember is half a dozen lines. That's all a scene is, and when I first started in this business I was as nervous as you are, but I found a way to calm my nerves down."

She left the room and came back bearing a small box in her hand. She sat down close beside him and opened it; Bobby stared down into it at the white powder in small cellophane envelopes. He had seen enough of it in his time, and he had an inherent fear of it. He had tried marijuana and popped a pill or two, but he had seen too many people destroyed by this innocent-looking white powder. Shaking his head he said, "No, that's not for me."

"All right. Have it your own way. I believe in letting people do what they want to do."

Bobby watched as she put some of the powder on the bottle top, leaned over, and inhaled it through a straw into her nostril. She leaned back then, her eyes half closed, and she was silent for a long time. "You might as well go," she said.

Bobby half rose and then slumped back. "Look, I'm afraid of that stuff. I've seen people absolutely ruined by it."

"So have I. I've seen people ruin themselves with alcohol too. It's a risk, but you'll have to decide whether it's worth it. For me it was. I only use it when I'm doing a movie. Didn't you notice how relaxed I was today?"

"Sure, but I thought that was just—well, you were a professional."

"I still get tense and uptight. I couldn't make it without this." She turned to him and pulled him down. Since she was half reclining, he was pressed against her closely. Her lips were soft and moved against his, and her hands roamed along his back. Then she pushed him back and said, "That's enough." She sat up, and Bobby was caught by the abruptness of her movements.

"I don't have time for failures, Bobby. Go on back to your concerts. You're doing well. Maybe you don't need the movies."

Bobby suddenly realized he did need the movies. He turned and looked at her. "I do! I've got to do it, Lannie! I've got to make it in the movies!" He looked down at the powder and struggled with his thoughts. Finally he got up and paced the floor, wondering what his parents would say; then the thought came, *They probably think I'm already on heroin. They think the worst of me, it seems.* He worked himself up into a feeling of self-pity; all the while Lannie Marr was watching him with a small smile, as if she had seen this before.

Bobby finally said, "You really think it will help?"

"Try it tomorrow. It won't take much, but it just sort of makes you loose and easy. That's all that's wrong with you. You're so tensed up you can't do anything."

"All right. I'll try it—but only just to get me through the beginnings. I'll pick it up soon, and I won't need the stuff."

"Sure. That's the way to look at it." Then she raised her arms and said, "Now, come to Momma, baby . . ."

★   ★   ★

By the time the picture was finished and released, Bobby and Lannie were in the midst of a torrid affair. All throughout the making of the movie he had kept saying to her, "I'll just have the stuff this one time, then no more," and she had always agreed with him. He found out quickly, however, that the more he took, the more he required, and by the time the picture was released and was proclaimed a hit, Bobby Stuart was in the grips of the white powder. He always had Lannie beside him urging him to more parties, which always involved more dope. He was also besieged and offered the moon by those who wanted to capitalize on his fame. Caught up with Lannie Marr and the crowd she ran with, Bobby simply gave in and became what he never thought he would become, an addict, both of dope and of the arms of a woman, and of the fabulous offers of dollars that seemed to flood in from every side.

From time to time Bobby would seem to sense that something was dreadfully wrong—but then there was always Lannie whispering to him, driving those thoughts away. So he hit the big time in Hollywood and became a star.

Part 2

Sowing
(1965–1966)

6

SENSATION AT THE PROM

Prue stood looking at the canvas, cocking her head to one side and delicately applying a little deeper red to the lips of the child in the painting. Always when she painted there came over her an intensity, and she seemed to forget the world except for that tiny fragment that lay before her and the canvas on which she tried to capture what she saw. With a sigh she looked up and saw that Pearl Swanson was watching her with a puzzled light in her eyes.

"Well, that's about the best I can do today, Pearl," she said.

"Can I see?" Pearl Swanson was one of those women of the Ozarks who married very early and had known nothing but a life of grinding poverty. Her daughter, Melody, had that fresh, sparkling beauty that children sometimes have, even in the middle of such poverty. Max Swanson worked at what he could get, having had no education and no training, and for now he was working with timbermen in the woods doing difficult labor in a hard and dangerous job.

As Pearl and Melody came over to look at the painting, Prue's heart went out to them. She took in the shack that had a dirt floor and no inside plumbing, and the red hands of the woman swollen with hard labor and thought, *She has so little and I have so much. I ought to be whipped for ever complaining about anything!*

She watched as the woman and the child stood before the canvas on which she had painted their picture and remembered how Pearl had come by their house selling vegetables out of the back of Max's old truck. The Deforges had little need of them, but she knew her mother would agree so she had bought practically their whole stock. Pearl Swanson's gratitude was so great that an acquaintanceship had been struck, and Prue conceived the idea of painting the pair in an attempt to capture the spirit of the Ozarks. It was not a new idea, for she had painted a few toothless old women who still wore their dresses down to their ankles and used the branches of gum trees as their snuff stick. It was Prue's favorite subject, and somehow she hoped to capture the hard poverty of these people, like the Swansons, and at the same time the beauty of simplicity in Pearl's face and the fresh, blossom-like features of two-year-old Melody.

"It looks mighty good, Miss Prudence," Pearl said, shaking her head. "I swan! I don't know how you do it. Just take that there brush, and look at somethin', and there it is right on that paper." She smiled, and traces of her early beauty were apparent.

"I'm glad you like it, but it's really not as good as I'd like. I may have to come again." She took a five-dollar bill out of her pocket and handed it to Pearl.

Pearl took the bill, held it as if it were fragile, then folded it up and put it into the pocket of her apron. "You come back anytime. Me and Melody will be glad to pose. Won't we, Melody?"

Melody looked up with her round, blue eyes and nodded vigorously. Pulling away from her mother, she ran over to the sack of peppermint candy and other treats that Prue had brought and popped a peppermint in her mouth at once.

Getting into the ancient Dodge that her father managed to buy as a second car, Prue started back toward the house. It was May in the Ozarks, and the trees were filled with blossoms; she noticed the dogwoods, the wild cherries, and the apple trees as she passed by the orchards. The smell of rich earth and evergreens came to her through the open window and she inhaled deeply. However, her mind was on the painting. "I didn't get it right," she said to herself. "I couldn't get the way Pearl had her arm around Melody."

She thought about the painting all the way home, and when she pulled up in front of the house, she started inside with it; then she heard the sound of an engine and saw that Mark had pulled in behind her and jerked his car to a stop. Quickly Prue put the painting back into the car in its canvas wrapping and turned to Mark. "Hi," she said. "How's everything with you, Mark?"

"Oh, getting ready for the prom. That's what I came over to talk to you about." He shifted uneasily, for somehow since he had kissed her the night he had brought her home from the Texaco station, there had been an awkwardness in his manner. She was somehow too much a childhood playmate, and he had vague feelings of wrongdoing about the caress. Still, he had thought about her a great deal, and now he said, "Getting geared up to do the senior prom."

"I'll bet Debbie's spent a lot of time picking out her dress."

"Well, you know Debbie. She really likes clothes."

"Are you two going to get married, Mark?" It was the first time she had ever asked Mark directly, and although Debbie had no ring, everyone seemed to be sure that she would have one soon enough. She watched as Mark pulled his cap off and ran his fingers through his hair in a gesture of frustration, or so it seemed to her.

"I don't know," he said. "Not for a long time; I've got some things to do first."

When Prue said nothing, he added, "But I came over to ask you if you wouldn't like to go to the prom. Have you been asked yet?"

"No, I haven't."

"Well, that won't be any problem," Mark said quickly. "I know half a dozen guys that would like to have a date."

"How tall are they?" Prue said, a tiny smile turning the

corners of her generous lips up. When she saw Mark hesitate, she said, "Don't worry about me, Mark. I don't really want to go."

Mark hesitated, then shrugged. "All right, but if you change your mind let me know. There are always some fellows who wait till the last minute. Good-bye, Prue."

He went at once to Debbie's house, and as he pulled up he felt a moment's reluctance. Debbie's mother was very society minded, and the house was like a museum. He told Debbie once, in a jocular fashion, "Your mother ought to make people take their shoes off like they do in China. Or is it Japan?" Debbie had not found that amusing, and he had not referred to it again.

Moving up the porch, he rang the bell, and when Mrs. Peters opened it, he said, "Hello, Mrs. Peters. Is Debbie around?"

"Yes. Come in, Mark." Mrs. Peters was a small woman, overweight from rich foods. She had been pretty as a girl, Mark supposed. In fact he knew it, for he had seen pictures. She had looked exactly like Debbie when she was a young woman. This had given him some pause, and he had tried to visualize Debbie as a thirty-five- or forty-year-old woman. Mrs. Peters was all right, but she sure needed to lose some weight.

"Have you decided about the football scholarships, Mark?"

Mark hesitated, then said, "I've been thinking about it a lot, Mrs. Peters."

"Well, I know it would be thrilling for you to go to some of the schools in the East, but I'm hoping you will go to the University of Arkansas. It's so close to home, and we'll get to see you and Debbie so often."

"Well, that may be," Mark said noncommittally. At that moment Debbie came in, and for the next half hour he was subjected to the latest on dresses for the prom. This was rather boring to Mark, to whom the prom was just another dance, but Debbie put special emphasis on it, and he made himself show all the interest he could possibly work up.

"I guess we'd better get started if we're going to catch the movie, Debbie," Mark said, looking at his watch. He managed to maneuver her out, and Mrs. Peters gave the inevitable warning about "Drive safe, and have her home early; Mr. Peters will be here, and you two can talk about the university. He went there, you know, and played football."

Mark had heard this at least a hundred times, but he managed to keep himself from looking bored. "Yes, ma'am. We'll be in early."

They went to the movie, which was not particularly exciting, and as soon as they were out, Debbie said, "Let's go down to Cranston's and get something to eat." Mark agreed, and he sat there eating a hamburger, drinking a chocolate malt, and listening to Debbie talk rapidly about the prom. Who was going with whom, and who was not going with whom. Finally they left, and when they pulled up at the Peters' home, he shut off the engine and said, "Debbie, I've got to talk to you about something."

Debbie turned to him, her eyes wide with expectancy. "Why, yes, Mark," she breathed, moving over closer to him. "What is it?"

Mark had his mind on other things, or he would have noticed that Debbie was waiting for him so expectantly that it could only mean she was thinking that he might be about to propose. But Mark said, "I've got to tell you something that I haven't told anyone else—not even my parents."

"Yes?" Debbie's lips were parted as she moved even closer and reached out to hold his hand. "What is it, Mark?"

"Well, I know everyone's expectin' me to go to college, and I could go on a scholarship, but that's not what I want."

Debbie sat absolutely still. This was not what she had expected. "What are you talking about? Of course you're going to college!"

"Debbie, listen to me. College is right for some people. It's

probably right for you, but I want to be a writer, and I've come
to the conclusion that you don't learn to write in college. Not
the kind of writing I want to do."

"Of course writers go to college! What's the matter with
you, Mark? Everyone's depending on you. I'm going to be
there, and we're going to have a wonderful time." She spoke
earnestly, and Mark sat silently, listening, but when she
ended, his voice was stern.

"I may go to college after a year, but I'm taking a year out
to travel this country; I hope I can get a job with somebody
as a reporter. Even if I can't, I can write, and after it's over I'll
know whether I'm fit to be a writer or not."

Debbie was furious. She, her mother, and her father had
made careful plans. Both of her parents were planners, and
Debbie had inherited their inclination to take over where others were concerned. At first she pleaded with Mark to listen
to reason, telling him why it was foolish to waste a year. The
scholarships wouldn't be there a year later; he wouldn't have
any money. Even if he did come, she'd be a sophomore, and
he would be only a freshman. On and on she went, and finally
she said, "So, Mark, you see it's impossible, don't you?"

Mark turned to her, and there was a determination in him
as he said, "I'm sorry, Debbie, but my mind's made up. I'm
going to do this. It may mean we'll have to postpone our plans
for a while, but—"

"Why didn't you tell me this before?" Debbie pulled away
and sat glaring at him. "It's not fair, and you're being totally selfish!" She went on for some time, expecting him to
change his mind. She had always been able to sway Mark.
This time, however, she saw that her attempts were hopeless.
She drew back from him and stepped outside the car, saying,
"I'm not going to take this as your final answer! We've got
our lives planned, and you can't just break those plans! You
have to think about other people!" She turned and walked
away, leaving Mark to stare after her feeling defeated and
frustrated.

For the next week a state of unarmed warfare existed between Mark and Debbie. She was totally determined that he would go through with what she had considered the best plan, and Mark was just as determined not to do it. At one point he was dragged into the presence of Mr. and Mrs. Peters, who threw their weight behind Debbie, and all he could do was sit with his head half bowed and his teeth clenched. But he had finally said, "I am sorry if it disturbs you all, but I feel this would be the best thing for me, and the best for Debbie too, in the long run. I need to find out who I am. Can't you see that?"

The Peters could not see that, and at the end of the week when Debbie encountered Mark in the hall at school, she said briefly, "I'm sorry that you've been so stubborn, Mark, but until you come to your senses, I think it's best that we not see each other." This had been the plan that her parents and she had agreed on, confident that it would bring Mark to his senses. Then she added quickly, "I also think it might be best if I went to the prom with Harry Findley."

Mark stared at her helplessly. "But, Debbie . . ." he began.

But she shook her head and said, "I'm sure a little time apart will make you see reason, Mark." She turned and walked away, and Mark, feeling as if he had been hit in the stomach, turned too and wandered down the halls, missing his next class and wondering how he had ever gotten himself into such a predicament.

★   ★   ★

Prue was shocked when two days after Mark's breakup with Debbie he told her what had happened. She was feeding the tiny fox that a neighbor had found in the woods, a vixen, and she looked up with astonishment from inside the pen where she kept the tiny animal. "What did you say, Mark?" She rose at once and stepped outside, saying to the fox, "No,

Pulitzer, you stay in." Then she turned and said, "You and Debbie have broken up?"

"That's about it. You want to hear the gory details?"

"If you want to tell me." Prue saw that he did want to talk, and the two walked slowly to the edge of the woods that flanked the Deforge farm. They sat down on a log, and Prue listened as Mark recounted the incident. When he was finished, he looked up at her with despair and said, "I guess you think I'm nutty, don't you? Everybody will. Giving up all those scholarships to go traipsin' all over the country."

Prue reached out and put her hands over his. "If that's what you want to do, Mark, and you think it's right, do it! But I believe you ought to talk it over with your parents, and all of you make the decision. It's a family matter."

Mark looked relieved. "Well, gosh. It's good to hear you say that, Prue. I been thinking I was the world's worst punk. I'll tell you, those fights with Debbie and listening to her parents just about did me in."

They sat there talking on and on, Prue mostly listening to Mark's plans to travel the United States. It did not disturb her, for she knew if he went to college she would not see him often anyway. Finally, when he mentioned he was not going to the prom, she said instantly, "I think you ought to go, Mark."

"Why? What fun would it be?"

"Well, it's sort of the end of your high school career, and besides, I don't want Debbie to think that she's defeated you. You ought to get a date and go with your head up."

"No, I wouldn't want to do that." He looked at her and smiled warmly. "You're good medicine, Prue. I was about ready to jump in the river, but it makes me feel good to know that at least one person thinks I'm not completely off my rocker."

Later that night, after supper, Mark called his parents together for a conference. They listened carefully as he explained what he wanted to do; finally Les said, "Is it really what you want, Mark? You'll be giving up a lot, like college and football."

"Those things are important for some people, Dad, but honestly, they don't mean a thing to me." He looked at his mother and said, "Mom, I don't know how to tell you this, but I've always wanted to be a writer. It's all I ever wanted to do; I could spend four years at the university, but I've read what I think are good writers. They didn't learn it in college. It was something inside of them, and I think if I don't try this, I'll always think I missed the boat."

"Then you ought to do it, son," Joy said. She came over, kissed him, and said, "I've seen something in you for a long time, and I've been waiting for you to tell us about it."

"Well, I didn't think you'd understand, but I was wrong. I should have come to you."

They talked for a long time, and finally he mentioned not going to the senior prom, and he also related what Prue had said to him.

"Prue's absolutely right," Les said. "You don't want to go off like a whipped cur."

"Yes, and I know exactly who you should take." Joy smiled. She looked at her husband and said, "Are you thinking what I am?"

Les said, "Who would you really like to go with, Mark, of all the girls you know?"

Mark hesitated, then blinked with surprise. "Why, Prue. I have more fun with her than anybody."

"Then you'll ask her, and we'll get her ready for the prom."

"But it's only two days. She can't get a dress—"

"You do the asking, I'll do the paying, and your mother will take care of the dress," Les said forcefully.

★   ★   ★

Prue put down the phone with a dazed expression on her face. She stood there for a long time, but her mother did not seem surprised. "Mom, didn't you hear what I said? Mark wants me to go to the prom with him!"

"Yes, and his mother and I have already talked about it. The three of us are going to Fort Smith today, and we're going to find a dress that will make every other girl's dress at the prom look like an old dishrag."

"Mother! You mean you knew?"

Violet slipped over and put her arm around her daughter. She was forced to look up to her, but she squeezed her hard, saying, "It was Mark's idea. He said he'd rather take you than any girl he knew, and I think he's showing good sense."

★   ★   ★

When Mark pulled in front of the Deforge house and got out of the car, he felt rather strange. "All these years, and never once did I think I'd be taking Prue Deforge to the senior prom." He was wearing a tuxedo, and when he knocked and Violet Deforge answered the door, she looked at him and let out a long whistle. "Well, aren't you the handsome thing, though. Come in. Prue's about ready."

Feeling more awkward than ever, Mark stepped inside, where he found Dent waiting. Dent grinned and said, "I like your monkey suit. How'd you like to wear one of those every day?"

"I'd hate it," Mark said, pulling at his collar, "but everybody's got to wear one. I wish—" He stopped abruptly, for Prue appeared on the stairs, and he stared at her as if he had never seen her before.

The dress hunting expedition to Fort Smith had taken all day, and considerable cash and persuasion to get Prue fitted. But as Violet took in the sight of her daughter coming down the stairs, she thought, *It was worth it!*

Prue's dress was made of a light lavender taffeta that complemented her dark hair and eyes. It had a low, rounded neckline with a white bead trim and a high waist that fit snugly under her bosom, where it was accented by a darker lavender ribbon tied in the front. Long, see-through sleeves ended at the wrist in white bead trim; the skirt was narrow with a small slit up the right side to the knee, and the bottom of the dress barely touched the tops of her lavender bead-trimmed shoes. Her hair was done up into a looped bun with several small ringlets escaping around the sides and the nape of her neck.

Prue came down the steps, walked right up to Mark and said, "I'm ready."

Mark swallowed hard and said, "You sure are! You look beautiful, Prue. Just beautiful."

Prue flushed and shot a quick glance at her mother, then at her father; then she laughed and said, "You're beautiful too!"

Mark handed her the orchid he had brought, and they went through the ceremony of pinning it on Prue's dress.

Mark said little as they drove to the prom, but he kept looking at Prue in a state of shock.

He was not the only one, for when they entered, a murmur went around the room. They were somewhat late, and everyone turned to see them.

"The word is out that Debbie and I have broken up," Mark whispered as they walked into the room. He saw Debbie standing with her date, and she was glaring at them furiously.

Prue made quite an impact that night. It was as if she was a stranger whom the young men had never seen before. Mark let many of them dance with her but finally said, "No soap, you guys! Go get your own date!"

As they moved around the floor to the sound of the orchestra playing Elvis's newest hit, "You're the Devil in Disguise," Mark pulled her a little closer and said, "I can't get over it, Prue. I always think of you as nursing a sick squirrel, or out grubbing in the garden. You look like—you look like a fashion model."

"They're all skinny and bony, aren't they?"

He caught the humor in her eyes and grinned. "Not you," he said. "You're just right. Have you noticed how we just fit?"

"That's the only reason I like you, because you're so tall." Prue did not realize how provocative she was. Her eyes were sparkling, and her clear complexion glowed. Mark's mother had bought her some perfume, and the saleslady had warned them, "Be careful. It's dangerous."

They enjoyed the dance and finally made their way home. Mark pulled up in front of Prue's house, got out, went around and opened the door, then walked her to the porch. "Your folks have probably gone to bed," he said, seeing the dark house except for the porch light. "I guess they must trust me."

"Yes, they do. They think you're something else, Mark—" Then she added, "and so do I."

"Do you, Prue?" He hesitated, then said, "You know what?"

"What?"

"Ever since I kissed you that night, I've been feeling guilty. It was like—well, I don't know. It was like I kissed my sister almost. That's sort of the way I always thought of you."

"I am *not* your sister!" Prue said with finality.

"No, you're not. I think I'm going to kiss you again. Do you mind?"

Prue did not answer, but her silence gave assent. She felt his arms go around her, and his lips came to hers, then she responded to his kiss. She stepped back finally and said, "Good night, Mark. It was a wonderful evening."

When the door slammed, Mark was still standing there somewhat shocked at his reaction. "It's like another person. She's not the little kid that I dug fish bait with." He went back to the car feeling ten feet tall, and as he drove away he looked back at the house and muttered, "Prudence Deforge, you have certainly grown up!"

7

A FUNNY WAY
TO SAVE THE WORLD

A beam of sunlight, which seemed as thick as a bar of gold, slanted down through the window to Jake Taylor's right. It struck the hammer-headed yellow cat on the far side of the room, and the huge animal lifted his head, opened his jaws, and yawned cavernously.

"I wish I didn't have any more to do than you, Punk," Taylor murmured; then he leaned back in his swivel chair, stretched hugely, and imitated the action of the feline. He was a tall, rangy man of thirty-nine, strongly built. His reddish-brown hair and sharp brown eyes complemented the old scars around his eyes and the puffy ear that was a memento of his prize-fighting career while a young man. He had risen to the top of his profession in the world of journalism and now controlled the editorial policies of the Hearst Newspapers.

Stretching again, he leaned forward and began marking the paper in front of him, stopping when the intercom buzzed.

"A gentleman to see you, Mr. Taylor. His name is Mark Stevens."

"Well, send him in, Elaine."

Taylor rose from his chair, moved around the desk, and as the door opened and a young man entered, he put out his hand. "Hello, Mark," he said with a smile. "What brings you to Chicago?"

"I'm a friend of Prue Deforge's and I'm here to see you, Mr. Taylor. I'll get right to it. I'm here looking for a job."

Taylor waved Mark to a chair across from his desk, resumed his own seat, then studied him. What he saw was a young man of about twenty, lean and muscular, with the moves of an athlete. He had a youthful appearance with a shock of tawny, yellow hair, deep-set gray eyes, a wide mouth, and high cheekbones. There was a seriousness about the young man that caught Taylor's attention, and he sat there talking for a few moments asking about his background and about Prue and her family. Finally he picked up a pencil and balanced it on his finger for a moment, then said, "What kind of a job?"

A rash grin appeared on Mark's lips. "The only kind you've got to give, I guess, sir. I want to be a journalist."

"Why?"

The question caught Mark off guard, and he shifted uneasily in his seat. He had prepared a speech in his mind long ago, what he would say when he confronted the editor, but now the single question had demolished all of that. "Why, I think it would be a good thing to do," he said simply.

Taylor grinned and tossed the pencil on the desk. He leaned forward, put his forearms flat, and shook his head. "I'm afraid most people don't think of journalism in quite the terms you do, Mark. As a matter of fact, I get called some pretty scandalous names from time to time. What do you mean that you think it would be a good thing to do?"

"Well, people are swayed by words, aren't they? And the words they read are in newspapers. I know there are a lot of crummy newspapers around, and crummy writers too, and—" he hesitated, humor dancing in his eyes, "and I suppose some bad editors, but I look on it as a calling."

Interested in what the young man was saying, Taylor began to pry at the boy's mind. He said finally, "You understand that as noble as our profession is,"— and here he grinned wryly— "it doesn't pay much."

"I'll be willing to work for anything. I've been going around the country now for almost a year, just bumming around but writing about the things that I saw. I've written about dirt farmers in Arkansas, oil rig roughnecks in Oklahoma, Orientals in Los Angeles, steel workers in Pittsburgh—just ordinary people. Listening to them, taking notes." He reached down and opened up the small briefcase he had brought; removing a folder, he said, "I brought some of the stuff for you to look at."

Taylor took the folder, opened it at random, and began reading. He did not move and was so still that Mark shifted again nervously in his seat and bit his lip with anxiety. He had thought of nothing since graduation from high school but working for Jake Taylor, and now that he was here, it all seemed highly unlikely. He had little experience, and the Hearst Newspapers were at the top of the journalistic world.

Jake rose and closed the folder. After making a phone call, he headed for the door. He picked up his hat, stuck it on the back of his head, and pulled on a suede sports coat. "Come on," he said.

"Where we going?" Mark asked in bewilderment, rising from his chair.

"Going to take you home and show my family off to you."

The two men left the newspaper office, and at the parking lot Taylor waved at his blue Thunderbird. "My wife Stephanie calls it my other wife," he said with a grin. "I've only gotten six traffic tickets so far, but I managed to have most of them arranged."

When they arrived at the Taylor home, a brick two-story on the lake, the wind cut into Mark as they moved to the front door. "Does it always blow like this?"

"I think it's a law of nature," Taylor said. "Come on in. Stephanie will be glad to meet you."

Stephanie greeted Mark warmly. She stood looking up at him. "Well, come on in and meet the real bosses of the Taylor household." She proudly introduced Betsy, a five-year-old with curly blond hair and brown eyes, and Forest, age two, who regarded Mark owlishly out of wide blue eyes.

During dinner Stephanie was surprised to learn that Mark knew her brother Bobby. She brought Mark up-to-date on the latest in Bobby's career. They also talked about Prue and her family.

"You're staying in the guest room," Stephanie announced firmly after dinner. "And no talk about a motel."

Mark laughed, his teeth white against his tanned skin. "I won't argue," he said. "I'm just about broke, and I've slept everywhere you can imagine, from a flophouse in Denver to a barn in Minnesota. I appreciate your hospitality."

★   ★   ★

For three days Mark enjoyed the best eating he had had since leaving home. Stephanie was a wonderful cook, and he grew very fond of the children, who constantly demanded his time. He went to the office with Jake for two of those days and got his first real insight into how a big newspaper works. It was exciting to him, but he kept waiting for Taylor to say something about the job.

Finally, after supper on their third day while Stephanie was putting the kids to bed, Jake looked up from the television set where he was watching *Ozzie and Harriet*. "I like to watch this program," he observed. "It's what family life ought to be like but usually isn't." He shook his head, and there was a look of wonder in his eyes. "God had to be in my life to bring me to a woman like Stephanie. I was an irreligious dog. It was her grandfather Amos who brought me to know the Lord. I think about him almost every day. He was a great man. I think he had more to do with the rise of the paper than Hearst himself, although Hearst would deny it, of course." He turned abruptly and said, "All right. You're hired."

The suddenness of the statement caught Mark off guard,

and for a moment he could not say anything. He heard the voice of Ricky Nelson in the background, but his whole mind was on what Jake Taylor just said. He finally cleared his throat and said, "I'll do the best I can for you, Mr. Taylor."

"You can call me Jake when nobody's around, but it's not going to be exactly like you thought."

"What do you mean, Jake?"

"Ordinarily when somebody comes to work for the paper, we start them in going through all the operations so they see the overall picture, but I've been reading through that sheaf of writing you did, and I've got an idea for a series of special stories. I'm going to give you a special assignment." His voice grew stern, and he said, "If you can't make it, all bets are off. You understand that? You have to pull your own weight."

"That's fine, Jake," Mark said quickly. "All I want is a chance. As I told my folks, if I can't make it, I want to find out now."

His statement pleased Taylor, who went over and turned the television set off. He had put a great deal of thought into this project and had great hopes for it. "Here's what you'll do. You'll travel around, just as you have been, and write stories of special interest. The one you wrote about the blind woman in Cincinnati. We can use that just like it is. I liked that story," he observed, clasping his hands together. "Most of us never think what it's like to live in a world without sight. Somehow you caught it. How did you do it, Mark?"

"I put a blindfold on, and I didn't take it off for two days," he said. "I've still got scars from running into things, but it gave me a little insight into folks with that handicap. It wasn't the same, though," he observed. "I could take off the blind-fold at any time, but blind folks can't do that."

"You're right about that, but your writing caught the pathos of it and also the courage of that lady. I'm going to pretty well turn you loose on your own, but your first assignment is all set in my mind." He spoke for a few moments, then smiled. "You'll leave tomorrow on this one."

That night, Mark sat down and wrote a short letter to Prudence.

> *Dear Prue,*
>
> *Well, it's happened. I'm a newspaperman—at least for a month. When I came here my knees were literally knocking. If Jake Taylor hadn't given me a chance, I would have gone somewhere else and tried to find a place to work. But he's hired me and is giving me the chance to do what I really want to do.*
>
> *I'll be coming to see you soon, for my first assignment is a humdinger. I think Jake is doing it just to test me, because of all things, he's ordered me to go to Mississippi and cover a bunch of baton twirlers. They have some kind of a school for that there, which I didn't even know existed. Anyway, that's where I'm headed tomorrow.*
>
> *We've talked a lot about me, what I want to do. I guess I have big ideas about saving the world, but how on earth am I going to save it by writing about teenyboppers twirling sticks?*
>
> *Anyway, I look forward to seeing you. I think about you a lot, Prue, and miss you a great deal.*

He hesitated for a moment and signed it, "With warm regards." Then he scratched it out and put, "Love, Mark."

★   ★   ★

Mark was glad to be back in the South, and when he got off the bus at Oxford, Mississippi, after a three-hour ride from Memphis, he walked around the town, taking it all in. He registered at the Old Colonial Hotel, then after unpacking his single suitcase, moved outside. He soon saw that it was like so many other small southern towns, with a sleepy square centering the life of those men who came to sit on benches, play checkers, and decide how the country should be run. He noticed two public drinking fountains, one boldly marked, "For Colored." His mind ran over the civil rights struggles that had taken place led by Martin Luther King, and he shook his head, thinking, *That won't be there very long.*

He was anxious to see author William Faulkner's house, and he asked two men sitting on a bench playing checkers, "Which way to Faulkner's house?"

One man slowly lifted his lean arm and pointed without moving his eyes from the board, mumbling, "Thet a'way."

"Thanks," Mark said wryly, then decided to go to the campus of Old Miss first. It was not difficult to find, nor was the Dixie National Baton Twirling Institute, for the first student he asked said, "Over there in that field behind that big building."

Mark nodded his thanks and moved on, walking along the wide pathways. The classes had already begun, he saw, and he was somewhat taken aback by what appeared to be hundreds of young girls out covering a field. They were all dressed in abbreviated skirts, and he could hear the voices of the instructors melding together as he approached.

He paused for a time to watch one pudgy girl no more than twelve, it seemed, spin her baton with phenomenal ease. It looked like a silver airplane propeller blurring, and as it went into the air it caught the sunlight. He moved forward and said, "Who's in charge?"

Without missing a beat, or a spin, or a revolution of her baton, the girl, who was chewing gum at almost the same speed of the baton, gave a nod saying, "Mr. Henderson. Over there."

Mark walked in the direction of the girl's gesture and stood for a while as a rather short young man with dark hair and dark eyes watched the spinning batons. "Mr. Henderson?"

"Yes, I'm Henderson."

"My name's Mark Stevens. I'm here to cover the twirling contest for the Hearst Newspapers."

Henderson's eyes lit up. "Well, that's fine. Real fine," he said in a southern accent so thick you could cut it with a knife. "Let's go over in the shade, and I'll be glad to tell you whatever you want to know."

When they reached the shade, Mark said, "Just tell me a little bit about the basics, and remember, I don't know anything about baton twirling."

"Right. Well, first of all you got to know that it's the second largest girls' movement in America."

"What's the first?"

"Why, Girl Scouts, of course. I want you to get this in your paper, Mark. There are three reasons why it's a popular sport. First, you can do it by yourself. Second, it doesn't require any expensive equipment, and finally, you don't have to go a million miles to do it. You can practice in your own backyard, or in your own living room."

Mark could see the young man was highly enthusiastic and said, "Don't be offended, Mr. Henderson, but what's the point of it all?"

"The point of it all? Why, the point is these girls can master a complex skill. It gives them all self-confidence, poise, ambidexterity, and discipline coordination."

Mark wanted to ask, *But how is that going to help these girls when they get out in the world? Not much call for baton twirling.* However, he did not, for he saw that the young man was full of the sport, or hobby, or whatever it was. As he listened, jotting down his notes, he discovered that there were multitudinous categories: advanced solo, intermediate solo, beginners' solo, strutting routine, beginners' strutting routine, military marching, and ad infinitum. He also discovered that the girls who came to the institute were divided up strictly into age groups; the winner in each category would receive a trophy, and the first five runners-up, medals.

Finally he left Henderson, who was called to his duties,

and stopped a young woman who appeared to be about sixteen and who was wearing an even briefer costume than the other girls.

"Do you design your own costumes?" he asked.

"I sure do. Do you like this one?"

"Very nice. Do you find that the costume has anything to do with your efficiency as a twirler?"

"Well, of course, I do!" the girl said quickly. "Back home we got these little skirts that sort of flare out, and of course, they're short, but I don't want anything gettin' in my way."

Mark wanted to observe that the costume she wore could not possibly get in anyone's way, but he refrained.

He moved on through the field and saw a pretty girl of no more than eight tossing a baton at least sixty feet straight up. She caught it behind her back, not moving an inch.

"How long did you have to practice to do that, miss?"

"Oh, about an hour a day for six years."

"You're certainly good at it. What's your goal in baton twirling?"

"I want to be the best there is at the High Toss and Spin."

"How many times does it spin?"

"Well, I'm up to seven," she said, "but I'm going to get more."

Mark spent a pleasant afternoon with the young women, took several pictures, then visited William Faulkner's house and his grave.

Standing over the grave, he said, "Well, Bill, I wonder if you're turning over down there with all these teenyboppers treading on your turf." He thought about the great writer for a moment, and then he said, "No, I think you would have found it amusing. So long, Bill." He turned and walked away and was glad that night to catch a bus headed for Fort Smith.

★   ★   ★

Prue had put on her most disreputable outfit, for she wanted to do some work on the barn. The outfit consisted of a pair of ratty old jeans that had belonged to her brother and that she had to hold up with a pair of his crimson suspenders. Her blouse was faded and patched, and she thought as she pounded the nails into the barn, *I look like Huckleberry Finn!* Her thick hair was tossed in the wind, but she did not notice. She loved to work on the farm and had become an expert in most of the things that needed doing. She picked up a board, held it in place, tapped a nail with the hammer, and was banging it in when she heard a voice calling, "Hey, Prue!"

Turning, she saw that Mark Stevens was rapidly approaching at an easy lope. He was wearing a pair of brown slacks and a light blue shirt, and the sun caught his hair as he came to stand before her. "I see you're all dressed up for my return."

"Mark Stevens, I hate you!" she said, throwing the hammer down and running her hands through her hair in a hopeless gesture. "You always manage to catch me when I look like a tramp!"

"You look good to me, Prue." Mark smiled. "I'm glad to see you."

Prue's face flushed, and she said, "Come on in. Mom made a chocolate cake last night, and there's still some ice cream left."

When they were inside and Mark had greeted Violet Deforge, the two of them sat down, and he plunged into the cake, smiling at Violet. "The best cake I ever had in my life."

"You always say that, Mark." Violet smiled. "Flattery is your strong point. Come to supper tonight. We want to hear all about your new job."

The two, after Mark finished his cake and ice cream, walked out and headed toward the woods. As they ambled slowly down the old pathway that led to the creek, Mark looked around and said, "I've missed all this. It's good to be back."

"We've missed you too."

Mark looked at Prue, saying, "Well, you're a senior now. How does it feel?"

"How did it feel when you were a senior?"

"I felt like I was a prisoner serving his last days."

His remark amused Prue, and she laughed. She had a fine laugh, full-bodied, but not at all masculine. Her eyes squeezed almost shut, and she looked at him and said, "That's the way I feel. I think everyone does."

"What's Debbie doing now? Have you heard?"

"She's dating the first-string quarterback at the University of Arkansas."

"It figures."

Prue shot him a quick glance. She wanted to ask if he grieved over his breakup with Debbie but said nothing. Finally she said, "How long will you stay, Mark?"

"Oh, maybe as much as a week." He told her about his job, that his time was pretty much up to himself and he could make his own decisions. They reached the creek and walked along it, tossing stones in, and once a large fish of some kind broke the water not twenty feet away. "I'd like to get you on the end of a line, buddy," Mark said.

"They've been biting good, Mark. I come almost every day."

"I'd like to come with you sometime."

Prue was pleased, and the two ambled along, stopping beside a willow that hung out over the creek. "Do you remember when we used to swim here?"

"I sure do. We must not have been more than ten or eleven."

"You were twelve, and I was eleven," Prue said instantly.

They talked for a while about those days, and finally Mark worked up the courage to ask, "Have you got a steady fellow now?"

"No."

The brevity of her reply disturbed Mark, and he said, "I

can't understand what's wrong with the guys. They must be idiots."

"Well, I'm the dumbest girl in school, and most of them are two or three inches shorter than I am. What do you expect?"

"I told you so many times! Don't put yourself down, Prue!"

"All right. I won't then."

They spent the afternoon reminiscing, and the woods rang with the sound of their voices and their laughter.

At long last Mark said, "I guess I better go home and spend some time with my folks."

"I'll make you a cherry pie tonight." She was looking up at him and said wistfully, "It's nice to look up to somebody."

"It's nice to look down at somebody." Mark reached out, pushed the curls away from her face, and said, "It's good to be back, Prue."

Prue did not answer. She was conscious of the touch of his hand on her cheek. It disturbed her somehow, for she knew that it was only a friendly gesture. Turning, she said, "Come on. I'll race you to the house."

8

"Make Me a Chocolate Pie!"

A ll right! Come and get it, Bucky!" Prue called out as the small black bear came tumbling out of the doghouse that had become his bed. Perhaps *small* was not the correct word, for although he had been no bigger than a kitten when she had taken him to raise, a gift from neighbor Tom Hankins, now the bear was as large as a big Labrador. His black fur glistened, and his snout seemed to quiver as he came up to Prue, reared up, and pawed at her, whining. He snapped at the pieces of leftover roast that she fed him, and Prue laughed. "You're the greediest thing I've ever seen. Now, get down! I've got work to do."

But the bear followed her everywhere she went, rearing up on his hind legs and seeming to beat time with his paws. Prue stopped from time to time, reached into her mackinaw pocket, and fed him peanuts, which he loved. He ate them, shells and all, and continually begged for more.

Dent Deforge had been watching the scene, leaning on the fence that held two dozen Black Angus cattle. He ambled over and said, "Prue, that bear's getting too big for a pet."

"I know, Dad," Prue said quickly. "He'll be going back to the wild pretty soon."

"Those things can be dangerous."

"Bucky? Why, he wouldn't hurt a flea!"

"Not you maybe, but when he gets a little bigger and he encounters a child it might be different."

Prue stroked the bear's head and said sorrowfully, "I hate to let him go."

Dent reached into his pocket, pulled out a bag of ginger-snaps, extracted two of them, and stuffed them in his mouth. As he put the bag back he chewed slowly, then shook his head, saying thoughtfully, "You've got to learn to let things go."

Something in his words caught at Prue. She turned from the bear, shoving him down, and looked up at her father. "I don't have much to let go, Dad," she said quietly. "No boy-friends, no career. I guess Bucky's all that I can let go of."

"Don't talk like that, Prue," Dent said, concern bringing a frown to his face.

"All right, I won't, but I'll tell you the truth, I don't have any idea what I'm going to do when I get out of school. Who would hire me with my lousy academic record?"

"Books don't mean everything."

"No, not out here on the farm, but they do when you go looking for a job."

Dent shifted his feet uncomfortably, pulled out the bag of gingersnaps, and this time took three of them and offered her the bag. When she shook her head, he stuffed one in his mouth and chewed on it thoughtfully. "I guess you'll have to find something that doesn't call for straight A's."

"I can always work at McDonald's," she said, smiling. See-ing his worried expression, she reached up and patted his cheek. "Don't worry, Dad. I won't." She changed the subject, saying, "I'm going out to get some quail today. Do you have any shells for the twelve gauge?"

"Sure. They're in the cabinet by the hot water heater. Be careful. Don't blow your foot off with that thing." He smiled, for he knew she was an excellent shot, almost as good as he was. "Where are you going?"

"There's a covey over by the old Olson place. I won't even need a dog for them. The last time I went they flew up under my feet and scared me to death."

Dent laughed. "They do that, don't they? I always think something bad's got me. Well, I'm partial to quail. Bring back a sackful."

★　★　★

The breeze had died down, and the November sun was a pale, silver disk high in the sky as Prue moved cautiously through the open field. She held the twelve gauge lightly, and the thought passed through her mind, *If I were a little thing like Debbie Peters, I couldn't handle this gun.* The thought gave her satisfaction for some reason, but she put it out of her mind, concentrating on the clumps of dried grass that lay ahead of her. She had a hunter's instinct, her father having taught her a great deal, and now as she moved forward slowly, she wished she had brought a dog. However, her favorite bird dog, Sissy, was expecting pups any day, and she had thought it wise not to bring her.

The smell of burning leaves was in the air—crisp, and sharp, and acrid, and she knew someone was burning their fields and thought for a moment about the dangers of a forest fire. But she had no time to think further, for when she took one more step the long grass in front of her seemed to explode with birds, their wings making a miniature thunder as they rose. Quickly she pivoted, planted her feet, and swung the twelve gauge up. She shot three times deliberately, and three birds came tumbling out of the air, falling to the ground.

Lowering the rifle, she advanced, claimed the birds, and stuffed them into the canvas bag that hung from a strap at her side. "That makes eleven," she said aloud with satisfaction. "That ought to please Dad and fill his stomach."

Moving forward, she encountered no more birds until she came to within a hundred yards of the old house where the Olsons had lived. Here, again, a covey flew up. She was too far away to get an accurate shot, but she knocked one bird down. *If I had a dog, it would have been better*, she thought as she walked over to claim the bird. As she bent over to pick it up, she heard a voice and was startled. Whirling, she saw that a man had come out of the old two-story frame house and was saying something to her.

She saw that the man was lame, for he leaned heavily on a cane. He was a stranger, and she studied him as she did when she encountered anyone new. He was no more than five feet ten inches with light brown hair and dark brown eyes. His face was sharp featured, and there was a frown on his lips. "You're not supposed to hunt on this land," he said, stopping in front of her.

"I'm sorry," Prue said. "I didn't know anybody was here. It's been vacant since the Olsons moved away last year."

"Well, it's not vacant now. I've rented it."

Prue felt awkward and said quickly, "I'm very sorry. I won't do it again."

"Are you from around here?"

Prue turned and nodded. "Yes, sir. My name is Prue De-forge. I live with my folks about a mile across those fields."

"My name's Kent Maxwell." The man hesitated, and it was now he who seemed awkward and ill at ease. "I'm new here. I just moved in yesterday."

"I'm glad to have you. You'll have to come over and meet my folks."

Her words seemed to encourage the man, and he lifted the cane and swung it for a moment, almost idly. He was wearing what Prue called city clothes: a pair of wool light green slacks, a pale beige shirt, and a pair of brown loafers. He seemed strong enough; his upper body was well built, and she wondered what was wrong with his leg.

"I don't know anyone to ask. I was intending to go into town," Maxwell said. "What I need is someone to help me. Kind of a part-time housekeeper, and maybe someone to do some cooking. Do you know anyone like that?"

Prue thought for a moment. "Mrs. Rowden does some housekeeping, but she lives way over on the other side of us. It'd be a little bit hard for her to get here. I'll ask her if you'd like."

"You say you live only about a mile over that way?"

"Yes, sir."

"Are you in school or working?"

"I'm a senior at the high school."

Maxwell studied her for a moment, then asked, "Could you do some housekeeping and some cooking?"

For a moment Prue hesitated, then she said, "I guess I know how to keep house all right, and I can cook some, but I'd have to ask my momma and daddy."

"You could come almost any time you wanted, after school and on weekends. I can't keep up this big old house, and I don't want to." There was a discontented look on Maxwell's face. He was handsome in a way, his features neat, but his hair needed cutting, and there was a food stain on the front of his shirt. "I just moved in from Chicago. Don't know a thing about the country. Don't even know how to buy groceries." He smiled and seemed to look younger to Prue. "Ask your parents. I'll pay whatever the going rate is around here for that kind of work."

Prue nodded. "Yes, sir. I'll ask them."

She turned and walked away and felt his eyes watching her. She walked with a country girl's slide that covered the ground quickly, and as she moved back into the woods following the old trails, she thought, *Strange for a city man to come out and live in that big old house. He must rattle around in there.* She thought about his offer, and when she got home went at once to her father and mother, who were sitting in the kitchen. Dent was watching his wife cut up a chicken, and they both listened as Prue told them of her encounter. "I'd like to make a little extra money," she said, "if it'll be all right with you."

"I don't see anything wrong with it," Violet said. "What do you think, Dent?"

"Might go by and have a talk with him. If he seems like an okay sort of man, it might be all right."

★   ★   ★

Kent Maxwell answered the knock at the door, and when he opened it he saw that he was facing a very tall man in his fifties, probably, with a shock of black hair and a pair of steady gray eyes. "I'm Dent Deforge," he said. "Your neighbor over to the east."

"Oh, you must be the father of the young woman that was hunting birds."

"Yes, I'm Prue's father. Came by to welcome you." Dent held up a sack and said, "My wife sent some homemade bread. Thought you might find it good."

"Come in, Mr. Deforge. Glad you dropped by."

Deforge followed Maxwell into the kitchen, taking in the limited use of the right leg, but, of course, did not mention it.

"I've got coffee made, and I can eat some of that bread right now." Maxwell poured the coffee into large white mugs, took the bread out, and sawed off a heel of it. He went to the icebox, pulled a stick of butter out, and sitting down, began to spread it on the bread.

"I'll have to bring you some homemade butter," Dent offered. "I can't eat that store-bought stuff myself."

"Well, I don't know about the butter, but this bread is fine. Your wife's a good cook."

"Prue's a good cook too. Her momma's taught her. You're from the east, Prue tells me."

"From Chicago actually." Maxwell took another bite of the bread and chewing it, said, "I never have lived in the country, Mr. Deforge. I'm kind of at a disadvantage."

"Just call me Dent. Everybody else does."

"I'm Kent, then. I'm looking for someone to help me keep up this big old place and do some cooking. I've had TV dinners until I'm sick of them already, and I've only been here a few days."

"A man misses home cooking all right," Dent nodded. "How long do you figure to stay here?"

"I leased the place for a year. Bought what furniture the Olsons had left, and so far I like it." He took another bite of the bread, then when he swallowed it said, "It gets so busy in the city, it got to where I couldn't think. I needed a little peace and quiet."

"Well, you got that out here. This is so far off the main road you won't have many visitors. Maybe an encyclopedia salesman or a Jehovah's Witness following the power wires in. What sort of work do you do, if I might ask?"

"I'm a teacher, but I got a sabbatical—a year off to do what I please. I thought I'd go to Europe, but I finally decided to just stay here. Find the quietest place I could while I do some work."

"Well, we're glad to have you in the community. The church is right down County Highway 6. We'd be mighty proud to have you come and visit next Sunday. It's a good way to meet all the neighbors in the community. Election's coming up. I don't know how you vote, but I'd be glad to talk with you about politics."

"I don't know much about that," Maxwell shrugged his shoulders. "This war on poverty that President Johnson's started, I don't think it'll ever work."

"You're right there. You can't get rid of poverty by passing a law. The Lord Jesus says the poor you have with you always, and I reckon I've seen that." He hesitated and said, "I came over to meet you and welcome you but also to talk to you about Prue."

Something in Deforge's voice caught Maxwell's attention. He lifted his head and waited, saying only, "Yes? What about your daughter?"

"I don't know how to put this any way except to be honest. Prue's a young woman, and you're a single man. Prue's a good girl, and I hope you're a good man, but I don't know you yet."

Maxwell smiled briefly. He tapped his right leg and said, "In the first place, I'm not a woman chaser, and in the second place, even if I were, I couldn't catch a woman on this bad leg." Then he sobered up and said, "You don't have to worry about that. My word on it."

Deforge studied the man, then said, "I'll take your word, sir, and you and Prue can work out the details. I hope you and me will get to know each other better."

"I'd like that."

Dent left soon after, and when he got home he called Prue, who was out feeding the chickens. "I met your Mr. Maxwell. He's a little bit hard to know, but I told him the rules of the game."

Prue laughed. "Did you threaten to take a shotgun to him if he offered me any insult?"

Dent laughed with her. "Just about," he said. "I don't think you'll have any problem, so I said you'd be by to work out whatever workin' rules you have to."

★   ★   ★

Prue arrived at Kent Maxwell's house at nine o'clock the next morning. When he came to the door she said, "Dad told me he came by and talked to you. He said it would be all right if I would work for you."

"Well, that's fine. Come in and we'll talk. Come on in the kitchen." He limped through the house, down the hall, turning to the left where a wood-burning stove drove the chill out of the air. "I hate that stove," he said, "but it's all that was here. Sit down, Prudence."

"I can cut the wood for you. I do most of that at our house," Prue said quickly.

"How about some coffee?"

"That would be nice, Mr. Maxwell."

The two sat there and talked over duties and wages, and finally Kent said, "I work up in the attic." He waved his hand around and said, "You know housekeeping better than I do. Why don't you just do whatever you see needs doing while I go up and try to get something done. You might fix something to eat about noon, if you would, Prudence."

"Most people call me Prue." Getting up, she said, "I'll do the best I can for you."

Maxwell nodded and moved out of the kitchen. As soon as he disappeared Prue went to work. The old house had not been thoroughly cleaned for a year. Maxwell, obviously, had made some attempts, but the kitchen itself was in sad condition. Quickly she began to wash the dishes and then organized them in the cabinets. She put more wood in the fire after she had finished the kitchen, then started work on the rest of the house. At eleven she stopped work, came back into the kitchen, and surveyed the supplies. Evidently Maxwell had simply piled whatever he could think of into a basket and brought it out; everything was all jumbled together—cans, dried beans and rice, sauces, and what seemed like, in the refrigerator, an enormous amount of ground beef.

"He must have been livin' on hamburgers," Prue said with a smile. She pulled the ground beef out and found some Worcestershire sauce and tomato soup; she took out a carton of eggs and beat three of them in a bowl with a hand beater, chopped up an onion and some green peppers, and soon popped a meat loaf into the oven. Since the old wood-burning stove had no gauge, she simply had to guess at it.

While the meat loaf was cooking, she made a recipe she had developed herself: potato croquettes. She sang to herself while she was cooking, pleased that she had found something to do.

Finally at noon she went to the foot of the stairs, hesitated, then ascended to the upper level. It was a two-story house, and there was another flight of stairs leading up to the attic. She climbed these, knocked on the door, and said, "Mr. Maxwell, can you take time out to eat dinner?"

There was silence for a moment, then she heard his cane

tapping across the wooden floor. Stepping outside the door, he asked, "Dinner already? What time is it?"

"About noon. Everything's ready to eat."

As she descended the stairs, Prue walked more slowly than she would have ordinarily, not wanting to make him feel inferior. She had a natural courtesy, partly southern hospitality in its finest form, and was sensitive to the shortcomings of others. Maxwell, she had already discovered, was sensitive about his bad leg, and as they made their way to the kitchen, he looked around, saying, "Why, you've done a lot of work, Prue."

"Oh, it wasn't in really bad shape. It's a nice old house."

The two entered the kitchen, which was very large in the manner of old, southern houses, and Prue said, "I thought we might eat in here where it's warm."

"Something smells good," Maxwell said. He sat down and leaned his cane against the wall; then Prue walked over to the stove. Using two small towels, she took out the meat loaf in the rectangular glass dish, then did the same with the potato croquettes. She had put only one plate on the table, and Maxwell said, "Why, I'm not going to eat alone. Sit down, Prue."

"All right."

Prue had put out the salt and pepper, a glass of milk, and the bread that her mother had sent; now she took a plate for herself as Maxwell cut into the meat loaf, cutting an enormous square. He put it on his plate, along with two large spoonfuls of the potato croquettes, and began to eat hungrily. Even as Prue was filling her plate, he was saying, "Why, this is delicious. What kind of potatoes are these?"

"Spanish potato croquettes," Prue said.

"Where did you get the recipe? I never tasted potatoes this good."

"Oh, it's just something I made up myself. Not much to it, and they're good when they're cold too."

Prue was amused at how heartily the man ate, and finally he slowed down. "Can you make pie?" he asked.

"Some kinds."

"Can you make a chocolate pie?"

"Oh yes! I make pretty good chocolate pies!"

"Well, I'd like to have one of those."

"I'll make you one before I leave if you have the ingredients here."

The meal was pleasant. The weather had warmed up, and outside the sun was shining cheerfully.

As they ate, Maxwell asked a few questions about Prue and listened as she spoke of her life. He noticed she did not ask him and thought, *That must be part of the southern culture.*

Finally he rose and picked up his cane. "That was excellent. After you get the dishes cleaned up, come upstairs to my workroom. It's a mess!"

"All right." Prue went to work at once cleaning up the kitchen and started the pie. She was very quick at such things, and soon she was able to leave and go upstairs. When she got to the attic room the door was closed, and she hesitated, then knocked.

"Come in."

Prue opened the door, and when she stepped in was stopped dead still. The roof had skylights in it letting the sun in, and near two large windows at one end, Kent Maxwell stood before a canvas. He had a board of some kind in front of him on a table, and a paintbrush in the other. He turned around and said, "Come on in, Prue." He waved the paintbrush and said, "Look, this place is worse than downstairs. It's where I stay most of the time, and I'm embarrassed that it's such a mess."

Prue glanced around, noticing the soft drink bottles, milk cartons, and remains of the aluminum plates that had held TV dinners. Then she saw the canvases. Pictures everywhere! Some of them barely started, some of them half finished; she came forward hesitantly and looked at the picture he was painting. It was a landscape, she saw, and at once said, "Why, that's the pond over by the pecan orchard."

Maxwell nodded. "Yes, I can see it from the window over there." He turned and cocked his head at the painting. "I haven't got it exactly right."

Prue edged still closer until she was right behind him. "Oh, it's just right!" she said. "Look, that's the old hollow tree where the pileated woodpecker lives!"

"Pileated woodpecker? What's that?"

"Oh, it's the biggest woodpecker in the woods. A huge bird, black and white with a red crest."

"I'd like to get that in there. I've heard him, but I've never seen him."

"He's real shy," Prue said. "You could see him if you sit real still though, and he'll come back." Her eyes went back to the picture and she whispered, "That's so good. I never saw a real picture like that, only prints. Except for those we saw at the museum in Fort Smith."

Maxwell studied the young woman. She was wearing a brown skirt with a green blouse that buttoned up with large, brass buttons. He noted that the sleeves were too short, and he noticed, also, the excitement in her dark eyes. Her hair was pulled back and tied, but in the sunlight he caught faint gleams of auburn. Her lips were half parted, and he noted that, unlike most girls, she wore very little makeup. She had a strong face, not pretty, but the bone structure was what all really handsome women had, he thought.

"Could—could I watch you paint after I clean the room up?"

"Why, of course." Maxwell shrugged. He turned again to the painting, and with an intensity that he brought to nothing else, worked steadily. He was vaguely aware of the girl moving around the room cleaning up, but he forgot about her as he applied himself to the strokes.

Finally he leaned back, took a deep breath, and turned to see her on a stool, absolutely silent. "Most people pester me with questions," he observed. He turned back and made three or four more strokes that seemed to transform a blob of paint into a clump of flowers with brilliant red blossoms.

"How do you do that?" Prue whispered. "It's like magic."

"Do you know anything about art?"

"No, just what I learned in school."

Maxwell turned to face her, put the brush down, and picked up a cloth already stained with many colors. He wiped his hands on it and said, "I came out here, Prue, in the backwoods to get some bugs out of my system."

"What kind of bugs?"

"Art bugs, I guess. I've done nothing but paint and teach art for so long that I've gotten stale. It's not good to come to art that way." He spoke meditatively, and a faraway look came to his eyes. "You need to get away from art to come to it fresh. Not do it every day for a living."

"You teach people how to paint?"

"Yes." He stared at her. "I hope you're not one of these undiscovered, great artists." He laughed. "I get a lot of them." He did not notice the swift expression that passed across Prue's face, nor did he dream that she had been on the verge of asking him to teach her something about painting.

"No, sir, but I like to watch."

Maxwell liked the girl. She was a little bit strange—so tall and serious, but he found her interesting. "You make chocolate pies, and you can watch me paint all you want to."

Prue rose at once. "There's one downstairs. I made it before I came up."

"Well, let's go get it!" Maxwell limped down the stairs again, sat down, and tasted the pie that she put out on a saucer for him. He shook his head with wonder and said, "You make me a chocolate pie like this once in a while, and I'll let you watch all you please, Prudence Deforge."

A week later Prue was writing in her diary. It was late afternoon, and she had just come from cleaning Maxwell's house and cooking his supper. She had left early, and now she sat at her desk and wrote:

> *Mr. Maxwell doesn't know it, but he's teaching me how to paint, even if he never says a word about it. I watch him and see how he mixes paint, and then I watch how he holds his brush and how he puts the paint on in layers sometimes. It would be so much better if I could tell him that I want to learn, but I'm afraid to. He's been pestered by people who won't let him alone, but even if it's slow, it's something. I'm going to learn to paint if it kills me!*

9

CHRISTMAS IN THE OZARKS

C hristmas came in 1965 bringing with it a longing for better times. The country had been stirred, and shaken, all year long. The air strikes in Vietnam had escalated the war, and young men from all over America were going there to fight and to die. The civil rights movement continued to escalate, and in Alabama there had been a Freedom March that drew the eyes of the world.

Cassius Clay had beaten Sonny Liston for the heavyweight title, and in Watts violence had broken out as race riots exploded in the city.

Perhaps as the Stuarts gathered in the little town of Cedarville, which was the closest thing called a town to the old home place, they had come to put some of these things behind them as far as possible. But it was more than that. For all of the older members it was a hallowed time when they would come together and feel again the sense of family.

Amos was gone, and Lylah was growing so feeble that it was a matter of time before she would leave an empty place at the table. Owen, also, was feeling his age, and looking it.

Logan, Peter, Lenora, Gavin, and Christie were all in good health, and as they came from their homes they were all aware of the two empty places in their circle, but no one complained.

Not all of the younger Stuarts came, for they were widely scattered, and some could not afford the trip. Jerry and Bonnie were there, as were two of their three children. Stephanie had come with Jake and their two children. Richard and his wife, Laurel, and their family had come early.

This smaller group was having supper at the old home place, and Jerry said, shaking his head, "I been meaning to tell you that Bobby says he's going to be here."

Instantly Richard looked up. He was Bobby's twin, although not his identical twin. He had flown in from Los Angeles, taking time out from his work in a street ministry in the worst part of that city, and now he said, "When's he coming, Dad?"

"I don't know, but it's going to be a problem."

Bonnie, Jerry's wife, looked over and said, "How could it be a problem?"

"He's bringing Lannie with him."

A silence fell over the group. They were all aware, as was most of America, at least those who kept up with the world of rock stars, that Bobby Stuart and Lannie Marr were living together.

Jake Taylor shook his head. "That's going to be awkward, isn't it?"

Jerry's face was grim. "Yes, it is. I've taken two rooms for them at the hotel, although that won't fool anybody."

Bonnie came over and put her arm around Jerry. "It's all right. It'll do them both good to have Christmas here. I've never given up praying for that young woman."

Bobby had brought Lannie by on a brief visit once, but Lannie had been stiff and very formal. She was aware of the Stuarts' disapproval of the "arrangement" that she and Bobby had, and it had not been a good time for any of them.

Stephanie was sitting quietly, but finally she said, "I remember when we were all growing up together, just kids, you and I, Richard and Bobby. Life was so simple then, wasn't it?"

"Yes, it was," Richard said at once, "but I'm like Mom. I'm not giving up on Lannie Marr."

"All right. We'll all pray for her then. We've already prayed for Bobby so much that God's got to hear," Jerry said. He smiled and put his hands out. "Let's claim them both for the Lord right now."

★   ★   ★

The Palace Hotel, as was customary, was blocked out during the Christmas holidays for the Stuarts. They filled all the rooms, and on Christmas Eve the great supper was held with all of the children present.

The cooks had done their usual magnificent job so that golden turkeys, succulent vegetables, corn-bread dressing, and pumpkin and pecan pies filled the dining room with a rich aroma as Owen Stuart rose and tapped on his glass. The talking and laughter was so loud that he could not get their attention, so he raised his voice and said, "All right! May I have your attention!" Owen's voice, even at the age of eighty-two, was still full and powerful. Everyone turned around and William Lee, his son sitting next to him, stuck his fingers in his ears. "Hey, Dad! Watch it! You're going to deafen me!" Laughter went up and Owen smiled benevolently, then began to speak. "Well, once again we meet at the good old Palace Hotel, and our thanks to our host, and to all the cooks, and to the fine, young folks who are serving us. Let's have a big round of applause for all of them." He waited until the applause died down, then said, "You know, I'm told that some Jewish people have the tradition at some of their ceremonial meals that they leave an empty place at the table—waiting for Elijah who is coming back." He looked around and said, "We could set an empty place today for Amos, but as I have said so many times, we haven't lost him. For when you lose something, you don't know where it is, and we know where Amos is—with the Lord Jesus." He smiled then and said, "We Christians never say good-bye, for we're only separated by a moment." He looked around the table and said, "So, here we are, Lylah. It's been a long time since we sat at this table as children, hasn't it?"

Lylah was eighty-five now and fragile, and her voice was not as strong as it had been when she had been on the stage or in motion pictures. But there was still a spark of fire in her, and she said, "It has been a long time, Owen, and I thank God that I'm able to be here today." She looked over and named off her other brothers and sisters. "Logan, Peter, and Lenora, Gavin and Christie. Christie, you're the baby of the family now. How old are you? Sixty-nine?"

Christie Stuart Castellano smiled and put her hand on her husband's arm. She and Mario both had white hair but were in good health. Christie said, "God has been good to all of us."

Lenora, at seventy-five, spoke up from her wheelchair. "I would have wheeled myself all the way from Chicago to get here. I look forward to it all year, and like the rest of you, I thank God that we are all together again."

Owen smiled at his brothers and sisters, then said, "I usually ask the blessing, but tonight I'm asking a younger member, one of the new generation, to do that chore. Reverend Richard Stuart, I can't tell you how proud we all are of you for the work you are doing in Los Angeles. There are others in this country who are more famous, but none doing the work of God more faithfully than you, my brother, in the terrible parts of that large city. Richard, ask the blessing."

The meal continued, and after it was over Richard sought out Bobby. He asked, "Where's Lannie?"

Bobby appeared to be embarrassed. "She went to her room."

"I wish she had stayed. We could get to know her better."

"I don't think she's feeling too well."

Both of the men knew that this was not so, and Bobby tried to smile. "I can't lie to you very well, can I, Richard? I never could."

"Naturally she must feel a little uncomfortable. It's all strange to her."

The two went outside the hotel and walked up and down the streets of the small town, speaking of unimportant things. Finally when they had come to the park, which was vacant because of the temperature, Richard said, "Bobby, I want to talk to you about the way you're living. I know you don't want to hear it, but I'm going to say it anyway." He spoke for a few moments about Bobby's lifestyle and finally said, "Even if I weren't a preacher, I'd hate to see you throwing your life away. Look at you, Bobby, you're full of drugs right now. You're living an immoral life, and there's only one end to that."

Bobby felt Richard's hand on his arm, and for a moment tears came to his eyes, but he blinked them away and jerked his arm back. "I didn't come here to get preached at, Richard! You keep your religion, and I'll keep what I've got!"

Richard watched as Bobby turned and walked angrily away. He went inside and sat down beside his father. "I tried to talk to Bobby, but he wouldn't listen." He shook his head sadly. "He's headed for a hard awakening someday."

Bobby went upstairs, knocked on Lannie's door, and then stepped inside without waiting. She was lying on the bed, and he knew she was doped up. He reached over and pulled her up to her feet. "Sober up!" he said. "We're getting out of here!"

Lannie murmured, "These people all talking about God! They're nothing but a bunch of religious nuts!"

Bobby, for the first time since he had known Lannie, reached out and slapped her. "Shut up!" he said. "You can't talk about my family like that!"

Lannie was barely conscious of his words, and she felt her face stinging from his slap. She stared at him as he pulled her suitcase out and began throwing her clothes in it, and finally when he pulled her up and forced her to get dressed, she could barely function.

Without stopping to say good-bye to his relatives, Bobby

walked outside, thankful that no one saw Lannie, as he practically had to carry her to the car. He shoved her inside, slammed the door, then moved around and got behind the wheel. Starting the Cadillac, he pulled away, but he turned and looked at the hotel, and something rose in him, bitter and harsh. Shaking his head, he drove out of town and stopped only when he could drive no farther. He went inside a liquor store and bought two fifths of bourbon, checked himself and Lannie into a motel, and got dead drunk, unable to face his thoughts or his memories.

10

GRADUATION GIFTS

Although Kent Maxwell had opened the two large windows, his workroom was still overly warm. April had come to the Ozarks bringing hot weather, and now, wiping the sweat from his forehead, Maxwell tossed down his brush with an irritated gesture on the rickety table beside his easel and walked to the third window. It had been stuck tight ever since he moved in, but up until now two windows had been adequate to cool the attic space. Placing his hands on the top of the wooden frame, he shoved with all his might, bracing against his good leg. The window resisted for a moment, then shot upward unexpectedly, breaking free from the dried paint that had held it. Maxwell grunted with satisfaction, but when he released the window it immediately slid back down. Irritation flickered in his eyes, and he muttered, "Got one of those ropes and sash weights. Rope must be broken."

His eyes swept the room, and he moved over to pick up a two-foot-long piece of wooden lathe, which he used to prop the window open. He walked over to one of the other windows, whose sash weight did work, and stood looking out over the countryside. He had had the screens replaced, for the old ones had rusted out years before. Now the bright aluminum net caught the rays of the hot sun and divided the landscape before him into a series of tiny squares. Always interested in visual impact, Maxwell muttered, "I wonder what it would be like to paint over a screen like this where all the little squares show." He toyed with the idea, thinking of techniques and ways to make such a picture come to birth, then shrugged his shoulders, speaking aloud, "It would probably be a hit. I'd be rich, and a hundred thousand half-baked artists would go around painting through screens."

The radio, which he always left on while he was painting, continued to fill the studio as he gazed out the window. The Beatles worked their way through "Eleanor Rigby," followed by Pete Seeger pounding out his anti–Vietnam War protest song, "Waist Deep in the Big Muddy," and this was followed by the strange song by Arlo Guthrie, "Alice's Restaurant."

With a grunt of displeasure, Maxwell limped over to the radio and turned the knob until he got Simon and Garfunkel singing "The Sounds of Silence." Maxwell paused, his eyes thoughtful, as he listened to the strange melody and the rather eerie words of the song. It had the power to make him sad somehow or other, although he could not understand why.

He moved back to the easel and was irritated when the music was interrupted by the daily five-minute newscast. As usual, the war news was bad. In dulcet tones, the local newscaster announced, "The death of U.S. servicemen exceeded those of the Vietnamese enemy in the war zone. . . ." He immediately followed with an account of a parade in New York on Fifth Avenue, the largest demonstration yet against the war. Maxwell listened as the announcer said, "More than twenty thousand people took part. Counterdemonstrators, some of them veterans of other wars, threw eggs from the sidewalk, and several dozen fought with the protesters at Eighty-Sixth Street. Police made seven arrests. Thousands of other protesters marched in Washington, in the Midwest, and in California. And in Boston today, fifty high school students shouted, 'Kill them! Shoot them!' as they fought with anti-Vietnam protesters after four of them had burned their draft cards."

Enduring the newscast, Maxwell waited until the music came back on. This time it was The Byrds, a trio he rather

liked. As they belted out "Mr. Tambourine Man," he muttered, "I like songs that don't have any social value. That's
what music's supposed to be."

The painting he was working on was one that he took great
pride in. It was a portrait of Prudence that he was creating
from memory. It was a memory that was very real to him, for
ever since he had seen the young woman one day, her hair
blown by the spring breeze as she sat outside under the blos-
soming peach tree, the picture had been taking place in his
mind. He had included, as a background, the line of foothills
that lifted themselves above the horizon and framed her face,
and he painted her from the waist up, her head tilted slightly
to one side and the beginnings of a smile on her lips. Now
he was working on the eyes with a tiny brush, trying to capture the light that he occasionally saw appear when she was
pleased. He could not remember what he had said that had
pleased her at that moment and wished that he could.

As he worked on, infinitely meticulous with the tiny brush,
he realized that—not for the first time—Prue's visits had been
a breath of fresh air to him. He had not made friends among
the neighbors, although several had called. Neither had he
gone to church nor any of the political meetings that some
of the locals delighted in. Most of his time he spent either
outside limping for relatively short distances around the place
or inside painting. The nights, when the light had gone, he
spent reading or listening to his collection of records.

It was a lonely life, and the appearance of Prudence to
clean the house and to cook for him had been a welcome
break. She came more often than was necessary, and after
doing her work she would inevitably sit as still as a statue
and quiet as a stone behind him as he worked. Her silence
and patience amazed him, for he had not seen such a thing in
the very young in all of his experience. Her presence did not
disturb him, and he had found himself explaining what he
was doing, dissecting his craft and speaking of the difficulties
that he encountered.

He had been delighted to discover by voicing his problems to the dark-haired young woman who sat watching him so quietly and steadily with her dark eyes that sometimes the problem resolved itself. He had also given her books on the history of painting and had made a startling discovery. She did not learn quickly from books, from the text that is, but she memorized every picture, every painting, that appeared in the book.

He heard a sound and quickly identified Prue's voice, for she always called as she came up to the house. He moved the canvas to an oblique angle of the room, covered it carefully with a piece of dry, thin canvas, and then moved to the window. "Hello," he called. "Come on in, Prue." He caught her quick smile and the wave of her hand, then turned and left the studio to meet her downstairs. *I won't tell her about the painting*, he thought. *It'll be a nice surprise for her when it's finished.*

Prue had entered the house by the time he hobbled down the stairs, and he saw she was holding up an object. The sun behind her blinded him temporarily, and he blinked as she said, "Look what I found." Moving out of the sunlight and letting the screen door slam behind her, Prue stepped forward, and Maxwell saw that she had a small cage built out of some kind of mesh. Inside was a red squirrel that chattered and held on with his claws.

"Where did you get him? You haven't been climbing trees, have you?"

"Oh no! Daddy found him while he was out hunting. He was just a little thing, and must've fallen out of the nest. I've been nursing him with a medicine dropper. He's so sweet." She undid the latch, lifted the lid, and reached inside. The baby squirrel chattered fiercely, then she put him on her shoulder. He held tightly with his claws, looked around, then sat up and appeared to wash his face.

"Doesn't he bite?"

"No. Not a bit." The squirrel turned and moved quickly, clinging to her shoulder but rising up and touching her ear with his nose. Prue giggled and pulled her head down. "That tickles," she said.

Maxwell, always the artist, instantly had a thought. "That would make a good picture, that squirrel perched on your shoulder like that, but I'm not sure I could do it."

"Why not?"

"Oh, I'm not very good with animals. I'm better with people."

The squirrel was nibbling at Prue's ear. She reached up and put her hand in front of him. A thought had come to her, and she had almost spoken it: *Why, you're not good with people at all!* But she was glad that she had kept the words back. It was true enough, of course. It had not taken Prue long to learn that Maxwell was not good with people. It was as though he had made the decision not to have friends or to let anyone get close. This puzzled her, for with her he was amiable and witty, and after the first stiff meetings could tease her and laugh at himself. But he was a man of mystery to her, for he never spoke of his past. She wondered, of course, if he had a wife and children, if he had family, and why he had chosen to seclude himself in the outback of the Ozark Mountains when he was obviously a city man. However, she filed this statement and then reached up and plucked the squirrel from her shoulder. "I just brought him to show you, but you can keep him for a pet if you want to, until he's old enough to turn loose."

"No. I don't want to take care of anything, Prue. He's cute, but I guess I've got all I can do taking care of myself—along with your help."

"All right. I'll take him home again." Putting the squirrel back in the box, she fastened the lid, but she took some shelled peanuts out of her pocket and put several of them inside. "There's your snack," she said, then she glanced around and put the cage down on the large oak table in front of the living room window. Coming back, she said, "I got a letter from Mark."

"That's your reporter friend?"

"Yes. Oh, it's so exciting. He's been traveling around working for a newspaper, writing stories, and they're doing very well in the paper." Her eyes were bright as she pulled the letter out and opened it, her eyes following the writing very slowly. "He says he's coming here this week." She looked up and when he saw the expectation in her that brightened her countenance, he said, "Bring him by. I'd like to meet him."

This was unexpected for Prue, but she said at once, "I think you'd like him, Mr. Maxwell, and you two would have a lot to talk about. He's so interested in everything. I bet he'd like to do an interview with you and put you in the paper."

Instantly Maxwell shook his head. "No, nothing like that, but maybe you could bring him over and cook supper for us both. He's a bachelor, I assume."

"Oh yes. He's just a year older than I am. We went all the way through school together. We were best friends, I guess you might say." She folded the letter and tucked it into the pocket of her blouse. "Well, I'd better get started cleaning."

"Come on up when you get through," he said.

"Are you sure it doesn't bother you?"

"Not a bit, but you can make a chocolate pie, as usual, to pay for the privilege."

★   ★   ★

Mark did arrive three days after Prue's conversation with Kent Maxwell, and she brought him the next day for the promised visit. The two of them walked over, and she listened as he told her some of his latest assignments. When they got to the house and were invited in by Maxwell, the first thing Mark said after Prue's introduction was, "It's an honor to meet you, Mr. Maxwell. I saw some of your paintings at the Art Institute in Chicago. I thought they were wonderful."

Maxwell stared at the young man. "You like painting?" he asked.

"Well, I'm no expert, and I don't dig the modern stuff much."

"Good," Maxwell grunted. "I'm relieved to hear that."

"Your paintings somehow catch my attention. I don't want to sound like a flatterer, but the one of the two old people in front of the tenement holding hands—I can't get it out of my mind. It said more to me about old age and poverty than a lot of words that I've read."

"Well, thank you," Maxwell said. "Maybe while you're here I can show you some of the new things I'm working on."

"That would be fine. I'd like that."

The visit turned out very well for a time, but at some undefined point, at least in Mark's and Prudence's minds, Maxwell changed. The two of them had been laughing, and Mark had reached over and pulled her hair, and she had thrown herself at him trying vainly to wrestle him to the floor. They were used to such scuffles, but Maxwell stood back stiffly with disapproval in his eyes. From that moment on he was less hospitable and almost gruff. As Mark and Prue left the house, Mark had a puzzled expression on his face. "Is he always that—changeable?"

Quickly Prue shook her head. "He's really very nice to me. I don't know what's wrong with him."

"Do you like working for him?"

"Oh yes. The pay's good. Not much work around here, you know. What are you doing here, Mark? You didn't say in your letter."

They had now reached the edge of the treeline, and the tall firs swayed gently in the breeze overhead, while underfoot the thick carpet of pine needles made a soft, spongy surface.

"I've come to take you to the senior prom, if I'm not too late."

"Oh no. That would be fine," Prue said quickly. She had had two invitations to go to the prom, but both of the seniors were shorter than she. Her eyes grew warm as she said, "I'll look forward to it."

★   ★   ★

"What do you mean you can't come the rest of the week, Prue?" Kent Maxwell had been working on a watercolor, something he did not feel he did well, and he was irritable. Prue had been sitting quietly watching him, and finally, in a rare instance, had broken her vow of silence and told him she would not be able to come and clean house for the rest of the week. Now he turned and faced her. "What am I supposed to do? Live in a pigpen?"

Prue grinned at him, shaking her head. The movement swept her black hair across her shoulders, and she answered pertly, "You're not going to live in a pigpen! It's just the senior prom. Mark's going to take me." Her lips softened then, and she said, "I guess the senior prom and graduation mark the end of something for me."

"I guess so." He hesitated, then said, "Don't you young people send out invitations to graduation?"

"Oh yes."

"I didn't get one."

Prue bit her lip. "I didn't want to send you one, Mr. Maxwell. It's almost like begging for a gift."

"Send me one," he said.

"All right, I will; but you don't really have to give me anything."

"I've already got your gift. Do you want it now or later?"

Prue was startled. "Why, I don't know. Do you have it here at the house?"

"Right here in this room." Maxwell studied her for a minute and said, "I think I'll give it to you now. I won't be here much longer, Prudence."

This startled the young woman, and she stared at the neat

features of Maxwell, noting that he needed a haircut. "Where are you going? On a vacation?"

"I'm going back to Chicago to get back to work."

"Oh!" Prue said with disappointment. "I thought you would stay here."

"No, this has helped me to be here. I've calmed down, and a lot of it's due to you, Prue." He studied her carefully and said, "You have a quiet way about you. You've made life a lot different for me. I would have been lonely if you weren't here. I'll be lonely anyhow. I'll miss you."

"I'll miss you too, Mr. Maxwell."

"Will you?"

"Why, of course, I will. It's been fun coming over, and helping you, and watching you paint."

"Maybe you can come to Chicago and visit. I'd like to show you the town."

"Maybe so. I've got relatives there—but it's a long way."

"Well, in any case, let me get your present." Maxwell moved over to the corner and picked up the easel bearing the frame covered with light canvas. He set it down so that it caught the light and turned to her. "Here it is." He removed the canvas and heard her quick intake of breath. When he turned to her, her expression was all that he had hoped. Her eyes were opened wide, and her lips were parted with surprise, and shock, and pleasure. "Do you like it, Prue?"

"Oh! Like it? It's beautiful!" She moved slowly forward, her eyes glued to the picture. "But I'm not that pretty."

"That's an insult! I paint what I see!" Maxwell answered, smiling slightly. "It's a good painting. I could get a lot of money for this in a show."

"Oh, I couldn't accept it!"

"Then I'll cut it in pieces. I'll refuse to have boorish people looking at one of my good paintings." Whipping out a pocket-knife, Maxwell made a motion to the canvas. Prue screamed and jumped toward him, grabbing his hand. "Don't you dare!"

she cried. Her grip was strong, and he smiled at her, saying,
"Then you'll take it?"

"Of course I will. It's the nicest present I've ever gotten!"

"I'd hoped it would be."

Maxwell and Prue studied the painting for some time, then
he said, "I didn't have time to get a nice frame made for it,
but maybe you can do that."

She said, "I'll wrap it up in this canvas and take it home, if
you don't mind. I'll bring the canvas back." She turned to him
and put out her hand. "Thank you, Mr. Maxwell."

"Couldn't you say, thank you, Kent?"

Shyly Prue smiled. "Thank you, Kent," she said obedi-
ently.

★   ★   ★

The picture was a source of admiration from everyone.
Prue's parents could not believe it and had insisted on buy-
ing the finest frame available at the local framing shop. They
hung it over the mantel in the living room, and Mark came
to see the unveiling. Standing before it and looking up, he
shook his head. "There's some sort of white magic in painting like that," he said. "There you are, young and beautiful,
and when we're both old and gray, you'll still be young and
beautiful in that painting."

Prue flushed at his words, the rich color rising to her neck
and cheeks. She had such a clear, fair complexion that she
showed her emotions in this way.

"I'll miss Kent," she said, looking at the painting. "It's
been interesting to watch him paint, and he's so lonely too."

"Maybe you and I can take a trip to Chicago and see your
relatives there. You could spend some time with Stephanie
and Jake and their kids. They'd be glad to have you."

"I don't know. It costs so much."

"Maybe you'd like to get a job there. I'm in and out all the
time," Mark said. "It would be fun."

"I don't know about living in the big city. I'm just a country girl, Mark. Besides, I couldn't get a job there. What am I fitted for? I can work at McDonald's here as well as I can there, and that's about all I can hope for."

Mark shook his head. "You'll find your way." He looked up again at the painting. "I've seen you look like that a thousand times, Prue. With your head turned to one side and your hair blowing in the breeze. I wish I could have that painting."

"Well, you can't. Daddy said he'd shoot any burglar that tried to take it." Prue laughed.

"Are you ready for our triumph at the prom?" Mark asked.

"Have you got a tux?"

"I'm afraid so. I hate those monkey suits, but we'll have a good time."

They did have a good time at the prom. They stayed until the last dance, then he drove her home, and as they approached the outside of the house, he said, "I've got your graduation present for you. If you're sweet, I'll give it to you now."

"I'm always sweet," Prue said, looking up at him. "It must be small if you have it in your pocket."

"No, it's the biggest present you'll ever get." He reached into his inside pocket and pulled out an envelope. She opened it and saw two tickets. "It's a ticket to Disneyland in California."

"But I can't go to California."

"I'll bet you can," Mark grinned. "Your parents have a present for you too. A graduation present. They told me I could give it to you, but you'll have to be sweeter than you have been to get it."

Prue reached up, pulled his head down, kissed him firmly on the lips, then drew back. "There," she said breathlessly, "is that sweet enough?"

He reached out and said, "Now, that was nice, but say something sweet to me."

Prue's eyes crinkled as she grinned. She leaned forward and whispered, "Marshmallow!"

"All right, I see I'm not going to get any more goodies. Your parents are giving you a trip to the coast. You'll be staying with your great-aunt Lylah, and I'll be covering the Republican Convention there; Ronald Reagan thinks he's going to win the nomination."

"Oh, Mark! Not really?"

"Your parents will tell you about it, but it shows what a strong, upright fellow I am, that parents would risk their daughter in his care all the way across the country and back." He laughed at her expression and said, "It'll be fun. You'll get to see Mickey Mouse, and I'll get to see Ronald Reagan. Right after graduation we'll leave."

Prue said, "It's the best present they could have given me, and you too, Mark." She leaned forward, kissed his cheek, and said, "You are sweet. The sweetest man I know," then she turned and went into the house, her face flushed, and Mark laughed.

"That'll be a down payment," he called out as the door closed quietly.

11

"I Don't Have a Life!"

The trip from her home in the country to Los Angeles was a pure delight for Prue Deforge. Just packing was an exotic adventure for her. She had never been on an airplane before, and when the airliner took off, she reached over and grabbed Mark's arm, watching the ground disappear beneath her.

Laughing, Mark patted her hand. "You're cutting off my circulation, Prue! Just lean back and enjoy it."

Prue watched with fascination as the earth seemed to move away from the airplane, rather than the other way around. "Look at how small the houses are," she whispered, "and the cars; and the people look like little ants." Finally she accustomed herself to the motion of the plane and was highly entertained by the in-flight movie, an Alfred Hitchcock thriller called *Torn Curtain*. She sat with her eyes fixed to the screen and whispered, "Isn't that amazing? Seeing a movie this high up in the air!"

They arrived at the John Wayne Airport in Los Angeles, and as the plane landed, Prue's hand gripped the armrest until her knuckles were white. Mark laughed. "Let her down easy, Prue. That pilot needs all the help he can get." After the touchdown Prue relaxed, and the two got off the airplane and were met by Adam Stuart, who shook Mark's hand firmly, then turned to Prue and smiled. "I'm glad to see you, Prudence. Mother's been looking forward to having you. We've got a full schedule planned for you. Congratulations on your graduation."

"Thank you, Adam," Prue whispered. She had always been fascinated by Adam Stuart, having been told of his feats of daring in World War II, and also because he was the natural son of the famous Baron von Richtofen. She allowed herself to be escorted into the limousine and soon found herself at the home of her great-aunt Lylah Stuart. The house was in an exclusive neighborhood, but the grounds were more impressive than the home itself. It was set off away from the main highway, shielded by huge shrubbery and towering palm trees, the likes of which Prue had never seen before. The house was California style—white stucco, modernistic, with a flat roof—and the inside was luxurious.

After welcoming her, Lylah said, "It's a small house. Only four bedrooms. I believe Doris Day's has fourteen bedrooms."

Adam laughed. "Who would want to have thirteen guests? Let Doris handle it. You're staying with us, Mark," Adam said. "Come along, and we'll let these ladies begin their gossiping sessions."

Lylah smiled but shook her head. "I haven't noticed that women gossip any more than men," she said. "Now, you get along! Remember, you're all coming over here for supper tonight."

Adam shook his head. "Are you sure you want those two lively teenagers too?"

"Of course, dear; bring them along." After the men left, Lylah said, "Come along out on the deck. We'll get some sunshine." They moved outside, and Prue was charmed by the view. The house had been set to get a view of the ocean, and she took in the green waters, the blue sky, and the fleecy white clouds. "It's so beautiful! Could I go swimming in the ocean?"

"Well, I can't go with you, my dear," Lylah said, "but I'm sure Mark would be glad to take you. I don't know what you'll wear though. These swimming suits they're selling now are a disgrace." She shook her head in disgust, saying, "They're like the movies and some of the television shows just beginning to come on. I'm embarrassed to watch some of them. Here, sit down, and we'll have some iced tea, or would you rather have a soft drink?"

"Tea will be fine, Aunt Lylah."

For the next hour Lylah entertained her young guest. She had been briefed by Dent and Violet on some of Prue's problems: that she had not done well in school, and that she considered herself too tall and not at all pretty. Now as she examined the young woman, she thought, *She doesn't know how attractive she is. The day of the tall woman is here. All the models dwarf ordinary women in height.* She examined Prue's dark hair and her sleek figure and finally said, "I wish your parents could have come with you. I love to have family around, and Dent and Violet need a vacation. Maybe we can plan for it later on in the summer."

"That would be wonderful. Mom would love it, and so would Dad. They haven't gotten around much. They've never been to California, I don't think."

"I'll call them and see if we can't fix something up. I don't see why we couldn't have the reunion out here sometime, but then, everyone's so stuffy about traditions." She sighed, leaned back in her chair, and closed her eyes. "But I'm the same way. It's been the joy of my life, those reunions at Christmas."

After a time Lylah said, "You must be tired. Why don't you go take a shower and lie down for a while. Adam and his family won't be here for a few hours."

"How old are his kids now?"

"Suzanne's eighteen, a grown-up woman almost. And Sam is sixteen, an outlaw if I ever saw one. Oh, he's not really mean. Just so full of life that it's hard to keep him down. They're the pride of my life. I'd be terribly lonesome without them." She smiled, saying, "Go along now. You've got a heavy dinner date tonight, and tomorrow, I understand, Mark's taking you to Disneyland."

"That's right. I've heard so much about it. I'm excited about going."

The dinner that night was fun for Prue. She had always liked Adam's wife, Maris, although she had not been around her except at the reunions, and Suzanne and Sam were charming. Sam had greeted her with an exclamation, "You sure are tall, Prue!"

At one time Prue would have been terribly embarrassed, but now she said, "There's six whole feet of me. I hope you'll be this tall in a few years."

"I want to be as tall as Mark," Sam announced.

Mark enjoyed this, and after dinner he and Prue played board games with Sam and Suzanne. When Mark left with Adam and his family, he said, "I'll be around at about ten in the morning. Wear comfortable clothes, Prue. It's a job seeing Disneyland."

★   ★   ★

The next morning Prue obeyed Mark's injunction and wore a pair of white shorts, a deep blue T-shirt, and a pair of white socks with her white Adidas walking shoes. She had a pair of dark sunglasses, forced on her by Lylah, and a white straw hat tied under her chin. "You'll need it to keep the sun off," Lylah said. "Have a good time."

As Prue walked inside the huge park, Mark gave her a breakdown on the operation. "Disneyland opened in 1955," he said. "That first year four million visitors checked in here at Anaheim, and they've been coming ever since."

"It's so big!" Prue exclaimed, and as they began their journey she could not see enough. She took a ride down an African jungle river, rode a rocket ship to the moon, and went on a submarine journey, which reminded her of the Disney film *Twenty Thousand Leagues under the Sea*.

She loved Sleeping Beauty's castle, the pirate ship flight to Peter Pan's Never Never Land, and the trolley cars on Main Street.

Every corner of the park was filled with something, and Prue was dazed by the food facilities suited to the contrived themes with waiters dressed in period costumes, wastepaper baskets—painted to look like part of the landscape, and menu language designed and adapted to the particular fantasy being spun.

Finally, after her feet had grown tired, they stopped to eat hamburgers. The restaurant was an idealized Tom Sawyer's island as a Mississippi riverboat plied its way through muddied waters. "The food's not much," Mark said. "No better than fast-food stuff, but you can't beat the setting."

Afterward they visited a Wild West saloon complete with chorus girls and cowboys shooting up the bar, and in Tomorrow Land the architecture blended into a futuristic, spaceport setting.

At the end of the day they wearily made their way back to the car Mark had borrowed from Adam, and as Prue leaned back, shutting her eyes, she exclaimed, "I've never seen anything like it, Mark! It was the most fun I ever had!"

"I've been trying to write a story on Disneyland," Mark said. "Interviewing the kids who work there, the people who run it. Why do millions of people like to go to that place?"

"Why, the kids like going on the rides and seeing Mickey Mouse."

Mark turned and grinned at her, his deep tan making his teeth look very white. "That's too simple for a story. There's got to be some deep, psychological reason why we all like to play Tom Sawyer or go through an African jungle. At least in my story it'll be that way." He grew serious and said, "I think it's escapism like so many other things, most of the movies and the plays we see, the songs we listen to. We Americans can't stand ourselves, that is, to be alone. Have you ever noticed that you never go into a room with somebody just sitting there, no radio, no television? Just sitting there?"

"I do that sometimes."

Mark turned to look at her with surprise. "So do I, but we're in the minority. Anyway, that's what the story will say." He drove her home and said, "Tomorrow another treat. We're going to see Bobby. He's making another movie, and we've got permission to go watch him."

"Oh, that would be interesting."

Mark pulled up in front of Lylah's house, got out and opened the door, and said, "You go in and get a good night's rest. You haven't started yet." He reached out and ruffled her hair, for she had taken her hat off and was holding it in her hand. "Don't get too close to any of those talent scouts. They might make a movie star out of you. I wouldn't want to lose my country girl."

★   ★   ★

Watching the making of a film was intriguing to Prue. Mark had seen some of it before, and he spent his time watching Prue's expression.

When Bobby first appeared and greeted them, then turned to go to makeup, Prue glanced at Mark, saying, "He looks so much older."

"It's a hard life. It puts the miles on pretty quick."

Prue nodded. "When I saw him in his last movie he didn't look over twenty-two or twenty-three. He's actually about thirty-one or two. He does look bad, doesn't he?"

"Yes. His parents must be pretty worried about him. Have you seen them?" Mark asked.

"Not since the reunion at Christmastime. His dad talked pretty straight about Bobby. No trouble with Richard, of course. We'll see him too, doing his street work ministry. Aunt Lylah made arrangements for us."

"Oh, I'd like that."

They spent most of the day watching a musical number being filmed. On-screen Bobby was filled with life, and his eyes flashed, and he seemed young. But afterward, as they sat in his dressing room and he invited them out, he moved almost like an old man. "We'll go out and party a little bit. Maybe meet some movie stars," he said.

Mark shook his head. "Maybe another day, Bobby. We've got a date to go out and see Richard's work. Have you been out there?"

Bobby shook his head. "No," he said briefly, and made no other comment. The question seemed to offend him, and he grunted and shrugged. "Give me a call while you're here." Turning to Prue, he smiled and seemingly could turn on the charm at any moment. "You've grown up into a mighty handsome woman, Prue. Maybe I can get you a screen test."

"No thanks, Bobby," Prue said. "I guess I'll just keep on being a country girl."

As they left the studio and made their way to the rougher side of Los Angeles, they talked about Bobby, and when they arrived at the two-story building that housed Richard's ministry, they saw a big sign that said "Jesus Saves" boldly plastered across the front. "The American Civil Liberties Union tried to get them to take that down, but Adam hired a fancy lawyer and made 'em cry uncle. I was at the trial. He made those New York lawyers look pretty sick," Mark said.

"Well, I'm glad," Prue said angrily. "The very idea! Telling someone they couldn't put up a sign about Jesus!"

"It's going to get worse than that, I'm afraid. That ACLU is the worst thing that ever happened to America. They're for liberty for anybody who's godless and hates righteousness."

They found Richard inside preparing to go out and preach on the streets. He was wearing typical California laid-back clothes and looked thin but healthy. He greeted them warmly, then insisted they come with him.

Prudence had never seen any such thing as street preaching, but when they got there several of Richard's co-workers began to sing, accompanying themselves with guitars. Where they came from, Prue didn't know, but a crowd gathered, most of them dirty and rough looking, indeed. When Richard got up to preach, she could see little effect, but it did not bother him. He preached as if he were in Madison Square Garden.

When the sermon was over, many of the street people stayed for prayer, although some mocked and laughed. Prue watched as Richard and his wife, Laurel, prayed with a prostitute who was so eaten up by drugs that she could do nothing but sob. Finally Richard came over and said, "We're taking Eileen home with us to stay at the shelter for a while."

"Do you think you can help her?"

"Jesus can," Richard said. He asked about Bobby, and listened to their report with pain in his eyes. "It kills me to see him going down the drain the way he is. All the money he makes has blinded him. And that Hollywood glitter, it's destroyed so many people." Tears came into his eyes, and he said, "I guess I've prayed a million prayers for my brother, and I'll pray a million more, but somehow God's going to come through on him."

★   ★   ★

Prue's time in California sped by quickly, and to her surprise, she enjoyed the Republican Convention. Mark was there explaining what it all meant, and to her shock, she was introduced by Mark to the candidate himself. "Mr. Reagan, this is a fine young Republican from Arkansas."

Reagan's eyes crinkled, and he extended his hand; somehow Prue felt that he had closed all the rest of the world out and was looking only at her. After asking which part of Arkansas she came from, he said, "Oh yes. I've been at Jasper. Floated the Buffalo River once. Beautiful country! Arkansas produces the best-looking young ladies in the country, I always say."

Afterward Mark said, "Boy, he sure got your vote, didn't he?"

"He's so—so natural, Mark. Why, he's just like anybody else. Not like a big movie star or a politician at all."

"You know, I think you're right, and he's going to beat some folks bad, although nobody much believes it. Ronald Reagan may not have been the greatest movie star in the world, but I've got an idea he's going to turn America around someday."

★   ★   ★

Finally, on June the third, after Prue had bid Lylah farewell, she was standing in the airport saying good-bye to Mark. She was tired, for he had kept her going every minute, but now she was saddened, and something about her silence showed it.

"You hate to leave the big city, Prue?" Mark asked.

"It's just—well, I don't know what I'm going to do, Mark. I'm not really fit for anything. I don't have a life."

"Don't be silly! As for being fit for something, you can cook, and clean house, and make a man feel good when he's low. You can be a wife, and that's the biggest job a woman can have."

"Do you really think so, Mark?"

"Sure, I think so." A voice said, "Flight 426! Last call for boarding!" and he reached out and hugged her, whispering in her ear, "It's been swell. I wish I could go back with you, but I have to cover the convention. I'll be coming down your way before you know it." Then he kissed her on the cheek and stepped back.

Prue walked back on the plane sadly, the thrill of flying gone. She knew that somehow the business and excitement of Los Angeles had affected her, and although she loved the farm, and the woods, and her pets, still she saw nothing in the future. A pang came to her as she realized that even Kent Maxwell was gone now, and he had played a big part in her life. As the plane sailed over the fleecy clouds, she sat back and closed her eyes, wondering what in the world she would do with herself for the rest of her life.

12

MAXWELL GETS A SHOCK

For a week after Prue arrived back home, she was troubled with echoes of the exciting world of Los Angeles that she had experienced. Her parents noticed that she was quieter, but neither of them mentioned it. They knew she was worried about what she would do for a job and was dreading taking a minimum wage job at a fast-food place, which seemed to be all that was available.

On Monday morning she got a call that surprised her. "Hello, Prue. This is Kent."

Instantly Prue's heart felt a sudden impulse of gladness. "I thought you had gone back to Chicago."

"I am going back, but I need to get the house cleaned up. I like to leave things neat. Could you come over and help me today?"

"Oh yes! I'll be over by ten o'clock."

She hung up and told her mother she was going to help Maxwell clean house. She was about to leave when she suddenly remembered she had promised Pearl and her daughter, Melody, that she would bring the portrait she had done of them. She had touched it up a little bit, and though not satisfied with it, knew she could do no more. Wrapping it and sticking it into an oversized shopping bag, she left the house and jumped into the old Pontiac. She stopped by Pearl's house, but no one was there, and the front door was locked.

"I'd better not leave it on the steps. Someone might take it," she said to herself. Going back to the car, she put it in the front seat, made her way to Kent Maxwell's, and got out at once. One of the car windows was jammed in the open position, and she was afraid that the storm clouds that were coming in from the south might bring rain. Picking up the picture, she went inside the house and laid it right beside the front door.

"Prue, is that you?" Maxwell came from down the hall and put out his hand. When she took it, he said, "How was your trip to L.A.?"

"Oh, it was fun. I got to see a lot of things."

Maxwell noticed that she looked listless, which was unusual for her. *Some trouble,* he thought. *She's just not herself.* Aloud he said, "Well, let's see if we can get this house cleaned up. My plane leaves tomorrow at one fifteen."

Prue worked hard that morning cleaning the house, stopping at one o'clock to fix lunch. They sat down to eat it, and he said, "We'll pack up all these groceries so you can take them home with you. I don't think I can take them on the airplane."

"All right."

Kent leaned back in his chair and studied her. "What's wrong, Prue?" he asked. "You look so sad."

"Oh, it's nothing. I just don't know what to do with myself."

"I think we get that way after we get something we've looked forward to for a long time. For you it was graduation. For years you looked forward to it, and now it's over, and you feel sort of empty and don't know what to do."

"Why, that's right! How did you know that?"

Kent lowered his head and studied the slice of pie in front of him. He did not answer for so long that she thought he did not intend to. Finally he said, "I've never told you about myself, have I?"

"No. You haven't."

"All my life I looked forward to having a home and a career. I got the career, but then I didn't get the home."

"What happened, Kent?"

"Before I went to Korea I married a young woman. While I was over there she found somebody else, and I guess—" He stopped abruptly and shook his head. "Not too original, is it?"

"I'm sorry, Kent." Prue reached over and put her hand on his. "I really am, but you'll find someone."

Kent looked at her hand, feeling its warm pressure, lifted his eyes, and saw the genuine compassion in her face. "You're a sweet girl, Prudence," he said. He started to say more, then apparently changed his mind. "Now, let's finish getting this house cleaned up, and then I'll take you out and we'll have a party celebrating the good things that are going to come to you."

"All right." Prue rose and began to clean the dishes. Kent left and walked down the hall. He turned to go up the stairs when an object caught his eye, a canvas shopping bag beside the front door. He turned with his limping gait, curious, and walked over, thinking it might be one of his paintings, but he did not remember putting it there. He picked it up, held it for a minute, then muttered, "Why, this must be Prue's." It was obviously a painting, and curiosity came to him. Glancing down the hall and not seeing Prue, he slipped the pad out of the bag and stood there staring at it in astonishment.

The painting was not perfect, but as he stared at it he felt the power, and the warmth, and the humanity of it. An Ozark woman and her daughter were smiling out at him, and in their faces he could see both the fear of the poverty that was reflected in the shack outlined behind them and the hope in the woman's eyes for something better for her little girl.

For a long time Kent Maxwell stood there simply looking at the picture, his eyes soaking it in; then, taking it up, he turned and hobbled down the hall, his cane tapping on the floor. When he stepped inside the kitchen and Prue turned from the sink where she was washing dishes, he held up the painting and said, "Who did this, Prue?"

Prue turned slightly pale. She dropped her head and stared at the floor, and when she finally looked up there was fear in her eyes. "I–I did."

"I thought it might be that way." Kent stood there taking the girl's features in and seeing the panic in her eyes. "You should have told me that you were an artist, Prue."

"Oh, I'm no artist!"

"You're wrong about that." Kent looked at the picture and studied it for a long time, then he looked up and smiled. "I've had students who have studied for ten years that couldn't do it this well. You've got something in you that God put there. Something that I couldn't teach you."

Prue was staring at the man with astonishment. Her lips were parted slightly, and she shook her head in disbelief. "I've never had a lesson in my life."

"I know. It shows in some of the things I see, but they are things that can be learned. But the life, the vigor, and the vitality of what you've done here. Prue, you've got to come with me to Chicago."

"What?"

"I can get you a scholarship at the institute where I teach. You have relatives there, don't you?"

"Yes, I do. But you can't be serious, Kent. I've never gotten good grades."

"That doesn't matter. Do you have any more paintings?"

"Oh yes. I've got lots of them."

"Where are they?"

"At home in my room."

"What do your parents think about your painting?"

"Oh, they don't know about it. They know I draw and paint a little, but I never show them anything very much."

"Come on. We're going to see them right now."

Prue never remembered much of the interview with her parents. She took Maxwell to her home, and he simply took over. When Prue took him to her room and unlocked the armoire, he almost shouldered her aside and began to pull the paintings and drawings out. "Help me arrange these around the room where I can look at them all!" he commanded, and soon her room was filled with paintings, and her mother and father who had come in were staring at them, amazed.

"Why, we didn't know you could paint like this, Prue!" Dent said with reproach. "How come you never told us?"

"I didn't think they were that good, and besides—" She could not finish, for the paintings had been her private life, and she felt ashamed at having kept this away from her parents.

Kent understood, however, and said gently, "It's all right, Prue. I know a little bit about that. Sometimes we just can't share things with others." He turned to Violet and Dent and said, "You know I teach at the Institute of Art in Chicago. You can check on my credentials, but I want to tell you that in all my years of teaching I've never had a student with the promise that Prudence has. With a few years of hard study, she could be a great success in the world of painting. I can get her a scholarship so that it wouldn't cost anything except her living expenses, and I understand you have relatives there, so she wouldn't be alone."

The conference did not last long. Dent and Violet listened to Maxwell as he explained what it would mean—Prue leaving home, going to the big city, and studying hard for at least two years. His eyes were alight, and his excitement was obvious.

Finally Dent looked at Violet, and some unspoken communication passed between them. Dent walked over and put his arm around his daughter. "I don't know about all this, Prue. What do you think? Do you want to go?"

Prudence stood there, a thousand thoughts going through her mind, but it was as if a door had opened. After a long silence she said, "I've never been able to do anything too well, and I've been worried about what I was going to do. All my friends are going to college or going to take jobs, and I felt so left out." She turned to Violet and said, "Mom, I want to do this, but only if you and Dad say it's all right."

Violet felt tears rise in her eyes, and pride. "If Mr. Maxwell says you have a talent, and you want to go, then I think God is opening the door to you."

They moved to the living room, where Maxwell outlined the program and then after a time said, "You talk it over with your parents, Prue. If you want to go, I can cancel my flight and get a later one. We could go together. You'd have time to call your relatives in Chicago. I hope you do it—you have a great talent, and you need to share it with the world."

Late that night, after a long talk with her parents, Prue sat down and began a letter. Her hands were trembling and she had to stop once, for although she was not a weepy girl, the suddenness of it, and the enormity of it, swept her.

> *Dear Mark, I'm going to Chicago. . . . and I'm going to become a painter studying under Mr. Maxwell . . .*

She signed the letter, folded it, put it into an envelope, and put the stamp on it; then she rose, walked over, and looked out the window. It was dark outside, but a sickle moon was throwing its light down upon the earth. She looked at the outline of the mountains and thought about her life, and then her shoulders began to tremble again. The tears came and she whispered, "Maybe I can be somebody!"

Part 3

THE FACE OF WAR
(1967–1968)

13

THE STAR

Mark Stevens was not favorably impressed with Las Vegas. He had arrived two days before he planned to spring his surprise on Elvis Presley and spent most of his time walking through the glittering casinos that had made the city a mecca for suckers. "You see one casino, you've seen them all," he muttered to himself as he walked down the long aisles of slot machines, pausing from time to time to stare at the faces of those who were frantic to lose their money. Although most of the eyes of the players were glazed with an identical stupor, he saw little similarity between the players. Some who plugged their coins into the one-armed bandits were very young; more than one, he suspected, were below the legal age to be in the gambling palace. Many of them were older people, faces lined with years of hard work. Others were middle-aged, probably working people; still others looked wealthy.

He paused beside one machine and watched a woman with an inexpensive-looking print dress thumb coin after coin into the slot. Examining her face carefully, Mark tried to detect some joy but could find nothing but a sense of desperation. She was a heavyset woman of some thirty years of age, he judged, and her brown eyes were tinged with a combination of hope and despair. Each time the wheels rolled in front of her eyes and came to a clicking stop, she heaved a sigh, then plugged another coin into the slot. Finally she hit some fortunate combination, and the coins poured in a cascade of jangling silver into the receptacle provided for them. Mark expected to see her cry for joy, but she simply scooped them up, put them into a canvas bag she wore at her side, and continued to play with the same sense of futility.

Shaking his head in wonder, Mark moved on and finally came to the huge room that featured all sorts of enticements for people to lose their money at a more rapid rate than the slots. He moved from table to table and for the next two hours talked to as many people as would give him the time. Few of them were ready to do this, however. They had come to gamble, not to give interviews to a reporter.

He hovered at the back of a crowd watching a small, well-dressed man with a good tan as he bucked the roulette wheel. The player had a large stack of chips in front of him, but after an hour they were all gone. He stood up and muttered, "Well, that's it," under his breath, then turned and shoved his way through the crowd. Mark followed the man, who went to the bar and sat down; seeing the seat next to him was empty, Mark plopped down beside him. He listened as the man ordered a drink in a shaky voice, and he himself ordered a Coke. The man drank the double Scotch down and sat there clenching the glass tightly.

"No luck today?" Mark asked. He scarcely expected an answer, but the man turned his head and said bitterly, "I've lost everything! What am I going to tell my wife?"

"Where you from?" Mark asked, hoping to get the man talking. He could see that there was a sense of bitterness, frustration, and fear etched in the man's eyes, and the lips were pale and trembling as he answered.

"Denver," he muttered. "I'm in the wholesale hardware business." He turned quickly, hailed the bartender, and ordered another double Scotch. When it came before him, he drained it down as if it were tap water. Bracing his shoulders against the shock of the alcohol, he bowed his head and did not speak.

"Sometimes it's not such a good idea to come to these places," Mark said gently.

For a moment the man was silent, and Mark saw that his shoulders were trembling; then he saw, when the man turned to him, that there were tears in his eyes. "I've got a good wife and three kids, and I had a good business, but I got hooked on gambling. I've lost everything—the house, both cars, all my savings. This was the last of it. I came here to make a big killing and pay everything off, and I swore and promised God I'd never come back again—but now it's all gone."

Mark wanted to say something to comfort him. "Never too late to quit a thing like this," he murmured. "If I were you, I think I'd just go home, tell my wife what happened, and ask her to forgive me; then I'd never bet a penny on anything for the rest of my life."

"You think I haven't done that?" The voice was bitter, sharp, and terse. Pulling a handkerchief out of his pocket, the man wiped his face, then stood up, and without another word to Mark walked stiffly across the room, shouldering people aside. He disappeared, and Mark stood up, a sense of disbelief in his mind over what he had just seen. He looked over the room that was swarming with people and thought, *They're all alike. Come to make a big killing, and most of them don't do it. Don't they know that the only way this kind of a place stays open is to set the odds so the house wins?* He moved out of the casino, taking a breath of fresh air, for there was a staleness and an odor of death in the place to him. He had planned to write an article on the casinos and what made people throw their hard-earned money away, but now he wondered about it. *That fellow could have read a hundred stories telling about the evils of gambling. Probably has, but it didn't stop him. I wonder what makes human beings do foolish things like this?*

★   ★   ★

Feeling like Secret Agent 007 in a way, Mark Stevens examined himself in the mirror, straightened the white collar of his shirt, and ran his hands along the sides of the uniform sleeve. He stared in the mirror and laughed aloud. "You're a fool for trying this! You'll never get away with it!" But the challenge stirred him, and he left his room and made his way to the hotel where he had discovered Elvis Presley was due to hold a champagne breakfast for a few select guests. Ever since Mark heard that Elvis was going to marry Priscilla Beaulieu, a scheme had been formulating in his mind. Elvis was big news, and anything he did, no matter how mundane, was good for snaring readers. As he piled up the information about the champagne breakfast, Mark had beat his brains trying to figure a way to get in on it. He knew, of course, that the breakfast would be more closely guarded than the United Nations, but there was no chance, whatsoever, that the guards would admit anyone who even looked like they might be a reporter.

Late one night, an idea had come to Mark. *Why don't I disguise myself as a waiter, slip in, and do a little waiting?* It had been a fruitful idea. He had learned quite a bit as an investigative reporter and had discovered that the Williamson Corporation would cater the affair. It took a little effort, but he managed to find one of the waiters who would be serving, and had, without seeming to do so, wheedled out of him the name of the company that provided the uniforms for Williamson people. It had not been too difficult to go to that place, pretend to be a waiter, and get a uniform. He had also discovered the timing of the breakfast and the dining room where it would be held. So, now as he gave himself a final look in the mirror, he muttered, "All they can do is throw me out!"; then he left his hotel room.

He moved down the street in a waiter's uniform, attracting no attention whatsoever. When he reached the Featherstone Hotel he entered by the service entrance, and by keeping his eyes open and making no more than two or three false entries, found a group of men all wearing the same uniform he had on. He had arrived just in time, for they were all carrying silver trays loaded with food and alcoholic drinks of all sorts. No one paid the slightest attention to him, so he simply picked up a tray from the table and joined himself to the line that was moving out of the service room.

The line proceeded down a short corridor where the elevator waited. Mark got on, and the fellow next to him winked and said, "This is something, gettin' to see the King, ain't it now?"

"Sure is," Mark said. "You like Elvis?"

"Never seen him, but my fourteen-year-old has got every record he made. Myself, I don't like his singing much. I'm a Perry Como man."

The elevator came to a smooth halt, the door opened, and the line formed. Mark managed to find a place at the rear as they moved into a large room with panels of glass at one end allowing in the bright May sunshine.

The tables that had been set up were covered with spotless white linen; Mark took time to observe the man in front of him and began to put the food on the tables. The guests were coming in even now, and he searched the incoming group but did not see Elvis. He lingered as long as he dared, but a tall man with a white carnation in his lapel said, "All right. Go get the rest of the food and the drinks."

Mark was forced to leave, and the crew of servers made their way back down to the service room, loaded up, and then returned to the dining room. As soon as Mark entered he saw Elvis sitting at the center table. He was wearing a black tuxedo with a white carnation in his lapel. His black hair was well combed, and a lock hung down on his forehead. He was turning to speak to his bride, who was one of the most beautiful women Mark had ever seen. He had seen her picture, of course, and now that he saw her in person, he understood the fascination that Elvis had for her. She was wearing a white chiffon gown embroidered with tiny pearls. Her black hair cascaded down her back, and her dark eyes flashed as she laughed at something that Presley said.

Mark had determined to stay in the area, and when the

rest of the crew filed their way out he ducked behind a pillar and began to take mental notes. He listened, trying to pick up some of the conversation, but he knew he would never get close enough to Presley and his bride, nor could he just walk up and begin speaking to him. As he waited, he really hoped that Presley would make some sort of speech and perhaps the bride as well.

He remembered reading that the couple had met in 1959 in Germany while Elvis was serving with the U.S. Army. The bride was the daughter of an Air Force Lieutenant Colonel and had attended high school in Frankfurt. Both Elvis and Priscilla were from Memphis, Tennessee.

Finally someone cried out, "Let's hear a speech from the new bridegroom, and the bride!"

Elvis grinned as the applause, and calling, and cries continued. Finally he stood up and waved his hands, his face flushed as he said with his thick southern accent, "I'm not makin' no speech on my weddin' day. All I got to say is I'm glad I kept myself for my bride, and I'm glad she kept herself for me." He turned and said, "You want to say somethin', honey?"

The bride shook her head but lifted her voice, saying, "Thank you all for coming, and for being so kind."

Mark stood behind the pillar as the breakfast continued. Finally, in desperation, he thought, *I've got to do more than this.* Taking a deep breath, he moved out from behind the pillar and walked along the lines of tables. He came to stand slightly to Elvis's left and cleared his throat. When Presley turned around, Mark said, "I'm sorry to bother you, Mr. Presley, but I did want to congratulate you on your wedding. I hope you have the happiest marriage in the world."

"Why, thank you, pal," Elvis said. He stuck out his hand and Mark took it, and then the famous grin flashed. "With a girl like this I think I've got a pretty good chance."

"I'm sure you do, and to you, Mrs. Presley, may you be very happy in your marriage."

Priscilla Presley smiled brilliantly and said, "Why, thank

you very much. It's so nice of you to come and wish us good fortune."

Mark started to say something else, but he felt a hand grip his arm; he turned around to face a large man whose eyes were hard as flint. "You're not one of our waiters," he said.

Mark started to speak, but he was pulled away. He turned back and called out loudly, "Have a good life, both of you!" The man's grip was like iron. When they were outside came the inevitable question. "What are you? Some kind of a reporter?"

"Not a very good one," Mark said cheerfully, "but at least I got to wish the bride and groom a good life."

"Get out of here before I bust your back!"

Mark left the hotel, went back to his room, changed clothes, and then took the uniform back and got his deposit. A sense of satisfaction filled him, and he thought, *Well, at least I got to shake hands with Elvis. That's something.*

★　　★　　★

Mark had come to Las Vegas to see Bobby Stuart's opening at the Sands. He wasn't disappointed; it was a smash, as he had thought. The crowd had been standing and begging for more, and Bobby gave them encore after encore. He used some of the hit tunes, including, "You Can't Hurry Love," made popular by the Supremes, and James Brown's "I Got You." Then he did "Turn, Turn, Turn" by the Byrds and the Rolling Stones hit "Paint It Black."

After the performance Mark went backstage and was finally permitted into the huge dressing room. As usual, Bobby was surrounded by his group: D. J. Heinzman, a tall, lanky man who played rhythm guitar; Ossie Peabody, black and militant, the drummer; and Jimmy Franz, small and eager with blond hair and blue eyes. He took a lot of abuse as the gofer.

Faye Harlow, a pretty young woman with reddish blond

hair and gray eyes, looked as if she was high on drugs, and the rest weren't far behind.

Bobby appeared to be on something too. His eyes were bright and glassy, and his laugh was high and artificial. Finally Mark got him off to one side, and the two had a talk, of sorts, although it was hard to talk with anyone as stoned as Bobby Stuart.

"I like your writing. I read all I can get a hold of, Mark," Bobby said, his speech slurred.

"Thanks, Bobby. I really came down here to do a piece on you."

"Is that right? Well, go ahead. What are you going to call it?"

"Just 'Bobby Stuart.' Thought I might give the fans an in-side view of what it's like to be the acquaintance of a famous star."

Bobby talked for some time, but much of it was disjointed, and finally Mark understood that he would get nothing out of Bobby Stuart when he was in this condition. He suggested that the two have breakfast.

"Breakfast? Man, I don't get up in time for breakfast! Maybe at noon. Come around, and we'll see."

A sadness filled Mark as he saw the wreckage in Bobby's eyes. He got up and left, and nobody paid any attention. They were all busy with their drugs and their liquor.

★   ★   ★

"I liked the story you did on Las Vegas, Mark." Jake Taylor was thumbing through the pages that Mark had left with him the previous day. They were sitting in Taylor's of-fice, and now Taylor looked up and said, "I think you've got some good stuff. Not too happy with the one on Bobby Stuart though."

Shifting uncomfortably, Mark shook his head. "I guess I'm too close to it, Jake. I talked to him twice, but I couldn't think of anything very good to write. He's changed a lot, I think, since he hit the big time."

"It happens to most of them, especially in the rock business. How many *old* rock music stars do you know? Most of them off themselves or wind up in a nuthouse OD'd, their brains fried from drugs. Stephanie hates it. She really loves her brother."

"Deep down he's got something good in him, but it's like he's caught in a whirlpool that's sucking him down, and there's nothing you can do about it."

They talked for a while about Bobby Stuart, and then Jake said abruptly, "This Vietnam thing gets worse all the time. I see where U.S. jets bombed Hanoi for the first time yesterday."

"The protests are getting stronger. I don't see how the president can take much more of it."

"It looks like he's determined to win over there. Did you see where Muhammad Ali got indicted for draft evasion? Gonna lose his title."

"Yeah, I saw it." Mark shifted uncomfortably, then said, "I may get caught up in the draft, Jake."

Taylor's eyes turned careful. "What would you think about that? Would you go, or would you run off to Canada like so many have?"

Indignantly Mark shook his head. "I'd never do that. I don't want to go, but if I get the call I'll have to."

The two men sat there, each of them thinking about the 125,000 young American men who were already putting their lives on the line in Vietnam. They also thought of the college students who had never heard a shot fired in anger, who were burning their draft cards and protesting vociferously at every opportunity.

Finally Jake shook his head. "It's a bad time for America. It looks to me like a no-win situation." Then he moved around and slapped Mark on the shoulder. "But I'm glad you feel like you do. I'd go myself if I wasn't an old man and didn't have a family."

14

ARTISTS NEED TO SUFFER

Standing stiffly before the easel, a brush clutched in one hand so tightly that her fingers ached, Prue stiffened her back and blinked back the tears that burned in her eyes. She was intensely aware of Kent Maxwell standing behind her, looking over her shoulder at the painting, and she was even more aware of the harshness of his voice as he continued to speak of the flaws of the painting. Despite herself, tears escaped from her eyes and rolled down her cheeks, then fell on the paint-smudged smock that she wore. Desperately she tried to think of something else, but Kent's voice penetrated her thoughts, and she could not shut it out.

"And don't you see that you have the colors all wrong in the hair? Look at it! It looks like a smudge where you've cleaned your brush out! The woman's hair is auburn, for heaven's sake, and you've made it a cross between a carrot red and a dull maroon. Have you learned nothing at all in all these months about mixing color?"

"I'm sorry," Prue whispered. "I did the best I could."

"No, you didn't do your best! You've got more in you than this, Prue, and I'm not going to put up with your slipshod ways any longer!" Reaching out over her shoulder, Maxwell snatched the brush, reached down to the palette, smeared it in the dabs of paint there, then with a rough gesture swept the brush across the hair of the woman that Prue had put on the canvas. "There," he said, "that's the way it is! Get your highlights just here—and here. She's not wearing a wig!"

Suddenly Prue could stand it no longer. She turned and walked stiffly away, headed blindly for the door of the studio. It was late, and there were no other students, and she was exhausted not only from this day's long arduous work, but from the days, and weeks, and even months that she had thrown herself into learning the art of painting. Her eyes were so blurred with tears that she bumped into an easel containing an enormous painting, knocked it down, and as it fell with a crash she turned and attempted to catch it. She struggled to pick up the canvas and free the easel and felt Kent's hand on her arm pulling her up. She turned her face away, but he held her tightly by her forearms. "What's this?" he said with surprise. "You're not crying?"

"No! I'm not!"

But Kent had seen the tears on her cheeks, and he stood there for a moment silently. His mind flashed back over the history of her stay in Chicago. He had not been wrong, he knew, in his estimate of Prudence Deforge's talent. It was enormous, and he had come to feel that the greatest thing he could do for the world of art was to see that she developed it. This had not been an entirely happy fixation, for he had rushed her through training that would have been difficult for most students to complete in years. Every day he stood beside her, laying out her work, and at night when she wearily left the studio to go to her small apartment, he had loaded her down with books and sketch work to bring back the following morning. To him it had been a delight to see her blossom, for she was not a lazy girl.

Now, however, as she stood before him, her eyes shut, he saw the lines of strain and the dark shadows that fatigue had put under her eyes, and his conscience smote him.

"I'm sorry, Prue," he said quietly, not releasing her arms. "Come and sit down."

"No. I want to go home."

"You can go home in a moment, but I need to talk to you." He pulled her to the couch, limping heavily, then sat down.

It was an old couch, three cushions badly in need of repair, and the black and gold coloring had long since faded into a general leprous gray. The studio itself was large, and all the lights were out except over Prue's easel, so that the two sat in a half darkness over beside the wall. The sound of traffic came through to them, the honking of taxis and the muffled roar of the engines that was always present in Chicago. From outside the huge windows on the north end of the studio, the lights of Chicago winked on and lit the skyline with a myriad of lights that sent a glow up to the ebony sky.

Kent fumbled in his pocket, came out with a handkerchief, and said, "Here." She took the handkerchief, wiped the tears away, and then handed it back without a word. She was as miserable as she had ever been in her life, and at last she said, "Nothing I do ever pleases you. I just can't do it, Kent. I can't!"

Her words and the pathetic expression in her eyes as she looked at him troubled Kent, and he said quickly, "That's not true, Prue. You do many things that please me. I don't always tell you—which I should. You see, I've had so many students who don't have anything in them to give. I have to try to find something nice to say about their work, and sometimes it's a job. But with you, I see so much in you that has to come out, and I just, well—well, I forget myself. I know I'm a slave driver. I know I've asked more of you than any teacher ever ought to ask of any student, but don't you see it's because of the great desire I have to see you become all that you can."

Prue sat there listening quietly, and she tried to think of the hours that he had given to her since she had arrived in Chicago. It was June now, 1967, and she remembered that it was almost exactly a year ago that she had left the farm and come to live in Chicago. She had been frightened by the big city, but Stephanie and Jake had been very kind to her, and she had grown closer, also, to Christie Castellano and her husband, Mario. Both these families—her relatives—had encouraged her and taken her in, and it had been Christie who found her an apartment close to the Institute. She thought, also, of how Kent had been at her side constantly, not just giving lessons, but showing her around the city through the myriad of museums and taking her to some of the shows.

"I know I'm ungrateful," she said, "but I try so hard, and it never seems to come out right. I just can't do what you want me to do."

Looking at her for a moment in silence, Maxwell said, "This is going to sound trite, but I'll say it anyway. Artists—most of them—have to suffer, Prue. Art, for most of us, doesn't come easy. It's like—well, it's a little bit, I think, like having a baby." When she looked up at him in surprise, he laughed shortly. "Not that I've ever had any babies, of course, but I know the theory."

"I don't understand what you mean."

"Well, a baby comes in a miraculous fashion. There's nothing there, and then suddenly in the body of a woman, there's life. But that life is so small and tiny no one would even know it's there." Kent leaned back, and his face grew intent as he tried to express himself. He had given lectures many times, but now he wanted this young woman before him to understand herself, and so he continued by saying, "That life has to grow, Prudence. The mother has to see that it stays alive, and finally after months it's born. There it is. She's holding it in her arms, nursing it, caring for it, bathing it. But it was only after nine months of waiting and after, sometimes, tremendous agony that she has that child." Waving toward the painting that Prue had been working on, he said, "When did you get the idea for that painting?"

Prudence glanced across the room at the canvas. It was a picture of a young woman she had seen at the canning factory near Cedarville. The woman had just come from work, and her garments were stained with the juices from the berries that she had been working with, as were her hands. Prudence had taken one look at her and seen the fatigue in her face, but when the young girl saw a young man her face lit up with excitement, her eyes glowing. Prue had tried to catch that in the painting, and now she shook her head. "Why, it must have been two or three years ago, I suppose."

"So, it's been in you all the time, and now you're trying to bring it to birth, and it's not easy. You got the hair wrong. That means you have to go back and do the hair again. It may not work." Kent made a gesture of despair. "And I know enough about that. I've had enough malformed paintings to know that sometimes it just doesn't work, but you know what, Prudence? You paint a bad painting the same way you paint a good painting. You give it all that you have."

Prue sat listening to him, from time to time glancing up at his face. As he talked about art he grew excited, she observed, and now she said, "Maybe I don't have whatever it is that makes a great artist. I just can't seem to get the fundamentals right, Kent."

Maxwell considered this for a moment, then without a word rose and limped across the room. He reached the bookshelf that was cluttered with books and pamphlets of all kinds, searched for a moment, then came back with a volume in his hand. He sat down, switched on the light, and said, "Did you ever read any Robert Browning?"

"No."

"You ought to. He speaks of art better than any man I ever saw. Let me read you this."

He thumbed through the well-worn volume and said, "This is a poem called 'Andrea del Sarto.' It's a poem about a real artist. One they call the faultless painter. It's a long poem and I won't read all of it. It's what's known as a dramatic monologue. That means del Sarto himself is doing the talking. He's talking to his mistress, who is not really in love with him, and he tries to explain his art. He tells her this:

> 'Behold Madonna!—I am bold to say.
> I can do with my pencil what I know,
> What I see, what at bottom of my heart

> I wish for, if ever wish so deep—
> Do easily too.'

"Do you understand that, Prue? What the artist is saying?"

"It sounds like he's saying he can paint whatever he wants to."

"Exactly right! And del Sarto was called the faultless painter. When he painted something, it looked almost like a photograph of it."

"That would be wonderful. I've seen some paintings like that."

"But great paintings are never like a photograph."

"They're not?"

"Why, no. They're something else. There's something in them that, despite the flaws, makes them great paintings, and the people who paint like that, I don't even call them artists. I call them photographers." Kent turned to her, looking up from the book. "You see. There's such a thing as genius. Nobody knows what it is. How could Beethoven write a symphony when he was nine years old? Someone asked him how he did it, and he couldn't tell them. That's genius! But del Sarto knew that something was lacking in him. Oh, he was a fine craftsman. Show him a dog, and he could paint that dog to the eyelash. Show him a bowl of fruit, he could recapture it. But there was no fire, no genius in his paintings." Looking back he said, "He goes on to say of these men that do have genius:

> 'There burns a truer light of God in them,
> In their vexed beating stuffed and stopped-up brain,
> Heart, or whate'er else, than goes on to prompt
> This low-pulsed forthright craftsman's hand of mine.'

"Why, I think I know what that means!" Prue exclaimed. "It means he didn't have a heart!"

"Exactly! That's close enough! He goes on throughout the

poem to tell how he admires these men. Even though their paintings are not technically as good as his, there's something great in them. A light and a vitality that he cannot emulate—and finally he says a line that has become sort of a motto with me, Prue. Right here. See, I've got it underlined. Read it out loud for me."

Prue leaned over, and as she did so her loose hair brushed against Kent's cheek, and underneath the smell of paints he detected a faint fragrance that she always wore. Her arm was pressed against his, and he took a deep breath, forcing himself to listen as she spoke.

"Ah, but a man's reach should exceed his grasp or what's a heaven for." Prue turned and her eyes were wide. "What does that mean to you, Kent?"

"It means that no matter how hard I try, I'll never really get it. The best painting I ever painted wasn't as good as it should have been." He reached over and put his arm around her shoulders. "Do you understand what I'm talking about at all, Prue?"

Prue was conscious of his arm around her. He had never, in all the months she had been under his tutelage, touched her or shown any sign of romantic notion. Now, however, her breath came somewhat shorter, for she did not know how to handle this. "I–I think I do. You drive me so hard because you want me to be the best painter I can be."

"That's right," Kent said quickly. He squeezed her and said, "You're the finest woman I've ever known, Prudence. Not just the talent you have, but you're the sweetest, most understanding, and most gentle young woman it's ever been my privilege to know."

Prudence did not know how to respond to this. She felt her cheeks growing warm under his praise, and his hand tightened on her shoulder. Quickly she forced a laugh, saying, "Well, I'm sorry to be such a crybaby." She rose suddenly. "You won't see me breaking down again. I hate weepy women."

Maxwell stood, his face bearing some sort of emotion that

he seemed to keep bottled up. "Well," he said, "I'm glad that you don't think I'm a Simon Legree."

"No. I'm grateful every day of my life for all you've done for me, Kent."

"Gratitude. I *hate* that word!"

"You hate gratitude?"

"Yes. Not that I hate to give it to someone, but somehow I hate to receive it from you. I'd rather think of us in a different light."

This seemed to Prudence to be dangerous ground, and she said, "Well, of course, we're more than teacher and student. We're good friends too."

"You understand then that I'm just trying to bring out what God has put in you."

This surprised Prue, for he was not a man who spoke of God often. "Do you really believe that? That God puts things in us?"

"Why, of course, I do! I'm not a pagan, Prue! I'm not a Christian either, but I've seen enough to know that men couldn't be what they are without God. Why did he choose you to put this talent into? Why did he choose me?" He shrugged his trim shoulders, saying, "I don't know the answer to these things." Then as if the conversation troubled him, he said, "I'll take you out to dinner. It's late."

"All right. Let me get cleaned up."

The two of them took some time, for paint soaked into the fingers and under the nails. Prue was in the restroom scrubbing furiously at her hands when she heard muted voices. *Who could that be at this hour? Maybe a student come to talk to Kent.* She dried her hands, ran her comb through her hair, then stepping outside was surprised to see Mark Stevens.

"Mark! I didn't know you were in town."

"I just got back." Mark came over and stood before her. "You all through for the day? I'd hope so. It's pitch dark out there."

"Well, yes. I had to do a little extra work tonight."

"Well, you worked enough. Come on. I'm taking you out to eat."

Prue suddenly felt trapped. She shot a quick glance at Maxwell, who was getting his coat. He turned as he slipped his arm into the sleeve, and when he saw her face, he studied her with an odd expression.

"I just promised to go out and eat with Kent."

"That's fine," Mark said cheerfully. "All three of us can go. That be all right, Mr. Maxwell?"

"No. You two go ahead."

"I don't want to bust up your party," Mark protested.

"That's all right. I'll see you tomorrow, Prue." He turned, saying, "Lock the door when you go out." He limped out, and Mark turned back with puzzlement. "What's wrong with him?"

"Oh, he doesn't take to big parties," Prue said.

"Big parties? The three of us?" Mark grinned. "Well, now we're a big party of two. Come on. I'm hungry enough to eat the north part of a southbound hog."

★   ★   ★

Mark took Prue to the Ivanhoe Restaurant, which was disguised vaguely as a medieval castle. When they were seated Prue was amused to see that the waiters, some of them, were wearing suits of armor. The one that came to them had trouble keeping his visor up, and it came crashing down, hiding his face several times. He tried to speak, also, in what he considered an Old English dialect but was almost totally incomprehensible.

Mark laughed at the sight and ordered for the two of them; as they waited he began to talk about the restaurants he had seen across America. He was wearing a pair of black slacks with cuffs at the bottom, a white and gray striped, cotton shirt worn with the top button undone, and a gray sports coat, and he looked tan and fit.

"I'm doing a piece on different kinds of wacky restaurants," he said. "Food's not really the thing anymore. A restaurant has to have some kind of a gimmick. Some of them are Old English pubs with names like Ye Old Bull and Bush—that's in Atlanta. Also in Atlanta there's The Abbey Restaurant, where the waiters come dressed as monks. There's a Magic Castle Dinner Club in Los Angeles, where stars like Cary Grant and Paul Newman are members. Bookcases are creaking, stools mysteriously revolve when customers sit on them, and food is served in bubbling cauldrons or a magician's top hat."

"I don't think I could pay any attention to the food at a place like that."

"Nobody else can either. Like I said, it's not the food that people go for but the atmosphere."

"Tell me some more of them." Prue found it relaxing to be away from the studio. She always felt good around Mark, who had stopped in many times when he came back from his travels. Now she sat back in her chair and sipped her water occasionally as he continued.

"Well, in Boston, a fellow named Anthony Athanas built this gigantic seafood restaurant right on a decrepit pier. He has a lobster fisherman tromp through the dining room with his catch, and the customers go crazy." Mark laughed and shook his head in half wonder and half disgust. "He even hired a one-legged doorman that he fitted with a wooden peg leg, but I guess the worst of all is New York's Auto Pub. The customers sit in bucket seats and are served by beautiful waitresses in racing uniforms. The lighting is racing helmet lamps. You can even choose a table in the Classic Car Lounge and sit in an old Stanley Steamer."

Mark talked steadily until the food came, and then they both ate hungrily.

When they had finished their steaks, Prue said, "Tell me what else you've been doing." She sat there and listened as Mark spoke of his other work, and finally she said, "I read everything you write, Mark. You're a wonderful writer."

Mark looked up and smiled. "Thanks a lot. That means a lot coming from you, Prue. I wish I knew more about painting. Your stuff looks wonderful to me, but what do I know. What does Maxwell say? How are you getting along?"

"Oh, he's never happy with what I do. He always thinks I need to do more."

"Sounds like a real slave driver."

"Oh, he's not that. He's just so anxious for me to succeed." She leaned forward now, and her face was filled with a secret excitement. "Someday he says I'll have a show, a one-woman show right here in Chicago." Her dark eyes glistened, and a spirit glowed in her like live coals. Mark had always known Prue was a girl with a great degree of vitality and imagination, but these things had always been held under careful restraint. Now, since she had come to Chicago, she had blossomed. As she leaned forward, he appreciated the supple lines of her body. She was in that first maturity that follows girlhood, and the light in her eyes now held some kind of laughter, and she was enormously pleased.

She laughed and said, "We've been talking too much. I'm tired. Come along and take me home."

They left the restaurant, and when they reached her apartment she invited him in. It was a very tiny apartment. The living room area, which doubled as Prue's bedroom, was painted a light green and had hardwood floors with a large area rug in tones of gold, green, and red on which a gold-toned couch that folded out into a bed had been placed; a chair covered in well-worn green leather, a coffee table, and two lamps completed the room. The kitchen, which was situated behind the living room area, had limited counter and shelf space, but there was a small table with two chairs that had been placed in the far corner of the room by the old white refrigerator. On the far side of the room was a short hallway with two doors; Mark surmised one led to a bathroom and the other to a closet.

Prue fixed coffee, and while Mark was drinking his, she said with a pleased light in her eyes, "I've got a present for you." She moved out of the room for a moment, then returned bearing a painting. "This is for you," she said.

Taking the painting, Mark stared at it with a distinct sense of shock, for he was staring at a portrait of himself. He recognized the setting instantly, for it was his home. He was sitting on the fence, arms braced against the top rail, and the wind was blowing his hair. It must have been in fall, because the trees on the hills behind his house were touched with yellow, and gold, and red. He looked young, and happy, and she had caught the smile on his face.

Prue stood looking down at him as he stared at the painting. She felt a moment's disappointment, for he said nothing, and she thought, *He doesn't like it.* But then he looked up and there was awe in his gray-green eyes. "This is wonderful, Prue," he said quietly, almost in a whisper. His eyes went back to the painting, and he shook his head so that a lock of his tawny hair fell over his forehead. "I don't see how you did it."

"Oh, it was from a snapshot I took. You probably don't even remember it."

"I look so *young*!"

"Come now, Grandpa. Don't trip over your long, gray beard." Prue sat down beside him, and together the two studied the painting.

"Is it oil?"

"No, it's acrylic."

"I don't know the difference, but it doesn't matter." He could not get enough of gazing at it, and after a while he said, "It's the best present you've ever given me, Prue."

"I'm glad you like it. I wanted to keep it for myself, but I can always do another one."

Mark held the picture lightly in his hands. Finally he said, "I'll get it framed tomorrow, but I don't have any place to keep it the way I move around. You keep it for me until I get a place of my own."

"All right," Prue said.

They talked for a while longer, and at long last he got up,

saying, "I'll be here for two or three days. Can you get some time off?"

"At nights, maybe."

"Take tomorrow afternoon off. We'll go out to the park somewhere and maybe have a picnic." He was standing now, and she had risen to stand beside him. He handed her the picture, and leaned over, and kissed her on the cheek. "Thanks for the present."

He turned and left abruptly, leaving Prue standing there holding the painting. She listened to his footfalls, and when they faded, she sat down and stared at the painting.

15

"You Grew Up and I Never Knew It"

Jake Taylor sat behind his desk, fingers locked behind his head. He stared across the room at Mark Stevens, who was leaning back in the oak chair going through a sheaf of papers he held on his lap. Mark looked up and asked, "So you want me to do a piece on this war protest movement?"

Jake nodded. "It's been done before in bits and pieces. *Esquire* did a pretty good run on it, but most of our readers don't read *Esquire*."

"I don't know how to approach the thing, Jake."

"You'll find a way. You always have." A smile twisted his lips crookedly, and he added, "Anybody that can write a piece on baton twirling can do a war protest. You won't have any trouble finding one. This blasted thing's spread all over the country. First it was just a few nuts out in California. Well, I'm not too surprised about that. Everything loose rolls to California, as they say. Then it started spreading in the other liberal colleges across the country. Worked its way down to the high schools, and now I'm not going to be too surprised if preschoolers don't toddle out in their diapers carrying signs."

"You feel pretty strongly about this, don't you, Jake?"

"Don't you?"

"Well, as a matter of fact, I do." Mark shifted in his chair impatiently, and there was a smoldering light of anger in his gray eyes. "I think we made a mistake going in there in the first place, but now that we're in I think we ought to push it on through."

"You'll never see that, I don't think. The Second World War we had men like Eisenhower and Patton." He brooded on the matter for a moment, then shook his head. "Sometimes I think nothing good happened to this country after George Patton died."

"Oh, come on, Jake! It's not that bad!" Mark protested.

"It's bad enough! I hate to think what the history books will say about this decade. The sixties have produced nothing much but a war that we can't call a war, a bunch of squalling babies running off to Canada when they're asked to fight, and the rest of them cutting their classes to carry signs and scream about the war."

"Well, I'll give it my best shot, Jake." He began shuffling the papers together but paused when Taylor said, "Watch your rear, Mark."

Surprised, Mark looked across at the rangy editor. "What do you mean by that?"

"Well," Taylor shrugged, "all of the newspaper stories are about the police beating up on the protestors, but we've had quite a few cases of where it happened the other way around."

"Oh, I know what you mean." The two men thought of the reporter who had gone to cover one of the protest movements in Los Angeles at UCLA. He had made the mistake of letting the protestors know that he was a reporter and had been badly beaten. Now Mark chewed his lower lip thoughtfully. "I think I'd better get myself wired for this one."

"Not a bad idea. And, you don't have to go to UCLA. They're having a protest out in the park today. It's supposed to be a big one."

"All right. I'll take it in."

"Come over for supper tonight. We're having squash casserole."

★　★　★

Mark looked down at his chest, where the wire leading from the tape recorder in his baggy trouser pocket was taped. He stood before the mirror, holding a roll of adhesive tape in his hand, and carefully ran the wire up his neck. It was the smallest microphone wire he could find, but it was still obvious. He carefully taped the little microphone, a little larger than a shirt button, to his cheek parallel to the right side of his lips and saw that the wire itself was firmly anchored. Then he took a large bandage and placed it over the microphone. The bandage ran down his cheek and under it, and he studied it carefully, then turned and picked up a white turtleneck shirt. He slipped it on and pulled the neck up over the bandage. "It looks pretty good," he murmured. "Like I tried to cut my throat or something. Now, let's go for a trial run." Reaching into his pocket, he snapped on the tape recorder and said in a normal voice, "I'm going to risk my neck with a bunch of hairy, juvenile war protestors. If I'm going to get beat up, I'd like to at least have a chance to record. This is a test."

He shut off the microphone, pulled it out of his pocket, ran the tape back, then put it on Play. He waited for a moment, then his voice came out of the tiny machine, which was no larger than a package of cigarettes. He listened and noted that it was fainter than usual but perfectly understandable. He nodded, ran the tape back, pushed Record, then the Stop button.

"Well, that ought to do it," he said.

Leaving the house he drove to the park, noting as he got out that the park itself was already overflowing with people. As he moved toward the bandstand, where he assumed the speakers would yell their invictives against the government and the president, he noticed that the crowd was an eclectic one. Some youngsters seemed to be no older than twelve or thirteen, while at the same time quite a few elderly people were moving toward the bandstand. The vast majority of the crowd, however, was made up of what appeared to be hippies, bearded and wearing clothes that looked like they'd been thrown away as rejects by the Salvation Army. Mark wondered why so many people would interrupt their lives. But the war was a burning issue. Those who were opposed to it vociferously demanded its immediate end, while others felt that America's reputation was on the line. He thought about the ferment that stirred across the country, and the grim thought came to him, *The country has never been this divided since the Civil War. If we divided up the people today, half of us would be for the war and the other half would be against it. I don't see any good end to it. . . .*

It was not his purpose to hear the speaker, for he knew what the rhetoric would be. The story, he had decided, would be based on the protestors themselves. Who are they? Where did they come from? Why are they so vehemently opposed to the war? Questions like this he had filed in his mind, and he began talking to a diminutive teenager who stood next to him. She was smoking marijuana, and the acrid smell of the joint was sharp in Mark's nose.

"It looks like a good rally," Mark said.

The girl, who had dishwater blond hair that needed washing, turned to grin at him. Her teeth were not good, and she obviously had not bathed that morning. He noticed also that her fingernails had dirt under them, and her fingers were stained yellow with nicotine.

"Yeah," she said, her speech slightly slurred. "You come out to these things a lot?"

"Not much," Mark said. "I have to work for a living."

"Yeah?" she said. "What do you do?"

"I sell paper supplies."

The girl giggled. "What a drag," she said. Her eyes took him in in a speculative fashion, and she said, "What do you say after the meeting we go out and celebrate?"

Mark nodded. "Might be all right," he said, thinking that

she was just doped enough to tell him the absolute truth about herself.

The meeting started, as had the others, with a sixteen-year-old philosopher who wore a guitar and was singing Pete Seeger's and Bob Dylan's protest songs. He was a mediocre performer, but the crowd did not seem to notice.

Mark felt he should get more reactions from the people, and he winked at the girl. "I'll see you after the meeting."

"Yeah. We'll have a party."

Mark moved around the crowd and noticed that the attention was not strictly paid to the protestor doing the singing. He passed through a motorcycle gang and eyed them carefully as a prospect for future interviews.

He began talking instead to an older woman who stuck out like a sore thumb. She was neatly dressed; her silver hair looked as if it had been done by an expert hairdresser, and as he moved to stand beside her, he said, "Hello. It's a big crowd today."

"Yes it is." The woman turned to look at him, taking in his white turtleneck and clean-cut appearance. "You don't look like so many of these other people," she said. "I wish more of our kind would come out here."

Wondering what "our kind" was, Mark decided it meant not hippies. "I guess our kind are working," he said.

"What is your job?"

"I sell paper supplies for the Acme Printing Company."

The woman nodded briefly, listened to the song, and then her lips tightened in a bitter line. She stood there silently, and finally she turned to Mark and said, "This horrible war! This is all I can think of to influence the president to stop it."

"You don't think we should go on?"

"With this terrible thing? Of course not!" She stared at him with antagonism beginning to show. "You don't believe in the war, do you?"

"Well, I suppose the president's having a hard time. We're

into it, and it seems wrong to just pick up and leave after all the soldiers who have died."

The woman turned to face him, her voice rising. "My son was killed six months ago in this useless slaughter!" Her voice got out of control, and those standing around began to look at Mark. There were scowls, and the crowd began to grow restless.

Mark saw he had gotten himself into the wrong light, but still the woman was voicing what many respectable Americans felt. He continued to play the role of a man who was not totally in favor of stopping the fighting, which proved to be a mistake.

"Well, looky here. We've got a patriot."

Mark turned quickly to see that the black-jacketed motorcycle gang had moved closer to form a semicircle around him. Three of them were of rather average size, but the speaker was a huge man about six foot four and weighing, Mark estimated, close to three hundred pounds. The sleeves of his jacket were cut off, leaving his arms free, and they bulged with heavy muscles. He was, Mark figured, a wrestler and a weight lifter. He had the ponderous strength of one of those, and his small eyes were glittering with a reptilian ferocity. He came right up, and Mark could smell the rank odor of marijuana, and sweat, and stale beer. The man reached out and grabbed Mark's arm, his grip like a Stilson wrench. "You're one of the president's men, are you? Why ain't you over there fightin' if you're such a patriot?"

Mark tried to free himself, but without breaking loose violently, it was impossible. He eyed the others who all wore identical clothing, what amounted to uniforms. "I didn't say I was in favor of it," he began lamely. "I just don't see—" He was cut off, however, for the four began laughing raucously. Another member of the gang, a small man with a feral appearance in his thin face, took his other arm so that Mark was pinioned. He began to curse, and Mark knew that he was in a poor situation. Quickly he glanced over the crowd, and from his superior height saw policemen wearing riot helmets and carrying sticks.

Got to get out of this quick! He decided to draw his strength into one motion and rip himself free from his captors. He threw his arms up violently, heaved himself backward, and threw his smaller assailant off balance so that he staggered, but it was only with a second effort that he managed to rip himself free from the gorilla-like grip of the other. He turned and made one or two steps toward the police, but a mighty blow struck him at the base of his skull. It drove him to the ground and sent the world around him in a kaleidoscope fashion. He knew what was coming next, and he rolled into a ball to avoid the kick. It caught him on the kidney, and the pain made him gasp; then he turned his head to see a boot coming toward him and tried to roll away. But it caught him in the temple, and the world exploded in a huge, orange burst of light. . . .

★　　★　　★

When he awoke, Mark lay for a moment in utter confusion. His head was pounding as if someone were striking it with a railroad spike tapped by a sixteen-pound sledge. He groaned, and voluntarily lifting his hand, felt the bandage around his head. But in lifting his arm, pain suddenly raced through his chest, and it caught his breath for a moment.

Slowly he opened his eyes and saw that he was in a hospital. There was no mistaking the stark bareness of the room, the single bed that he lay on, and the sterile, shiny white walls and ceiling. Memory came to him, and he muttered, "They must've had a holiday kicking me." He took a breath, and as he did the pain came back again. He lay there for a moment, then saw the cord with the buzzer looped around the aluminum rails. Reaching out very carefully, he punched the button, then let the arm fall back. Almost at once the door opened, and a short, heavy young man of about twenty-five moved across the room and looked down at him. "Well," he said, "you're back with us. How do you feel?"

"Like I was hit by a truck."

"That might have been better." A grin touched the chubby face, and the speaker's blue eyes considered Mark. He reached over, took his pulse, then leaned over and peered into his eyes carefully. "Well, you're lucky," he said. "No broken bones, and no concussion, it looks like. But you do have some ribs that are sprung and cracked pretty bad."

"How long have I been here?" Mark licked his lips, which were dry, and tried to sit up.

"Better not try that," the nurse said. "I'll crank you up a little bit." As he manipulated the controls, Mark slowly came to a half-sitting position. He said, "They brought you in about six hours ago. I was in the ER, and you were in bad shape! You want some water?"

"Yes, please."

Mark gulped down the water, some of it spilling down his chin, and the nurse chattered on happily, giving a list of Mark's injuries, which were not encouraging. Even as he spoke, the door opened, and Jake Taylor walked into the room, his face tense with worry. "How is he?" he asked the short nurse.

"Going to live, but he's not going to be much good for anything for a couple weeks." He turned and left the room, saying, "I'll be back to give you some medication after your visit."

Jake shook his head. "Well, this wasn't the best idea we ever had, was it?"

"No, it wasn't. If I had kept my mouth shut, it would never have happened." He recounted how he had gotten into such a condition and said, "I guess I'm not much of an investigative reporter."

"You're coming home with us. Stephanie's got something for what ails you. She always feeds us chicken soup, no matter what kind of sickness we have."

Mark was glad that he would not have to stay in the hospital. That afternoon he went home with Taylor, and for the next week he moved slowly and carefully. As usual, he enjoyed Betsy and Forest, and he spent hours playing board games with them.

It was on the fifth day of his stay at Stephanie's that Jake came home with a small package of letters in a rubber band. "I stopped by and picked up your mail. These came for you at the office," he said, tossing them on the table. He sat down and began to recount the affairs at the paper, paying only scant attention to Mark. Finally, however, he looked up and saw that Mark was staring at a single sheet of paper, his face pale. He had discarded all the bandages, but there was still puffiness and discoloration on his right temple. Jake did not like to pry, but Mark was so obviously shaken that he asked, "What is it, partner? Bad news?"

When Mark looked up, his eyes were filled with grief. "My best friend in high school, John Tyler. He's been killed in Vietnam." His voice was tense. "This letter's from his mother; she's a widow. John was her only son." He was silent for a moment, then he dropped the paper and clasped his hands together. "John was a good guy," he said. "He played tight end at the University of Arkansas on a scholarship. I was going with him—that was always the plan, but I decided to do something else. I–I hadn't even heard that John had joined up."

Taylor sat there, understanding some of the pain in the younger man. He had lost a good friend himself in Vietnam, and finally after a time he said, "This war! It's chopping our men to pieces."

Mark appeared not to hear. "He always loved dogs," he said. "Every stray dog in the world that he found, he would take 'em home. His mother was so aggravated with him, but he never gave her a minute's trouble." He lifted his eyes and stared out the window for a moment, then murmured, "And now he's dead. It's all over. He'll never get married, never have those kids he should have had."

Taylor sat there for a while, but he saw that Mark did not want to talk. He moved into the kitchen and told Stephanie the news. She stood there with compassion in her eyes. "The poor boy," she said. "And Mark's taking it hard, you say?"

His brow furrowed and he shook his head. "He's not going to shake this off so easy."

★　★　★

Jake Taylor was right. Mark could not shake off the death of John Tyler. He stayed at Jake's for another two days, saying little, and he was glum and lifeless. Mark knew he was casting a pall on the place. Thanking Jake and Stephanie, he moved back to his apartment, but he found no peace there either.

One night he stopped at Prue's apartment after he'd been walking the streets. She was surprised when she opened the door. "What are you doing out at this time of night, Mark?"

"I've got to talk to you, Prue." Mark stepped inside as she invited him in, and sitting on the couch, he began to speak of what had happened. Prue took her seat beside him, her eyes filled with compassion. He ended by saying, "I've decided to join the Marines, Prue."

Shock ran through Prue Deforge, and a wave of fear followed. She could not speak for a moment, so disturbed his statement had made her, then she said, "Mark, don't do anything rash."

"I've got to do something. Oh, I know it's foolish, and I won't change anything, but I've got to do *something*."

Prue had a swift thought. "Let's go home. You can talk to your dad. He was a fighting man in the last war. He can give you some good counsel."

Mark looked up with surprise. "And you'd go with me?"

"Of course I would. I'd like to get away and rest for a while anyway."

★　★　★

Mark's parents were surprised to see them, for they had not announced they were coming. Prue whispered, "Come to my house after you have talked to your father," and Mark agreed.

Mark said nothing for the first day of his visit, but late the next afternoon he drew his father aside outside and said, "I've got to talk to you, Dad." The two of them walked slowly down the path that led to the lower pasture, and Mark poured out his problems to his father. He finished by saying, "I'm joining the Corps, Dad, if you think it's right."

Les Stevens stared at this tall son of his, and memories of combat came rushing back to him. It had always been his fervent hope that his son would never have to face death the way he had. Now he saw, however, that the dreaded moment had come. He began to speak, talking about the country and the bad things that had happened; then he added, "I guess you know my line about things like this."

"You mean what Stephen Decatur said?"

Les nodded. "That's right. To our country may it always be right—but right or wrong our country." He reached out and put his hand on his son's shoulders. "You're a man now, Mark, and you have to make your own decision, just like I did. Just like every man does. I'm ashamed of the decisions that some young men I know, men from this town, have made. I hate like blazes to see you go, but if you do, I'll be right behind you. And proud of you too."

Mark felt a warmth flow through him, and he said huskily, "Thanks, Dad—I guess I needed to hear that."

"We'll have to tell your mother. She'll take it hard."

They went inside the house, and it was difficult. Mark left half an hour later, his head down. His mother said little, but he saw the pain in her eyes. Crossing the highway, he made his way down the Deforge driveway and found Prue sitting on the front porch. It was late afternoon, and shadows were growing long. She came down and said, "Did you tell them?"

"Yes. It wasn't easy."

"Let's take a walk, Mark," Prue suggested. They moved down the path to the stream where they had had so many walks before, and when they got to the creek, they stood for a long time, letting the silence of the place sink into them. The swifts were doing their acrobatic dance in the air, turning and rolling, and for a while they watched them.

Finally Prue whispered, "We had so many good times here, didn't we, Mark?"

"We'll have them again."

"No, I don't think we can ever be that happy." Prue shook her head. "That's strange, because I had an unhappy childhood, always too tall, always doing so poorly in school." She turned to him, and the fragrance of her hair was like a drug to him. Her face was lifted, and she said quietly, "You helped me through some hard times, Mark. Even though you were always going with other girls, and so popular, and I was a nobody, you always had time for me."

"You're not a nobody now." Mark studied her face, her dark eyes and dark hair. There was such character in her face, in the full lips and the deep-set eyes that observed him with such warmth. Her figure was the envy of so many girls now, and he thought of the angular leanness that had been hers when she was growing up. Something took him then, coming to him as almost a revelation. He said quietly, "You've grown up, Prue. I've been thinking of you for so long as the girl I grew up with. All arms and legs, and always sort of sad."

"That's what I was. I guess I still am."

"Not now," Mark said. The summer heat lay across the land, but it had grown cool now. From far off came the sounds of cattle lowing, and the cry of a night bird was a melodious melody that came to them as they stood there.

Prudence looked up at Mark, and a longing came to her. All of her life, it seemed, she had been alone except for her parents—and for this young man that stood looking down at her. She had known for a long time that she was in love with Mark Stevens, but it had been a hopeless love. One that she never thought would be returned. He had always been the popular one, the one all the girls wanted to go with, the star quarterback, the hero, and she had been just Prue Deforge, an object of ridicule for so much of her life.

Now, however, as she stood there breathing the fragrance of the land and looking up into his face, she knew that he might never come home again, and a great pity came to her. She suddenly knew the hungers that come to a lonely woman and recognized that she had put childhood and adolescence behind her. With a boldness that slightly shocked her, she reached up, put her arms around his neck, and placed herself against him. She felt the shock run through him as her soft curves flattened out, and she pulled his head down and whispered, "Kiss me, Mark."

Mark put his arms around her and lowered his head. Her lips were soft and yearning and willing under his. There was an innocence in them, but at the same time the fullness of a woman's passion. She held him tightly, and the touch of her lips and the clasp of her arms stirred him as he had never been stirred before. He clung to her, pressing her closer still, and as he did, the old hungers revived and seized him. He lifted his head and whispered, "Oh, Prue, there's such a sweetness in you."

"Is there, Mark?" She looked up, and he saw that her eyes were filled with tears.

"Why are you crying?" he asked.

"I can't help it." Her voice was almost inaudible, and she did not move back but seemed to cling to him for strength. She held him for a moment longer, then said, "Oh, Mark, be careful!"

He looked down at her and kissed her again, this time gently, then he simply held her as she put her head on his shoulder. They clung together without speaking for a long time, both of them knowing that this might be the last time anything like this would ever take place in their lives.

16

A SURPRISING EVENING

M ark Stevens' introduction to the Marine Corps began
with a sergeant whose rich, blasphemous oath shocked
him to the core. He was a man of middle age with a pot
belly that spoiled his posture. He wore the Marine dress
blues and over this a regulation, tight-fitting overcoat of forest
green. As the sergeant spoke, Mark had the thought that blue
and green were the two colors his mother told him did not
match, but the Marines had decreed otherwise, and later on,
the gaudy dark and light blue of the Marine dress seemed to
blend in well with the soothing green.

"When you get to Parris Island," the sergeant was saying,
"forget you ever had any other life. You will anyway by the
time they get through with you over there. You're going to
hate them," he said. "Your sergeants, your officers, and maybe
even each other. You'll think the officers are the stupidest,
rottenest bunch of men who ever lived, but if you want to
save yourselves a headache, listen to me—do what they tell
you and keep your big mouths shut!"

Mark was to remember the sergeant's words. He remained
silent all the way on the trip to Parris Island, joined by Marine recruits from all over the country. They were crammed
into passenger cars pulled by a diesel, and comfort was left
behind in Washington. As the train moved through the darkness to the clickety clack of the wheels over the joinings of the
rails, Mark realized that somehow this business of becoming
a marine was already having a vital impact on him. He had

heard of boot camp and knew that the Marines believed in the toughest of all training, and the man who had it the roughest was the most admired.

When they arrived at Parris Island, they tumbled off the train, became a training platoon, were assigned a number, and given into the cruel hands of the drill instructor, who began bellowing at them instantly.

Mark felt his ears blistered by the profanity, and he studied the sergeant carefully, for he knew that his fate would be in his hands. He whispered to the man next to him, "He's not as big as a freight car—but he's not a whole lot smaller either."

Sergeant Tippit's voice was as big as his body. It seemed to reach out and physically embrace the squad, and Mark felt the rough sound of it down into his very bones. He loved drills, Sergeant Tippit did, and Mark forever carried a picture in his mind of the sergeant striding a few feet apart from his men, arms stretched out, hands clenched, head canted back, and his whole body ceaselessly bellowing out the drill.

Mark quickly learned that a naked man has no pride, no identity, no past, and no future. When he was stripped at the quartermaster's, defenseless and not knowing what was coming next, he somehow lost his character with his clothing. The quartermaster swarmed over the recruits with a tape measure, and then the clothes seemed to be thrown at him from all angles: caps, gloves, socks, shoes, underwear, shirts, belts, pants. Mark emerged with a number, surrounded by sixty other human beings, but somehow the parts seemed to have no meaning except in the context of a whole. Glancing around he saw they all looked alike, and when they passed through the barbers and emerged with their heads as naked as marbles, they had lost one other portion of their identity.

Constantly they were screamed at and told that they were half baked, that they were no longer civilians, that they would never make Marines and would probably die during the training.

When they were not being screamed at, drawn up at attention, they were marching. Everywhere, always marching. To the sick bay, to the water racks, to the marching grounds. Mark grew accustomed to the sound of thousands of feet slapping the packed earth, grinding to a halt, rifle butts clashing. He seemed to have the sound of Sergeant Tippit's voice in a small tape recorder that had been implanted in his skull. "Right— right shoulder ahms!" Slap! Slap! "Start your pieces, hear me? Start your pieces, you hear? I want noise, blood! Present ahms!"

No one cared about anything but discipline, or so it seemed to Mark. He had expected talk of the war, of how to survive in Vietnam, but they heard no fiery lectures about killing the gooks. The drill instructors were like sensualists, who feel that if a thing cannot be eaten, or drunk, or taken to bed, it does not exist, and all Sergeant Tippit cared for was drill, drill, drill. Once he marched Mark's platoon straight into the ocean, and when some men faltered, his screams could be heard a mile away. "Who told you to halt! I give the orders here! Nobody halts until I tell them to!"

Mark, fortunately, had continued marching until the water was up to his chest, and when he was directed to about-face found it very difficult to do underwater. Nevertheless, he and a few others who had continued marching straight into the sea thought they saw a glint of approval in the eyes of the gigantic sergeant.

As the training went on, Mark found that he could endure the hardship of marches, the obstacle field, the blistering sun, the screaming constantly in his ear. What he found most difficult of all was the lack of privacy. There was no such thing as privacy. Everything was done in front of a hundred or more men. Rising, waking, writing letters, making beds, washing, shaving, bathroom functions—all were done in full view of a thousand eyes. Mark had vague memories of those times when he would be by himself for hours, and days, and if he missed any part of civilian life, this was the element that he most longed for.

Mark's finest hour came on the firing range. He had always been an expert shot, and he seemed to have a natural flare for it. With the gunner instructor at his elbow, he shot bull's-eye after bull's-eye and qualified without difficulty for an Expert Rifleman's Badge, which added five dollars a month to his twenty-one-dollar regular pay. After five weeks of basic, Mark Stevens had been made over. The change had taken place. He was a veteran. One day he passed a group of incoming recruits still in civilian clothes looking cheap, shoddy, and unkempt, and he had joined the squad, who cried with one voice, "You'll be sorreee!"

When they were ready for the second phase of their training, the members of the squad were classified. The enlisted man who interviewed Mark was bored out of his skull, obviously. He asked questions rapidly—name, serial number, rifle number—and then asked, "What did you do in civilian life?"

"Newspaper reporter."

"Okay, you're in the First Marine Division. Go out and tell the sergeant."

"Some aptitude test." Mark grinned at Speed Carswell, a tall, lanky Kentuckian who was also an expert rifleman.

"I guess being a newspaper reporter qualifies you to kill VCs," Carswell replied.

Mark and Carswell joined a few others from the squad as they moved to the second phase of their training. Along with Carswell, he formed a friendship with several more. All the time, during this period, his company became like a clan, or a tribe, of which the squad was the important unit of a family group. Each squad differed from the other because the members were so different. Mark noticed that they had no "inner conflict," as the phrase goes. They knew soon that they would be in the jungles, and that their lives would be in each other's hands. *This*, Mark thought, *tends to make a man want to get close to his buddies*.

The days sped by, and Mark trained, and drilled, and

learned to read maps, and listened to lectures. He wrote letters home now, and received some too, living for them. He got more than most and wrote more than most. While the others were going into town partying, getting drunk, and chasing the young women who inhabited the saloons and dives, he kept a journal and used his tape recorder, for he knew that one day forgetfulness would come and wipe the things out of his mind that he was experiencing. He sent the tapes home to Prue, asking her to file them but not listen to them, for some of the things were rough, and he knew she would be shocked. He determined to keep a journal, as one man had done in World War II; *Guadalcanal Diary* had revealed the heart of a young warrior better than a thousand stories could.

He wrote down not only what happened outwardly but what was happening on the inside: how he was being made into a killer, which he hated, but which was necessary. You could not fight the Vietcong with a law book, or a medical diploma, or a typewriter. They had to be stopped with the weapons forged by war, and as the weeks dragged on Mark felt himself becoming that kind of individual who could be trained to point a rifle at an enemy and blow his brains out.

At long last, almost imperceptibly, the day came, and Mark found himself with thousands of other men on board a troop carrier. He recorded the instances and experiences of the voyage, and when he first set foot in that far country where men were dying every day, something closed about his heart like a fist, and a coldness swept over him. He looked at the faces of the veterans waiting to take the transport back and saw a stark despair; he wondered if he would come back in this condition—if he, in fact, came back at all.

He moved forward as the officers barked commands, and as they moved toward the dark green jungles that lay just off the beach, his thoughts were of his home, of his parents, and of Prudence Deforge. And then, as a man folds a treasure up, puts it in a strongbox, and locks it, he put these memories away, and holding his rifle advanced toward the crucible of battle.

★   ★   ★

For a long time Prudence stood before the painting that she had been working on for weeks, staring at it with a hopeless droop to her shoulders. "It's just not right," she said, staring at the half-done painting. The painting itself was a scene from her past, a picnic out by the Buffalo River, where she had gone with her Sunday school class. There had been a baptizing connected with it from her church, and she had seen the pastor, Brother Crabtree, waist deep in the bubbling waters of the river, his hand resting on the back of a young girl's head and holding her folded hands with his other. She had wanted to catch the immediacy of that moment, for it remained in her mind as clearly as if it were a picture. The young girl about to be baptized was her friend, Amy McPherson, who had been converted at a revival meeting at the church. Amy had been frightened of water all her life, and she had confided to Prue that "I'll just die! I know I will! He'll let me drown!"

Prudence could almost hear Amy's voice after all these years, and she had hoped to catch something of that fear in the young girl's face, but it had proved impossible. Even the scene itself did not seem exactly right. The water did not express the rushing flow of the spring torrents that the Buffalo had. The canoe in the background with the two fishermen looked stilted and artificial, like a picture on a calendar in a funeral home somehow. With a sigh she shook her head, took the painting down, and moved across the room. Other students were there now, and one of them, a short, well-shaped young girl from Ohio named Kim Kelly, said, "No luck, eh?"

"Just couldn't do it."

"It goes that way sometimes." Kim shrugged. She herself had absolutely no talent and had been at the Institute for three years. No one could ever convince her, and she had withstood the most blistering lectures from her instructors with apparently no effect. Now she continued to smear paint recklessly on the canvas, and Prue could barely identify the subject, which appeared to be a thick-legged horse out in a pasture with grass that was blue-green with touches of yellow.

Prue tried to think of something pleasant to say, and said, "That's an interesting color, that grass, Kim." Then she moved on, having made the young woman happy, for she got few compliments.

It was almost four o'clock, and the fingers of her right hand were stiff, but no more stiff than her emotions. She was tired inside as well as out, and after cleaning up, she pulled her coat from the rack and headed for the door. "You're leaving early." She turned to find Kent Maxwell standing there, his eyes showing disapproval. "Let me see the picture."

"It's not worth looking at!"

"I'll decide that," he said coolly. He stared at her so straightly that she shrugged and said, "All right, but you won't like it." She moved back through the room, Kim giving Maxwell a brilliant smile as he passed and asking, "How do you like this, Mr. Maxwell?"

"It's terrible. Is that supposed to be a horse, or a moose, or an elephant?"

Kim laughed and said, "Anything you want it to be."

"Fool girl!" Maxwell muttered under his breath as they arrived at Prue's painting. When she put it on an easel and stepped back with resignation, he stared at it. "Why don't you like it?"

"It doesn't do what I wanted it to do."

"It's not bad," Kent said. "Just not up to your usual standard." He began to make a few critical comments and then turned to face her. "You know what I think?" he asked.

"What?"

"I think you're tired. Remember, I told you once that you could get too much art? That you need to come to it fresh instead of as a chore that has to be done? Well, I think you've reached that point."

The hum of talking filled the large room, and the light

filtered down through the north glass. The smells were as familiar to Prue as anything by now, so that this studio had become her medium. She lived here, or at her apartment, with a few brief excursions outside. Now she shook her head, saying wearily, "You may be right. I'm awfully tired."

Abruptly Maxwell said, "Let me get cleaned up. We'll go out and uncoil a little bit."

"Oh, I'd rather not. I just want to go home."

"Well, I won't let you. Wait until I get ready."

An hour later they were sitting in a Chinese restaurant named The Bamboo Palace. Kent had ordered for them both, for he discovered that she had rarely eaten in a Chinese restaurant. Soon their plates were filled with succulent vegetables, sweet and sour pork, moo goo gai pan, delicious crab cakes, and spicy fried rice, and he was instructing her, "Put just a little of this mustard on there. Not too much."

Prue took the spoon and put a generous dollop of mustard on her fried rice, then took a bite of it. For a moment, it seemed that the top of her head was being blasted off, and she could only stare open-eyed, unable to get her breath.

Kent grinned. "I told you to use a little. It's pretty potent stuff."

Prue grabbed the glass of water before her, drank half of it down, then gasped. "That stuff's the hottest thing I've ever tasted."

She continued eating cautiously, avoiding the hot mustard, and the soft Chinese music seemed exotic and strange to her ears. "All those songs they sing," she said once, "sound just alike."

"I imagine those we sing sound alike to them. You know we Caucasians think all Orientals look alike, but I don't imagine they do to each other." He was watching her carefully now, his eyes half hooded, noting the fatigue in her features. He continued to talk gently, hoping that she would relax. "I have a Chinese friend who told me once, when we have a baby we know what we're going to get. Dark hair, and dark eyes, and yellow skin. When you Americans have them, you don't know what you'll get. Blond hair, brown hair, red hair—blue eyes, green eyes, brown eyes." He grinned and said, "There may be something in that."

As the music jangled on with its eerie rhythm, so different from that of the Western world, Kent began to speak of art. "You remember the poem of Browning, Prue? The one about the faultless painter?"

"'Andrea del Sarto'?" Prue nodded. "Yes. I got a copy of Browning. I've read that poem over and over. Some of his poems I don't understand, but that one is a good one."

"Have you read 'Fra Lippo Lippi'?"

"No. I haven't gotten to that one yet."

"You'll like it," Kent nodded. "I don't have it with me, but I've almost got it memorized. It's another poem about a painter. Browning was a lover of art and culture, and he knew more about the nature of art and the philosophy of art than most of the modern critics, all of them, I might say."

"'Fra Lippo Lippi.' What kind of a name is that?"

"Italian," Kent said. He took a bite of sesame chicken, dipped it in sweet and sour sauce, and put it into his mouth. "This is good," he said. "I wish I could have it every day." Then he shrugged, saying, "The poem is about a young Italian boy, a beggar, who is taken off the street. He's an orphan and has to make his own way and almost dies of starvation. The monks want to take him in and make a monk of him. There's one portion where he speaks of the kind of eye that I think that an artist has to have—quick, and sharp, and looking in the very heart of things. In any case, they took the boy in and found out that he could paint." He laughed then and looked pleased.

"What's funny about that?" Prue asked.

"Well, back in those days, in the Renaissance, painting was all very ethereal. You've seen pictures of where the Virgin, and Joseph, and the baby look like plaster saints? No reality at all."

"Yes, I always thought that was odd."

"It was the way they did it back then. Lippi didn't want to do that. When he first painted, and the priests came to look at it, and the prior, they were shocked. How does it go? Let's see:

> "How? what's here? . . .
> Faces, arms, legs, and bodies like the true."

Prue laughed. "That must have been quite a shock for those monks to see real arms, and legs, and flesh and blood bodies."

"It was, but the lines that I want you to underline I think you'll like." He quoted the line softly:

> "However, you're my man, you've seen the world
> —The beauty and the wonder and the power,
> The shapes of things, their colours, lights and shades,
> Changes, surprises—and God made it all!"

He looked embarrassed then and said, "You think me an irreligious dog, no doubt, but that's what I believe. God made this world in all its beauty, and as artists somehow we've got to show it."

"I didn't know you felt like that, Kent."

"It's hard for me to put into words. You remember the Ash Can School of Art."

"Yes. I thought it was ugly and hideous."

"They like to paint garbage cans and the garbage that was in them and the ugly things of the world. Well, those things are here, but that's not all that's here." He leaned forward and said, "God has put in you the gift to show the beauty that he made. You show it in your paintings of the Ozark people— where they live, where they work—and somehow when I look at your paintings I see into the hearts of those people. I see their goodness, their struggles, their flaws as well—but I've learned to love them through your work."

Prue flushed. It was the most extreme compliment that Kent Maxwell had ever paid her. It was also what she longed so desperately to put into her paintings. She wanted to show the world the beauty and the dignity of the people of the Ozarks. Now she could barely speak she was so full of pleasure at his words. "Every time I see a painting of a place that I've seen, even though I've seen that place a million times, the painting holds me. It sort of brings it back to me," she said quietly.

"That's what art does. It reminds us of good things and teaches us things. I would guess that as you painted these people you learned about them."

Prue glanced up startled, for this was a secret, or she had thought so. "That's right, Kent. Somehow when I try to get them on canvas, I seem to see deeper into their hearts."

They talked for hours, and finally they left the restaurant. He took her to her door and said, "It's been a wonderful evening."

"Thank you so much. I feel better now."

"We're not through yet. We've got to talk some more."

"Would you—would you like to come in?"

"Yes."

Prue opened the door, and the two went in. After they hung up their coats, she put the coffeepot on and came to sit by him. As soon as she sat down, he said, "Prue, I want you to have a show."

His words seemed to paralyze her. "Oh no! Not yet! I'm not ready! I'm not good enough!"

"That's for me to decide. You're not as good as you will be," he said earnestly, reaching for her hand. "But you're good enough. I'm setting it up for two weeks from today. Don't be afraid," he said quickly, seeing the panic in her eyes. "You're better than you know, and it's time for you to share what God has given you with the world."

It took nearly an hour before he could convince Prue that this was the right thing. At last she took a deep breath and said tremulously, "If that's what you want, and if you think I'm ready—"

He nodded confidently. "It's your time." He talked for some time about the details, then suddenly fell silent. He remained so for so long that she said, "What's wrong, Kent?"

"I'd like to tell you a little more about myself."

"Why, if you want to."

Prue sat listening quietly as Maxwell spoke, slowly at first, and always with pain. He spoke of his marriage, and in his tones there were echoes of grief.

"Remember my telling you about my wife? Well, when I went off to Korea I hadn't been there for more than six months before I got a letter. She had fallen in love with another man. She wanted a divorce."

"Oh, Kent—" Prue reached over, took his hand, and held it between both of hers. "I'm so sorry," she whispered.

He looked down at her hands and then lifted his eyes. "That was it. I never saw her again; then I got this leg blown out from under me and became a cripple. When I came home I didn't have faith or love for anybody." He continued to speak of how he had thrown himself into his career, and finally he said, "Prue, I was an angry, bitter man when you first met me."

"Not that bad, Kent."

"Bad enough." He took a deep breath and turned to her. "Prue, something has happened to me, and you're at the heart of it. I don't hate my ex-wife anymore. I don't know what you had to do with it, but something about being around you and seeing your sweetness and your goodness. It restored my faith. I've even started believing in God again."

"I'm so glad, Kent. You've done so much for me, but I've really done nothing for you."

Suddenly he reached forward and pulled her toward him. His move was so swift that she could not, at first, understand, and then his lips fell on hers, and he pulled her closer. His arms were strong, and she lay in them, and for a moment she was completely shocked and confused. Finally he drew back and said clearly, "I love you, Prue, and I want to marry you."

The silence of the room seemed deafening to Prue as she sat there, his arms still half around her. She remembered how closed off he had been for months, but now there was a pleading in his eyes and she could not think of what to say. Finally she sat back and said gently, "I never thought of such a thing, Kent!"

"Didn't you? But I'm not a man who shows his feelings much. I wish I could do it more. I'd hope you would see that side of me. If you marry me, I know you will."

She hated to hurt this man, for he had been so kind to her, but she knew what she had to say. "I can't give you an answer."

"I didn't expect you would. Things never come easy for me, Prudence, but I love you, and I hope you'll come to love me. This has been sudden for you." He stood and picked up his cane; she stood too, and they were silent for a moment. Each of them knew that they could never go back to what they were before; they had crossed some sort of an invisible line and nothing could be the same again.

"Good night," Kent Maxwell said abruptly.

"Good night, Kent." She walked with him to the door, and when he left, she closed it and leaned against it. She felt confused, and somehow afraid, and could not think clearly. His proposal had taken her completely off guard, and now she stood there leaning against the door, wondering how she could face him, and what would come of this strange evening.

17

Success!

A s Prue entered the Morgan Museum, a sense of inade-
quacy washed over her. Her one-woman show had been
well advertised, and it had given her an almost eerie
feeling when she had seen the announcement in the
paper with her picture staring out at her. As she walked up
the white marble steps with Kent Maxwell by her side, she
felt a weakness in her legs and could not say a word.

Maxwell turned to look at her and saw the paleness of her
cheeks. Taking his left hand, he held her arm and smiled re-
assuringly. "It's going to be great, Prue," he smiled. "You're
going to be a famous artist before this day is over."

"Oh, Kent, I'd like to turn, and run away, and hide!"

Pausing, he held her and they stood in the middle of the
steps. The Morgan Museum towered over them, its modernistic curves and angles scoring the blueness of the sky as
it was outlined. Several people passed them by, stopped to
look at the two, noting the tall young woman and the man
who held on to her arm while balancing on a cane with his
right hand. "You've got to learn to put your head down and
go right at it. Smile! Show the people that you're the artist!
You created all these works! They're the ones who ought to
be humble, not you!"

Prue tried to smile, but it was not a good effort. "I just don't
feel very victorious," she said. "I wish I had your confidence.
You always seem to know what to do."

"You're wrong about that. I don't always know what to do,"

Kent said, "but I don't let anybody know about it. The worse I feel and the more inadequate I feel, the more I smile and the louder I talk." He hesitated, then said in a more gentle tone, "It will be all right, Prue, after the first fifteen minutes. Come along."

"But what do I *do*, Kent? Just stand around?"

"Don't worry about that. You won't have time to think much. Everyone will want to meet you, and we're going to have some pretty big guns here."

"Well, that doesn't encourage me any!" Prue said.

They reached the top of the stairs and entered through the revolving doors that hissed as they made their majestic sweeps. They were the biggest revolving doors Prue had ever seen. Ordinarily there was room for only one or two people, but these were so enormous she could walk through without being afraid that the door behind her was going to clip her heels. When they emerged, it was like stepping into the future.

"This is where the shows take place. Pretty fancy, isn't it?" Kent said as he led her across the black marble floor.

Prue saw that the room was already occupied by people going around to various stations where her works were exhibited. Some paintings were on the wall, and some were on modernistic sculptured bases created out of alternating black and white marble. The light flooded in from overhead through enormous skylights, and each painting had its own lighting system. The walls were pure alabaster white, and the ceiling rose majestically and had a cathedral feel to it.

Stopping before Prue's painting of Pearl and her daughter, Melody, Kent motioned to it with his free hand. "It looks different here, doesn't it? How do you like it?"

"I don't know. It doesn't look like the same painting." She studied the painting, which was framed simply enough, but somehow being set off on the expanse of the white wall in its dark frame, and with the lights cast on it from every possible direction including the sunlight from overhead, the painting seemed to glow with a light that it had not had in the studio. "It's like I'm seeing it for the first time," she whispered.

"That's the way it is with a good exhibit. Look. You can see the lines of fatigue on Pearl's face the way you never could in any other setting. And the girl. Look at her. You can see the yearning in her eyes for things in life that she never had, and probably never will have. It's a great painting."

He grinned at her and said, "I wish I could afford to buy it myself."

"How much is it?" Prue asked.

"Ten thousand."

"Ten thousand dollars?" Prue gasped. "Why, you must be crazy! Nobody would pay that for that painting!"

"It'll be worth ten times that someday. Some of these people," Kent said, "don't know much about art, but they're investors, speculators. They find young artists who are on their way up, buy their paintings while they're cheap, and then make a killing when the artist gets a big name."

"Cheap? I wouldn't call ten thousand dollars cheap!"

"You've got to get used to the big time." Kent studied her carefully, then said, "I don't know if anybody will buy it or not. These one-man, or one-woman, shows are strange. Sometimes they don't go over at all, and you have to be ready for that, Prue."

"Why, I am ready for that," Prue said. "I just hate to think of all the time and money you invested in me, for this show must have cost a fortune."

"One painting will pay for all of that," Kent said. "Sometimes the things get hot."

"What do you mean 'hot'?"

"I mean the paintings start going, and sort of a panic sets in. People are afraid they won't be able to have anything, and they snap up all the rest of the paintings. That's what I'm hoping for here."

He broke off abruptly and said, "Look. There's Art Kensey over there."

"Who's Art Kensey?"

Maxwell laughed and shook his head in despair. "You really aren't with it, are you, Prue? Art Kensey is the most influential art critic in Chicago. He'll be coming over to meet you pretty soon. Remember now, be cool."

But Prue was anything but cool. Her face felt hot, and as she stood next to Kent she had not the faintest desire to speak to Art Kensey or anybody else.

"Here he comes. Don't pay any attention to his ways."

Kensey was a tall, muscular man who looked more like an athlete than an art critic. He had a shock of salt and pepper hair and appeared to be about fifty. His eyes were alert, and he put out a huge hand, saying, "You must be Prue Deforge. I'm Art Kensey."

"I'm happy to know you, Mr. Kensey."

"How are you, Kent?"

Kent took the man's huge hand and smiled. "I'm doing fine, Art. I'm glad to see you here."

"So this is your protégé?" Kensey grinned at Prue. "He took me out and bought me a steak the other night. First time he's ever offered to buy me anything. I take it it was in the nature of a bribe."

"You know better than that, Art," Kent protested.

"You never bought me a steak when I was reviewing your shows. But it was a good steak." He studied the young woman, who was not at all what he expected. He had heard she was from the Ozarks, and he had seen enough of her work to know that her specialty was the mountain country—its people, its scenery—and he had expected someone like a young Grandma Moses, a country girl. What he saw was something quite different, and as Kent watched him, he was glad that he had taken Prue in hand, as far as her dress and appearance were concerned. He had gone with her on a shopping trip and then visited a beauty salon, where he had given specific instructions to the hairdresser.

What Art Kensey saw was a young woman, at least six feet

tall, who was wearing a royal blue crepe dress that had cut-away shoulders, a high neckline with pearls decorating the band encircling her neck, a snug-fitting bodice, and a skirt that flared out delicately to where it ended at midthigh. The dress set her figure off admirably, and as Kensey studied the sculptured contours of her face, the high cheekbones, the beautifully coiffured hair, and the enormous, dark eyes, he said, "You don't look like most of the other artists that I see around. More like a high-fashion model."

"I don't know whether to thank you or not for that." Prue smiled. She liked the man and was surprised. He seemed not at all distant but warm and friendly. "Most of the models I see look like they're refugees and haven't eaten in a month."

"You don't have to worry about looking like them," Art said. "Now, tell me about yourself."

Kensey found that Prue apparently had no ego, which came as something of a shock to him. He was accustomed to being bombarded by artists eager to convince him of the value of their work, but Prudence Deforge was a modest young woman who spoke softly and seemed to have no idea of her own importance.

Others began to come around to meet Prudence, and Kensey stepped aside to let them have their chance. He stopped long enough to say to Maxwell, "I think you've got a winner there, Kent. You'd better hang on to her."

"I'm doing my best." Kent smiled enigmatically. "I can't wait for the reviews. You've already looked around. What are you going to say about Prue's work?"

"You know better than to ask me that! I never reveal what I'm going to say."

"Come on. Just between us."

Kensey raised his eyebrows. "You're really interested in this girl, aren't you, Kent?"

"Never mind that. What about her work?"

"It's good. She's young, and there are some technical flaws that I'll have to mention." His eyes sharpened, and he looked over at the young woman, who seemed to be doing very well in meeting people. "She's almost too good to be true, isn't she? I guess they don't grow them like that here in Chicago, or New York, or Paris." He turned and said, "You know her strengths, and you know her weaknesses. Five years from now she'll be a lot better, but she's got it, Kent, and that's what I intend to say."

A sense of relief rose in Kent Maxwell, and he said, "Thanks, Art. Thank you for coming."

★　　★　　★

Christie Castellano entered the display room hauling her husband, Mario, as if she were tugging at him, saying, "Hurry up, Mario."

"What's the hurry, Christie?"

"I don't want all the paintings to be sold."

"I don't think they'll sell that quickly." He opened the buff-colored brochure that listed the paintings and their prices and shook his head and whistled. "She's not giving them away, that's for sure! Look at these prices!" Castellano had been one of the most successful lawyers in Chicago. He was, however, far prouder of his wife, Christie, and his two children, Maria and Anthony, than he was of his fame as a crack tax lawyer. His sharp black eyes studied the paintings as they moved along toward where Prue was standing with a tall, lean man, and he said, "They're good, aren't they? I hope she makes a bundle."

Mario stopped in front of Prue, and when she turned they saw that she was flushed with excitement.

"I'm so glad you've come, Aunt Christie and Uncle Mario."

"Why, we wouldn't miss your show for anything in the world," Christie said. Her eyes turned to the man standing beside Prue. He had a vaguely familiar appearance, and Prue said, "I want to introduce you to Mr. Vincent Price. Mr. Price, this is my great-aunt Christie and her husband, Mario Castellano."

"Vincent Price?" Mario gasped and moved to face the tall man with the bony face, the sleepy eyes, and the wide mouth. "Why, I think I've seen every movie you ever made!"

A laugh began deep in the actor's chest, and he put out his hand, smiling. "I bet you say that to all the actors you meet." He was a suave, cosmopolitan man, and as Prue had found out, an expert in art. She had gasped too when he had walked up and introduced himself, and she said almost the same thing as her uncle.

Mario shook his head. "No. I love old movies. Don't care much about the new ones."

"I was just telling Mr. Price my favorite film of his was *Laura*."

"That's mine too," Christie said quickly, as the actor bowed slightly and smiled. "I know you must be very proud of giving so many people pleasure."

Before Vincent Price could answer, Mario said aggressively, "Well, that wasn't my favorite picture. I like those horror films you made. With all the dark, dank castles, and secret passageways, and lots of blood and violence. And the vampire ones were the best of all."

Price found this amusing, and he stood there speaking to the three in a very warm, natural manner. Then he turned and said, "Miss Deforge, you're standing on the brink of a wonderful career. I bought two of your paintings. Number 7 and number 22, and I shall get a great deal of pleasure out of them, I assure you."

"Thank you, Mr. Price. That makes me feel very good, indeed."

The actor nodded to the three of them, then turned and began to go around the display again.

"Oh, it's been so exciting," Prue said. "Paul Newman was here, and Richard Daley, the mayor. I didn't care for him much, but Mr. Newman was very nice."

"Have you sold any paintings except for those that Price bought?" Castellano asked.

"I don't know. Kent takes care of all of that, but it's been so wonderful. I was scared to death when I came in, but it's going very well."

Christie nodded with approval. There was an assurance in Prue, and when she and Mario left—after having bought a painting that Mario had liked—she said, "Prue's different. She's lost that awkward, half-scared look she had."

"She was a homely little thing when she was growing up," Mario said. "I remember at the reunions she always kept back. A strange girl, I thought, but she's a knockout now. It's a wonder she hasn't married."

"I think she's still got a crush on Mark Stevens. She's always been sweet on him."

"Too bad he had to go to Vietnam."

"Yes, and I hope and pray God keeps him safe."

★   ★   ★

Prue was sitting at her desk in her new apartment. Her diary was in front of her, and she looked around the spacious room with the enormous windows that looked down on Chicago. She still did not feel as comfortable in it as she had in her small apartment, but at Kent's insistence she had taken it. "You can afford it," he said, "after selling eighteen pictures in your first show. I think that's a record."

All the rooms in the apartment were large and were painted a pure, crisp white. The ceilings were white, also, and had little swirls etched into them and were adorned with sparkles that caught the glints of the sunlight coming through the large window beside her desk. The desk was made of wood, painted black, and had been placed in a corner behind the large dining area, and a black and brass desk lamp sat perched on the upper left corner. She glanced around the room and took in the black iron and glass dining table, the black chairs, the black-and-white tile floor, and the all-white kitchen, far too modernistic for her taste at first, but Prue had come to like the clean look and feel of the place. Looking to her left, her eyes took in the sunken living room area. It was covered with a red and black carpet and was furnished with red and black furniture. Huge plants in glossy black containers decorated the corners of the room, as well as the entrance to the long hallway leading to the bedroom and the bathroom. Along one wall was a built-in mirrored shelf unit that held Prue's small supply of books, and here she had placed some of her prized mementos from her home in the Ozarks. The walls had had abstract paintings hanging on them when she had moved into the apartment, but now the walls were filled with an array of pictures that she herself had painted.

She was writing a letter to Mark:

Dear Mark,

I wrote you about the success of my first show. Well, I don't know how to tell you what I've been feeling lately. You may find out sometime, but I've become a little bit famous. Isn't that funny? Gangly, shy Prudence Deforge, a famous artist. It scared me a little at first when the art critics would come to interview me, but I did what Kent said. I just told them the truth. Some of them think I'm putting on a country act, which amuses me, but I had my picture on the cover of a magazine! It was called Art News, *and it said under it, "The new genius of the art world." I thought that was ridiculous, Mark, but it did make me feel very good.*

She wrote on page after page, pouring herself out. She hesitated, then wrote:

One thing I don't like about all this. I'm getting invited out all the time now, and mostly by men who want to date me. You remember Maxine Baker in high school? She was so

pretty, and she was elected Miss Stone County, then later
became Miss Arkansas. She told me one time that she didn't
know whether men were asking her out because she was
Maxine or because she was Miss Arkansas. Well, I feel like
that. I had to get a private phone number I was getting so
many calls. I haven't gone out with any of them though. I
don't think they're interested in me, just in what I do. And
that's not right. People should be admired for who they are,
not for what they do.

Her fingers grew tired, and finally she wrote:

I must close. I got a call from Bobby yesterday. He's going
to be in Chicago, and I'm going to his concert. I'm worried
about him, Mark. You know what he's like. He's real
famous, but it hasn't made him happy.

I never stop thinking about you, Mark, and I'll never stop
praying for you either. Almost every night I think about the
last night we had back home when you kissed me—or when I
kissed you, I guess would be closer to the truth—back by the
creek. I wish we were there right now. We will be someday.

She started to put "With warm regards," and finally just
signed it, "Love, Prue." As she sealed the envelope, she
thought about how many thousands of miles it had to go and
wondered if it would ever catch up with Mark. A sense of sadness came to her as she thought of him and so many thousands
of young Americans risking death and undergoing tremendous hardships. As she held the letter she breathed another
prayer, "Oh, Lord, keep him safe. Bring him home again!"

★　　★　　★

Prue had not exaggerated the change in her lifestyle. She
could no longer go down to the studio and work under the
tutelage of Maxwell as before. Now that she had become a

successful professional artist, the students all went out of their way to get closer to her. Somehow they seemed to feel that her success was transferable, that somehow she could make them successful too. Students who had never spoken to her before the show now showed every intention of becoming her good friend. Prue found this disgusting and finally had to stop going to the studio except after hours.

She had complained about this to Kent, who had said, "That's the way of the world. The crowd worships success, and you might as well get used to it."

Prue felt she would never grow accustomed to it, and she threw herself into her work. Kent asked her, more than once, if she had changed her mind about marrying him, and she had difficulty answering him. The man had done so much for her, made her a new life practically, and Prue found it hard to hurt anyone.

In her diary she had written: "I wish I could love Kent, but I don't really, and I don't know how to tell him so. He's so lonely, and I'd give anything if he could find a woman he could share his life with—but I know in my heart it won't be me."

The fruits of success had been great. She had a bank account now and had bought a car—not the sports car that Kent had urged her to buy but a rather sedate Chevrolet that she liked very much. She had never been one to like clothes very much, but now she enjoyed going shopping once in a while, although her tastes were simple, and she did not have to go to Saks or one of the other expensive stores.

She wrote home to her parents regularly and spent much time with Jake and his family and Christie and Mario. She had a great sense of family, Prue Deforge did, and sometimes the longing to go back home and find the peace and tranquillity of the mountains became overwhelming. She did go back once on a quick visit just for a few days and found that word of her success had preceded her. She was invited to homes that she had never even seen the inside of before, and everyone seemed eager to have her as a guest.

Finally she had said to her father, "Dad, I liked it better before. All these invitations. They don't really mean anything."

"I'm glad you see it that way, Prue, and I'm glad to see that you haven't changed." Dent's eyes twinkled and he said, "Except to become rich, healthy, and good-looking."

"Oh, Dad, don't say that!"

"Well, it's better than being poor, sick, and ugly, isn't it?" He laughed. Then he came over and put his arm around her. His eyes were soft, and he said, "I can't tell you how proud I am of you, Prue. Your mother and I, it's all we can do to keep from crowing like roosters. As a matter of fact, I do quite a bit, and she has to keep me down."

Prue hugged him. "Thank you, Dad. It's always so good to know I can come here, and you and Mom haven't changed."

"Have you heard much from Mark?" Dent asked.

"I write him a lot, but his answers come pretty spaced out. I know that he doesn't have time to write, and I know he's not telling me the truth about how bad it is over there."

Seeing the worry in his daughter's eyes, Dent said quietly, "Well, your mother and I are praying for him." He hesitated, then said, "You love that fellow, don't you? I think you always have."

"Yes, Dad. I guess I have." She could not lie to her father, for the two were very close. She twisted her hands nervously and said, "I spend a lot of sleepless nights worrying about him."

"We pray for him every day," Dent said. "We'll just have to put him in God's hands."

★　　★　　★

Bobby Stuart grinned broadly as Prue opened the door, and he stood there, his auburn hair long and his eyes sleepy. "Well, it's my famous relative, Prudence Deforge. The greatest artist since Michelangelo or anybody else."

"Bobby! Come in," Prue said. She took his hands, and he leaned over and kissed her on the cheek.

"How have you been, Prue?"

The two sat down and talked for a long time. Bobby listened and kept his blue-green eyes fixed on the young woman's face. She was excited, and there was a difference in her.

"You're different, Prue," he said, when she finally stopped.

Startled, Prue said, "You mean because I've had success?"

"I guess that's part of it. Success is a dangerous thing." A frown clouded his eyes, and he passed a hand over his forehead. "In a way, I think it's different than drugs."

Prue stared at him, knowing that he had had his troubles with drugs. It had been well enough publicized. She saw the unhappiness in his face and said quietly, "What's wrong, Bobby?"

"Same old thing. I'm on a merry-go-round, and I can't seem to get off. That's what success does," he said glumly. He leaned back in the overstuffed chair and closed his eyes. "Everybody loves you. Everybody wants a piece of you, but they don't really. It's not you they want. It's something else."

"I know," Prue said quietly. "I've had a little taste of that."

"You're going to get more. It's just beginning for you." Stuart now was past his first youth. He was in his thirties, with years of success in concerts and films, and his records were selling by the millions. He had all that a man could want— but still there was an air of unhappiness and uncertainty. He never showed this, Prue understood, in public, but now in the quietness of her apartment she saw the lines on his face and the twitching of his mouth, which indicated unhappiness somehow.

Bobby sat up, and leaned over, and took her hand, holding

it for a moment. "You're a special person, Prue. You're not like everyone else." He hesitated, not mentioning the fact that he had run through dozens of young women and some not so young. They had been readily available, and now he said, "Women seem to lose their minds, or their hearts, or something. They go crazy over rock stars. I'd give anything to find one woman like you that's real. Prue, you're good-looking enough to tempt any man. I'm just trying to tell you that right now you're standing on the brink. You're going to be tested more than you know."

"Oh, Bobby, I don't think—"

"I know. You think you can handle it. I thought I could too. But it's strange about power, and money, and fame. They get in your blood just like heroin or alcohol. You don't ever intend to get caught up in it, but you do. How many Hollywood stars do you know who are still plain, simple folks?"

"Well, there's Jimmy Stewart—"

"That's one. Now name ten more. Five more for that matter." He shook his head and grinned ruefully. "You can't, can you?" He sat there quietly, and the two talked long into the night. Prue had known he was unhappy but had never plumbed the depths of his misery. He was overweight now, and hard living had marked him. She noticed that his hands began to tremble after about an hour, and when he got up and said, "Well, I've got to go," she knew he was headed for a bottle or drugs of some kind.

"Bobby," she said, standing up and moving before him, "isn't there some way you can change your life?"

"Did you ever know anybody to change their life, to throw away millions of dollars and everything the world has to offer?" His voice was bitter, and he suddenly leaned forward and kissed her cheek. He hesitated, then said, "Don't change, Prue. Please don't change. It's too late for me, but I'd hate to see anything happen to you. I think too much of you—and of Mark."

He turned and walked away abruptly, and Prue understood

that drugs had created a craving in him. When the door shut, she felt the tears rise in her eyes, and for a long time she felt miserable and defeated. The thoughts of Mark fighting in Vietnam came to her, and she whispered aloud, "Mark's not in any more danger than you are, Bobby."

18

MEN OF HONOR

The segment of the Los Angeles Police Department that housed the vice squad was busy, as always. The large space, which most of the detectives used for their work, was cluttered with desks, chairs, computers, and telephones that seemed to ring incessantly. Some officers wearing their guns and shoulder holsters would speak in a staccato voice over their phone, slam the receiver back into the cradle, then plunge into the debris of paperwork that covered their desk. A constant hum of voices would, at times, lift into what amounted to a roar, but the officers had become so accustomed to it that they paid it little heed.

From time to time, informers and witnesses would appear, stepping through the large door on the east end of the room, and Lieutenant Mario Scarlotti had long since noticed that no matter why they came, a look of guilt and fear usually leaped into their eyes. Scarlotti had stepped out of his office, just momentarily, and his hard, gray eyes swept the room, ticking off his squad, making notes somewhere deep in his brain for future reference. His very presence was enough to cause a furor of activity on the part of several officers who had been standing at the water fountain, laughing and telling jokes. They scurried back to their desks trying to look serious, which was not difficult. All of them had heard Scarlotti peel the potato of several of the vice squad's detectives, and they knew that it was not his policy to call a man to one side. He read him off where he caught him, even if it was in the middle of the squad room, and his voice could carry for two country miles.

"Sergeant! Come into my office!"

"Yes, sir." A tall, thin officer with a Russian nine millimeter in a clipped holster on his belt rose with alacrity and kicked his desk chair back in a sudden motion. He had light blue eyes, a crown of brown hair leaving most of his scalp bare, and a thin mustache over a rather narrow mouth. Otto Krugman knew his superior well, and he wasted no time crossing the room toward the door.

"Time for the boss to straighten you out, Otto." Larry Taylor grinned. "You've been gettin' out of line lately. Tell him to go chase himself."

"I'll let you tell him that, Larry," Krugman said. "You had a pretty full life, I guess." Reaching the door, he stepped inside the office that, unlike the squad room, was completely uncluttered. It was a room not more than twelve feet square, the furniture being a single desk with a straight-backed chair behind it and another straight-backed chair placed exactly in front of it. The desktop contained an in-and-out basket, double stacked, a gold Cross pen and pencil lying on a pad in front of Lieutenant Scarlotti, and nothing more.

Keeps that desk stripped for action, Krugman thought as he came forward and sat down opposite the chief of the vice squad. He was the only man in the unit who faced Lieutenant Mario Scarlotti without apprehension. The two of them had been partners for a long time—both having served together as uniformed officers in a patrol car. Being a uniformed patrolman in the city of Los Angeles tended to either make men hate each other or trust each other completely, and so it was with Krugman and Scarlotti. They did not socialize, for they were almost completely different in their habits and lifestyles. However, each of them could remember times going into dark alleys when the other had held his life, and a firm bond of trust had been formed.

"I've been working on the Anderson case—"

"Never mind that, Otto." Scarlotti shook his head. "That's not what I want to talk about." Scarlotti was forty-one years old, and his dark hair was cut short, and his eyes, almost black, were capable of practically burning holes through steel—at least through criminal and recalcitrant police officers! He was a bulky man with a weight lifter's build, and as he placed his hands flat on the desk, Krugman noticed automatically the hard edges along the little finger and the cutting edge of the palm. He well knew that Scarlotti could bust a two-inch oak board with those palms, and he remembered several times when human flesh had broken easier than the oak. He waited silently, knowing his man. Scarlotti took counsel from no one but let plans formulate in his mind until they were complete. Then he would call in his detectives, one at a time, and give them a complete program ready to execute.

"Otto, I'm not happy with the work we've been doing on drugs."

"Nobody is," Krugman shrugged.

"That's right, but they're going to be because I'm going to make a big noise."

"You gonna call in the Marine Corps, Lieutenant? That's what it would take to police just part of this city. You'd have to put an officer in every crack house in the city, and you know how many that is."

"I know." Scarlotti nodded. "It's like trying to keep a ship afloat that's got about fifty holes in it. Every time you plug one, another one starts, and in the meanwhile all you can do is keep bailing." He leaned forward, and his eyes burned with an intense fire. He lived for his department, for his work, and apparently the only joy he got out of life was seeing some criminal put behind bars. It had been the regret of Scarlotti's life that capital punishment had gone out of favor, so that now all he could hope for was long sentences and no paroles. He hated to see men sent to the state penitentiary. He loved the federal prisons, for there was no parole from a federal prison.

Krugman sat there watching the wheels go around, almost, in his chief's eyes. He had learned to read the man, and finally he was rewarded as Scarlotti said, "I'm going to make a big noise, Otto. So big that it'll make every newspaper in the country."

Interested, the sergeant leaned forward. "We going to move in on that Colombian that's set up here? We know he controls the flow of drugs pretty much. If we could nail him."

"We'll get him, but he's not ready yet. We have to have him standing over the body with a smoking gun. No. What I have in mind is something a lot simpler."

A knock came at the door, and Scarlotti lifted his voice. "Get away from that door!" Then without breaking the pattern of his speech, he allowed the corners of his lips to turn up in a smile. This, in another man, would have been the equivalent of a huge burst of laughter, but Otto had scarcely seen Lieutenant Mario Scarlotti laugh. He wondered what was in the man's mind, but whatever it was he knew that it would probably work. Scarlotti did not sponsor failures in the department, and Krugman knew this was something that the lieutenant had worked out completely.

"We're going to bust Bobby Stuart."

The statement came as a mild shock to Otto Krugman. He digested the essence of it, then shook his head. "From what I hear, it shouldn't be too hard to set him up."

"We don't have to set him up. I've already had an inside man looking at the thing. He's doping all the time now. If we can nail him, that'll pass a message along to the young people of this country."

Krugman wanted to argue. He wanted to say, "How many rock stars have already been busted, and how many kids have quit doping because of it?" He had long ago learned that once Scarlotti had his mind made up, it would take an act of Congress to stop him. So he simply said, "How are we going to work it?"

Leaning forward slightly and picking up the gold Cross

pen, Scarlotti stroked it with his forefinger and thumb. It seemed to give him a sensual pleasure, and his eyes were almost dreamy as he said, "It'll be in every tabloid and newspaper in the country." Then he blinked and began to speak rapidly. "Here's what we'll do, Otto. . . ."

★   ★   ★

The party was at Ossie Peabody's house, and it had been limited to no more than twenty people, but each one of these twenty seemed to have brought a friend so that the house was packed with partyers. Ossie moved among his guests wearing a pair of chinos and a lavender T-shirt with the sleeves cut completely out. He was sleek and smooth and, as most of the others, his eyes were glazed. He murmured greetings to several guests and stopped once to put his arm around a young woman and whisper something in her ear. She looked up at him, gave him a blinding smile, and nodded with promise in her eyes. Moving on, Peabody stopped at the bar, and a young Filipino dressed in a white uniform served him a glass of brandy. He tossed it back and sat on the stool surveying the room, which was filled with smoke.

"Good party, man." Bobby Stuart had come up to stand beside the drummer, and the two spoke for a time about various guests. Finally Peabody looked over at Stuart, and something troubled him. "You look washed out, babe," he said, shaking his head. He leaned forward and examined Bobby's eyes carefully. He noted the pale lips and then the trembling of the hands. "I think you maybe had enough," he said under his breath. "You don't look too good."

"Must have gotten some bad dope," Bobby said. He knew that he had drunk too much, and when one of the guests had offered him some pills that promised the biggest kick he had ever had, he had taken them. It had provided a sharp uplift, but then the effect passed over, and now he felt nauseated. "I think I'm going to be sick," he muttered.

"Come on, babe." Ossie Peabody was the self-appointed caretaker of Bobby Stuart. He had been with him longer than anyone else, and only he was aware of the deep depression that seized Bobby periodically. It was Ossie who nursed him through some screaming fits that came after bad drugs, and now he took Bobby Stuart's arm and piloted him through the crowd. He had almost reached the door of his bedroom when suddenly he was aware of shouting and screaming. Wheeling quickly, his eyes narrowing, he saw men piling in through the door and muttered, "Uh-oh! It's a bust, Bobby! Somebody here must be a snitch. Quick, empty your pockets of those pills."

It was too late. Stuart was growing sicker by the moment. The room was swimming, and the pills he was holding dropped to the floor. He was aware of a tall, bulky man with a pair of dark foreboding eyes who had come to stand before him. "You're under arrest, Mr. Stuart, for possession of a controlled substance."

"Hey, man. It's just a party—" Ossie began. But one glance from those eyes, which were almost reptilian, shut him off. He recognized Mario Scarlotti, and said under his breath, "We're in it now, Bobby. This is one tough cop!"

Bobby reached for his wallet. He was ready to throw up, and his head was spinning. Taking out a roll of bills, he shoved it toward the policeman and said, "Here, Lieutenant. Go buy yourself a Cadillac."

Ossie whispered frantically, "Shut up, man!" He jerked the arm back, but it was too late. Scarlotti took the money, then turned to face Ossie. "It'll be nice to have you witness against your friend. The charge now is bribing a policeman. Come along."

"I gotta—call my lawyer."

"Oh, I'm sure you'll have plenty of law there downtown. You can make your call, and you can have a bank of lawyers." Scarlotti's eyes narrowed. "But you're going down on this one, Stuart."

As Bobby was escorted outside, each of his arms in an iron grip of burly policemen, he threw a desperate glance at Ossie Peabody, but for once the self-assurance was gone. Ossie dropped his eyes and shook his head, and Bobby Stuart knew that he was in bad trouble.

★ ★ ★

The courtroom of Judge Bess Fryerson was perhaps the most controlled space in the city of Los Angeles. Judge Fryerson was a small woman of fifty with iron gray hair and direct blue-gray eyes, which she put on Bobby Stuart now as he came to stand before her. She was a wife, a mother, a grandmother, and had been elected mother of the year two years earlier. Those outside of the courtroom knew her for her charm, for her generosity, and for her willingness to help in any cause that was worthy. She was widely admired by almost everyone—except those unfortunate men and women who came to stand before her as Bobby Stuart now did.

"She's not a hanging judge," one of the lawyers had told his client. "That's too slow. She's a guillotine judge, and heads have rolled out of her courtroom by the bushel baskets."

"Do you have anything to say before I pass sentence?"

Bobby had been well drilled by his lawyer, Errol Baker—Baker, at least, was one of his lawyers. As Lieutenant Scarlotti prophesied, the bust had been highly publicized; the bail had been set at one million dollars, which Bobby had managed to make, and he had been on the program of good behavior ever since his arrest. Baker had told him, however, "It's like locking the door after the chickens have been stolen, Bobby. The damage is done, and that dear lady is going to throw the book at you."

As Bobby stood before Judge Fryerson, his mind seemed to scramble frantically. *How did I get into all this?* he thought. *I can't go to prison. It would kill me!* He looked up at the judge with a speech ready, the one that Baker had grilled him on, but somehow nothing came. The trial had proved conclusively that Bobby had been guilty of using drugs, although Baker had foiled the attempt to prove that he had been selling them. This was ridiculous, for he had never sold anyone any sort of drug in all his life. He wanted to say, "Judge, you can't put everybody in jail in Los Angeles that uses drugs," but that thought died stillborn, and he remembered Baker's admonition. "Don't try to sweet-talk that lady on the bench. Don't try to outthink her. Don't try anything. Just tell her that you are guilty of using drugs, and you didn't know what you were doing when you were offering Scarlotti a bribe."

"Your honor," Bobby said, his voice so thin that those spectators in the rear of the courtroom had to lean forward, "I've pleaded guilty to attempting to bribe a police officer, and, of course, I was on drugs when I did it." The eyes of Judge Fryerson bored into his, and panic came to him. *She's going to put me in jail for a hundred years.* He cleared his throat, then shook his head. "I was drunk, your honor, or I would never have tried such a thing. I don't even really remember it. I know that's no excuse, but it's all I've got. I—I would ask for you to show leniency."

Judge Fryerson had been prepared for more than this. She had never known a rock star, and all during the trial she had been mildly shocked by the manners of Bobby Stuart. He was quiet and subdued, not at all the smiling, frenzied young man she had seen on her screen so often. Secretly she was an admirer of rock music, and Bobby Stuart had been her favorite.

She had also been aware of Stuart's family, for his father, Jerry, and his mother, Bonnie, had been in the courtroom and had served as character witnesses. She had also been aware of Bobby's twin brother, Richard, whom she had met and whose work she knew. He was a genuine young man, Richard Stuart. The judge had pondered over the two young men whose pathways had gone in such different directions. Judge Fryerson had become interested in the family and was impressed with their credentials. Many of the Stuart men had served their country in the wars, and most of them were exemplary citizens, with the exception of Stephen Stuart, who had spent some time in prison.

All of this passed through Judge Fryerson's mind. She had fought with her own conscience, for she never allowed sentiment to interfere with her sentences. Now, however, she looked at the young man who was waiting, his head held high and his lips pulled tight in a line of fear. She wondered if her original idea had been the best. She had a mind that worked like chain lightning, and sitting there she made an instant shift toward a much lighter sentence.

"Mr. Stuart, you've been tried and found guilty, and there is no question of that decision. Your plea that you were under the influence of alcohol and drugs is nothing to the point." Judge Fryerson hesitated, her eyes turning toward Jerry and Bonnie Stuart. She saw the agony in their eyes and wondered what it was like, as a parent, to be in their position.

"You have more responsibility than most men, for all over this country young people look to you. You have failed miserably to show them what a man of honor should be. . . ."

Bobby stood there facing the judge as his lawyer had instructed him, keeping his eyes on hers, and shame filled him as she continued to enumerate the failures of his life. Despair came to him then, for he could see but one end.

Finally Judge Fryerson said, "I sentence you to five years in the penitentiary." She waited until the murmur had gone over the room, for it was a stiff sentence for a celebrity. She saw Bobby Stuart's mother drop her head and knew that she was weeping; then she said, "Against my better judgment, I am suspending your sentence, and you will do community service during the period of your sentence." She saw relief wash over the face of Bobby Stuart, and she leaned forward and said, "Mr. Stuart, I know this sounds very good to you right now, but I will be in touch with your parole officers. I am going to work closely with them, and let me say, if you step outside the line one time—one drug offense, one charge of any sort—you will be inside prison walls, and you will serve all of your term. Is that clear, Mr. Stuart?"

"Yes, your honor," Bobby whispered, "—and thank you for your leniency."

Once again the judge looked over at Bobby's parents. "You have a fine family, and you have been a disgrace to them." The judge's voice rang like cold steel, not loud, but it entered into Bobby Stuart's soul like a sword. "I am giving you a chance to become a decent, respectable member of this family. It will be your last chance, I think, Mr. Stuart." Judge Fryerson picked up her gavel and smote the surface of the desk in front of her. "This court is dismissed!"

Bobby turned blindly, tears in his eyes, as his lawyer whispered in his ear, "It's great, Bobby! It's great! Couldn't have been better."

But Bobby paid no attention, for his parents were there, his mother's arms around his neck and tears on her cheeks. He looked into his father's eyes and saw the relief—but he could feel only shame. Others came, and he did not hear them, for he was saying deep in his heart, *I can't take another fall. I couldn't stand it—and neither could my family.*

★ ★ ★

Corporal Mark Stevens had become reconciled to the fact that the men who ran the war did not themselves understand it. When General Westmoreland had been asked to comment, he had said, "This is a different war than the Americans have ever been asked to fight." When asked, "How is it different?" he had sputtered, "It's just different."

The Battle of Hue had been a hellish struggle for individual and corporate survival. It was not the bloodiest battle of the Vietnam War, but it was the hardest and bitterest, and even the coldest chronicles somehow revealed the white-hot fury of the battle that had raged.

Now, after Hue, there had been some lessening of the pressure, and Mark was sitting on the ground with three members of his squad wondering how they had made it through alive. He studied the face of Harold Stasom, the tall, blond wheat farmer from Minnesota; his glance moved to Johnnie Mayfield, a minor league pitcher for the Arkansas Travelers, and finally to Ike Cantor, an aluminum siding salesman from Detroit. The four of them were survivors, and bitterness rose up in Mark as he thought of the men who were not here but who had been carried away in body bags for burial back in the States.

The jungle around them brooded, it seemed, with some sort of tenacious threat that never left. Mark had forgotten what a full night's sleep was like, and glancing at the strained faces of his buddies, he knew they were all stretched out tight.

Johnnie Mayfield was speaking of his days as a pitcher. He was a left-hander, and said, "I'm gonna play for the Washington Senators one of these days. You guys will say, 'I knew him when he was only a hero in Nam.'"

The others all grinned, and Ike Cantor said, "I guess I must not have been there. When was all this heroic stuff that you pulled?"

"Why, you just don't pay attention, Ike. I must have saved your life at least a dozen times, and you never even noticed."

Ike Cantor summoned a grin and shook his head, saying nothing. He had a wife back in Detroit and a baby son he had never seen; Mark knew that his mind was preoccupied with his family, and he wished that the mail would come with good news.

Harold Stasom picked up a handful of dirt and let it run through his fingers. He watched the thick, gray soil as it fell to the ground and said in a discouraged voice, "I'd hate to try and farm this land."

"Tell us again about that farm of yours," Johnnie Mayfield said. "We haven't heard it but about a thousand times."

"Go on and laugh." Stasom shook his head. "It's all I want. Just let me get back to that farm and grow some wheat."

The four men sat there knit together by the dangers and horrors of war. Finally after a time, Captain Sipes appeared, walked over, and stood looking down at the four men, keeping them at ease. "How's it going, Corporal?"

"Fine, Captain." Mark nodded. He was aware of the officer's eyes fixed on him, and he tried to sit up straighter. Lately he had been falling asleep even with his mess kit full of food. That was during the daylight hours, but during the night he often had nightmares, and Stasom or Mayfield would have to hold him down until they passed.

Sipes finally said, "That's good." He turned, walked away, and went at once to the command tent, where he found a short, stocky lieutenant named William Jefferson. "Lieutenant," he said, "I think Stevens has gone almost his limit."

Jefferson looked up in surprise. "Why, he's the best man we've got in the company. Always out there on point, ready for any patrol."

"I think he's pushed himself too hard. Look at his eyes sometime." Sipes nodded. "He looks just like Bristol did before he went off the deep end."

Lieutenant Jefferson paused, thinking. He finally scratched his bearded face and said, "You're right about that. I had noticed he's moving slower, but we all are."

"Well, just keep your eye on him." He hesitated, then said, "I want him sent to R and R just as soon as this next patrol is over."

"Yes, sir, and the rest of the squad too?"

Sipes hesitated. "I think we can work that. They've been together a long time. Yes, set it up right after this next patrol."

"Shouldn't be much of a problem. Don't expect any VCs in that area."

★　　★　　★

Moving carefully through the jungle under the tall trees, Mark was strangely at ease. He was happy, or as close as he had come to it in some time, for Lieutenant Jefferson had prompted him. "Just one more milk run of the patrol, Mark, then you and the rest of the squad go back of the lines for R and R." He had grinned, seeing the light in Mark's eyes. "You could use a little of that. I guess we all could."

Now as they moved forward, Mark walked upright, and his eyes were not as alert as they should have been, for the lieutenant had spoken of this patrol as being mere routine. They were fanned out but came to a thick portion of jungle with one trail. "I'll take the point," he called out, and he watched as the squad formed behind him. He started moving through the trees, looking up at the sun that glittered through, almost blinding him. He thought suddenly of Prue and wondered what she was doing at this exact moment. He had learned to take refuge in thoughts of his family, and now as he seemed to see her strong features, her dark eyes, and black hair, a smile touched his lips.

The shattering outburst of fire came as such a shock that for one split second he could not think; then his training came to his aid and he whirled, saying, "Ambush! Take cover!"

But then as he looked down the line, he saw all three of the other squad had been cut down by the automatic fire. He saw a flash of movement up in a tree and opened up on it. He saw one body fall but had no more time. The fire was increasing, and he ran back and fell down beside Harold Stasom. "Harold!" he cried out. He rolled the man over and saw that a bullet had taken him in the temple. Stasom's eyes were open, and Mark knew he was dead. Rage and anger came to Mark then as it never had, but he moved along until he found the other two men, Mayfield and Cantor, also dead. Madness came to Mark Stevens then. He was aware of shouts from behind him, that help was coming, but he straightened up, walked back into the fire of the VC, shooting when he saw a flash of movement knowing that he was a dead man, but not caring. The loss of his three friends had pushed him over the edge, and he wanted to kill every Vietcong he could before they got him.

He never knew when he went down; he felt no pain at all. One moment he heard the sound of firing as the sun was coming through the trees in golden bars; then he was firing his automatic weapon, and finally there was nothing.

★   ★   ★

He heard voices murmuring very close to him, but when he opened his eyes he could not see. "Why is it so dark?" he said. Instantly hands were on his chest, but they could not hold him. He reached up and found that his head was bandaged but not his eyes.

"Take it easy, Marine!" The voice was steady, but Mark was filled with panic. "Why can't I see?"

"Don't worry. I'm Doctor Johnson. You took a wound in your head, and it's disturbed your vision."

"But I'm blind! I can't see anything!"

The two doctors that bent over Mark stared at each other. Doctor Johnson shook his head as the other started to speak. "These things happen sometimes. Probably the optic nerve has been jarred."

Mark let the hands force him back down on the cot, and Doctor Johnson said, "Just lie still. You're not badly hurt, Stevens, and your vision will come back."

Mark lay back. He could hear the activities in the field hospital. In his mind he could see the bodies of Mayfield, Stasom, and Cantor all dead, and yet he was alive. He was not aware of it, but tears began to flow from his eyes and run down his temples.

Johnson continued with his work, and an hour later Captain Sipes came to his office. "How is Stevens, Doc?"

"I can't figure it out." Johnson shook his head. "He got a pretty bad head wound; we had to put some bones together and a little steel plate in, but he says he can't see. I can't figure it."

"Were his eyes harmed?"

"Not a bit of it. Be careful. Go on in and see him. Try to reassure him. I don't think it's physical, although I can't be sure until we get an X-ray."

Sipes nodded, then went down the hall to the ward. He moved down the row of cots, saw Stevens, and went over and sat down. "Well, Mark, I'm glad to see you made it." He tried to make his voice cheerful, but there was something wrong. Something dreadfully wrong. "How do you feel?"

"They're all dead," Mark whispered.

Sipes knew what was going on in Stevens' mind. *These fellows go through so much they're like brothers*, he thought. He bit his lip then said, "I'm afraid so, Mark."

"They're all dead—and I'm alive. Why's that, Captain?"

"Nobody knows about these things." Sipes laid his hand on Mark's shoulder and said, "You've got to pull yourself out of this, Mark. You'll be going home before long. You'll be all right then."

Mark's eyes were open, but they were staring blindly to the left of Captain Sipes. There was something disconcerting about it, and Sipes could not speak for a time. He did not know how to talk to this man who had suffered the loss of his three closest friends in an instant. Finally he said, "Well, you just have to go from where you are, son."

"All dead except me," Mark whispered. Bitterness changed his voice, and he lifted his head and stared with blind eyes at the wall, saying, "I deserve to be dead—not just blind!"

Part 4

HARVESTTIME
(1969)

19

"WHAT GOOD AM I TO ANYBODY?"

D
ecades get old just as do the human beings that dwell
in them. The sixties seemed to age suddenly. In 1968
violence scored the nation bringing grief to hearts everywhere. Martin Luther King was assassinated, and Robert
Kennedy was shot to death while pursuing the presidency of
the United States.

Lyndon Johnson, worn down by the increasing pressures
against the Vietnam conflict, refused to run again, knowing,
no doubt, that he would be soundly defeated. His refusal to
run spurred a hot contest for the presidency, which was won
by Richard Nixon but only after the Democratic convention
was torn by vicious riots on the floor of the great hall.

Those looking for good news were cheered when Apollo 8
orbited the moon, and for a time, at least, America had genuine heroes to look up to.

The last year of the decade was not a happy one. As a matter of course, the great ones passed away from the scene, including the great novelist John Steinbeck and the great leader
of World War II Dwight Eisenhower.

The world seemed to deviate into violence. Cuban skyjack-
ings became epidemic, and violence raged in Ireland. Bombs
ripped marketplaces in Jerusalem as Yasir Arafat led the Pal-
estinian forces in the never-ending battle in the Middle East.
To offset this man, Golda Meir became the fourth Premier of
Israel, the first woman ever to serve in such an office.

All over the broad land of America things seemed to be

falling apart. The old ways were maintained by a remnant, but homes and marriages were under attack by movements that seemed determined to replace the Judeo-Christian ethic with a morality that was almost nonexistent. The beer commercial that became famous was "You only get one trip around, so live it with all the gusto you can!" License plates began to appear urging people "If it feels good—do it!"

As the century wound down, the people of God were searching desperately for a foundation, something that would keep their children and grandchildren from following the pathways that led to destruction. Billy Graham preached to more people than any other man in history. His message was so simple that many learned theologians looked down upon him, but wherever he went, when he spoke the words, "I want you to get up out of your seats . . ." people rose and came flooding to the front of the arenas to give their hearts to Jesus Christ. It seemed to many that though it was a dark hour in America's history, still, the light of God's promises was there waiting to be seized. Many hoped for a sweeping revival, not only in America but in the whole world.

★   ★   ★

As always, when Mark first awoke, panic shot through him like a bolt of lightning. All his life he had awakened quickly from even the soundest sleep, opening his eyes totally aware of his surroundings. Now, however, as he opened his eyes and the world remained black as ebony, terror ripped through him. Lying there with his eyes wide open, his body tense, and a screaming in his mind, he heard a sound of music, and time and place came rushing back to him.

Marty Robbins was crooning "El Paso," the singer's fruity voice made metallic by the cheap radio that Oscar Tatum kept by his bedside. Slowly Mark relaxed, and as the panic disappeared it was replaced by bitterness. He rolled over and buried his face in the pillow, almost like a child who had been threatened with punishment. But he could not shut out the sound of the country western song, and soon Robbins was replaced by Johnny Cash singing "A Boy Named Sue." Rolling over and sitting up, Mark waited for Oscar to speak, and when his roommate's voice came, rich and thick with the sounds of Mississippi, he knew there would be no sleep left.

"Climb out of that bed, Mark! Time to go get us some bray-fuss." Ossie could not seem to pronounce *breakfast* correctly. In his slurred, southern dialect, the word, along with others, was almost unintelligible.

"I don't want any breakfast," Mark muttered. He groped around on the table beside his bed for the glass, and with his other hand managed to find the water pitcher. He poured some water, drank it thirstily, then stood up and began his pilgrimage to the bathroom that he and Oscar shared with two other patients. Oscar said, "Sho you want bray-fuss! We gonna have ham, and eggs, and grits. That no'count cook done promised me grits. Hard to find grits in Chicago, but he said he'd come up with some."

Ignoring Oscar's cheerful prattle, Mark felt the wall until he touched the edges of the doorway to the bathroom and then moved to the sink. He had been at the Veterans Hospital in Chicago for only three days, and they had not been happy ones. He opened the door of the medicine chest, pulled out his safety razor and a can of aerated shaving cream, and put them beside the faucet. He filled the sink with water, found the fresh washcloth where it always was, and the soap. He washed his face, listening as he had to as Oscar turned the radio up; Roy Acuff was singing the classic "Great Speckled Bird." Mark winced at the whiny voice of the star of the Grand Ole Opry and tried to shut it out.

Grasping the shaving cream can, he squirted some in his right hand and applied it to his face. He groped until he found the razor again and began shaving. He found himself struggling, peering ahead trying to see the mirror, but all was black as the deepest midnight. He had discovered how hard it was to shave; this had come as a shock to him as had many things. He was so accustomed to looking into the mirror that it was second nature, and now he found that his blindness made the act of shaving even more difficult than others. He managed to cut his chin, but he finally washed off the shaving cream, put the razor and soap back into the cabinet, and found the comb. He ran it through his hair carelessly, again finding himself looking in the mirror. *What do you expect to see?* he asked himself bitterly. *You're blind as a bat, and what does it matter what you look like?*

Finishing his abusing, he returned to the room and managed to drive the toes of his right foot against his bed. He cried out sharply in pain, then caught his breath.

"You better watch where you're goin', Mark," Oscar said quickly.

Mark felt the man's touch on his arm, and violently shrugged away from him. "I don't need any help!" he said.

"Of course you don't. You get into yo clothes, and we'll go get some bray-fuss."

Mark put on his summer uniform and felt around until his hand encountered the cane that was propped against the wall. Oscar said, "Let's go, Marine," and Mark heard him moving across the floor. He had never seen Oscar Tatum, but he could tell that he was a big man by the sound of his feet, and when he had shaken hands with him it was like putting his hand in a wrench. Oscar had broken the ice by saying, "Maybe you don't like black folks."

Mark had summoned a grin, saying, "When you're blind, there aren't any black folks."

"Guess that's right. Maybe we ought to blind everybody that don't like folks whose skin is different."

"That wouldn't be the answer," Mark had said. "What's in a man's heart is there whether they can see or not."

Oscar had tried to get acquainted with Mark but had found it difficult. Time and again he tried to talk about Mark's problem, but Mark had shut him down shortly, leaving nothing to be said.

As they moved down the hall, Mark was aware of the sounds of voices and of footsteps on the tile floor. He had discovered that his hearing had sharpened. He had always heard that when you lose one sense the others kick in to compensate, and now he realized that he could hear the thin, tinny voice of Charlie Masterson even though the marine was probably fifty feet behind him and dozens of others were talking loudly. Masterson was talking about the women that he had had in Chicago before he had gone into the Marines, and Mark picked up every word of it.

As they moved along, Mark kept the cane in front of him, but he was aware that Oscar was staying close beside him. He wasn't putting his hand on him, just walking so close that their arms brushed. Mark knew this was the big marine's way of offering help without seeming to do so, and he had a quick surge of gratitude but said nothing.

Skillfully Oscar managed to lead the way to the line of men who were going to pick up their food. He handed Mark a plate and flatware, talking rapidly about the days when he had played defensive guard for Old Miss.

Mark moved down the line with his plate out and felt the weight of food being put in it. When he got to the end of the line, Oscar saw to it that he had a mug of coffee, then said, "There's two places over there." Mark felt, as always, as he walked across the floor that he was about to step off a precipice or into a wall, but somehow when he got to the table with Oscar's help, he found himself seated and propped the cane against the seat.

"I'm gonna go get us some of them grits that no'count cook promised. You wait right here."

Mark sat there listening to the talk of the patients around him. They sounded happier than they should have, for he knew from his brief stay there that some of them were terribly wounded. Some were on crutches, and some were in wheelchairs, but cut off as he was by his lack of sight, he had difficulty keeping them straight. He had heard of blind people who knew voices so well they could recognize people after meeting them only once, but that was not true of him thus far. He wondered hopelessly if he would ever be able to recognize voices like that.

"Here he is! He done got us some grits!" Oscar's big voice boomed, and Mark felt the table shift as the big man sat down. "Now, here's the drill," Oscar said. "You got eggs at twelve o'clock, hash browns at twelve fifteen, bacon at twelve thirty, jelly over here beside your plate, and toast, and here's your grits right out on the right side."

Mark had learned to hate mealtime. He had not realized how much sight was a part of eating; he touched the plate with his left hand, put his fork down to what he assumed was the top, brought it up, and was disgusted to find it empty. He was certain that Oscar was watching him, but the marine said nothing. Making another try, Mark managed to get a heaping forkful of eggs to his mouth and groped until he found the toast and began to eat.

"How you like them grits? They ain't as good as Mississippi grits, but they're probably good enough for an Arkansas redneck like you, Mark."

Mark thought of the time when someone had made fun of Oscar being from the South. He had not seen what had happened, but there had been a sudden outcry of pain, and the prankster had begged for mercy. "I just squoze his neck a little bit," Oscar had told him. "His mammy didn't learn him no manners, I reckon."

Mark had no appetite and toyed with his food until finally he reached for the orange juice and managed to knock it over.

"Hey, that's all right! I'll get that!" a voice on his right came abruptly, and Mark felt like a fool. He rose, and without saying a word made his way out of the room, managing to bump into a table and upset more eating ware.

Oscar watched as he left and turned to face the patient who had offered to clean up the orange juice. "He ain't doin' no good, Phil."

Phil Quincy looked at Oscar and said, "He's better off than some."

"He sho is, but he don't know that."

"Does he ever talk about how he got blinded?"

"He don't talk about nothin' much. Be better if he would."

Mark left the building, using his cane to tap as he found the big doors that led to the outside. One of the attendants called to him, "You want me to go with you, Marine?" but he didn't answer.

As soon as he was outside, he felt a little better. It was April, and as he moved along the walk he could smell the grass, rich and fragrant, and he heard the sound of a lawn mower going. He had always liked the smell of fresh cut grass, and now he paused for a minute to savor it. The sun beat down on his face, and he looked up at it, his eyes wide open—nothing.

Moving slowly and sweeping in front of him with the tip of the white cane, he was aware of cars passing on the highway. They were a long way off, but he could hear the big diesels as they went into a lower gear to pull up a hill. The thought came to him, *I'll never drive a car again*, and somehow this hit him hard. He had always loved to drive, and now he realized that it was one of those things he had always taken for granted. Since he had lost his sight, every day brought some bitter revelation to him, and now he put that inside the little part of him that stored all the bitterness of things he would never see again.

For twenty minutes, he walked along the perimeters of the hospital, having learned the sidewalks, and finally came to a bench that an attendant had taken him to one time. His cane struck it, and he groped with his other hand until he found it, then slumped down, and holding the cane with both hands on the handle, leaned forward and put his chin down. For a long time he sat there not moving, thoughts running through his mind of days gone by. From time to time he would think of Vietnam, but he had learned quickly to turn away from that and force his mind farther back into the past. He thought of the time Bobby Stuart came to the high school and how the two of them had gone deer hunting.

His thoughts then went to Prue, as they often did. He found that he could picture her in his mind so those memories were clearer than any others. He could call up her strong features, her dark eyes and black hair, and for a time he sat there remembering their days together growing up.

Something suddenly touched his hand. It was wet and cold, and he jerked upright and sat there rigidly. "What's that?"

A muted wuffing sound came, and he realized that it was a dog, a rather large one apparently since his hands had been as high as the crook on his cane. He reached his hand out tentatively and said, "Hello, boy," and instantly a rough tongue began to lick his hand. Putting the cane aside, he reached his other hand over and found himself stroking a massive, broad head. "Must be a big Lab or something like that. A short-hair, anyhow. What are you doing here, boy?" he said, and the dog again said, "Wuff!" and at once reared up and put his feet on Mark's legs and licked him in the face. Mark had always loved dogs, and he allowed the animal to remain in that position; he stroked him, noting the rather stiff, short fur. He thought of the dogs he had had at home during his youth and muttered little endearments to the huge animal.

Finally a voice said, "Max! Come on! Stop bothering people!"

Reluctantly Mark felt the pressure on his legs disappear, and then the dog was gone. "Maybe when I get settled somewhere I can get one of those guide dogs," he murmured. "Even if they're no good for guiding, I'd like to have one."

Time ran on, and twice as he sat there people passed by speaking to him, and he had responded, but they had gone on. He was glad of it, for he had no desire to talk to anyone. After a while he heard a rapid patter of footsteps, and it puzzled him. It sounded like a child, and although he knew children sometimes came to visit, he was somewhat surprised when a youthful voice said, "Hello. What's your name?"

Mark turned his face in the direction of the voice and said, "My name's Mark. What's yours?"

"Heidi. I'm five years old."

"Are you? Well, I'm twenty years older than you are."

"That's old!"

Mark grinned despite himself. "I guess it is. What are you doing here, Heidi?"

"My mummy brought me to see my daddy. She's gone inside now, and she told me to wait here."

Mark felt a small body settle beside him, and turning, he thought he could smell perfume. "You're not wearing perfume, are you?"

"Yes I am. My mummy said I could wear it today. The kind that Daddy likes. What's wrong with you?"

"Oh, I got hurt," Mark said quickly. "Do you go to school?"

"I go to kindergarten. I brought some books. Maybe you'd like to read one to me."

Mark felt a book pressed into his hands, and for a moment could not answer. The girl said, "You can read that one. I like it the best of all."

Mark swallowed, then shook his head. "I'm sorry. I can't do it. I can't read the book for you, Heidi."

"You mean you can't read?"

"No. That's not what I mean. I can't—" He had trouble getting the words out and felt foolish being so backward with a child that he would never see again. "I can't see. I'm blind."

"Oh! I didn't know that! Did you get hurt in the war?"

"Yes, I did."

The child was silent for a moment, then she said, "Well, I'll read it to you, Mark. My mummy's read it to me so much

I know it by heart." Mark felt the book leave his hands, and the child began reading a story about a little train that had difficulty. Something about the little engine that thought he could, thought he could, thought he could. Mark sat there listening as the childish voice went on, and finally the story ended with the little train being successful.

"There! Did you like that?"

"That's a good story."

"Mummy says that if you try hard enough you can do anything you want, but I don't know if that's right or not."

"Better listen to your mummy."

"She says Daddy's going to get well because she's going to ask Jesus to make him well." The voice hesitated, then Mark felt a small hand come and touch him. Turning his hand over, he held the child's smaller one; after a few minutes she said, "Why don't you ask Jesus to let you see?"

Mark could not answer. A thickness came to his throat, and he had to pause and clear it before he could say, "That sounds like a good idea."

"Oh, there's my mummy! I've got to go."

"Thank you for reading the story to me, Heidi."

"That's all right. Now, you be sure to ask Jesus to let you see."

Mark sat there, and as the sound of her footsteps diminished, he thought about what she had said. He was shocked to find that there was a hardness in his heart. Although he had been moved by the child's words, he knew that something was different in him. He was not the same man he had been. He had lost some tenderness, some softness, and now there was a hard wall that seemed to surround him as thoroughly inside as the blackness did outside. He rose and tapped his way along the walk, and as he went he kept hearing the child's voice saying, "Why don't you ask Jesus to let you see?"

★   ★   ★

Dr. James Pennington leaned back in his chair and chewed on the eraser of his yellow pencil. Realizing what he was doing, he looked down with irritation and saw that he had bitten it off. Shaking his head angrily, he tossed the pencil into a wastebasket, yanked open the drawer, and pulled out another from the supply he kept. He tapped the pencil against his open palm and said to the young marine sitting across from him, "Sergeant, I've looked over your X-rays and the reports of all the tests we've made." He hesitated for a moment, giving Mark a chance to speak, but when only silence met him, he said, "We can't find anything organically wrong with your eyes."

"Then why can't I see?" Mark demanded, his voice grinding and hard.

Pennington removed the eraser from between his teeth and tapped it on his palm again. The young marine who sat there was the first case that he had ever had like this. Carefully he said, "As I said, we've done all the tests that we can think of, and there's no reason, physically speaking, why you can't see. There's no point doing more tests, but I want you to see Major Franz."

"The shrink?"

"Well, yes. He is a psychiatrist."

"No thanks!"

Mark's abruptness caught Pennington's attention. "Don't be a fool, Sergeant! He may be able to help you!"

"I don't think so!"

"You're just being stubborn! Look! Have you ever thought about how many of your buddies didn't get back at all, and here you've—"

"You don't have to tell me that! Every one of my patrol was wiped out! I was the only one left!"

Pennington was shocked by the ferocity in the young marine's voice. He had talked with Stevens twice before, and now as he stared at the young man he was baffled. "You can't blame yourself for that. Now look, I want you to see Major Franz today."

"Is that an order, sir?"

Pennington hesitated. If Mark Stevens' trouble lay in an area other than physical, he knew that he might be making matters worse by forcing him to see a psychiatrist. "No, it's not an order," he said. "Just a suggestion, but one I think you should take."

"I'd rather not."

For a time Pennington sat there trying to convince Mark Stevens, but he had other patients to see and finally shrugged his shoulders. Looking down, he saw that he had bitten off another eraser and angrily threw it into the wastepaper basket. "All right. Come back to see me next week."

"What for?" Mark rose and made his way out of the room. He had learned to navigate better in the week that he had been at the hospital, and as he slammed the door behind him, Dr. Pennington shook his head, muttering, "He's carrying a big load, and I don't think he even knows it."

Mark made his way back to the room and found Oscar listening to Loretta Lynn sing "Stand by Your Man." "How do you stand that country western mess?" he said.

"You don't like country western music? I thought you was from Arkansas."

"I like folk music," Mark said, sitting down on his bed. "But just the titles of those songs are awful."

"What's awful?"

"That one for instance. What's the name of it?"

"That one? That one is, 'If I Told You You Had a Beautiful Body, Would You Hold It against Me?'"

Mark grinned despite himself. "You don't see anything wrong with that?"

"No, I don't see nothin' wrong with it!" Oscar shook his head. "You ain't been raised right. Anybody that don't like country music ain't got much goin' for him. Here's a letter for ya. You want me to read it?"

"I guess so."

Mark sat back and listened to Oscar tear the envelope. "It's from Prue Deforge. That yo main squeeze, Mark?"

"Just read the letter."

"All right. She say: 'Dear Mark: I was glad to hear that you had been transferred to the hospital in Chicago. I heard from Jake that you arrived here last week. I've been out of town, but I will be by to see you as soon as I can get there . . .'"

Oscar read the letter, which was three pages long, and said with admiration, "That's a fine lady you got there, Mark."

"I don't *have* her!" Mark said sharply.

Oscar looked over quickly and saw the frown on the young marine's face. "You want me to read it again?"

"No."

"I'll just fold it up then and put it in this here drawer." As he closed the drawer, he said, "She sounds like a nice lady. Not like some I had." He waited for Mark to respond but saw that he had lain down on the couch, his face turned upward, his eyes open and unseeing, his mouth hard, and he shook his head thinking, *He sho is a hard case! If I had me a nice lady like that, I don't reckon I'd be as stubborn as he is!*

★   ★   ★

Prudence sat across from Dr. Pennington, listening carefully. When the physician finished his explanation, she asked, "I really don't understand, Doctor. If there's nothing wrong with his eyes, then why can't he see?"

"He refuses to see a psychiatrist, but I think his problem is mental, or perhaps emotional. It certainly isn't physical. He never had any vision trouble before, did he?"

"Why, never! He can see farther than anybody I know, and he was always a great shot in the woods while hunting."

"Well, all I can say is physically we can't find anything wrong with him. Have you talked to him since he was wounded?"

"No. I've written him many letters, but he stopped answering them. Of course, if he can't see, he couldn't write." She was sitting tensely in the seat, and there was an urgency in her dark eyes that riveted the doctor's attention. She leaned forward and said, "Can't you do *anything* for him?" He shook his head helplessly.

"Maybe you could help him," Pennington said. "These things are peculiar. It's not my field, you understand, but I've got the feeling that he feels terrible because all of his buddies were killed on that last patrol he was on. We've seen that before a time or two and never saw it take this form, but emotionally it's hard on men. You know how it is, I'm sure, how close men get on the field of battle. And then when they lose a buddy, somehow they get to thinking it should have been them, and then they're guilty, or think they are."

"But what could I do?"

"I'm not sure—perhaps nothing. He needs love, and assurance, and all I can say is it will take the good Lord himself to bring him around."

Prue rose after a few more minutes of conversation, thanked the doctor, and then left his office. She made her way down the hall, and when she got to Mark's room, she hesitated. She had not seen Mark in a long time, and a whole war stood between them. Still, he was the same Mark, and lifting her head, she knocked on the door.

"Y'all come on in!"

Prue stepped inside and saw a huge marine seated at a desk working a jigsaw puzzle. He stood up at once, and his white teeth gleamed against his black skin as he said, "I'll bet you're Miss Prue, ain't you now?"

"That's right."

"I'm Oscar Tatum. I try to keep this here fella straight." He waved over toward Mark, who was standing beside an open window. He had turned, and for a moment Prue could have sworn he was seeing her. He seemed to focus on her, but he did not move. Quickly she moved over to stand in front of him, saying, "Mark, it's so good to see you."

"Hello, Prue."

When Mark did not move, Prue felt a moment's panic. Then she stepped forward, took his hand, and squeezed it. "I wish I would have been here before, but I was out of town."

"That's all right." Something in Mark's voice was different. Prue could not identify it, but there was an adamant, harsh quality to it. His eyes were open, and although he wore dark glasses, she felt somehow that he was seeing her, though she knew this was impossible.

"Well, I'll just step outside and let you folks do your talkin'," Oscar said. He winked at Prue, saying, "You ought to stay over for supper tonight. I done talked that cook into givin' us some good ole turnip greens. Now I'll go tell him how to cook 'em with some salt meat."

"He seems very nice," Prue said as the door closed.

"He's all right," Mark responded. "You want to go for a walk?"

"Yes. That would be nice. It's so pretty outside today."

Five minutes later the two were walking along the sidewalk, and Prue was finding the conversation very difficult. She had run through all the news she had of her family, and he had commented only briefly.

"How's the painting going?" he asked.

"Oh, very well! I had another show in Philadelphia. That's where I was."

"Sell lots of paintings?"

"A few." Prue proceeded to talk for a time about her work, and finally they came to a large grove of oak trees that were in full bloom, the leaves stirring in the breeze above them. "There's a little bench there," she said. "Let's sit down. My feet hurt. I have on some new shoes."

"All right."

Prue took Mark's arm to lead him to the bench and felt the muscles tighten under her grip. Still, there was no other way for her to lead him there, and she was relieved when they sat down. "I talked to Doctor Pennington," she said.

"Have you? So have I." There was a bitterness in Mark's voice, and he kept his head down as he said, "He says there's nothing wrong with me. That's a little odd since I can't see a thing."

"He thinks maybe—" Prue hesitated, not knowing whether it was wise to repeat what Pennington had said. At last she said, "He's very concerned about you."

"He wants me to see a shrink. I guess he thinks I'm crazy. Maybe I am."

Prue laid her hand on Mark's arm. "Don't talk like that," she said urgently. Her eyes searched his face. For a long time she sat there not knowing whether it was wise to repeat Pennington's words or not, and finally Mark said, "I guess you better be going, Prue. We'll be going in to supper pretty soon. You wouldn't like it."

Mark stood up abruptly, and Prue followed suit. The grounds were empty except for a man trimming a hedge over by the main building. Quickly she said, "I thought about you every day that you were in Vietnam, Mark, and I prayed that God would bring you back."

Mark turned to face her. "Well, I'm back," he said, his voice clipped. And then he felt her arms go around his neck and felt her lips touch his with a soft pressure. He immediately reached up, took her arms, and stepped back. "It's time for you to go, Prue. I can find my way back." He turned and left, leaving Prue standing there staring after him with tears in her eyes. She turned slowly and left, making her way back to where she had parked her car.

"He's so—shut off!" she murmured. "And he's gotten bitter. He was never that way before."

★　　★　　★

Kent Maxwell knew something was troubling Prue. He had been working with her on a new technique, and at last he said,

"What's wrong, Prue?" He put the brush down and shook his head. "You're not listening to a word I say."

Prue was wearing a smock that had been washed many times but contained all the faded colors of the rainbow. She shook her head abruptly and moved with a discontented air to the window of her studio. She had moved out of her expensive apartment and rented a place that served both as an apartment and a studio. Now she looked down on the neighborhood below, saying nothing.

Maxwell came over and turned her around. "Is it trouble? You've been out of sorts for a week."

For some reason Prue had never found it right, or fitting, or convenient, perhaps, to talk to Kent about Mark. She had gone back to the hospital day after day but was getting no encouragement. She had talked to Mark's parents and to Jake; everyone was at their wit's end about Mark.

Seeing that she was not about to speak of what was on her mind, Maxwell said, "When are you going to marry me and let me take care of you, Prue?"

"I don't know. I can't talk about it now." Frustration swept across Prue, and she turned away from Maxwell's intense gaze. "Why don't you give up on me?"

"I'll never do that," he said.

★　★　★

That evening Prue went to the Taylor house and was relieved to find Jake gone on a story. After the kids were in bed, she sat down and told Stephanie everything that was on her heart. "It's so hard, Stephanie," she said, wringing her hands, squeezing them hard. "Mark will hardly talk to me. He's bitter, and I don't know what to say to him."

"What about Kent Maxwell? Is he still after you to marry him?"

Prue shifted and looked up quickly. "How did you know that? I never told you."

"Yes you have," Stephanie said. "In everything but words. What are you going to do about it?"

"I don't know. He's done so much for me. I owe him so much."

"You can't marry a man because you're grateful to him."

"I know, but—"

"Look. You know how some dogs have to have their tails bobbed—cut off?"

"Why, yes."

"Jake tells a story about a man that loved his dog so much he hated to hurt him. The tail had to come off, so the first day he cut off an inch of it, the next day another inch. He cut off an inch at a time until the tail was gone."

"Well, that's awful!" Prue said, and then she laughed ruefully. "I see what you mean. It would be better just to make a clean break."

"If you don't love him, that's what you should do. You're not doing him any favors, Prue, by dragging the thing out."

Prue stayed until Jake came in, then went home but did not go to bed. She walked the floor thinking of Mark, of Kent, of herself, and finally said bitterly, "I'm going to write a book sometime about how to dump an unwanted lover."

At last she went to bed and had barely drifted off into a sleep when the phone rang.

Groping for the phone, she picked it up and said, "Hello?"

"Prue?"

"Who is this? Is it you, Mother?"

"Yes. I have bad news."

Instantly she thought of Mark and could not breathe or speak for a moment. Finally she controlled herself and said, "What is it?"

"It's Logan—he passed away to be with the Lord this afternoon at two o'clock."

A great emptiness spread through Prudence Deforge. She had loved her grandfather, and now the thought that she would never see him again on this earth seemed unbearable. She spoke to her mother for a while about the arrangements, then hung up the phone. Knowing she would not go back to sleep again, she went over to stand by the window and looked down on the neighborhood below. She prayed for a long time, and as she prayed a peace seemed to come to her. She had no direct word, but somehow she knew that her grandfather's death was tied to the salvation of Mark Stevens.

20

PRUE TAKES OVER

April passed, bringing with it the warm, clear, sunny skies of May. Mark spent hours walking in the warm sunshine until he learned every walkway in the vicinity of the hospital. He hated to stay inside. The television was a deadly bore—even worse because he could not see it. The comedy shows he had once thought at least mildly amusing now seemed stupid and vulgar, and the obvious laugh tracks that blasted from the set drove him from the recreation room.

The time got even harder when Oscar Tatum said one afternoon, "I'll be leaving you tomorrow, Mark."

The words jolted Mark. Although he had been surly with his fellow marine, he had grown deeply fond of him. He knew Oscar wanted to help, but since no one could give him his sight back, he had been short with him. Mark finally said, "I hate to see you go."

"Well, when you get back to Arkansas, I'll be in Mississippi. They butt up against each other, you know." Oscar came and put his huge hand on Mark's shoulder and squeezed it almost fiercely. "I'm leavin' my phone number with you, and you get in touch as soon as you get back home. You hear me?"

★   ★   ★

Oscar's departure left a vacuum in Mark's life. The other patients seemed occupied with their own problems for the most part, and to those who did try to make conversation, Mark found he could not respond.

Prue came daily, and Mark would walk with her, listening as she spoke. She brought him cassette tapes and a machine to play them on, which was his biggest consolation. He was sick of the Beatles, and Elvis, and the whole rock scene, and the radio either offered that or country western music, which he did not like. It reminded him of Oscar, and despite himself, when the country western music came on, he thought of the gentle giant who had offered friendship—which he had turned down.

Doctor Pennington gave up all pretense of being able to help Mark, and at one appointment said bluntly, "There's nothing wrong with you physically. I've told you that all along, Mark."

"Don't be ridiculous! Seeing is a physical thing, isn't it?"

"Well, yes, but in your case there's no reason physically, scientifically, why you can't see. Something's blocking your sight all right, but it's something in your heart."

The words had jolted Mark, although he had not responded to Pennington. *Something in your heart.* The words echoed in his mind day after day, and during the long nights when he lay awake listening to his tape player with an ear microphone so he would not disturb his new roommate—a silent man named Jack Mackenzie who did not say a dozen words a day—he thought of them again. *Something in your heart—something in your heart.*

As the days passed, he did not improve in his ability to perform even the simplest functions. The physical therapist, an ex-medical student before he joined the Corps, said in disgust, "You haven't ever accepted the fact that you can't see, Stevens! That's the reason you don't learn to do things better!"

Mark could not argue, for deep down he knew that the therapist was right. He could not bring himself to face up to the fact that he would never be able to see again. Somehow, despite the hardness that had come upon him, he nurtured a hope that one day his sight would return. He clung to this hope as a man in a lifeboat out on an endless sea hopes for the sight of a ship, or an airplane, anything to bring relief.

And so the days and nights passed. Sometimes he thought that all was hopeless and he wanted to end it all, but that was no answer. When his family came, or Prue, he sat silently as they talked. Once his father urged him to come home, and he had said bitterly, "What am I good for?"

★   ★   ★

"Hey, man! It's me, Bobby!"

Mark pulled the earphone from his ear and had to smile. "It couldn't be anybody else. Come in and sit down."

Bobby Stuart shut the door and slumped across the room, dropping down on the bed where Mark was sitting up listening to his tape player. "How you doin'?"

"Great."

"Yea," Bobby said. "Yea, I bet. I should have been here before, but you know me. I never do what I'm supposed to do."

"You're not in jail. That's good news."

"I will be if that judge has her way," Bobby said. "You know what they done to me, don't you?"

"Prue gave me a blow-by-blow description. If you make a single misstep, you're in jail."

Bobby snorted and moved his hand across his face. There was a nervousness to his manner that Mark could sense although he could not see. "That's right, man. That's right," Bobby said, his voice in a shrill staccato. "Man, I'm afraid to spit in the street anymore! You know what she's got me doin' for community service?"

"What, Bobby?"

"Pickin' up trash down on the east side. Can you dig that? Bobby Stuart pickin' up trash!" He got up and walked nervously around the room, speaking rapidly. "They got some-body watchin' me all the time. You know what it's like down there. There's dope everywhere. Why, I've been offered ev-erything from a joint to heroin, and I think some of the Feds may have put somebody up to it. They want to put me behind bars. Make an example of me, you know?"

"Stop pacing around. Sit down and take a load off your feet." Mark waited until he heard Bobby collapse into the chair next to the wall, and said, "It's pretty bad. Worse for you because you had more to lose."

Bobby blinked and said, "What do you mean by that?"

"I mean you had it all, Bobby. Money, cars, fame. Every-body wanting to meet you. Pretty hard to lose all that."

Bobby again moved his hand across his face. It was as if he was trying to brush cobwebs away, and he leaned forward and said, "I'm off dope, and it's about to kill me! I don't even smoke cigarettes anymore. They'd find out, and when they did they'd put me in jail. I couldn't stand that, Mark."

Mark sensed the tension in Bobby and asked, "Do you perform any?"

"Perform? Man, I can't even whistle in the shower! It's all gone!"

"I can't believe that."

"You better believe it, man. I don't know whether it's be-cause I quit cold turkey and I got the shakes all the time, or because that female judge wants to see me back in jail. I don't know what it is. I know I'm losin' my mind. Sometimes I wake up and don't care what happens to me."

"I know what that's like."

Instantly Bobby shot a glance toward Mark, who was sitting quietly on the bed dressed in fatigues. "Hey," Bobby said, as he reached over and tapped Mark's shoulder. "Here I come with all my troubles, and you got the real problems. I can't believe it. You can't see nothin'?"

"Not a thing."

"Aw, they got ways of helpin' people in hospitals. Why, I'd

give a million dollars, I guess, to hospitals. It looks like they could do *something*!"

"I don't think they can. They'd like it if they could, but so far zero." Mark swung his feet over the bed and said, "Come on. Let's go for a walk." He picked up his cane and the two men left the hospital.

They walked for over two hours, Bobby talking in a spasmodic fashion. Once they sat down on a bench, but after ten minutes he said, "Come on. Let's walk. I'm losin' my mind."

"Sit down, Bobby. You have to learn to live with this. Just like I have to learn to live with what I've got."

"Look," Bobby said, "I know it's bad for you. A thousand times worse than it is for me. You got yours in an honorable way. All I've ever done—" He halted and slumped on the bench. He said nothing for a long time, and Mark simply waited.

Finally Bobby said, "Well, some visitor I make. I come out to cheer you up and don't do anything but cry in my beer—wait a minute. Not real beer in case I'm bein' bugged. That's how bad off I am, but I don't want to bother you anymore."

"Come on back to my room. We'll talk some more. Maybe play some tapes. Do you have to be anywhere?"

"Not today. Tomorrow I've got to be pickin' up gum wrappers."

The two men went back to Mark's room. Word got out that Bobby Stuart was in the hospital, and soon men started finding excuses to come by and visit.

Bobby whispered, "Get 'em out of here, Mark. I just don't feel like talkin' to anybody."

Mark said, "All right, fellas. A little privacy, if you don't mind." He waited until the room was cleared, and then went to sit down, but had no more got there when he heard a knock on the door and Prue's voice saying, "Mark?"

"Come in, Prue."

As Prue stepped inside, Bobby rose up and tried to grin at

her. "Hi, Miss Prudence," he said. "Good to see you. You're lookin' great."

Prue came over and looked at Bobby, whose eyes had dark circles under them. "You look terrible, Bobby," she said.

"This is my *good* day. You ought to see me when I really look bad."

Prue shook her head, reached up, and laid her hand on Bobby's cheek in a maternal gesture. She seemed cool and collected, but there was an excitement in her that both men sensed.

"What's going on, Prue?" Mark said. He was still standing and had turned to face her, turning his head slightly to one side to catch her words.

"I came over to talk to you."

"I'll just fade on out," Bobby said, but as he turned to go Prue's voice stopped him.

"No, Bobby. Now that you're here, I think it might be good for you to stay too."

"Are you sure about that?" Bobby asked, lifting one eyebrow.

"I'm sure," Prue said. "Sit down. I've got something to say that may take me a while."

Bobby grinned suddenly. He was thirty-five now, but he still had his boyish grin. "Don't tell me you have bad news," he mocked. "Why, I haven't had anything but good news for so long I don't know how I'd take it." Nevertheless, he went over, plopped himself down in a chair, and waited. Mark sat down on the bed, saying nothing.

"I've just come back from Logan's funeral," she said gently.

Mark dropped his head. "I guess I should have gone with you to give you some support. But I couldn't, Prue. I just couldn't."

"I should have gone too," Bobby said. "After all, he was my relation." He stared at her, his mouth pulled down into a mournful expression. "I don't very often do the things I'm supposed to do. How was the funeral?"

Prue stood before the two men and related the circumstances of her grandfather's funeral. It had been, she told them, the biggest funeral they had had in Strong County in years. "I never knew Logan had so many friends. The church was packed, and it could have been filled three times, I think. Finally the pastor simply went outside and held the funeral in the open from the church steps. It was a wonderful sermon he preached, about how much Logan served the Lord Jesus Christ all of his life."

"Were all the family there?" Bobby asked quietly.

"Most of them. Lenora couldn't come. She had the flu, and Lylah really shouldn't have. She's not well these days, but she came anyway. Your folks were there, of course."

She hesitated, then said, "I think of Logan so often. He was such a good man."

Bobby listened as she spoke for a while about the family, then he said again, "I should have gone."

Prue hesitated only for a moment, then said, "I talked a lot to Richard. He was there when Logan died, and you know he talked about you two a lot."

"About me?" Bobby said, opening his eyes wide with astonishment.

"Yes, about you. He thought a lot of you, Bobby, and of course, Mark, you were just like a grandson to him."

"What did he say?" Mark demanded.

"He was afraid for you. Both of you."

"Well, I guess he had reason to be," Bobby said. "Is that all he said about us?"

"He said," Prue spoke very quietly, "that you ought to get away from here. That's what Richard told me. Just before he died he said Logan had prayed for both of you, and he was afraid that the life would get you here."

"He's right about me. It's got me pretty fair already," Bobby muttered. "But where would I go?"

Prue took a deep breath and said, "To the Ozarks. Both of you."

Mark lifted his head with shock. "Back to the Ozarks? No, I won't do it."

"Wait a minute," Bobby said. "What would we do there?"

"Get away from everything that's here," Prue said. "You don't know, Bobby, but you remember, Mark, how quiet it is there."

"It's quiet in this hospital," Mark said stubbornly.

"That's not the same thing." Her voice grew suddenly tense, and she said, "You've sat here feeling sorry for yourself long enough. Richard said Logan prayed for you and told him that God had given him a promise. That he was going to work on your life, and you too, Bobby. And he told Richard that the two of you ought to come to the hills, for a while anyway."

"Well, that lets me out. I couldn't go anyway," Bobby muttered. "That judge wouldn't let me go for a million dollars."

"I'll see the judge, and I'll have Jake Taylor go see her. They're pretty good friends, you know. You'll have to do some sort of community work there, but I think you ought to go."

Mark sat still on the bed, thinking over what Prue had said. "How would we get there, and where would we stay?" he asked finally.

"I've got it all planned," Prue said eagerly. She had expected Mark to lash out at her, but now she saw that he was bending. "I'll get three one-way tickets to Fort Smith. We'll get on a bus there, or rent a car, and we'll go to Logan's house. It's empty now. We'll stay there, and we'll wait until the Lord does something."

For a moment bitterness rose up in Mark, and he wanted to lash out at Prue, asking why God had let him go blind, but the silence grew in the room and he was aware that the other two were looking at him.

Finally Bobby said rather timidly, "I'll go if you will, Mark."

Prue went over and put her hand on Mark's shoulder. "Please come, Mark. Just try it. You remember how quiet it is there. We can go walking down by the river, and you'll have time to think."

The silence seemed to swell in the room. Bobby's eyes met Prue's, and both knew that Mark was engaged in some deep inner struggle.

Oh, God, Prue prayed silently, *don't let him turn me down! This is his last chance!*

Abruptly Mark stood, took a deep breath, and shook his head as if he were coming out of deep water. "All right," he said quietly. "I'll go. I don't think it will do any good, but I'll go."

Prue kissed him, then twirled and ran to Bobby, throwing her arms around him. "You stay right here. I'll go get Jake, and we'll go to the judge, and I'll get three tickets. We're on our way home!"

21

BACK HOME

A s the airplane landed, Mark found himself tensed up and turned to whisper to Prue, "Let's wait until everybody else gets off."

"Of course, Mark," Prue answered. She knew at once that he hated going through anything unusual and different, and she squeezed his arm as they waited for the passengers to disembark.

"All right. I think we can go now," she said. She rose and waited until Mark, who had been sitting by the window, moved out, and nodded toward Bobby, who fell in behind Mark as Prue led the way.

"Thank you for flying Delta," the stewardess said with a smile as they left.

The steps leading down from the plane were steep, and Prue wanted to say, "Be careful," but she knew that Mark would resent it. She slowed down so that he bumped into her, and she said, "I'm always afraid of these steps. They're so high." She moved slowly, glancing back to see Bobby following Mark, ready to lend a hand if necessary.

As the three arrived on the ground, Bobby said, "Come on. Let's get us a van."

"You don't want a car?" Prue asked with surprise.

"No. Let's get a van. More room to move around in. Besides, I'm a little bit tired of cars."

Mark found himself wedged in between the two, and it was Prue who said, "You two wait here. I'll go rent the van."

The two of them waited in the small waiting room of the Fort Smith Airport, and she came back soon. "They've got a Ford Econoline. Is that all right, Bobby?"

"Just about my speed."

The three of them made their way outside. As Bobby loaded their bags, he said, "Prue, you better drive. You know the roads on these hills better than I do."

"All right."

Prue got behind the wheel, and Bobby got in the backseat and immediately lay down, saying, "I'm gonna catch me a little rest. I never let all my weight down on those airplanes. Don't see how they stay up."

Mark moved into the front seat, rolled the window down, and said, "Let's not have the air conditioner on."

Prue started the engine. "No, it's cooler today than usual."

She pulled out of the airport, and soon they were on the highway that led through the Ozarks. She said nothing but leaned over and turned the radio on. At once they were treated to a noisy rendition of country western music, and Mark said wryly, "I guess we're home again."

"I don't know. I've gotten to where I sort of like country western music," Prue remarked. She swerved to miss an armadillo that leaped straight up in the air and then scurried for the side of the road. "Once you get used to it, it's not so bad."

"I guess you could say that about rheumatism."

Prue laughed. It was the first attempt at a joke that Mark had made in some time, and as they moved along over the twisting roads, she enjoyed the air rushing through, blowing her hair back.

"Must be about plowing time," Mark remarked.

"Yes. We're passing some of those big tractors. I think one of those things probably costs more than a whole farm back up in the hills where we come from." She spoke from time to time of the rivers they crossed, and the small towns. They took Highway 71 up to Fayetteville and then turned right on 412 passing through Huntsville. Mark swayed from side to side with the movement of the car. Once, the right wheel of the van hit a pothole, which made Bobby grunt. Mark said, "I see they still haven't fixed the roads." Prue called off the names of the small towns—Rudd, Alpena—and when they came to Bellepoint, she remarked, "I think we have good names here in Arkansas. They're so peculiar."

"You mean like Bald Knob? That's peculiar, I guess."

"Yes, or Toad Suck Ferry. I always liked that one."

The two talked for a while about strange names in Arkansas, and Mark laughed, saying, "I always liked Booger Holler. That had a certain ring to it. I wanted to use it once in a story, but they told me I couldn't. They said it was nasty."

They moved along roughly, and finally Prue said, "Almost home now." She rounded a bend in the road and said, "There's the house. It looks a little bit lonesome now, and it'll be that way with Logan gone."

Pulling up in the front, she sighed. "Well, we're here."

Bobby got out, stretching stiffly. "You got a key to the place, Prue?"

"No, but it's in the mailbox. I'll get it." She walked out to the mailbox twenty feet down the road, opened it, and pulled the key out.

"They sure are trustin' folks around here. You wouldn't do that in New York or Chicago," Bobby remarked. He yanked open the doors and began pulling the luggage out. Prue said, "Come on, Mark." She walked beside him, noting that unconsciously he allowed his arm to touch her to give him a sense of place.

"Got to fix these steps," Prue observed, as they approached the flight leading up to the high porch. Mark reached out at once and found the railing, and made his way up. He turned at the top and said, "I imagine you can almost see our houses from here."

"Right, and we'll go see your folks, and mine, sometime. As soon as you like."

"Not for a while, Prue," Mark said quietly.

"All right." Taking the key, she unlocked the door. "Come along, Bobby." Leading the way inside, she said, "There are two bedrooms downstairs and one upstairs. Let me have the one upstairs. I always liked it. It looks out on the front yard. You and Mark can fight over the other two."

Once they were settled down in the old house, Prue drove to the store and came back with a load of groceries. She immediately began fixing a meal, and the two men sat out on the porch rocking slowly in the cane-bottomed rockers.

"What time is it, Bobby?" Mark asked.

Looking at his wristwatch, Bobby grunted, "Almost seven o'clock. It sure stays light a long time in the summer around here."

"What do you think about all this?" Mark could hear Prue in the kitchen and wanted to get Bobby's true feeling.

The question caught Bobby off guard. He stopped rocking and ran his hand through his hair, then shook his head dolefully. "Shoot. I don't know, Mark. Can't be any worse than what I had in Chicago pickin' up popsicle sticks for eight hours a day. What do you think?"

"Well, it's a nice place. The weather's good. It'll be a little bit hot without air-conditioning." He stopped suddenly and listened hard. "Listen, those are katydids. I'd forgotten they were so loud."

Bobby listened hard and said, "We didn't have those where I grew up, or at least I never heard them."

Mark said quietly, "You remember when you came here and we went hunting?"

"Yea, and I went out and got drunk and messed it up with some girl. Whatever happened to her anyhow?"

"I don't know."

"I hope she doesn't have any big brothers around, or maybe a pa with a shotgun. I bet they haven't forgotten it."

"I'm guessing they probably have."

Bobby took out a package of chewing gum and pulled one out. "Want some Juicy Fruit?" He handed Mark one of the sticks, peeled one, stuck it in his mouth, and began to chew rhythmically. "I remember that time," he said finally. "You and I had a good time hunting. I wish we hadn't done anything but that."

"No sense going back and wishing things were different. You can't change the past."

"I know," Bobby said. He began to rock back and forth, his fingers drumming nervously on the arms of the rocking chair. "I wish you could. I surely wish you could. I think back when Richard and I were growing up. The folks were always so proud of us. Well, they're still proud of Richard. I'm the one that would have been better off if I had been put to sleep."

"Don't say that, Bobby. You're young yet."

"I'm thirty-five. That's old enough for a man to have done something with his life."

Mark turned his head toward the voice, and said, "Well, you have done something. Everybody in America knows who you are."

"They know I pop pills and ruin young girls. That's what they know."

Mark considered the bitterness of Bobby Stuart's tone. He felt more or less the same way and had for some time, but he had never said so to Bobby. Now he said, "I guess you've got as much talent as anybody in show business. What would have happened if you had gone another way?"

"I guess I could have been another Pat Boone if I had known God, but I don't."

At that moment Prue stepped out, holding the door open. "Come and get it. Supper's ready."

The two men rose and made their way into the dining room. Bobby sat down, running his hands over the old, polished oak. "You must have had many a meal here," he said. "I'm sure it won't be the same without Logan."

"No it won't, but he had a good life. You'll be hearing about him from the people around here. They really loved and respected Logan Stuart."

Prue sat down, and then without waiting, bowed her head and asked a brief blessing. The two men both bowed their heads, and when she was through Prue said briskly, "Well, Bobby. You start work tomorrow. Your community service."

Bobby had lifted a forkful of mashed potatoes to his lips, but he halted and lowered it. "You mean you've already got that lined up?"

"Oh yes. I took care of it on the phone."

"What am I going to do? Clean up papers on the highway?"

Prue shook her head. "You better eat hearty. I hope you like pork chops."

Bobby took a bite of the mashed potatoes, then tried some of the pork chops. Surprise came to his eyes, and he said, "Hey, this is good! I didn't know you were such a good cook! I thought you just painted pictures."

Mark was glad that Prue had simply filled his plate and put it in front of him without comment. Now he said, "What is Bobby going to be doing?"

"He's going to work for Pearl Riverton."

"Work for a woman? What does she do?" Bobby inquired, washing down another mouthful of pork chop with a sip of foamy milk.

"She runs a foster home for youngsters in a daycare center in town." Prue smiled, and then mischief came to her eyes. "I expect she'll have you changing diapers."

Bobby suddenly choked. "No way! I'm not changing any diapers!"

"I expect you will if that's what Reverend Pearl tells you to do. It's that or go back to Chicago and maybe to jail."

"Reverend?" Bobby stared at her. "You mean she's a lady preacher?"

"Sure is."

"What's her denomination?"

"She's a Pentecostal," Prue said, taking a bite of the fresh corn bread.

"Pentecostal. You mean she speaks in tongues and handles snakes?"

"I don't know about the snakes or speaking in tongues, but she says she's *Pentecost at any cost*." Prue laughed and said, "I've always liked Reverend Pearl."

"She got a husband?"

"No. She's a maiden lady," Prue answered. "Give her a chance. She's very firm but very fair. She's done a lot for the town."

They finished supper and listened to the radio for a while, and then Mark said, "I think I'll turn in."

"You better go too, Bobby. You've got your day with Miss Pearl early in the morning. You're supposed to be there at eight o'clock."

Bobby shook his head sadly and said, "I think I'd rather be back picking up gum wrappers on the streets of Chicago than doing anything for a Holy Roller woman!"

★   ★   ★

As Bobby pulled the van up beside the old, red brick building with the sign "Sunshine Daycare," he had the impulse simply to gun the engine and drive on by. The small town mostly occupied one main street, and the Sunshine Daycare Center was at the very end of it. It was set back off the road, and a few small children were already playing some game in the front yard. The building had two stories and a steep-pitched roof, and huge white windows all the way across the front. A white, freshly painted picket fence surrounded the structure and the front yard, and for a moment Bobby sat there with the engine in neutral.

"I got to do it," he sighed. He put the van in park, turned the key off, and piled out of the Econoline. As he moved through the gate, the children, about six of them, stared at him. They all appeared to be less than six years old, but Bobby Stuart knew little about children. "Where can I find Reverend Riverton?" he asked.

A blue-eyed, blond girl, no more than five, grinned, exposing a vast empty space in her front teeth. "She's in there," she said.

"Thanks, kid."

Bobby moved up the walk, aware that the children were watching him curiously. He walked up to the double doors, which were propped open, opened the screen, and stepped inside. He found himself in a wide center hallway with doors leading off right and left and a set of stairs at the far end. "Anybody here?" he called as he moved down the hall.

He came to a door marked "Reverend Pearl Riverton" with a homemade sign and knocked on it. A muffled voice answered, and opening the door, he stepped inside. From across the room, a diminutive woman with silver hair and a pair of tiny granny glasses peered at him. She was sitting at a desk as erect as any master sergeant in the Marines, and her hair was drawn into a bun on the back of her head. It seemed to be pulled so tight that it appeared to Bobby it was pulling her eyes into a slanted position, but then he saw she was simply squinting against the bright sunlight coming down through the high windows.

"Yes? What can I do for you?"

"I'm Bobby Stuart. Prue Deforge sent me."

Looking over her glasses, Reverend Pearl said, "Sit down," nodding with her head toward a single chair that sat in front of her desk. When Bobby perched himself in it watching her warily, she said directly, "I hate your music."

Bobby had expected anything but this. His eyes flew open, and he opened his mouth to say something, but then realizing that his fate lay in the slender hands of the woman across from him, he nodded. "Yes, ma'am, I reckon most folks your age would."

"It has nothing to do with age."

"No, ma'am," Bobby agreed, wondering how to answer the severe look she was giving him.

"I think it comes straight out of the jungle, and it's leading millions of young people straight to hell."

Bobby blinked with surprise at this stern admonition. To save his life he could not think of a thing to say for a moment, then finally he shrugged. "Well, I won't be making any music for a while."

"That's right. You'll be earning your keep around here. Let me see your hands."

"My hands?"

"Your hands!" Reverend Pearl said. "Let me see them! The palms!"

Bobby extended his palms, and when Reverend Pearl looked at them she made a disgusted sound and shook her head. "Not a callus on them! We'll change that!"

Again Bobby had the impulse to get away as quickly as he could from the Sunshine Daycare Center and Reverend Pearl Riverton, but necessity kept him nailed to the chair. "I guess you got the best of the argument, Reverend," he said. "I got some community service to do, and I guess I'll try anything you'll put me to."

Reverend Riverton got up, and Bobby rose with her. She was, he saw, no more than five two or three, thin, and had hazel eyes. Despite the heat she wore long sleeves buttoned at the wrist, and her skirt came almost halfway between her knees and the floor.

"Do you know the Lord God Omnipotent?"

Bobby flinched at the question but shook his head. "No, ma'am. I don't guess I do."

"The more shame on you. With all that God's done for you, and you don't even know him. Well, we'll have time to talk about that after you've done your work. Come along." She wheeled and marched out the door. Bobby turned and followed her. She led the way to a room that contained buckets, mops, soap, and various other items of cleaning equipment.

"Clean the building."

Bobby stared at her. "What part of it?"

"All of it. I haven't had any help here. Dust everything that can be dusted. Wash everything that can be washed, and mop everything that can be mopped. I'll be around to check on you from time to time."

Bobby stared at the buckets and mops and sighed deeply. "Yes, Reverend," he said meekly.

★   ★   ★

The rhythm at Logan Stuart's house fell into place very quickly. Bobby got up and went to work every morning after being fed a good breakfast by Prue. He returned every afternoon shortly after five looking exhausted and with a string of complaints against Pentecostal lady preachers. But as the week passed his nerves seemed to grow more steady, and in the evenings he would even sometimes sit at the piano and play old songs. Never rock and roll, but the real old music that seemed to come from dim memories.

Mark and Prue went nowhere except to visit their folks on the second day of their arrival. Mark had told them, "I need time. Just give me time," and they had all been quick to agree.

Now each day he rose early and went for long walks down the road alone, always coming back looking thoughtful. Prue was afraid that he would be hit by a car, but she never thought once of warning him. She began cleaning the house, cooking the meals, going to the store, and she herself would go to visit her parents during the day. Her father would ask her each time she went, "How is he today?" and she would reply, "No better, Pa."

Mark was wrapped in a cloak of isolation. He was glad to be back in the Ozarks savoring the hot summery days, the smell of open fields, and the fresh earth being broken by the plows. He walked in the woods with Prue, and she would mention the dogwood breaking into blossom and the cardinals that she saw from time to time.

In the afternoons he would sometimes go out to the pond behind Logan's house and fish, using night crawlers that Bobby had put in a large coffee can for him. He used no cork and quickly learned how to catch the thumping brim and the fighting bass that occupied the large pond. He even learned how to clean them, and often at night they would sit down to fresh fried catfish and hush puppies. The brim were white and tender, breaking off in flakes, and once Prue said, "I remember the first time I ever caught a fish. It was over at Jenkins Creek. You were with me, Mark."

Mark said, "Yes, I remember," but offered no more conversation.

It was in the middle of the second week when Prue was almost desperate. Mark seemed to be getting no better, and his parents were wild with worry about him. They wanted to see him but knew he was holding them off. She went to her home one afternoon to feed her pets, those that were still left, and brought back Miss Jenny, her canary. As soon as she brought her in the house, Mark lifted his head and said, "What's that?"

Going over to him, Prue said, "This is Miss Jenny, my canary. Doesn't she have a beautiful voice?"

Mark listened as the bird's melodious song arose, and he nodded. "I like that. I never had a bird."

"Would you like to keep her in your room?"

Mark hesitated, then nodded. "You'll have to show me how to take care of her."

It was some time before they had set up Miss Jenny's cage, and Prue had told Mark how to feed this tiny bird and change the paper in its cage. "She likes a slice of apple once in a while. Just cut it and slip it between the bars."

Mark sat listening to the bird, and finally he turned to her and said, "Thanks, Prue."

"Why, you're welcome, Mark."

Prue turned away, but somehow she felt she had gotten closer to Mark, and as the days passed he grew more and more attached to Miss Jenny. It was during this period that Prue began to pray for herself, and for Mark, and for Bobby. She had never known what it meant to pray so hard and so long. Some days she even fasted, keeping it from Bobby and Mark, and day by day as she prayed, faith began to grow in her; early one morning she was kneeling beside her window and something came to her so strongly that she almost felt as if it were an electric shock.

"It's going to be all right," she whispered. "Bobby and Mark. They're both going to be all right." She bowed her head, and as the tears flowed down her cheeks, she began to thank God for what he was going to do.

22

THE OLD RUGGED CROSS

Bobby Stuart had never found anything quite as aggravating as the time he put in working for the Reverend Pearl Riverton. The tiny woman seemed to have the energy of a dozen Dalmatian puppies, and she insisted that Bobby have at least half that much. Every morning he got up groaning and dreading his arrival at the Sunshine Daycare Center, and by late afternoon he found himself praying that the time would pass. Once he thought, *The first time I prayed in many a year—but it's the first time I've had a female Adolf Hitler running my life.*

"I think I'm gonna quit and go back to Chicago," he complained to Prue and Mark as they were eating breakfast one Saturday morning. He accepted four plate-sized pancakes from Prue, picked up a jar of amber sorghum, and baptized them recklessly. He cut the pancakes into four pieces, stuck a quarter of one in his mouth, and nodded. "These are good, Prue. Best pancakes I ever had." He swallowed, drank down half a cup of the strong, black, unsweetened coffee from the huge mug beside his plate, and continued to grumble. "I declare that woman is like nothin' I ever saw on this earth! Work, work, work! That's all she ever wants—except, of course, when she preaches at me!"

"She does that a lot, does she, Bobby?" Prue had cut her own pancakes up and put a small portion in her mouth. Bobby's complaining amused her, for without his knowledge she kept in close touch with Reverend Pearl and knew that Bobby was fulfilling his obligations despite his complaining.

"Preach at me!" Bobby exclaimed. "Two fellas were in the office the other day while I was mopping. One of them said, 'Did you ever hear Reverend Pearl preach?' and the other one said, 'I never heard her when she wasn't,' and I popped up and said, 'Amen, brother!'"

"Well," Mark said as he sipped his coffee, "if she's preaching at you, I guess you're getting a break from your detail."

"No such thing!" Bobby snorted. He crammed another huge portion of pancake in his mouth and said in a muffled voice, "She preaches at me *while* I'm working! If I didn't go off and get lunch down at the Dew Drop Inn, she'd preach at me while I was eating!"

"I don't guess a little preaching will hurt you." Prue looked with approval at Bobby and Mark. "Both of you are looking better. Lots of this good Arkansas sunshine and fresh air."

Mark continued to sip his coffee but did not respond. It was true enough; he did feel somewhat better, but he still had nightmares of the last patrol, and the faces of his buddies would come floating to him in the dream. Sometimes he went to bed at night feeling calm and peaceful, more than since he had been wounded. But then the dreams would come, and the faces would appear seeming to plead with him, or seeming to accuse him just for being alive, and he would wake up tense and confused, wondering why he had been spared when better men had died.

"Well, I get tomorrow off, anyway. She won't make me work on the Sabbath," Bobby said with satisfaction. He tossed his napkin on the table, picked up his coffee, drained the cup, and started for the door. "Got to get started. Old Simon Legree will have her whip out if I'm a minute late."

"Have a good day," Mark mocked.

Bobby turned around and stared at him. "You know I don't care much for what people say, but that kind of hacks me off!"

"What hacks you off?" Mark asked in surprise.

"That saying! Have a good day! It don't mean nothin'!" He scowled broadly and ran his hand through his thick auburn hair. His electric blue-green eyes seemed to flash, and his voice rose as he said, "Have a good day! Everybody says that! Nobody cares whether you have a good day or not!"

"I think it's just a way of saying good-bye," Prue offered.

"Well, why don't they just say good-bye then? You know what really set me off? When I left the trial with this muddy sentence that female judge laid on me, the guard at the door said, 'Have a good day.' I wanted to punch him out."

"Well, have a good day anyway, and I really mean it," Prue smiled.

Bobby's shoulders relaxed, and he grinned back at her, which made him look much younger. "All right. You two have a good day." He turned and left the house, got into the van, and drove away. The morning was cool for May, and he took in the men working in the fields he passed. Nearly all the houses out in the country had gardens, and women wearing cotton dresses and bonnets were out working in them. Many of them lifted their hands and waved to him as he passed, and he blew his horn in a signal reply. "You won't catch people waving to you in New York or Los Angeles," he said. "They're all afraid you're going to mug 'em." Then he suddenly thought, *All my life I wanted to live in those big places, and now here I am braggin' on the Arkansas hills. I must be losin' my mind. It's that woman's fault. She's gonna drive me crazy.*

He reached the daycare center, parked the van, and got out. He was surrounded at once by a group of children who were holding their hands up, and he reached in his pockets and began handing out candy. He had bought a huge stock that he kept in the van, and he kept his pockets full of it. Reverend Pearl had warned him, "Those children won't have a tooth left in their heads if you keep on feedin' 'em candy." However, she had not forbidden it, so he passed out the M&M's and silver-covered Hershey chocolates until he reached the door. "That's all," he said, shooing them away. "Go on now!"

Stepping inside, he went at once to work. Some of the old windows had sash cords made of cotton rope, and they had broken. Now the only way to keep them up was to prop them with a stick. He hated that for some reason and was determined to replace them all with nylon. He had not said a word to Pearl about this but had gone about it on his own. Once she came and looked over his shoulder as he replaced a rotten cord, and asked, "What are you doing that for?"

"I like things to work right," he said shortly.

"The Lord will probably come back before those wear out," Reverend Pearl said.

Bobby turned to her and said, "I wish he would, but in case he don't, these cords will last another hundred years, I reckon."

The two stared at each other, and she finally left him to his work.

After she left the room Bobby thought about Reverend Pearl. She had driven him out of his mind, for somehow her words had a power that he could not define. Usually they were brief words oftentimes connected with a Scripture. He had heard enough sermons while he was growing up, but he had been ashamed to even go into a church considering the lifestyle he had led for the past ten years. Now as he polished the flatware that the children used when they ate their lunches, he thought about her hazel eyes, which seemed to have the power of laser beams. *She seems to know what I'm thinkin', and sometimes I think she knows everything I've ever done.* His thoughts continued on the woman until suddenly Reverend Pearl herself came back in and said, "When you finish that, go out and bring in some sassafras roots. I been yearnin' for some sassafras tea."

Looking up with surprise, Bobby shook his head. "How am I supposed to know what they look like?"

"You don't know sassafras roots? Your education's been neglected. Come on with me." She marched out the door, and Bobby put down the hardware and followed her. The woods were only a hundred yards past the daycare center, and she marched him directly toward a small growth and said, "That's sassafras. Dig up the roots and bring 'em inside."

"All right, Reverend Pearl."

He began to work at the roots, aware that she was watching him. He said suddenly, "Well, I won't have to put up with you tomorrow, preacher lady."

"What makes you think that?"

"Why, tomorrow's Sunday."

"You don't get tomorrow off."

Bobby dropped the roots and straightened up, anger coursing through him. "What do you mean I don't get tomorrow off? It's Sunday! The Bible says you're not supposed to work on Sunday!"

"You're supposed to work for the Lord on Sunday," Reverend Pearl said defiantly, looking up at him. She was not much larger than some of the children that attended the daycare center, and yet there was a strength and a power in her that almost cowed Bobby Stuart.

"I don't think it's right! Here I've worked six days, and I ought to get Sunday off!"

"You mind what I tell you, Bobby Stuart! I've got a chore for you tomorrow!"

"Doing what?"

A rare smile played around the lips of the elderly woman. "Playing piano in church."

Bobby stared at her, his eyes flying open with astonishment. "I'm not playing the piano in your church," he said adamantly, "and that's that!"

"Yes, you are! I'd hate to turn in a bad report and hate to see you get throwed in the pokey, so you be at the First Pentecostal Church in the morning at ten o'clock."

Bobby wanted to stalk away and drive off leaving her flat,

but something made him say, "All right. I'll come and play for the service. What time is it over?"

"It's over when the Lord says it's over!"

"Well, could you give me an average?" Bobby asked in exasperation.

"On the average, we start when the Lord begins to move, and we stay until he's through. Usually about two or three o'clock. Sometimes a little later."

"You stay at church five or six *hours*?"

"People stay at them dumb concerts of yours that long, don't they? You be there at church like I'm tellin' you!"

"I don't have anything to wear to church."

"We only got one rule about clothes at our church," Reverend Pearl said, and her eyes twinkled with a light of humor. "You have to wear clothes; you can't come nekkid."

Bobby burst out into laughter. "All right, preacher lady. I'll be there. But what are you gonna do if I start playin' one of them Elvis Presley rock-and-roll songs?"

"You don't want to get struck dead. I wouldn't advise it."

Bobby spent the rest of the day mostly thinking of his chore the next morning, and that night after supper he broke the news to Mark and Prue. "Well, tomorrow will be a first for me—first in a long time, I mean."

"Tomorrow's Sunday. What are you going to do?" Mark questioned.

"Going to play the piano at the First Pentecostal Church."

Prue laughed suddenly, then said, "I'm sorry. It's not funny, Bobby."

"Well, it is in a way. Here half the preachers in the United States are tellin' their congregation how Bobby Stuart's leading young people to hell, and I'm going to church to play the piano for a lady Pentecostal preacher with a bun on her head so tight it makes her eyes squint."

Mark found this amusing and chuckled softly. "I think

it's a great idea. What do you say we go take the service in, Prue?"

"Oh, I'd like that," Prue agreed instantly.

"Aw, come on! You two don't need to come. I'll feel enough like a fool without you two there."

"No, we'll all three go," Prue announced. She sat there listening as Mark poked fun at Bobby, and at the same time there was something going on inside her heart. She had felt the Lord speaking to her about Bobby Stuart, particularly, which surprised her. She had been praying so hard for Mark, and Bobby had been on her heart, but not to the same degree. Yet, for the past three nights she had prayed fervently for him to find God and had wanted to ask, "Lord, why should I be praying so hard for Bobby? It's Mark I love and want to see redeemed." Now as she sat there on the porch listening to the whip-poor-wills calling their mournful tune, she prayed, "Oh, God. Maybe this will be the time. Do something in Bobby's life tomorrow at church."

★　　★　　★

The First Pentecostal Church was a simple white frame building, and the paint itself was none too fresh. Strips of it were peeling, and Prue made a mental note to see to it that the church was painted. She herself was not Pentecostal, but she loved Reverend Pearl, who had been a character in town for as long as she could remember. She had even attended some of the services there, so was familiar with the inside of the ancient structure. Bobby was not, however. He had put on a pair of clean blue jeans and a white shirt but wore no tie. His face glowed from a fresh shave, and his hair was brushed back carefully. As he looked around the auditorium—which consisted of one single large room with home-built pine benches with no cushions, a piano, two guitars, and a set of drums at the front—he grinned at Prue. "Well, they got guitars and drums. I won't be too much out of place."

Reverend Pearl, wearing a plain, gray dress buttoned up to the throat and at the wrists, came at once to where they stood. The auditorium was packed, and an odd expression glinted in her eyes. "Well, Mr. Bobby Stuart. Are you ready to play the piano to the glory of God?"

"I'll do the best I can, Reverend," Bobby said, looking around uneasily.

"You might not know some of these songs. Do you know anything besides rock and roll?"

"Oh yes, Reverend Pearl," Prue said quickly. "Bobby grew up in church. He knows all the old songs. All the old Baptist songs, anyway."

"Well, the Baptist songs are good. You can put a little pep in 'em."

Bobby followed the diminutive woman to the front and sat down at the piano. Mark and Prue took their places in one of the hard, uncomfortable seats, and Prue whispered, "Have you ever been at a Pentecostal service?"

"Never have."

"They're a little bit different from what you're used to, I think."

"I've heard they climb over the benches to get at you and drag you down the aisles."

"That's not true. Not of Reverend Pearl anyway. I heard someone say that once to her, and she said, 'If a body ain't got the gumption to get out of a pew and walk twenty feet to the front of a church, then he ain't ready for God.'"

Mark grinned despite himself. "I think Bobby's pretty shook up over this. I talked to him while he was shaving and he said he nearly cut his throat."

"He's very nervous talking about God. I think he's been running from the Lord most of his life."

"Yes, I think you're right. He's talked to me a few times about it."

"He has? I'm surprised."

"It's kind of a strange thing," Mark said quietly as the musicians were tuning up their guitars and Bobby was running his fingers over the keys in a quiet fashion. "Bobby puts up a hard front, and he's done a lot of things that aren't right, and the world has practically bowed at his feet, but underneath he's unhappy and very insecure."

"I've noticed that about young girls who are very pretty. The beauty queens. You remember Maxine Baker? She became Miss Arkansas. When we were in high school she was the prettiest girl there, but she told me one time she never was satisfied with the way she looked."

"I never knew that," Mark muttered in surprise. "I wonder why that is?"

"I think anybody who trusts in their looks or their talents would never really know whether people liked them for themselves or for something else."

Mark sat there listening to the congregation sing. Some of the songs were strange to him. One of them was called "The Royal Telephone" and urged people to call up God on the telephone. It struck him as humorous at first, but as the untrained voices of the congregation boomed out, he thought, *These people get some sort of blessing out of that. I guess it depends on how you grew up. They wouldn't get much out of a high church Episcopalian service, and I can't imagine what an Episcopalian would think of singing like this.*

He could not see Bobby, of course, but he could hear the piano as it wove its way through the melodies. He remembered Bobby telling him he had played in church for years before he became a celebrity. Even now with the crudeness of the singing, there was some sort of magic in the way that Bobby Stuart managed to play the piano. He knew that Prue felt it too, for he felt her arm pressing against his, and once she whispered, "What a great gift Bobby has, and how much of it he's wasted."

"How does Bobby look?" Mark inquired, having to lift his voice.

"He looks like he'd rather be anywhere in the world but here."

★　　★　　★

Prue's words described Bobby very well. He sat bolt upright at the piano and had no trouble with the music. There was a genius in him for anything connected with singing or playing the piano, but as the old songs continued for over an hour, he found himself becoming more and more miserable. One of them, he remembered, was the first hymn he ever learned to play. It was "At the Cross," and Reverend Pearl insisted on singing it again and again:

> At the cross, at the cross
> Where I first saw the light,
> And the burden of my heart rolled away,
> It was there by faith
> I received my sight,
> And now I am happy all the day.

The words seemed to hammer into Bobby's head—*And now I'm happy all the day*. He was very much aware that throughout the years he had become more and more unhappy, and now the thought came to him, *Where did I lose it? Back when I was a kid I was happy. When I first started playing for the public I was happy, but I lost it somewhere along the way.*

Reverend Pearl, at one point, called for those who were sick to come forward and be prayed for, and Bobby watched as several people came down. Reverend Pearl put her hands on their head or shoulders, whichever she could reach, and prayed at the top of her lungs, and he wondered if any of them actually were healed.

Finally the Reverend began preaching. She had a worn black Bible that she opened once at the beginning, and read a Scripture that Bobby did not remember ever hearing. She lifted the Bible up and held it, saying, "My text is taken this morning from the Gospel of John, chapter 12, verses 24 and 25. 'Verily, Verily, I say unto you, Except a corn of wheat fall into the ground and die, it abideth alone: but if it die, it bringeth forth much fruit.'" She looked up then and said, "Let me preach at you about that verse. Every one of you here are farmers. Let me ask you. If you took a grain of corn and put it in a glass mason jar and put the lid on it, and set it up on the mantel, and you waited a year to go back, how many grains of corn would you see in that mason jar?"

Several loud voices called out, "Just one, preacher! Just one!"

"That's right! Amen! Just one! And why's that? Jesus said a grain of corn has got to die before it's any good to itself or to anybody else. Now, let me ask you. If you took that same grain of corn out, dug a hole in the good, black Arkansas earth, put it in there and covered it up, something would happen; what would it be?"

The congregation answered, "It would die! Amen! Glory to God it would die!"

"Amen! That's right!" Reverend Pearl said. "That grain of corn might have enjoyed bein' in that mason jar, but there'd never be but one grain there. Never two or three or a hundred. Imagine with me that grain of corn could talk settin' up there in that mason jar. You know what he'd say? Why, he'd say, 'I reckon as grains of corn go, I'm about the top of the ladder. Look at how slick and pretty I am. I'm fat and healthy!' He'd feel mighty proud of himself. Matter of fact, you could take a bunch of grains—twenty, or thirty, or a hundred—and put them in a jar, and you could call it a church, but at the end of the year it would still be the same number because a corn of wheat has got to fall into the ground."

She went on for some time speaking of the uselessness of life outside of God and then said, "Now, just play like that grain of corn could talk again. Grain of corn, aren't you tired of being all alone? Come on out, and let me show you how to amount to somethin'. And then that grain of corn, I'd take him out and put him in the ground, and I'd reckon he'd think after a while, 'Well, it's all over. I feel myself dyin'. Sure wish I was back in that glass jar again.' Then all of a sudden when he's fallen all to pieces, he'd feel something between his shoulder blades. What is it? Why, it's a little root and it begins to go down, then he feels something else. It's a shoot. It begins to go up, and that root goes down, and that shoot goes up, and if you're standin' there watchin' you would see a tiny, green spear that would grow into a tall stalk of corn. And then you know what would happen . . . !"

"That's right, preacher. There would be nubbins, and then full ears of corn." The congregation helped the Reverend along.

"That's right. So, Jesus says a corn of wheat has got to fall to the ground and die, and that's exactly what Jesus done. He died so that you and me, and that everybody could live."

Suddenly she turned and looked right at Bobby Stuart, who was listening entranced. His heart seemed to pound hard as he looked into her eyes. "He that loveth his life," Reverend Pearl said slowly, "*shall lose it.* A lot of people have lost their lives. They're in a little glass jar, and they look good, and smell good, and talk good, but they're dead. And until they fall into the ground and die to everything they got, they're going to be dead. But the rest of the verse says, 'He that hateth his life in this world shall keep it unto life eternal.'"

Bobby felt his throat tighten as the small woman continued to preach, and finally she said, "Now, verse 26 tells us what will happen if anybody will give up on themselves and let God have his way. 'If any man serve me, let him follow me; and where I am, there shall also my servant be: if any man serve me, him will my Father honour.'"

Reverend Pearl closed her Bible and looked directly into Bobby's eyes again. "You've had the honor of the world," she said, speaking as quietly as if they were alone, "and what has it brought you? Happiness, or joy, or peace? None of those. You been honored by the world, but God wants to honor you." She stopped, and everyone in the congregation knew that there was something between these two—the gray-haired Pentecostal preacher lady and the idol of the rock world, Bobby Stuart. A silence seemed to fall over the entire building. Prue felt it, and so did Mark. They both almost held their breath. Mark was straining in the darkness to understand what was going on, and Prue had her eyes fixed on Bobby's pale face, which was twitching with emotion.

"The Lord's told me to have you, Bobby Stuart, sing 'The Old Rugged Cross.'"

Bobby swallowed convulsively, and Prue thought he meant to refuse. But he ran his hands over the keys and the old familiar melody filled the church. He played the song through once, and then Reverend Pearl said, "The Lord says for you to sing the words, son. Sing them words loud and clear!"

Bobby Stuart had sung in arenas where thousands of people listened, but he never had a harder time singing a song in his life. He knew the words and began haltingly.

> On a hill far away stood an old rugged cross,
> The emblem of suffering and shame;
> And I love that old cross where the dearest and best
> For a world of lost sinners was slain.
>
> Oh, that old rugged cross so despised by the world,
> Has a wondrous attraction for me;
> For the dear Lamb of God left His glory above,
> To bear it to dark Calvary.

Bobby sang the first verse, then the second, but when he got to the chorus, suddenly his voice broke. Prue reached over and grabbed Mark's arm. "Something's happening to Bobby," she whispered.

"What is it? What's going on?"

"God is convicting him."

Bobby tried to sing another line, but suddenly his heart seemed to swell, and he thought of his parents in their years of prayer, and his brother who loved him dearly. He looked up and saw Prue, tears running down her face, and he began to weep. His shoulders shook, and he could not speak. He looked helplessly at Pearl, whom he expected to preach loudly at him. Instead she came over, put her arms around him, and sat down on the piano bench beside him. He looked at her through tear-filled eyes and saw a kindness and a goodness in her eyes that he had never recognized before. She spoke then, and her voice was gentle, and everyone in the congregation heard her say, "Jesus is waiting for you at the old rugged cross, Bobby. I'm going to pray for you, and you're going to die. But you're going to come alive again and know honor from God, and happiness, and joy."

Bobby Stuart leaned forward, put his arms on the keys of the piano, and laid down his head. He heard the voice of Pearl Riverton praying, and soon he began to cry, "Oh, God, I can't stand it. Whatever I have to do, help me! Save me in Jesus' name. . . ."

23

ONLY A MINOR MIRACLE

The conversion of Bobby Stuart sent shock waves not only throughout the small Ozark community but around the country and even into foreign lands. Reporters, as is the manner of the breed, came from the big cities demanding details and discounting most of what they heard.

Jake Taylor flew in mostly to visit with Mark, of whom he had become very fond, but he also congratulated Bobby, saying, "You're not going to make most hard-nosed reporters believe that you're really going to follow Jesus Christ. They don't want to hear that."

Bobby grinned. "They'll just have to believe what they want to, but I know what's happened in my heart, Jake, and that's all I care about."

After a week all the reporters had left, and the magazines and TV stations were printing and broadcasting stories about Bobby. The *National Enquirer* and others of its sort, of course, had a field day.

Prue was reading one such account to Mark as they sat on the front porch after supper. It was a rather cynical article suggesting that Bobby was trying to win back his public after his drug bust. Lowering the paper, Prue exclaimed in disgust, "Why do they have to say things like that?"

Mark sat silently listening to the crickets chirp for a moment, then he shrugged. "Most of them aren't believers, Prue. They don't believe the Bible, and they think most Christians are hypocrites—but I know something's different about Bobby."

Prue smiled as she said, "All he wants to do is read the Bible and talk to Miss Pearl. He idolizes that woman now, I think. Well, that's the wrong word, *idolize*, but at least he has a world of confidence in her."

"I know," Mark said. "It took a miracle of God to bring Bobby back from where he was. I think he's going to be all right now. I don't know what will happen to his career, and I don't think he cares a bit."

"He doesn't seem to. He won't even talk about a performance."

"Strange how it all happened, isn't it? Of all the places for a public celebrity like Bobby to get saved, a Pentecostal church would be about the last place you'd think it would happen."

"God's ways are not our ways, Mark." She sat quietly for a moment, and the two enjoyed the evening breeze. A black-and-white cat emerged just then from his hunting trip in the barn. They had called him Conan the Barbarian because he seemed to be so wild and strong. Now he came and jumped up into Mark's lap and curled up. Mark flinched, but then he laughed and began to stroke the silky black fur. "Well, Conan. Did you have a mouse for supper tonight?"

"That cat really loves you, doesn't he?"

"Yes, he does. I've always been a dog man. Didn't think cats had much personality, but this one does. Don't you, Conan?"

The cat looked up sleepily, yawned hugely, exposing sharp white fangs, then closed his eyes and put his chin down on Mark's leg. He began to purr, a small miniature motor going inside his chest, and Mark laughed. "It doesn't take much to make you happy, does it? Just a mouse and a little petting every now and then."

They sat on the porch until Bobby came home. As he got

out of the van, they noticed he was carrying a Bible in his hand.

Sitting down, he said, "You two waitin' up for me? Afraid I'd go down to the pool hall and be led astray?"

"That's it," Mark said. "Where have you been? With Miss Pearl?"

"Yep! She's been trying to teach me something about Revelation." Bobby shook his head ruefully. "If I get a dog, I'm going to name him Revelation because I never understood dogs, and I don't think I'll ever understand this book." He continued to speak with excitement about what he had learned and finally said, "Well, I don't understand about all those beasts with seven horns and things like that, but I understand the last part of it. Jesus is gonna rule over the whole shootin' match. Why, he could come back any day. Did you know that?"

"That's what I've heard," Prue said slyly, squeezing Mark's arm.

"Well, that would suit me fine," Bobby said. He sat there for a while and then looked over at Mark and spoke in a voice filled with excitement. "You know, Mark. I've always heard that God healed people, and I've been reading about this blind man. If Jesus healed back in those days, he could do it again. I think we ought to ask God to heal your eyesight."

Mark sat absolutely still. He knew that Prue and his family had refrained from saying too much about the hope of his being healed, of his sight coming back, but coming from Bobby this was quite a shock. He could not answer for a time, and at last he got up and left, saying, "I think I'll lie down and listen to music for a while."

After the screen door slammed and they heard his bedroom door close, Bobby turned to Prue, a worried expression on his face. "I guess I hurt his feelings, but I didn't mean to."

"It's all right, Bobby. I'm glad you spoke up like you did. It means a lot coming from you."

Bobby Stuart leaned back on the cane-bottom rocker and

began to rock slowly. "I reckon it is kind of odd, isn't it? I've been away from God so long doing everything in the world. I worried about that, you know. All the stuff I did, drugs and women."

"You mustn't do that, Bobby."

"That's what Reverend Pearl says. She said when I gave my heart to Jesus he took all my sins, dumped them in the sea, and then put out a sign that said, 'No fishin', devil.'"

"She has a way of saying things, doesn't she?" Prue smiled.

"Sure does. You know, I'll never forget that morning in church at the piano with Miss Pearl praying for me. A few times the devil's come to me and told me I don't know what I'm doin', and sometimes I don't feel saved, but I go back to that little church, and I go in and point to that bench and say, right there's where it happened. I guess I may have to do that for a long time. I've got a lot to make up for."

Prue was touched by his openness. He was so different! There had always been a streak of arrogance in Bobby Stuart, naturally enough, for he had received the adulation of the world. But now there was a new spirit in him, and if Prudence Deforge needed any evidence of the reality of a conversion, she had it before her eyes.

"We do need to pray about Mark. He needs a miracle. A minor miracle, I guess, as far as God's concerned."

Bobby smiled at her and stopped rocking. "All right. Let's just ask God right here to give that old boy his sight back. Those doctors don't know everything, but God does."

Prue reached out, and the two held hands and prayed for Mark to receive his sight.

★   ★   ★

The next morning, after Bobby left for the daycare center, Prue washed the dishes, then went into Mark's room. He was listening to his tape player.

"Mark," she said abruptly, "I've got to talk to you."

Mark shut the music off and said, "What is it, Prue?"

Prue went over and sat down and put her hands on his shoulders. "I love you," she said simply, "but I'm not ever going to marry a man who is filled with doubts. You have to learn to believe God."

Mark stood up and turned to face her. "What are you talking about?" he said, his voice uncertain. His face was twisted with confusion, and he said, "What's all this talk about marriage?"

"We're going to get married someday. God's told me this a long time ago."

"He didn't say anything to me about it!"

"I think he did, but you haven't been listening. You know, Mark, I think back to the days when we were growing up and I was so tall and skinny. No more figure than a rake handle, and you were the star quarterback and the most popular boy in school. But I knew even then that somehow you would be my husband."

"Prue, I can't—" Mark's face was contorted. He said, "You can't marry a blind man."

"Do you love me, Mark? That's all that matters."

Mark suddenly felt a release of his spirit. He reached out and pulled her up toward him. She came to him, pressing herself against him, putting her arms around his neck. Her lips beneath his were soft and yielding, and yet at the same time demanding. As he held her, savoring the wild sweetness of her kiss, old memories arose, and at the same time hungers came of a man for a woman. He clung to her, as a drowning man might cling to a spar, for he had been lonely and lost, and now he realized with a shock that Prudence Deforge was the one stable element in his life. He lifted his head and said, "You can't marry a blind man and wait on him for the rest of his life."

"I love *you*—not your eyesight," Prue said quietly. "And besides, you've just seen a miracle. Bobby getting saved. I'm not sure I always hear God right. As a matter of fact, I know I don't, but somehow I just know in my spirit that God is going to do a miracle. That you will see again. Can you believe that, Mark?"

Mark reached up and stroked her hair. It was fragrant, and he remembered how black it was and longed to see it again. "I guess it's hard for me to believe much of anything since Vietnam, but Bobby is a miracle. You're right about that. I guess if God can save him from what he was, he can cause me to see again."

She kissed him and clung to him, and pressing her face against his, she whispered huskily, "We'll see God do a mighty work. I don't know when, but it will happen."

★   ★   ★

A strange peace fell over Mark Stevens. Ever since he and Prue had expressed their love for one another, there was a richness and a quietness in his life such as he had never known. He still could not see, but now she would come to him, kissing him and whispering of love, and that sank into his spirit in a soothing fashion, and he found himself coming to life again. It was as if in Vietnam he had died with the rest of his squad—except that he kept on walking, and talking. And now at night the dreams of his lost squad members did not come anymore. He remembered them, and now for the first time was able to dictate letters to Prue, to the families of the men that he had been bonded with in the struggle in the jungles. As he dictated the letters they came alive for him, and Prue whispered, "These are fine, Mark. They'll mean so much to the families of your friends."

Two weeks came and passed. June arrived, and heavy rains began to fall. Mark still could not see, but there was a steady confidence in him, and he and Prue talked about their future as if he could see.

"When will we get married?" he asked her once as they

walked through the woods. It had begun to drizzle that day again, and he could hear the creek as it roared along its bank.

"Any time you say, Mark."

He held her hand, squeezed it, and then turned and held his head to one side. "The creek is out of its banks, isn't it?"

"Yes, and Buffalo River is higher than it's ever been."

As they walked on, talking about the floods that had ravaged Arkansas, Missouri, and parts of Tennessee, Mark said, "I always loved the rain. I like to just hear it on the roof or be out in it. It doesn't matter if it gets me soaking wet."

"I guess you like that movie *Singing in the Rain* so much because of that one number where Gene Kelly dances in the rain."

"You're right," he said. "I've watched it over and over again just to see that scene."

The rains continued for several days, and on a Wednesday afternoon it appeared to clear off. "Let's go for a walk. I want to see how high the creek is," Mark said.

"All right," Prue responded.

The two left the house and laughed as their feet squelched in the mud making sucking sounds. "Going to ruin our shoes," Mark said cheerfully.

"They'll clean up. Smell that freshness. Rain always does that, doesn't it?"

When they reached the creek, Mark said, "It's way out of its banks. I can hear it."

"Yes, it is. If it gets much higher it's going to get into the Jemsons' house." The Jemsons were a large family that lived down the creek about half a mile. They walked along the banks, and Mark held tightly to Prue's arm. Once he said, "I don't mind holding onto you and trusting myself to you. Until I can see again, it's good to have a good guide."

They had gone half a mile when Mark said, "Do you hear that, Prue?"

"Do I hear what?"

"It sounds like children's voices."

"It is," she said, lifting her eyes. "There's two of the children from the Vine, Jimmy and Elaine. They shouldn't be out playing around."

"All kids like to play around creeks. We always did, didn't we?"

"Not when they were high like this. Come on. We'd better go tell their parents."

"How old are the kids?"

"Oh, five or six. You know those children. They're just stair steps." As they approached, Mark heard a cry from one of the children, and Prue said, "Mark, it's Elaine! She's fallen in!" They were only twenty feet or so away, and the boy was crying out, "She can't swim! Look! She's going to drown!"

"What is it, Prue?"

"She's fallen in, and the current's taking her down the stream! I'll try to get her, but you know I can't swim."

Mark did not hesitate. "I'll get her!"

"Mark, you can't!" Prue protested, but he yelled above the roaring waters, "Point me at her! Don't argue!"

Prue tried to plead with him, but he made straight for the stream. When he felt the bank crumbling, he threw off his shoes and hollered, "Where is she?"

"Straight ahead, but going downstream quick!"

Mark leaped into the creek and felt the current catch at him. He heard Prue screaming, "Just ahead to your left!" With strong strokes he propelled himself through the current, but the current swept so quickly he lost the sound of Prue's voice. He thrashed around trying to find the girl, and a sense of terrible helplessness overcame him. He knew the girl would drown quickly in waters such as this, and he cried out, "Oh, God, help me to get her! Help me to see!"

For a moment the hopelessness overwhelmed him, and then a grayness came. Not solid blackness as he was accustomed to, but a gray light. He cried out, "Let me see, God! Let me see!"

The light became brighter and brighter, then—he could see!

He saw the muddy brown waters of the river with the caps of white, and not ten feet away a red piece of cloth—the girl's dress! She was sobbing and crying, and he drove himself toward her, caught her arm, and pulled her upright. "Don't be afraid, honey! I've got you!"

The current carried them downstream, and as he made his way to the shallows, he picked the child up and started up the banks. His feet stuck in the mud, but he heard Prue's voice and saw her running toward him along with the girl's brother.

When Prue came to him, he looked into her face and saw that she was weeping. "You saved her, Mark!"

Mark held the little girl for a moment, set her on her feet, and then straightened up. He looked at Prue, and her eyes met his. Immediately her eyes widened, and he smiled and pulled her into his arms. "I can see, Prue!" he whispered.

"Oh, Mark!" Prue said as she threw her arms around him.

They stood there in the muddy banks, the water rushing past them, the boy and the girl both crying. Mark pulled back and looked deep into Prue's dark eyes. "You're beautiful, Prue," he said. He looked around at the rushing, muddy creek, at the skies overhead, at the green trees, and whispered as he looked back, "Everything is beautiful, but especially God, who has given me my sight back."

24

A NIGHT TO REMEMBER

July 20, 1969, was a day that most Americans would mark on their calendars, for at 4:17, Eastern Standard Time, Neil A. Armstrong and Edwin E. Aldrin Jr. piloted their Apollo lunar module named Eagle to a landing on the Sea of Tranquillity. They walked on the lunar surface six hours later. Armstrong spoke the first words from the moon, "Houston, Tranquillity Base here. The Eagle has landed." As Armstrong stepped down from the landing craft, he became the first man to step foot on the moon. He told hundreds of millions who were watching the scene on television, "That's one small step for man, one giant leap for mankind."

All the world was in the moon's grip. From Australia to Norway, from Kansas City to Warsaw, people pressed their ears to radios or watched the momentous events on television. The TV audience was estimated at six hundred million persons, one-fifth of the earth's population. Even in unfriendly nations the mission was reported favorably.

And so, as the decade of the sixties came to an end, most people would remember the moon walk as the most important event of the decade. But for a few people gathered in War Memorial Stadium in Little Rock, Arkansas, another event would always remain fixed in their memory.

★　★　★

Mark Stevens pulled the red Mustang up to the parking lot of War Memorial Stadium, and after shutting the engine off sat quietly on the rich leather seats. He turned to the young woman beside him and said, "Prue, I never thought I'd drive a car again, and now look at me driving a red sports car!"

Prue Deforge reached across the console and touched Mark's hand. She smiled at him, saying, "God is good." She turned and looked out. "It looks like the stadium is going to be filled."

Mark shrugged. "It's big news, I guess. Most people are watching the moon walk with Armstrong and Aldrin, but to me this is a bigger thing. Everybody's been wondering when Bobby would come back to his career, and I guess tonight's the night. Come on. Let's go try to find seats."

Twenty minutes later they were inside the stadium looking down at the platform that had been built in the middle of the football field. As they settled themselves, watching the band set up their instruments and the sound people working busily, Mark looked down and said, "I always wanted to play football here with the Razorbacks. Maybe I did the wrong thing."

"No. God's had his hands on you for a long time. He's been making you into a proper husband for me."

Mark laughed aloud. "You brazen hussy! You were after me all this time! Why didn't you just tell me what was going to happen?"

Prue smiled at him brilliantly.

"You look beautiful in that yellow pantsuit." He reached over and kissed her cheek and said, "And you smell good enough to eat. What is that perfume?"

"It's called *Mantrap*."

The two sat there laughing and enjoying one another, and finally Mark looked around and said, "Hey look! There's Jerry and Bonnie down there, and Richard and his family."

"I'm glad Bobby's family is all here. They've prayed for him so long. Look how happy they are."

Mark agreed, and the two sat watching as the stadium filled up. A small group of teenagers came to sit down in front of them, one of them a skinny young man with a strange haircut and earrings who said, "I heard he got religion, but I don't believe it."

Mark and Prue listened as the group expressed their distaste for Bobby's conversion. It had been well enough publicized, and now Prue's brow furrowed with worry as she said, "This is a rock-and-roll crowd. Do you think Bobby's going to play hard rock?"

"He hasn't said anything to anybody, but I think that young man there, and others like him, are in for a surprise."

Ten minutes later Bobby Stuart walked across the field. As the crowd caught sight of him, they all began to yell and scream, "Come on, Bobby! Let's hear it!"

★　　★　　★

Down beneath Prue and Mark, Jerry Stuart held tightly to Bonnie's hand. His face was pale, and he turned to say, "Well, here we go." He was gray-haired now, and his memory went back a long way. Even at the age of sixty-nine he had a youthful look in his eyes, and Bonnie reached over and kissed him. "He's going to do all right."

Richard Stuart put his arm around his wife, Laurel. The two smiled confidently. Richard leaned over and said to his father, "It's been a long time since Bobby came in late and you threatened to thrash him, but God's going to do something tonight. I just feel it!"

They sat there watching until Bobby mounted the platform and without hesitation walked over and picked up a microphone. He did not welcome the crowd, as was his custom, but immediately began singing, "I Have Decided to Follow Jesus."

A silence fell over the crowd. Most of them had come expecting to hear the old Bobby Stuart with, perhaps, a little Christian stuff added, but as Bobby's voice filled the stadium there was a difference, and everyone in the vast stadium knew it.

The young man with the odd haircut stood up and cupped

his hands over his mouth. "Come on! Let's have some of your old stuff, Bobby! Give us some real rock and roll!"

All over the stadium young people were calling for that, but Bobby continued to sing, "I Have Decided to Follow Jesus."

When he finished the song, he waited until the cries quieted down, then he said, "I know that you've come here to hear the songs I used to sing, but I've got a new song now. It's about Jesus Christ, and that's what I'll be singing from now on." Without apology he added, "Before I sing another song, I want to tell you about something that's happened to me."

The crowd listened silently, except for a few Christians who were calling out "Amen" as Bobby gave his testimony. He did not spare himself when he revealed the barrenness and the sins of his past. When he began to speak about Reverend Pearl and how he had found Jesus in a small, frame church, tears rolled down his face, and some of the crowd began to call out, "Spare us the sob stuff, Bobby!"

Finally he concluded his testimony and said, "I'm going to be singing some of the songs I used to sing, but some of them I won't sing anymore because I've left that kind of life. Right now, before I get into that, I'm going to sing one song that's meant more to me than any other in my life."

He walked over to the piano and began to sing, "On a hill far away stood an old rugged cross. The emblem of suffering and shame. . . ."

★   ★   ★

Prue and Mark watched as from all over the stadium, young people began to leave, many of them. They were angry and felt betrayed, and they cried out blasphemies and obscenities at Bobby, and the stadium thinned.

Bobby finished the song and then began to sing other songs, and those who stayed applauded wildly.

"I don't know what this all means," Mark said as they made

their way back to the car after the concert. They had gone down and talked to Bobby and to the other members of his family who were there, and now as they stood in the parking lot, which was almost empty, Mark turned and said, "Bobby's going to be all right." There was confidence in his voice as he added, "He'll lose some hard rockers, but he's going to reach some of them. He's got a powerful testimony."

"I think it's wonderful that he had the courage to do it. He's throwing away so much."

"But he's getting a lot too. He's getting everything as a matter of fact."

The two stood there in the empty parking lot in the dimness of the lights, and finally Mark gave Prue an odd look. "I guess I'm ready to hear about our marriage plans."

"Not so fast, Mark Stevens," Prue said. She put her hand against his chest as he tried to pull her close. "You're my first real beau, you know."

"What about Kent Maxwell?"

"That was never serious," she said. "I respect him, but I told him that there could never be anything between us."

"That's good news," Mark said dryly. "Now, about getting married."

"First you're going to have to court me."

"Court you?" Mark said in astonishment. "I've known you all your life."

"I want you to bring me flowers and take me out to nice places. I want you to be uncertain and miserable, and I want us to have some lovers' quarrels, and then we can make up again, and that'll be the good part." She looked at him, her eyes shining. As she slipped her arm around his neck and pulled his head down, she whispered, "I want to enjoy being courted, Mark Stevens."

Mark pulled her close, and as he lowered his head to kiss her, he whispered, "Well, let's get started."